SWEPT AWAY

"By Triton's will, you are a stubborn wench!"

"Wench!" Penelope stepped closer to Ram. "Listen, Neanderthal Man, don't you dare assume that you can just take—"

Ramsey wanted to shake her. She was too bloody independent for her own good, and she'd walk into a nest of trouble again if he wasn't careful.

"You are innocent to this, Penelope." His voice was edged, warning of the coming explosion. "And by the Gods, I will protect what *is mine!*"

"I'm not yours!" burst from Penelope's lips. "I'm not!"

Ram smothered the sting of her denial and said, "You were every bit as such last night."

She inhaled, eyes bright, posture stiff. "Of all the pompous, egotistical, self-indulgent—"

His arm shot around her waist, jerking her against his body, his lips descending upon hers with a crushing force, molding, shaping hers, his tongue prying open her teeth afore plunging inside. She shoved at his chest, twisting, and his mouth followed hers, his muscled leg insinuating atween her thighs. His hand dove down her spine, pressing her tighter to his length and in that fraction of time, she gave up.

And she sank into him, gripping his shoulders, raking her fingers through his hair. She answered him, reveled in him, for his touch bore the same soul-stripping fire as the evening before, taking her beyond sex and pleasure and into a plane of greedy passion and an unrelenting hunger she knew she'd never satisfy without him .

Books by Amy J. Fetzer

MY TIMESWEPT HEART
THUNDER IN THE HEART
LION HEART
TIMESWEPT ROGUE

Published by Zebra Books

TIMESWEPT ROGUE

Amy J. Fetzer

Zebra Books
Kensington Publishing Corp.
http://www.zebrabooks.com

ZEBRA BOOKS are published by

Kensington Publishing Corp.
850 Third Avenue
New York, NY 10022

First Printing: November, 1996
10 9 8 7 6 5 4 3 2 1

Printed in the United States of America

For
Jodi Greenfelder,
my sister of the soul.
Friends like you come along once in a lifetime.
Past lives included.

Acknowledgments

I'd like to thank the readers who took the time from their
lives to write to me, asking for Ramsey's story.
He came to life again because of you.

Dena Hawkins
Roberta Bitner
Tricia Conway
Rita Ann Conway
Maria Castrataro
Debbie Damiani
Shirley Edwards
Leanna Glen
Gail J. Hayes
Elizabeth Lammer
Dea Lindsey
Cheryl Malzahn
Janis Moore
Eileen Masterson
Phyllis Fugate
Jean Liebel
Carol Pasch
Becky Mossor
Iris Southwood
Ellen Smith
Maggie Tompkins
Loretta Harosia
Jennifer Newman
Sylvia Meadows
Frank Vulpo
Ann Hamilton
Heather Unikel
Maxine Wells

Betty Harriger
Carol Addeo
Isabelle H. Shields
Leta Gonzales
Tamyra Flory
Roseanne Tedesco
Reiko Peterson
Bonnie Kutch
Marti Smith
Melissa Carlson
Shirley Skeen
Angela Pense
Abbie Mercado
Melissa Justice
Heather Roberts
Nancy Patano
Helen Pratt
Susan Christina
Jill Thrower
Kimberly Preston
Diana Confresi
Chrisi Konrad
Jean Ussrey
Connie Ooten
Traci Noche
Crystal Harrison
Linda Gouvaia
Kim Charman

Chapter 1

South of the Tropic of Cancer
West Indies
1789

"They've attacked, Capt'n."

"I have eyes, Mister Cameron. And ears." Ramsey O'Keefe sighted down the spyglass, his fingers flexing with impatience. The bleached house rested atop a small mountain like the aging crown of a massive cake, layered with gardens and frosted with a high stone wall. Yet from his vantage point aboard a captured sloop, he saw only flames, orange tongues licking at the stucco walls and taking lives. "Damn you, Blackwell," he muttered under his breath. "Get your friggin' arse out of there." He lowered the glass and closed it with an angry snap, then handed it to his first mate without so much as a glance.

"Ready the skif."

"Aye, aye, sir." Men scrambled, yanking hemp rope and shifting the boom harness, practiced hands swinging the small boat out over the side of the ship lying dormant in the cove.

"Lower away and stand fast," Ramsey ordered, then paced, glaring intermittently at the smoldering fortress. Show yourself, Blackwell, he agonized as ropes slipped through tackle pulleys, ship mates gathering their strength to ease the dingy into the churning sea. Water lapped at the painted hull. Rigging creaked like old bones. And Ramsey paused, straining to see beyond the dark as sporadic gunfire cracked and the cries of dying men drifted to him. He tried to ignore it, studying the small inlet, certain the night's tide would carry them out as soon as all were aboard.

If only he could have prevented this. A grinding knot twisted in his gut, and with both hands, he gripped the polished rail, his knuckles draining of color. He felt helpless, desperate to be in the middle of the fray. For 'twould be his only assurance that his message had reached Dane in time, informing him that several of Ramsey's mates lay scattered in and around the fortress. But if it had not? Sweet mother, he did not want to consider that Dane might kill one of his crew simply for lack of recognition. Instinct warned him that Phillip Rothmere would tempt such a daring act and if 'twere not foul enough that the cocksure bastard had murdered Dane's sister and stolen the Blackwell fortune, now he held the greatest prize. Tess.

Damn you to hell, Rothmere, Ram cursed, shoving away from the rail. *If she's harmed, if her skin bears but one mark, by all that is holy, I will tear you—*

A sudden piercing scream sent the hackles rising on his neck and he snapped his fingers, the spyglass immediately produced. Ram sighted. Angry fire illuminated the entire house now, yet his gaze remained riveted to the crumbling mortar below a pair of windows.

"Give the signal to assault," he ordered, and the double shots rang across the water. On shore, his men climbed the steep embankment, and even in the distance Ramsey could hear the whirl of grappling hooks, the *clunk* and scrape as they caught on ancient stone. Within moments the Continental Marines were scaling the wall. He waited, seconds chipping away until light pricked the murky night. There! The tunnel; sealed off from a decayed staircase and emptying into nothingness. 'Twas their only escape. And the survivors had to repel down the wall to the beach below. 'Twould be no challenge for Tess for he'd seen her climb swaying rigging in a storm, but if she were injured? Ramsey squinted, yet could discern no more than dangling shadows splashed with torch light. The lack of clarity increased his frustration and he lowered the glass, handing it over to Cameron. Ramsey refused to watch, every unidentifiable sound toying with his nerves. He feared the worst, for Rothmere was a twisted animal, Satan incarnate, and Tess was his innocent hostage.

Oars slapped the water in brisk smooth rhythm, the muscles in Ram's shoulders bunching with each measured sound. He clenched his fists, knuckles cracking. The small skiff thumped the hull and Ramsey flinched violently, his gaze snapping to the railing. He stood motionless, his breath locked in his lungs til a dark head crested the wood.

He reached.

"Ramsey!" Tess cried as he pulled her over the rail, his big arms swallowing her in a bone-crushing embrace.

"God save us, lass," he murmured against her hair, then grasped her arms, holding her back to search her lovely features. "I thought—" He swallowed, looking her over once more and noting every cut and bruise. "I did not know—"

Tess gazed into his glossy eyes, incredibly touched by the emotion creasing his handsome face. "I'm fine, Ram. Really." She patted his cheek, her voice soft with pride. "You did good, O'Keefe. Thanks for sending Jamie."

"Ahh lass, *you* are most welcome," he said sincerely, catching her hand and dropping a kiss to her scraped knuckles. "Dane?" he asked and Tess saw raw fear flash in Ramsey's dark eyes.

"One wonders if you truly care," came dryly, "with the familiar way you are holding *my* wife." Ramsey looked up as Dane swung his leg over the rail.

"Blackwell!" Releasing Tess, he grabbed Dane by the shoulders. "By God, I knew the bastard couldn't lay you down!" Relief and reverence blended in his voice as the men stared, then succumbed to a backslapping hug. Ramsey stepped back, his smile slowly evaporating as his gaze shifted beyond Dane to the house engulfed in flames. "I gather he's dead?"

"Aye, Elizabeth shot him."

Ram cursed softly, plowing his fingers through his dark hair. "My God, man, what happened?"

"I shall enlighten you later, my friend." Dane's gaze shifted meaningfully to Tess. She picked at the torn threads of her gown, sullen, and Ramsey's heart tripped. She looked much the sad little waif.

Sliding his arm about her waist, Dane gave her a reassuring squeeze, and she lifted her gaze to his. Delicately, her trembling fingertips brushed his lips, her expression so possessive, so undeniably loving, Ram had to look away. Jealousy burned through his chest, yet 'twas not a jealousy of Dane for winning Tess, but an envy of the heart-wrenching love they shared in naught but a simple smile. He wanted that for himself, a woman he could lock horns with and still love, a woman he'd kill for, die for. Live for.

He assured himself his day would come. Aye, he sighed, but when? *When?* And would she be a'tall like the spirited Tess? Would she take him as he was, without tempting to change him? Would she—good God. You be in a fair mess of it, he thought, smirking at his own melancholy, then giving orders to weigh anchor as the last Marine boarded. Canvas unfurled, catching the breeze and moving the sloop quickly out of the cove toward the *Sea Witch*.

Ramsey turned back to find Dane studying him intently. "Is this a hidden facet of your character, Ram, disobeying direct orders?"

Tess glanced between the two men. "Uh-oh. Were you a naughty boy, O'Keefe?"

" 'Tis a reputation I strive for, madame." Lightly, he tapped her nose.

She rolled her eyes. "I'll alert the media."

Media? Ram mouthed, looking to Dane for explanation and receiving a puzzled shrug. Tess laughed, quiet and to herself and Ram was struck again with the notion that she held a secret power only she understood. And Dane was rejoicing in it.

" 'Tis well you seek some other profession, Captain O'Keefe, if this—" he gestured to the garishly painted ship— "is *your* sampling of a fit craft for a Marine."

Ram grinned devilishly. "Captured her right beneath Rothmere's pointed nose."

"Are you certain he didn't give it willingly?" Tess taunted.

"I've proof. See." Ramsey held up his bandaged finger like a child showing off his latest wound. "A kiss would speed the healing, me thinks," he teased, flashing her a roguish smile and wiggling his brows.

"You *sure* he's a Marine?" she said to Dane as she tossed her thumb toward Ramsey.

"Oftimes 'tis debatable, love," Dane murmured on a laugh, settling against the rail to watch the sparing match.

Tess's brows furrowed. "If you're here, Ramsey, who's commanding the *Triton?*"

"Is that not what a first mate is for, lass?"

"Gee. What a relief." She sighed dramatically against Dane, her silver eyes bright. "And here I thought you misplaced it."

Ram folded his arms over his chest. "Misplaced *her,*" he corrected and her expression instantly soured.

"Just like a chauvinist to refer to a twenty-four-gun frigate as a female."

He eyed her, puzzled. "A chau-vin-ist? What mean you by this?"

The wind ruffled her hair and she brushed back the loose strands. "Ought to be easy for you to understand. It's a man who more or less thinks with his—" she waved in the vicinity of his breeches.

Ram chuckled lowly, but Dane stared at her in utter shock. "Tess Renfrew Blackwell!"

"I know. *God's teeth, woman, but you're a bold wench,*" she mimicked deeply. "But you love it, pirate." She kissed him, hard and quick, then cast a sideways glance at Ram. "Triton is a *man's* name," she challenged.

"Aye, yet *her* name is truly *Triton's Will,* lass. The will to resist the lure of the siren, who is most definitely female." He was towering over, grinning hugely and adoring her quick retorts.

"I stand corrected, meek and subservient." Though she failed miserably to look it.

" 'Twill be a chilling day in Hades,'' Dane muttered, then let out an *oof* when she elbowed him in the ribs.

"*She's* to rendezvous with us later,'' Ram half-spoke to his superior. "Sailing away with cargo we commandeered from Phillip's warehouses.'' He winked at Tess, all three aware of her part in their success.

"Too bad he didn't have any paint in those crates.'' Tess glanced around. " 'Cause this tub looks like a floating pansy.''

Dane smoothed his thumb and forefinger over an imaginary moustache, hiding his smile. "Be kind, Tess. 'Tis transport out.'' Then to Ramsey he said, "She's your prize. You may keep her.''

"Bloody hell, nay!'' Ramsey gruffed, nauseated by the pale blue sloop and its ridiculously striped sails. He itched to scuttle her himself. And would.

"You know, O'Keefe,'' Tess said philosophically. "I half expected you to come crashing through the windows at any moment back there.'' She inclined her head to the house burning in the distance. "Knowing your flair for the dramatic and all.''

Mischief danced in his chocolate-brown eyes. " 'Twould have been a bloody disappointment to ruin a new pair of boots in that muck.'' He modeled his polished Hessians.

"Why, Ramsey,'' her hand fluttered to her heart—"I'm touched.'' She looked at Dane. "Can we hang him from the yardarm or something for that?''

"I'm afraid not, love, he captains this . . . ship.'' Dane's lips twitched, his pale green eyes shifting to Ram, waiting for the next barb.

"I fear I must ask for the portrait of you back, Tess. I find I'm sorely in need of a reminder—'' He leaned down in her face—"For 'tis the only time I've caught you with your mouth shut.''

"Do and it's pistols at down, O'Keefe,'' she shot back and Ram chuckled. Cheeky lass. "Dane'll be my second.'' She nudged her husband. "Won't you, babe?''

Dane smiled benignly, refusing to comment, not that 'twould matter.

"Or will an angry father beat me to the punch?''

Ram reared back, his crushed look spoiled by his sparkling eyes. "Ahh, but you're a cruel woman, thinking the worst of me."

She arched a tapered black brow. "If the breeches fit."

"You wound me, madame." He clutched at his shirt. "I believe 'tis a bit of Phillip that's rubbed off—" Ram ceased in midsentence as Tess's face went ashen and she twisted into Dane's embrace. God almighty, what horrors did she witness in those hours? He opened his mouth to apologize, then simply turned and walked away, cursing his thoughtlessness.

The *Sea Witch's* first mate approached him.

"Captain?" Gaelan whispered, glancing atween the couple and O'Keefe. "What shall I do with this?"

Ramsey frowned at the pile and grasped the familiar first, stuffing Tess's diamond pouch inside his shirt til he could return it, yet scowled as he accepted the small gilded box. Turning the tiny key, he flipped back the lid. Even in the indigo dawn he knew he held Dane's legacy: the Blackwell gems.

Chapter 2

1989
Universal Studios, Florida
Closed Set

"Why was Tess Renfrew driving *your* car, using *your* credit and residing in *your* state room aboard the *Nassau Queen?*" Justin Baylor rushed to ask, hoping to catch his prey off guard.

He didn't.

And she continued to stare at him, stirring her coffee, cat-like eyes unblinking.

"Cut! Cut! Damn it, Justin. This is our livelihood, not hers!" the director called angrily. "You're costing the studio money, so stick to the format. Clear?" he added from his seat beyond the camera and Baylor waved agreement, still looking at his guest.

"Sorry."

She smoothly arched a tapered brow. "Liar," she said and the single word held a wealth of warning. He was trying for sensationalism. And he wasn't going to get it. Not from her. She'd spent her life avoiding just that.

Settling deeper into the overstuffed white sofa, actress Penelope Hamilton crossed her legs, shooting a don't-even-think-it look at the makeup artist who saw the break as an opportunity to apply yet another layer of face powder. Jesus, they're like attack dogs, she thought, briefly leaning out to set the coffee spoon aside, her slim hand coming back to brush feather-light at the waterfall of straight deep red hair pouring over her shoulder and pooling on her lap.

She hoped no one noticed her trembling.

The last time she had agreed to an interview, she was eighteen and they'd crucified her. Never again, she thought, staring at the coffee cooling in her cup, her tight grip threatening to snap the delicate china. She took a deep breath and her touch loosened. She had to be careful. Her mind wasn't sharp enough today, constantly slipping to the last time she'd seen Tess; alive, taking on Penny's problems and running from two armed men itching to put a bullet in her back.

That was three days ago.

Not knowing what had happened to Tess chipped away at her composure.

A lump swelled in her throat, and she swallowed hard, forcing it down before tears could follow.

The call for quiet demanded through the studio, yanking her attention to the man sitting across from her in a matching chair, checking his notes. He looked up, his smile resembling a panther prepared to pounce and Penny wanted to knock his teeth in. He ought to wear a sign: DOES NOT PLAY WELL WITH OTHERS. He didn't want the whole truth, only dirt, enough to grab a headline, and she wondered whether this bout would go the round without bruises. For her the truth was muddier that he could ever imagine. And suppressing it just might have cost Tess her life.

The camera's red light flicked on.

"*The Gold Masque* sounds like another box office smash," Justin said, slickly plugging her next film. "Now, how about answering the questions on every fans mind?"

Here he goes again, she thought. "And that is?"

"Your past."

Eyes, dark green and feline, stared back at Baylor.

"Such as?" Frosty, remote.

"Any sisters, brothers? Lovers? Ex-husbands?"

A hollowness echoed through her heart as she said, "I was an only child and my parents are dead." Inwardly Penelope cringed at the half-truth. She'd no idea if she had family or even her real name, for that matter. Pathetic.

"Are you in love with anyone now?"

Her gaze sharpened, then immediately cooled. "No." She tilted her head, thoughtful, a sapphire earring winking in the artificial light. "At least not that I can tell." And the public didn't need to know, even if she was dumb enough to let anyone get that close.

"Ex-husbands?" Justin added quickly, now that he'd broached the subject.

"Marriage is nothing that can be ex-ed in my book," she said, her smile brittle as her nerves. I should never have agreed to this, she thought, fingering the tiny locket suspended from the long chain around her neck.

"Any prospects, then?"

Her chuckle, low and husky, wafted around him like dense wood smoke.

"You act like I'm on a hunt."

Justin smiled. The camera loved this woman and up close, he understood why. She was exotic, sensually sleek and mysterious.

"Well—your name's been linked with other celebrities like Mel Gibson."

"Now, Justin." Her tone scolded, her smile Mona Lisa faint. "He's a married man with a wonderful wife and six beautiful children." Envy blistered through her and she took a fortifying breath before quickly adding, "Do you honestly think he'd be interested in giving that up for me?"

His gaze flitted over the deep teal linen suit, simply cut and curve hugging. "About half the male population would. Like Josh Randell?"

Penny stiffened, guarded. "See, that kind of talk gets you into trouble. You speculate and the rumors fly." She waved a hand, Queen Mum elegant.

Damn. She wasn't going to give him anything juicy, Justin

realized, grinding his teeth. "Is that why you've given this interview, after being silent for so long?" He wanted to ask about Tess Renfrew again, but couldn't risk her walking out.

"I haven't been silent; the media prints whatever they want." Beneath the hot lights she felt perspiration form at the small of her back. "No one ever *asked* me for my views. And when my name was connected to all sorts of people I'd never met, I decided they would distort the truth even if *I* gave it to them."

"Is that why you opted for the on-screen interview instead of a printed article?"

Green eyes, sharp as glass, assessed him. "What do you think?"

"That you want to be certain your fans heard it from you."

"Very astute, Justin," she said, placing the cup on the low table and feeling as if she were leading him through this by that fashion statement of a tie. "Next question."

"Anthony Wainright."

Her rare smile warmed as she pulled a rose couch pillow close, staring briefly where she toyed with the pleated corner. "Anthony is Anthony. Welsh, austere, but a gentleman. We met while I was auditioning for summer stock." Or rather getting dumped from it, she recalled. "He appointed himself my acting coach and all around guardian angel." That comparison paled to what Tony meant to her now. "I was *very* young, untutored, and in dire need of a *bit of polish* as he would say. I suppose he saw me as a—"

"Diamond in the rough?" Justin interrupted.

"More like an unwaxed fruit, I think."

Justin laughed. Well, well, a sense of humor, finally. He glanced at his notes. "You've won three libel suits already, Miss Hamilton, and have one pending—"

"Not any more."

His brows shot up. "Really?"

She nodded slightly, razor straight hair shifting across her lap like a river of red wine.

"Will your settlement go to charity as the others have?"

"The homeless, yes."

"Why them? Why not AIDS research or cancer or—"

"This money doesn't go through channels until there is nothing left for the people who really need it now," she said with more anger than she should. "*I* see that it gets to the people standing outside soup kitchens. And before you ask, it's spent on better food, more of it, cots, blankets, and a grant if you want to call it, to get families on their feet again, somewhere else. Retraining or an apartment." She shrugged slim shoulders. "They decide with the help of counselors."

"Some say you're easing your guilt because you have so much."

Penelope leaned forward slightly, eye to eye, ignoring the knot twisting in her stomach. "No one chooses to live in shelters or paper cartons, Mister Baylor."

God, what a predatory stare, he thought, feeling like raw meat before a tigress. "And the single people? You help them, too?"

Her expression was tolerant. "Of course. The funding simply obliterates a couple of obstacles when surviving is a daily struggle; people trying to stay alive while surrounded by criminals ready to take advantage of the circumstance and tear apart the last of their world." Good God, get off the soap box, Hamilton, you've said too much.

And he noticed it. "You sound like you talk from experience?"

Penelope bristled, retucking her hair. "Be serious, Justin," she said, looking at him beneath half-lidded eyes.

"You're to be admired for your conviction, Miss Hamilton," he said, genuine.

"I don't do it to be admired." Great, after all these years did everyone think she was just some shallow bimbet?

"That leads me to ask why you don't live with the jet set in Hollywood?"

"Florida is my home. Hollywood is where I work." She stole a covert glance at her watch. "The separation keeps me—even."

"Yet you could certainly add considerably to your homeless charity with a celebrity fund raiser."

Her gaze thinned, her tone matter-of-fact. "Flaunting diamonds and laying out two thousand dollars for a gown so one can eat a thousand dollar-a-plate dinner on camera isn't giving because you *want* to help.''

He tapped his lips with his pen, then asked, ''Then what is it?''

''More like 'Look at me up here, aren't I the saint? Now let's see a little bowing and scraping for my efforts.' '' She swallowed, her tone softening. ''Why do the fortunate have to *get something* before they can contribute to our own needy?''

The lady hides those claws well, Justin thought, seeing her differently and hoping it showed through the lens. ''Why won't you allow cameras in your Victorian home?''

Penelope recalled her unmade bed, the pile of dirty laundry in the corner of her bedroom, and almost laughed at the idea of showing the viewing audience her lousy habits. ''I'm like anyone else in this business. I enjoy my privacy. When I clock out, I leave my job *and public,* at the studio.''

Justin sighed at her evasiveness, yet maintained his smile. Sounded damn lonely to him. ''You won an Academy Award and didn't show to accept it. Everyone thinks it's the grand insult.''

''Neither did Katharine Hepburn or Marlon Brando, Justin.''

He took the hint and glanced at his notes. ''In your last film, *Habits of Nature,* you portrayed a young woman who'd been raised in a secular convent struggling with the real world.'' Penelope nodded. ''Is it true you actually lived in a convent prior to doing the film?'' God, she looked ready to bolt.

''You've done your homework, Justin. And yes, I couldn't very well portray a novice if I hadn't any idea of the lifestyle. Can you imagine her turmoil, never to have seen a man that wasn't wearing a collar and surrounded by females devoted to one narrowed view of life, then suddenly,'' Penny snapped her fingers, ''violence, men, sex, drugs.'' She glanced down at her watch, then leaned forward and shook his hand. ''Time's up, Justin, thank you.'' Pulling free, she stood and turned away.

''Did you have Randell's child?'' he asked quickly, managing to get to his feet.

Penny froze, slowly looking back over her shoulder. Green

eyes bit into him like the jab of a knife. ''No. Did you?'' she said, then immediately strode from the artificial living room.

The director yelled cut and Justin Baylor tossed his notes on the table, admiring her graceful walk as she vanished beyond the studio wings. The woman was still a damn mystery.

A cameraman came up behind him, pulling off his headset as he laid a hand on Justin's shoulder.

''Christ, Justin, you're going to be goddamn famous after this airs.''

Penelope smiled benignly at the stagehand, then slipped into her dressing room and shut the door. She gripped the knob, fighting the emotions clamoring for escape. But the tears came, hot and quick, and she buried her face in a terry cloth robe hanging on the back of the door. Low, tight sobs jerked her shoulders, pulling like water hoisted from a well and she bit the cloth until her teeth ached, squeezing her eyes shut. Her body flexed. The urge to throw something, smash—*anything*— twisted inside her, struggling to pass unblemished as she sank to her knees and wrapped her arms around her middle. Penelope wept, out of terror and anger and tremendous guilt that had nothing to do with her first interview in ten years. And the horrible grinding ache held the same haunting pain of her childhood.

Oh God, Tess, what have I done?

Exhausted, she slumped against a chair, then pulled herself onto the seat, brushing at the dampness flowing down her cheeks. She sniffled, searching the vanity. No messages. Damn. Resting her elbows on the surface, her hands covering her face, she battled for control, then, shielding her eyes from the bright cosmetic lights, she reached sluggishly for the phone. Penny dialed, spoke briefly, then cleared the line and dialed again. She dried her eyes and blew her nose while she waited for the pick up.

''Tony? This is Penelope.''

''After all these years, my dear, I do recognize your voice. How went the interview?''

"Remind me to fire you for pushing me into it."

He chuckled shortly. "I'll make a note." A pause and then softly, "Any word on Tess?"

"No, damn it, and I can't stand another moment. Have Daniel ready the Lear, would you? I'm going down there. Today."

Crooked Island, Bahamas
1989

Ducking low, Lieutenant Bindar of the Bahama Air Sea Rescue Association rushed forward as the helicopter's blades slowed to a heavy whirl. The door popped open and a pair of stockinged legs appeared first, then their owner. The woman held tight to her broad brimmed hat, head bowed as the couple moved quickly away from the chopper. It lifted off after a wave from the pilot.

In silence she walked beside him, her heeled shoes tapping on the wood pier. Stepping onto the gangplank, he offered his hand, helping her onto the B.A.S.R.A. cutter, then relayed orders to cast off. The motor roared, the boat slipping easily into the current as he glanced at her, his heart thumping like a schoolboy's. Penelope Hamilton. He couldn't believe it. No matter how much she tried to hide her face beneath the white hat, he knew it was her.

Any man would.

"When will we be near the area where—where—" Penelope looked away, blinking. She couldn't even say it. Oh, Tess, what's happened to you?

"Just a short while, ma'am, two hours at the most."

She nodded mutely and Bindar resisted the urge to comfort the famed American actress.

"Can I get you anything, ma'am?"

"No, thank you. Is it all right if I stand at the bow?"

"Certainly. May I help you over the equipment?"

"That won't be necessary. I'd prefer to be alone, if you don't mind.

"Certainly ma'am. I understand." He turned away, leaving her to weave a path around ropes and gear to the bow.

Oblivious to the seamen working around her, Penelope stared at the rushing water, her heart clenching painfully. It should have been me. Me! She'd no idea their little identity exchange would have resulted in Tess's death. No, not dead; she wouldn't believe it. Not yet. The reports insisting she'd jumped off *Nassau Queen* were sketchy at best. And for God's sake, why did she do it? Penelope prayed someone had picked her up; a passing fishing boat, honeymooners out for a secluded celebration . . . but so far out at sea? Keep hope, she reminded again, though the more time passed, the slimmer their chances of finding a body.

From the pilot house Lieutenant Bindar watched her. Miss Penelope Hamilton was every man's fantasy; leggy, redheaded, and sensually reserve. Her navy blue dress was slim fitting and nautically piped in white, the broad white hat shielding deep green eyes he knew were rimmed in the thickest lashes. The stiff breeze whipped her long braid against her back, and she didn't seem to care that the spray soaked her shoes. Then suddenly she bowed her head and covered her face with her hands, her shoulders quaking miserably. And Bindar turned to the control panel, ordering right full rudder. He had a job to do; return to the last place anyone saw Olympic gymnast Tess Renfrew alive.

Chapter 3

West Indies
1789

Ramsey O'Keefe strolled the deck of the *Sea Witch*, inquiring after the captain's location and found Dane leaning against the bowsprit, his wife cuddled close, both looking nauseatingly happy.

"Duncan bade me to give you this."

The couple separated, barely. Still in each other's pockets, Ram thought, handing over the brittle missive to Tess.

At her quizzical stare, Ram said, "McPete said it fell out of your pouch when he was tidyin' the cabin."

Dane cleared his throat, his eyes on his bride.

That smile is bleedin' wicked, Ram thought enviously, aware of the telltale clothing the couple left strewn around the captain's quarters. A night of blistering loving, he imagined, turning his gaze to the sea, for he'd oftimes found himself enjoying the like with a tavern bawd or a lady. Yet recently a lusty ride atween willing thighs left him with naught but uncomfortable departures and mere physical gratification. Unfulfilled, meaningless. Almost painful. 'Twas never a concern afore, for 'twas all he sought, but the conquest for the sensual rewards atween the sheets had lost their challenge. And 'twas the caliber of females he'd spent company with that he'd questioned, only since meeting Tess. He wanted more.

"You okay, Ramsey?" she asked, shielding her eyes from the sun.

He drew his gaze back to hers. She was inquiring after his health, he decided. "Aye, do I not look fit?" He grinned, folding his arms over his chest, dark fabric straining against his bulk.

"Fishing for compliments, O'Keefe?"

"From you, lass?" he said in feigned astonishment.

She smiled sweetly. "Getting the pulp best out of you last week smartened you up, I see."

Ramsey chuckled. God love her, the lass is resilient. Rothmere had held her hostage, tried to kill her, murdered innocent souls afore her eyes, and she seemed unscathed by the events. What was it about the woman he found so intriguing, Ram wondered again, his dark gaze appraising her slim body encased in men's clothes. Her odd clipped speech? Her keen intelligence? Or did her allure lie beneath the fierce independence she wore like her skin, even though he knew she loved Dane to distraction? From where did she hail and how had she fallen into the sea in the first place? Dane had never said and Ram felt 'twas a well-guarded secret.

She was an extraordinary woman, different than any he'd met afore. 'Twas why he captured her in oils, to hold the image of this enchanting creature forever. And although he'd not so much as kissed the lass on her wedding day, Ramsey knew he'd lost more than a fine lady to his best friend. *As if you'd had a pickpocket's chance with the lass,* he reminded, stepping away to allow her privacy to read. He saw his affections for her doled into the chambers of her heart meant for a brother, for Tess instantly recognized him for the rogue he was, setting him in his place with her honest assessment, and for the first time since he was five and ten, made him consider what his future held. Or rather, lacked.

He supposed he'd her to blame for this blasted turmoil running amuck in his chest, then.

Women. Make a man see cross-eyed, he nashed, plowing his fingers through his hair, then resting his forearms on the rail. He stared at the ice-blue water rushing past the black hull as if 'twere a seer's crystal. Are you, in truth, finished with fencing brigands and hedonistic play, old man? And if you're believing a good woman will satisfy, are you prepared to search? You're not a young pup, so what chance have you now? Aught, he despaired, must be better than this wrenching loneliness, this . . . impatience for more. 'Twas damned unfamiliar.

And blast it, he was jealous. He was! Though he'd never begrudge Dane the happiness he found with Tess, Ram knew he'd not be so fortunate as to pluck the love of a lifetime from the sea.

Bloody hell.

Was he seeking what could not be found?

Ramsey lifted his gaze to the horizon, a grinding chill working up his spine. He rolled his shoulders, yet found no ease, and Dane's exclamation of his love for Tess brought a snarl to his lips.

"Friggin' newlyweds." He glanced to his side to glare at the couple, then straightened abruptly, staring beyond. "Sweet mother of God," he whispered, awed. "What in the bleedin' creation is that?"

Tess twisted around. "Jesus H—no!"

"Capt'n! 'Tis the wall—*again!*" a crewman wailed, terror scraping his voice.

Again? Ramsey stared, utterly spellbound by the black wall of mist stretching from the ocean's surface up into infinity. The dense smoke undulated, tentacles of mist reaching, following them across the sea, uncurling like a woman's delicate fingers. Ram swallowed. Curious, fearful.

"Prepare to come about!" Dane shouted, yanking Tess close to his side.

Crewmen scurried, frantic to adjust sail and spar, and Ramsey's gaze snapped to Tess, riveted by the horror on her flawless features, in her panic-stricken eyes. And Dane . . . by God, the man was desperate, bellowing commands, yet refusing to release his wife.

They've lain witness to this apparition afore, Ram realized, then climbed to the bowsprit for a clearer view. His heartbeat suddenly accelerated, a strange burning rushing with his blood, and he paused, dizzy, sweating, and gripped the rigging for balance. "God almighty!" he gasped for air, "what be this?" he demanded back over his shoulder.

Tess looked uncertainly up at Dane, then to Ramsey, then back at her husband.

"Tell him, love," Dane urged, his ears tuned to the creak of rigging as it shifted to bring his frigate away from the wall.

Tess's silver-gray eyes locked with Ramsey's. "It's the future, Ramsey."

His brows shot up, his fingers flexing on the ropes.

"I don't know exactly to where—but that," she glared at the curtain, "is a rip in time."

Ramsey jerked a look at the black wall, the sharp motion muddying his vision. He blinked. The future?

" 'Tis comin' closer!" a crewman screamed.

"Port, hard to lee!" Dane commanded. "Now!"

Eagerness tightened Ram's features even as he considered she could not be jesting. A cut in time? A doorway, mayhaps? He swung around to look at Tess as she begged her husband not to let it take her back. Back where? Home? Dane would perish from the loss and—sweet God above . . . *'Tis come to retrieve her.* All he knew of Tess and claimed odd, rushed through his brain. She was like none he'd ever known . . . but to not belong to this lifetime?

He returned his gaze to the wall, his stomach rolling violently. Was it possible? To step into another age? He licked his dry lips, a crushing sensation gripping him and a quick glance told him Tess felt it, too; a sudden piercing of flesh and sinew and muscle, sand-rough fingers clamping a vise on his bones, tugging. The wall neared, dense mist stroking the sea and the sensations intensified.

By Triton, 'tis calling me—nay, *begging* me to come experience what lies beyond!

"Your journey was long to find your heartmate, Tess," Ram rasped, his face bloodless with clawing nausea. "Mayhaps . . .

I must take the same," he forced moisture into his mouth, "to discover if such exists for me."

Her teary eyes widened with understanding as he gave her a jaunty salute.

"Ramsey! Noooo!" she screamed as he dove off the *Sea Witch* and into the raging water.

Ramsey burst through the surface, his powerful arms knifing through the water, drawing him nearer.

Dane cursed him.

Tess pleaded.

And King Triton's fury grew wilder, the sea's boiling swells propelling him closer.

Ramsey swam. He didn't look back, fearing he'd change his mind and be caught. Not til he reached the wall did he send them all a reassuring smile.

And so it begins, he thought, lifting his arm to wave.

A sudden tightness squeezed at Ramsey's chest, and he struggled for needed air. Misty arms wrapped round his torso, lifting him from the sea and pulling him backwards through the partition, his legs appearing severed til they passed fully through the black wall.

And then he was falling, fast.

Off the coast of the Caicos Islands
1989

Penny gripped the stern rail of the ship, frowning, swearing she heard someone scream, and for the length of a heartbeat the sun's warmth and radiance vanished, cooling her back. Tilting her head skyward, she blinked against the bright sunlight, then twisted slightly to look aft. There wasn't a cloud for miles. So what caused the quick darkness, she wondered, scanning the sky once more before facing stern.

Abruptly a sailor grabbed her shoulders, moving her bodily out of his way as he passed, the activity aboard the vessel suddenly frantic. A commanding voice warned her to hold on as the ship banked sharply to the right, retracing its path.

Then she saw the body floating in the sea.

And rapidly sinking.

A rubber pontoon dropped into the ocean, scuba divers and medical technicians jumping in the instant it blossomed with air. The outboard motor churned white foam as it heeled away from the ship and headed toward the body.

Oh, Jesus, please be alive.

Two divers immediately dropped backwards into the water just as the body sank below the surface. One diver remained submerged, pushing the victim towards the surface as a sailor aboard the pontoon reached out with a hooked pole, the end catching on clothing. Dragging the limp form back to the pontoon, several hands grasped the body, slipped on a preserver, then turned the victim over and felt for a pulse. A sailor instantly slid into the water and performed mouth to mouth, the rubber craft floating aimlessly as he forced air into unmoving lungs.

Penny watched, her entire body strung tight, her gaze frantically searching between the half dozen sailors for a glimpse. Then she heard it. First a cough, then a groaning gasp for air and the paramedic turned the dark head to the side as the half-dead survivor vomited into the sea. *Tess?*

She shook the rail, impatient to see something recognizable as the rescue team slid a back board into the water beneath the survivor. But there were just too many people. After securing the straps, a diver twisted toward the cutter, waving broadly, smiling. Bindar issued orders to come about. Penny's knees gave out, and the Bahamian captain lurched forward, but she caught herself, gripping the thin steel rail.

"God bless," Bindar murmured close to her side and Penny nodded. "I admit I never expected to find her, ma'am, let alone alive."

"Neither did I, Lieutenant." Stepping away, Penny straightened her hat, discreetly wiping her eyes as the pontoon and ship merged. She started for the port side, but Bindar gasped her arm, his heart doing a quick flip-flop at the sight of those hopeful green eyes.

"She may be, ah, the weather and days in the water—"

"I understand, but she's my only family."

Penny moved closer, yet stayed clear as they lifted a basket-type gurney onto the deck. The air rushed into her lungs and she stumbled back, her hand covering her mouth. Grief returned, pressing on her with an unforgiving force, threatening her breathing.

It wasn't Tess.

The sailors glanced between themselves and the man as she turned away, her sensitivity to his condition buried beneath her pain. Anger built, stirring new hurt and fresh guilt. Oh, God, the guilt. She'd needed to hope, for her own sanity, yet now the damning of even that fading light was gone. She lifted her gaze to find Bindar regarding her with open sympathy.

"I wished the hell you'd found nothing," she hissed softly and his eyes widened a fraction. "Do you know what this means?" She lashed an arm toward the survivor.

Bindar's gaze shifted briefly to the horizon. "Yes, ma'am, I do." He hesitated before asking, "Shall we call off the search?"

"No!" then softer, "No. There's still a chance." His expression said otherwise and Penny's heart shattered, bitter pain stinging through her chest. "A couple more days. I need answers, Lieutenant, and I'll pay for extra men, overtime, anything." Her voice softened to a whisper. "I *need* to know."

Bindar's shoulders sank and he nodded, then spoke into a hand radio as she tilted her face to the sky. Two search and rescue helicopters circled over head, rocking once before heading further out to sea. She cast a quick glance at the man, limp in the basket as a doctor worked over him. Hippie, she thought, with that long hair. Her outrage intensified, reality settling hard and before she said something else she'd regret, Penny strode toward the pilot house.

Sloane Rothmere. This was her fault. Whatever she planted in the package Tess stole for Penny . . . got her pal killed.

Chapter 4

Her shoulder braced against the wall, Penny worried the handle of the china cup, gazing out the porthole as the sea raced past. Droplets splashed the thick glass, melting into the clear surface, vanishing. Like Tess. Hot tears burned the back of her eyes, and she swallowed her despair. Unanswered questions tore relentlessly through her brain, angering her, frustrating her. For if Tess were alive, she would have contacted Penny. And grasping the empty hope that Sloane Rothmere might have her sequestered somewhere was useless. Sloane was clever, devious, the viciousness she pulled in college proving she had the talent for covering her tracks, with money, and Tess was last seen diving *off* the *Nassau Queen*.

Abruptly the door opened, and she flinched, yet didn't turn toward the visitor, gathering her frayed emotions under tight guard.

"The helicopters have returned to base, Miss Hamilton. The light, you know." She nodded, setting the cup on the small railed table before facing him. The lieutenant was half in, half out of the hatch.

"The man they found?" She felt obligated to ask, though in her present state she didn't want to hear details about *hippie*.

Bindar stepped inside, leaving the hatch open. "He's still unconscious, his condition guarded, I'm told. We'll make the best speed to shore, regardless."

"I see." She slid elegantly into a chair, ashamed of her insensitivity. Poor guy. It wasn't his fault. "Do you know who he is, at least?"

"That's the odd thing," he said, brows drawn as he settled into the opposite chair. "No identification a'tall, not even a label in his clothing."

"Is that so unusual?" Penny recalled when she wore what she'd found in someone else's garbage. "Not everyone can afford store bought clothes."

He flushed at her cutting tone. "That's not it, entirely," he soothed. "His are hand-stitched, every seam! No zippers, just buttons, rather crude wood buttons."

"I fail to see the importance, Lieutenant. Didn't he have any papers, a visa?"

Bindar shook his head. "But he has coins sewn into the lining of his coat."

Penny relaxed into the chair and crossed her legs. "Really?" she said archly, thinking the invasion of the man's privacy unnecessary.

"And heavy chains around his neck, gold soft enough to twist, knives in his boots, sheathed at his waist and an antique gun! Loaded!" It was clear the skipper thought this all very fascinating.

Penny didn't. She wanted Tess back.

A deep wrenching howl rumbled down the companionway like black thunder, drawing the skin up on her arms. Penny turned wide eyes toward the open hatch, then back to Bindar, who was already on his feet and moving. A med-tech skidded to a halt in the corridor, nearly slamming into his skipper.

"He's out of control, sir."

Ramsey woke with a jolt, his eyes snapping open, his chest expanding as he sucked air into his lungs. It tasted odd, he thought afore raked with a fit of coughing, a fire exploding through his chest. Hands held him down, and instinctively he fought.

"Try to relax, sir. You'll be fine."

English, Ramsey recognized, a snarl twisting his lips as he let loose a growl, his open palm smacking a man's chest, sending him back against glass-faced cabinets. The silver closet rattled with the impact, bursting open and dumping little boxes and jars. Something covered his nose and mouth, and Ram tore it off, flinging the clear mask aside as he sat up.

"Sir, please! Don't fight!" Two men in white uniforms pushed him back down.

"Bloody English bugger!" He took a deep breath and coughed. "I'll slit your friggin' gullet to your scrawny neck if you do not leave off!" Ramsey groped his boot for his knife, his fingers meeting the skin of his calf. Hell. No weapons. His instinct to survive brewed power, and a few well placed thrusts sent his assailants stumbling backwards.

He leapt from the high bed, glared at his opponents, then spit in his palms afore rubbing them together, broad fists primed to dress down a few English hides. 'Twas his favored pastime, he thought with a grin. One man stepped forward, and Ram sent him back with a sharp jab to the nose. He bled all over the white shirt, the poor sot.

"Now see here!" The skipper stepped into the infirmary.

Ramsey planted a hand on the man's chest and shoved, propelling him back over the raised threshold.

Penny looked down at the fallen skipper, then bent to help him to his feet. Bindar shrugged, adjusted his clothing and his dignity, then solemnly entered the infirmary.

"Dare you try again, runt?" Ramsey challenged, swaying slightly.

"Sir." Bindar held up his hands in surrender. "You've been injured. I'm sure it's been quite the shock, but please, we mean you no harm."

Ram scoffed. "Then give back me weapons."

"After this display?" He gestured to his battered men. "They've been locked in my safe."

"Does *me* no good, English pig!"

The skipper stiffened. ''I am Bahaman,'' he told him, and Ramsey caught his nearly-imperceptible nod. His fist shot out to the right and the sailor dropped to the deck.

Ramsey grinned, cocky.

''Stop it this minute! These men saved your life, for God's sake!''

Ramsey's gaze shifted past English, and he slowly lowered his arms, his attention on the red-haired woman stepping through the hatch. His gaze dropped immediately to the shapely display of long bare legs and thinly heeled white slippers. What a lovely bit of femininity this, he thought, bringing his gaze to hers. Cat-green eyes stared unflinchingly back and afore he could ponder overlong as to why such a comely lass wore so little afore so many men, something pricked his back. He swatted the burning sting, turning his head. An incredibly thin needle attached to a slim cylinder lay on the narrow bed, half-filled with amber liquid. Ram blinked, dizzy, his accusing gaze shifting to the crew, then to the woman. The room suddenly dropped, and he cursed them to hell as they eased him back onto the hard bed.

''Ought to keel-haul you for that, English,'' Ramsey slurred, drunkenly shoving at gentle hands with no success. At the mercy of the enemy was the last place Ram wanted to be.

The skipper sagged against the wall, blotting his brow with his sleeve. The doctor checked his vital signs.

And Penny stared, a bit stunned. He'd looked like a pirate just then, bare-chested and bronze, spoiling for a fight and arrogant down to his bare toes. And that hair, chestnut dark, wild and waving beyond his shoulders. She moved closer, unwillingly drawn to the flash of helplessness she'd caught in his cognac-brown eyes.

''Bloody unfair tactics,'' he mumbled, then turned his head, blinking her face into focus. ''Ramsey O'Keefe, m'lady. At your service.'' His grin was sappy, liquid. ''Mayhaps in a moment or two, I shall be—'' He was out, his smile lingering a moment longer than his senses.

Penny lifted confused eyes to the doctor.

He shrugged. ''His injuries are not serious now, except for

a nasty cut on his leg, from the knife lodged in his boot, I assume, and a bruise the length of his spine.'' The doctor refrained from discussing any more and ordered restraints.

''Is that necessary? He's docile.''

The physician's gaze shifted meaningfully to the wounded sailors, and she sighed agreement.

''Was he hallucinating or something?'' Her words came hesitantly. ''The way he talks is so archaic.''

''It's like his clothes and belongings,'' Bindar said, peering closer, keen on solving the mystery. ''Nothing fits.''

Penny felt sympathy for Mister Ramsey O'Keefe, and perhaps a little curiosity, but nothing more, yet she couldn't keep from just looking at him. He was handsome enough, rugged features, square jaw, his chest tight with ropey muscles; not the kind a guy gets from pumping iron, but sleek and sinewy from hard physical work. He was big, yet the snugness of his trousers, hemmed just below his knees, accentuated his lean hips and powerful broad thighs.

A beautiful man.

But drop-dead gorgeous flirts no longer affected her. The film industry overflowed with their share, and she'd been pursued by hundreds just as sexy and confident as this one.

Turning away, she informed the skipper that she'd wait in the wardroom til the *Diana* docked. Glancing over her shoulder before stepping out, Penny suddenly resented his presence.

Ramsey O'Keefe was here.

And Tess was gone.

Forever.

Chapter 5

The haze of drugs lifted, yet Ramsey remained still, waiting several minutes for it to dissipate completely. Opening his eyes slowly, he examined his surroundings. He was alone, aboard ship, and a glance out the porthole told him 'twas nearing evetide. His gaze moved around the room, his eyes slow to focus. The transparent mask lay discarded in a metal waste basket, the clear molded form cracked, but not shattered. 'Tis not made of glass, he realized, for 'twas light as goose down. He searched for the familiar, aught that would offer a bit of information, a clue. The cabin was crammed with trays of metal instruments—of which he recognized only one—boxes, basins, glass jars, and large metal cylinders with tubes and metal configurations attached to the top. A surgeon's quarters, he deduced, having found the cutter's necessary on occasion in the past.

Past.

Or future, he wondered with the lift of his brow.

Beyond wanting to know the century he visited, whose vessel carried them so swiftly, with such God-awful noise? And how was the air chilled like a New England spring morn when he knew 'twas summer beyond the . . . what hay? 'Tis a wall of iron! Itching to see for himself, Ram tried to sit up and found his wrists and legs shackled to the bed frame with wide leather straps. Ruddy English. 'Twas an indignity he supposed he deserved after dressing down thrice over. Ram strained against the straps, bending the metal bars, yet the thick leather refused to give.

Bloody hell, captive again, he thought, propping himself up on his elbows and examining the bed frame for a weak spot.

Afore he found it, one of the men he'd flattened stepped through the hatch, a cloth-covered tray in his hands.

"Release me."

The crooked-nosed young sailor briefly glanced down at his tray. "In a minute."

"Nay, now. And you'll not be sticking me with those again, lad, if you wish to see another morn."

Graves hesitated, then set the tray on a rack and methodically filled the syringe. "It's necessary, sir. That cut," he gestured to Ram's bandaged calf—"is already inflamed. The weapon was filthy."

"I never planned on usin' it on meself," Ram snarled, his implication clear.

The lad raised the clear syringe, squirting liquid. "It's only an antibiotic."

Ram frowned skeptically, unwilling to voice his ignorance of such a drug.

"Are you afraid of needles, sir?"

"Watch yer mouth, puppy, and get on with it. Since I've no hands to thrash your impudent hide."

Graves smiled, poised near Ramsey's arm. "Ever had penicillin afore, Mister O'Keefe?" His words sounded stuffed and nasally and Ram regretted pounding such a young face.

"Nay." Ramsey watched him swab the area with a bit of pungent smelling fabric, the stroke leaving his skin cool as he inserted the needle into his skin. It burned the more the sailor depressed the plunger.

"Are you going to—ah—" Graves swallowed—"thrash my hide again, sir?"

"Will you give me cause?"

"No, sir." Graves discarded the syringe and pad, then unbuckled the straps, his eyes widening when he saw the bends in the bar.

Ramsey rubbed his wrists, sliding off the table, grinning when the seaman flinched. "My belongings?"

Graves gestured to the neat stack of clothing and the large flat yellow parcel, and Ram snatched the lad's arm, examining the clock strapped round his wrist. 'Twas incredibly small without numbers and nay, 'twould not chime, he decided after putting the glass to his ear.

"Sir?" Graves drew his arm back, frowning questioningly, yet Ramsey ignored the look, realizing he'd misplaced his hand in front of the enemy.

"Where am I?" Ram asked, shrugging into his shirt.

"Aboard a Bahama Air Sea Rescue ship, sir."

Ram arched a brow at the boy, tucking in his shirt tail. "A rescue vessel? Solely for retrieval?"

"Yes, sir."

Ingenious, Ram thought, impressed. "Where bound?"

"We ought to be putting ashore any minute. Crooked Island, sir."

Ram recalled naught of the place, but 'twas no matter now. He'd *traveled* through time for certain, yet exactly to where and what century, he'd have to deduce on his own—without raising suspicion, or he'd no doubt find himself locked up in some asylum. Yet as he pulled on his jacket, the conveniences surrounding him were unmistakable; the refined simplicity of the medical instruments, the iron walls, and the lad's wrist clock his first solid indication, and he knew 'twas in the future he'd found port. But how far?

His back throbbed mercilessly, reminding him of the consequences of his recklessness, though the impact of hitting the ocean's surface was a small price for the chance to begin anew. Prying up the brass tongs, Ram flipped open the envelope and froze, a sense of repetition claiming the moment. He turned the packet over in his hands. 'Twas a larger version of the one Tess possessed, once filled with colored diamonds. His gaze glazed over his surroundings again, ending on the glass filled porthole. Be I in your century, lass, he wondered, drowning his excitement and dumping the contents on the examining table. Graves leaned closer, but Ram's glare sent him back.

Ram held his time piece up to his ear, shaking it. Water filled and ruined. Slipping it into his pocket, he sheathed his knives and decided not to bother loading the pistol; the powder was wet, the shot jammed, and what remained in the horn and pouch were damp. After shoving the gun in his waistband, he fingered his jacket lining, surprised to feel the heavy coins, then donned the chains.

"Where did you get those?" Graves asked, gesturing to the matte gold chains as Ram secreted them beneath his shirt.

"A prize from the turn of a card, puppy." Ramsey didn't mention the Spanish bastard tried twice to regain possession and ended up bleeding all over Ram's finest blade. Dropping onto a stool, he pulled on his boots, his chest tight, the air slow going in.

"Well, I see you're calmer now."

Ram glanced up, then leapt to his feet, smiling broadly, unreasonably pleased she was still aboard. The woman leaned against the hatch frame, eyeing him from head to boots, then shifting her gaze to the sailor.

"The skipper would like to see you, Mister Graves."

"Aye-aye, Miss." The sailor nodded, flushing a bit too much, Ramsey thought, as he slipped past the woman.

They stared, unchanged, unmoving, and Ramsey experienced an exciting tension flickering atween them. 'Twas his first opportunity to gaze at her without the confusion of drugs or people about him and he let his eyes roam freely. Her garments shaped her body, defining where hip ended and thigh began. God love the fashions of this century, he thought, for he knew he could gaze upon her willowy legs for an eternity. She was as lovely as he first imagined, slender grace and feline seductive. Aye, a fine piece of woman, he thought. Truly fine.

"M'lady." Ram bowed from the waist, holding her gaze, his sizzling look driving gooseflesh across her bare arms.

Penny masked his effect by shifting her position, resisting

the urge to check if her clothes were burning off her. Those eyes were just too seductive to be legal.

"Now you really look like a pirate." Yo he ho, she thought. He grinned, and something flittered in her stomach.

" 'Tis not the image I wish to leave in your memory, lass."

His voice was deep and rumbling, and though she knew she should leave, Penny remained, curious. "Where are you from, Mister O'Keefe?"

"I once hailed from Lexington, mistress, yet the sea is my home."

She laughed shortly. "You liked it so much you tried to drink half of it?" His smile sweetened, and the churning in her belly quickened.

" 'Twas not my intention, I assure you. From whence do you hail, m'lady?"

Her brows rose. He honestly didn't know who she was. Well, for heaven sakes. Penny wasn't conceited, yet rather keenly aware of the publicity usually following her. Movie buffs wanted to know where she dined, who she was seeing, where she shopped, anything—which was one reason why she cherished her privacy.

Yet here was a man who genuinely didn't know her from Adam. What a kick.

"Florida. Were you stranded on a deserted island or what?" She was trying to reason out his clothes and speech when she ought to keep her mouth shut.

"Mayhaps." He shrugged, slowly crossing the room, his head feeling drugged again. "Or mayhaps shipwrecked." He stopped inches afore her, his gaze lingering over her delicate features, his words low and raspy. "Or even dropped from the heavens just for you?"

She rolled her eyes, her tone flat. "Right." A practiced flirt, she thought again, noticing his flushed skin. "Keep it to yourself," she sighed, "that's your business, anyway."

"And may I be so bold as to ask what a—" Ram paused to draw in air—"lovely lass is doing aboard this rescue ship?"

Her expression clouded, an imprint of haunted pain, and Ramsey regretted his prying.

"We were searching for a friend of mine, lost at sea," came tiny and sad.

His voice gentled. "I offer my deepest sympathy, m'lady." He bowed slightly, but it took a second to right himself.

Penny straightened, lowering her arms and looking him over. "Are you okay?"

He frowned at her, her voice distant.

"Mister O'Keefe?" His skin turned a horrible shade of purple and she didn't hesitate, pushing the emergency call button. The alarm sounded, and she grabbed his arm when he tottered. "Here, sit down." Foot steps thumped down the passageway. Ramsey's knees wobbled. "Mister O'Keefe, can you hear me?"

Hunched, Ram looked to the side, his swelling face inches from hers. "Ohh, aye, lass, and a damn sweet—" he struggled to fill his lungs—"sound it is, too." Suddenly his eyes rolled back, his limbs slackening and unable to support his weight, Penny slid to the floor with him just as the doctor raced in.

"He can't breathe!"

A crewman pulled her from the deck and Penny staggered back against the bulkhead, panic charging through her veins. The doctor slid to the floor, stripping off Ramsey's coat to examine him, issuing orders and preparing a syringe as a tech administered oxygen. "Allergic reaction to the penicillin," he told them, injecting his patient. The ship thumped against the dock as a crewman spoke into the intercom, ordering a chopper.

"Take mine," Penny offered into the chaos, his laborous wheezing clawing at her composure. "It should already be on the warf."

The doctor nodded thanks as the techs slid Ramsey's unconscious form onto a stretcher, strapping him in. "Bring a trache-pac. We may have to cut him open."

A tracheotomy, Penny thought, touching her throat.

Dear God.

He was dying. Again.

Someone thrust a bundle into her arms, and she clutched Mister O'Keefe's possessions to her chest as they maneuvered the stretcher through the hatch. For an instant she remained frozen, staring after the medical team as they negotiated the narrow corridor til the skipper nudged her, handing over her hat and oversized hand bag, then urging her to follow. Stuffing the bundle in her bag, she jammed on her hat and climbed the passageway, emerging on deck in time to see them lift him into the chopper. Beneath the flood lights, the craft rose in a swirl of sand and pebbles the instant the door shut. Heedlessly Penny raced to the rail, clutching iron and watching the chopper lights fade before tearing down the gangplank. *Please don't die.*

Cameras flashed and popped in her face, lighting the dark, and instinctively she turned away, a swarm of photographers and reporters shoving microphones beneath her chin.

"Was that Tess Renfrew in the chopper, Miss Hamilton?"

"Was she alive?"

"Reports state she jumped off the *Nassau Queen*, was it suicide?"

"What condition did you find the body?"

Penny shielded her face with her bulky bag as the skipper put an arm around her shoulder, gesturing heatedly to his men. Sailors pushed the media back, clearing a path to a waiting car.

"Vultures!" he muttered, dropping into the seat, cameras flashing beyond the glass. "The airport, please," he told the driver, then looked at Penny as the sedan pulled away. "I gather you want to go to the hospital?"

"No. My hotel first." His brows rose. "I can't help Mister O'Keefe now, and I need to change into something less obvious. If anything," she inclined her head toward the rear window and the reporters hounding beyond—"to distract them. The last thing he needs is the press grilling him, too."

If he lives, she thought, staring out into the night, the memory of his teasing smile hanging bright amidst her grief.

Ramsey would rather die than admit to anyone he was terrified out of his mind. He couldn't move. Mind and muscle refused to cooperate. Faces loomed in his field of vision, then receded. He felt as if he'd smoked opium, having tried it once afore and thought it useless to be so incoherent.

Needles pierced his arm. Firm hands tried to suffocate him with the masks, forcing him to breath in foul-tasting air. A half dozen men and women in green shirts asked him questions he couldn't answer; half because he couldn't understand what they meant, half because he couldn't form the words. His breathing was painfully slow and wheezy, and he couldn't begin to follow the conversation beyond the urgency in their voices.

God almighty.

He regretted taking the risk; regretted leaving the comfort and familiarity of his own time. He wanted to go back. Desperately. To lie bare-assed afore strangers was humiliating, then to have them do things to his body he couldn't stop only served to heighten the disgusting sensation. He closed his eyes, trying to block the debasing feel of the man's hands on his prick. A catheter, he said. Whatever the deuce that was.

You be an arrogant fool, O'Keefe. You're in a strange time, a hellish place, with tubes and needles stuck in you like some pagan sacrifice. You're penniless, weaponless, and you're dying, man, alone.

Bloody hell.

Bloody friggin' hell!

Chapter 6

Penny stood before the glass window, staring at the man lying in the hospital bed, the gray-cased monitor by his bedside pulsing his steady heartbeat. He was just a stranger, arriving in her life when she sought only Tess and answers. But watching him go from flirt to dead man made her uncharacteristically vulnerable. And she didn't like it one damn bit, didn't want to get involved with anyone, especially Robinson Crusoe here. Her emotions were back under control now, and she cursed herself for allowing him to get to her, for even the thought of men and relationships were out of the question in her career. *Especially* in an industry that was fertile ground for breeding scandal and invasion and backstabbing hatred. She needed her seclusion too much, and though maintaining it was an every day task, her life was just fine as it was.

Keep saying that and maybe you'll believe it, a voice pestered, sounding far too much like Tess, and she shifted her shoulders as if to nudge it away.

Admit it bud, you're the loneliest woman on this planet.

There's a difference between alone and lonely.

Coward.

Penny rubbed her forehead, a headache starting. She hadn't

slept and though a tiny part of her would like to blame him,
nightmares kept her awake. I ought to be used to it after so
many years, she thought, wanting to leave and be done with
him. Yet, holding the man's possessions forced her to pay him
a visit. Five minutes and that's it, she decided. No concern, no
attachment. No emotion.

Yet she watched him, memorizing his features, something
breaking open in her chest and flooding through her blood
stream every time she looked at him. It pulled, this sensation
and it made her wary. Ramsey O'Keefe reclined, half-sitting, his
chestnut-brown hair side-parted and shielding his face, flowing
beyond his shoulders. Her gaze lowered to the white hospital
gown, the taut fabric defining the muscles of his chest and
folded arms. Nice arms. He didn't move a fraction and stared
off into space, pitifully forlorn.

Stop it. Don't care. Don't! That's what gets you hurt. Just
deliver the goods and split!

"Miss Hamilton?"

Penny turned, the man's white coat marking him the doctor,
as did the stethoscope slung across his neck and no doubt, the
illegible notations he jotted on a chart. "Are you a friend of
Mister O'Keefe's?" He gestured with the top of his pen to the
window, then wrote some more.

"No. Yes. Well, not really."

The doctor shot a skeptical glance between his patient and
the actress, then continued making notations.

"I happen to be on the rescue ship when he was found."

"I see."

No, you don't, she thought, glancing at his name tag; DR.
MARKUM. "What's our acquaintance have to do with anything?"

He scribbled, dotting i's and crossing t's. "Have you spoken
to him?"

"Only briefly," she said, frowning, recalling his definitely
archaic speech.

Markum straightened, giving her his complete attention for
the first time. "I'd hoped you could help me, Miss Hamilton."
He gently pulled Penny away from the nurses' station. At four-

thirty in the morning the halls were dark, silent, yet his low tone sounded loud. "There are things about Mister O'Keefe that cannot be explained."

She adjusted her overloaded shoulder bag. "Such as?"

Her cool attitude made him hesitate for a second. "He hasn't been immunized against any childhood diseases."

"Not one?"

He shook his head. "Not even the standards for a toddler, DPT, HIB, polio. And his teeth are a puzzle in themselves. Two have been pulled."

"An every day occurrence."

"I don't mean surgically extracted, they've literally been yanked from his head. And from x-rays we've determined his jaw was cracked in the process." Her eyes widened a fraction. "The rest are fine, a bit crooked for the loss of the molars, and a few cavities need to be filled." He shoved his glasses back up the bridge of his nose. "Our resident DDS reports that Mister O'Keefe has had several hairline fractures in his chin and cheek and his nose has been broken at least five times."

Penny's face ached by the time he'd finished. "What does he," she inclined her head toward the ICU unit, "have to say about all this?"

"Nothing. He won't answer a single question and has refused any further testing."

"He has a right to privacy, Doctor Markum."

For an instant the diagnostician had forgotten he was speaking to America's most reclusive actress. "Aside that the police need answers he won't give, I can't administer any medication without more information and tests." The physician slipped his pen in his coat pocket, leaving a mark. "According to a medical records search, Ramsey O'Keefe has never been treated, at least not by a licensed physician in the Grand Islands, nor the U.S.

Penny arched a brow. "Perhaps he's just done without."

"Then he has the strength of an ox, for that man owns enough scars to warrant being a cop or a war hero." Markum hesitated then, shifting the aluminum chart to his other hand and staring at his patient. "No, he's had treatment. And beyond his medical needs, he has several scars on his back. And I'd bet my stethoscope," his gaze shifted back to her—"they're the result of a whipping."

"An abusive childhood?" she rushed to suggest, the horrifying image of him restrained as the skin was stripped from his back forming in her mind. It had to be childhood. The incident in the infirmary said he'd never allow such a barbaric crime without a fight.

"They're too . . . fresh," he said grimly. "Regardless, I can't treat him further, nor release him, not after what he's been through. I *need* more information, Miss Hamilton, and he won't talk." His tone implied she could get the answers he needed.

Penny doubted that.

Shielding her eyes, she was rubbing her temples, thinking she ought to stay out of *hippie's* business, when she heard the unmistakable sound of a camera shudder. She started to slip into the room, then halted, catching a glimpse of O'Keefe through the glass.

He shouldn't be subjected to this because of me, she thought. Especially if what Markum said was true. Turning on her heels, she brushed past the doctor and crossed the hall, arms reaching, her body briefly disappearing into a darkened alcove.

"Come on, Miss Hamilton, just one picture," Dr. Markum heard and moved closer, frowning into the shadowed corridor. Miss Hamilton stepped back, yanking a slender blond photographer none-too-gently by his camera strap until he was beneath the fluorescent light.

"Somehow I knew it was you, Maxwell." Tired, almost amused.

"Who else?" He smiled, unashamed. "You're my life's work, Miss Hamilton."

"I bet that really disappointed your mother." Penny turned the camera back-side up.

"Nah, she's a big fan. Hey, you can't—"

She slapped his hand away. "Yes, I can. This is a private hospital." Penny easily flipped the lock and with tapered nails, plucked out the roll. "Private." She jerked on it, exposing the film.

Doctor Markum, along with several hospital staff, watched the exchange as he picked up the phone and dialed security.

"But you're famous," the photographer said.

Penny's eyes narrowed as she unclipped the camera strap and turned away.

"And the public has a right to know." He followed, groping for his Nikon.

"Get lost before I call the cops." She elbowed him aside.

"Who's the long hair in ICU, Miss—?"

"Drop dead, Max." Penny reached for the knob to O'Keefe's door.

"He sure doesn't look like he needs intensive care." Max shifted behind her, trying to take back his camera, but she blocked him like a linebacker. Finally he gave up. "Why all the secrecy? Is he your latest lover? It *has* been a while, ya know. And I hear he's a real space case." His tone was snide. "Or is he Tess Renfrew's killer?"

Penny faced him, head tilted. "You know, Max, I might disregard the fact that you work for a cesspool magazine and give you the exclusive on this. Since you've always managed to report the truth." His face brightened. "But that crack just cost you any chance."

He blinked, false innocence shaping his face. "Which crack? The one about your lack of lovers, or the one—"

Penny schooled her features, a mask of cool indifference she wore well. "All the way out of the building, gentlemen," she said to someone behind Max.

His shoulders sagged. He knew that *you've pushed too far today* tone. "Okay, okay, I'm going. But I'm not quitting," he warned, wagging a finger.

Penny handed the camera over to the guards. "I never expected you to, Max." She turned away. "It's your nature to be a royal pain in the rear."

His gaze dropped to her buttocks, his smile appreciative. "And it's such a nice rear, too, Miss Hamilton." The guards grabbed Maxwell, dragging him backwards down the hall as Penny slipped into the room. Letting out her breath, she sagged back against the door, then drew the blinds. At least it was just one of them this time.

She stared at O'Keefe, pulling the heavy bag from her shoulder. The weight of it jerked her arm and she rubbed the strap bruise, walking to the side of his bed.

"Hey, Mister O'Keefe? Are you awake?"

No response. Asleep, she assumed, dropping the bag on the floor and sliding into the bedside chair. I'll wait. She picked up a magazine, the pages crackling as she flipped distractedly.

"Go away, woman."

Penny flinched, glancing up. He didn't look at her and she imagined he was embarrassed by the swelling from the reaction.

"No, thank you." She returned her gaze to the magazine. "I'll wait here, if you don't mind."

"I do mind."

"Yes, well, you'll have to suffer my presence for just a little while longer." In truth, Penny needed only a few minutes for the guards to get Max off this floor.

"I do not-wish-your-company!" Tortured, raspy.

Penny looked up, slowly laying the magazine aside as she stood. "Are you feeling all right, Mister O'Keefe? Can I get the doctor for you?"

"Nay! 'Tis my wish that you simply *leave me in peace!*" By the blood of Triton, Ram despaired, was the woman so addle-patted she could not see 'twas embarrassing to have her here, in his room, when he was shackled to tubes and such? Sweet Christ, a damned bottle of piss lay not but a foot from her!

"Wish I could. But I've got your things, and well, there's this, ah—" Her gaze clung to the muscle working violently in his jaw. Something was definitely wrong. "Are you sure there isn't anything I can do for you?" An uneasy silence filled the air between them. "Mister O'Keefe?" His breath came quick and harsh. His tanned fists clenched and unclenched, crumpling the pristine sheets. And she nearly swallowed her tongue when he slowly turned his head, stunned by the rage in his dark eyes.

"Get me out of here." Precise and biting.

"Out?" Her brows rose. "Right now?"

"Aye!" By God, but it unmanned him to ask for *her* help.

She glanced over her shoulder to the unblinded windows. A pair of white nurses' caps peeked the high desk; computer screens pulsed green lines beyond them. She returned her gaze to his. "How much of this are you hooked up to?" She waved at his sheet-covered body.

Ramsey's skin darkened, and briefly he glanced away, humiliated. "A great deal, I fear."

"Yeah, me too," she agreed and he made a pained sound, sinking into the pillows. "If I help you," she couldn't fathom why she was even considering it, "what happens if you croak on me?"

He looked at her, his brows tight. "Croak?"

"Die. Keel over."

"I assure you, madame, I am quite fit."

Her gaze slid easily over him again. I just bet you are, she thought, then dropped into the chair. "I don't see how you can manage."

Ramsey folded his arms over his chest, certain if forced to spend another moment captive to those white knights of torture, he'd lose his sanity. "You need only show me the way out."

Her gaze shifted from the monitors, to the I.V.s, to the wires disappearing beneath his gown, then to the clear green oxygen tube stretched beneath his nose and she could only imagine what else was holding him in that bed.

"Impossible." She met his gaze and saw his disappointment. "Well, just look at you!" She waved at the bed.

With a viscous snarl Ramsey yanked at the oxygen tube until it snapped, then threw it aside, pure air hissing against blue tile. Grasping a handful of the gown, he tugged once and it gave, the ripping sound catapulting her to her feet. Before she could stop him he peeled off the two EKG leads on his chest, the monitor drawing a blank line, the alarm sounding as he dispensed with the third.

"Mister O'Keefe!" He tore the tapes from his forearm, footsteps thumping down the hall as he made to pull out the long I.V. needle. "Oh, Jesus. Don't." She slapped her hand over the area, their faces inches apart. "Okay. Okay! I get the message," she rushed to say. "You're serious. But for God's sake, don't pull anything else out."

Without so much as flinching, he yanked. Blood dampened her palm and she applied pressure, snatching up tissues as a nurse burst into the room.

Ramsey pointed to the door. *"Begone!"* he roared and the nurse's wide gaze shot to Penny.

She waved her off. "He's fine, obviously," she assured and the nurse backed out of the room as Penny switched off the beeping monitor. She looked at Ramsey.

And only his eyes shifted, the stare ice cold. "I believe they've stowed my clothing in the wardrobe." He gestured to the closet.

She hesitated, replacing her palm with tissues. "But aren't you, ah, well you know, attached?" Smoothly he arched a brow. "Nothing?" Her gaze darted down the length of him.

Ramsey leaned on his elbow, close, his dark eyes sparkling. "Mayhaps the lady would like to verify the fact?" He lifted the sheet lying on his bare stomach.

"Spare me the thrill," she said, deadpan, ignoring the effects of that smile and searching the nightstand for a bandage. God. He went from raging to lusty tease in the space of a heartbeat.

Ramsey studied her as she tended the scratch, his gaze roaming leisurely over the claret-red hair pulled high on her crown with a thin ribbon. Her skin was golden, smooth, yet he could see the light touch of paints enhancing her beauty. He'd like to see her without it. For that matter he'd truly enjoy viewing her shapely assets in naught but a smile—which she'd yet to bestow on him. And why in God's name was she wearing garments ten sizes too big, he wondered, eyeing the man's jacket pushed up at the elbows, her rose silk blouse disguising her plumper attributes. But 'twas her faded blue breeches that gathered his attention—and held it. He couldn't drag his gaze from their snug fit across her hips, and lower, the fabric outlining every curve and valley of her more softer parts. He swallowed. God save me, did every woman in this century wear such provocative garments? He lifted his gaze to find her glaring at him, her lips pressed tight, arms akimbo.

"Are you quite through?" she snapped and he flashed her an unexpected grin.

"Nay, lass, yet 'twill do for now." Her deep green eyes narrowed, and his smile broadened. "My clothing, please."

His high handedness irritated and she folded her arms in silent challenge. "If you're so hot to get out of here, you get them!"

"If you insist." He tossed the sheet back and climbed from the bed, naked.

"Oh, wonderful."

Reaching for the wardrobe, Ramsey glanced up, expecting to see her back and had the good grace to blush, for she stood with her arms folded still, looking him up and down just as bold as she pleased. Saucy wench, he thought, meeting her gaze. "Are *you* through, madame?"

"Get dressed, Mister O'Keefe, that's nothing I haven't seen before." Penny nearly choked on the lie. God, it was a crime to have a body like that.

"I am truly moved by your compliments, lass." He opened the door, blocking her view, a bit ashamed of his tactics. Was she a bawd, he wondered, donning his breeches and ignoring his slight dizziness. Nay, the lass was simply returning his jibe. Like Tess would. He grinned, bending to yank on his boots, intrigued. And he dared a little more. " 'Tis a shame the connoisseur finds naught to her liking."

"Watch your mouth, mister," she warned softly, smiling at his elegantly delivered payback, more than just those muscular tanned thighs burning across her memory. The closet door jolted and Penny moved closer. "O'Keefe?" She peered around the wood. "Damn." He was slumped against the wall, still standing, his eyes squeezed shut, his breathing heavy. "Here, lean on me." She slipped her arm around his waist, groaning as his weight sagged against her. "I thought you said you were *quite fit?*"

He straightened, blinking down at her. "Do forgive me the slight indiscretion, m'lady."

Penny wasn't sure which one he meant; the flasher scene or this, but his skin was warm where it brushed her cheek, rock hard beneath her hand on his bare ribs. And she noticed several shiny scars on his chest as she lifted her gaze to his. He smiled, slow and masculine, and her insides sang like a finely tuned violin. Max was right; it has been a while.

"What name have you, little one?"

She responded instantly to the whispered question.

"Penny—Penelope Hamilton." She hadn't had to introduce herself since her first movie hit the theatres. God, this was strange. And she couldn't shake the terrifying feeling that helping funny talking Ramsey O'Keefe, in any way, would somehow destroy her very private life.

Chapter 7

Ramsey was tempted.

God almighty, but he sorely itched to ply that sour mouth with long wet kisses, til she was breathless and wanting. And mayhaps smiling. 'Twould be easy enough. For her face was near, close enough to see the vivid starburst green of her eyes, feel the brush of her breath against his bare chest. Her body, lusher than he first imagined, was pressed to his side, warm and yielding and smelling exotically sweet, yet he resisted the allure, unaware of how a woman of this time—whichever the deuce it was—would react.

Her screaming like a banshee would not do just now.

And he needed her help.

His gaze drifted past her and he nodded beyond. "I believe 'tis time to make our escape, Mistress Hamilton."

She twisted to look. Two uniformed men walked away from the elevators. "Oh, splendid. The cops."

"I beg your pardon?"

She returned her gaze to his and as if just realizing how intimately they touched, smoothly disengaged herself and stepped back. "The police."

He continued to frown as he shrugged into his shirt, aware of the chill surrounding her now.

"The authorities," she clarified, grabbing her tote bag and pulling out his jacket.

"The constabulary, aye." Ram stood, stuffing the shirt tails in his breeches. " 'Tis an unpleasant lot, those."

It was her turn to frown, her eyes suspicious. "Have you committed a crime or something?"

Though Ramsey considered time-travel might be a sin, he denied the allegation, then pulled a ribbon from her hair as if 'twere his right. Vivid deep red silk cascaded over her shoulders, and she shoved it back, irritated.

Ramsey raked his fingers through his own hair and secured it with her ribbon, grinning hugely. Fiesty lass. "Nay, do not bind it," he said when she gathered her hair into a knot. " 'Tis a glorious sight, Mistress Hamilton." He lifted a deep-red lock, sanding it atween his fingers. "As if a fire's trapped inside every strand." He brought it to his nose and inhaled, closing his eyes.

She couldn't move, her gaze on his serene expression, its effect running like quicksilver to her heart. Then she yanked her hair from his grasp. "Your toys are bundled inside, Casanova," she muttered, shoving the rolled coat in his stomach. He just smiled that sappy grin and Penny turned away, striding to the windows. No attachment, no emotion, she reminded as she peered between the half tilted blinds. The police were speaking to Dr. Markum.

"Please hurry."

Completely dressed Ramsey slipped his knives into their hiding proper places, wincing when the blade tip grazed his stitched calf, then began loading the pistol.

She glanced over her shoulder. "What *are* you doing?"

"Arming meself," he said as if she should know.

She was entranced, watching his long fingers swiftly load the antique gun, then considered that thing might actually fire. "Do you plan to shoot your way out of here?"

"If need be." He rammed the shot home, then stuffed the pistol in his waist band.

He was dead serious, she realized, examining his expression. "Look, Mister O'Keefe—"

He flashed her an easy smile. "I'm called Ramsey, lass."

"Give me that." She held out her hand.

He scoffed. "Methinks you envision a fool here, woman."

She nearly laughed at his antiquated words. "Swear to me you won't use it." She didn't believe it would work, especially after getting wet, but just the same . . . "Swear to me."

He planted his hands on his lean hips, his belligerent expression implying she was insane to even ask.

"Terrific," she said, rolling her eyes. "A mutiny in the ICU." Voices grew louder and she glanced out the window, then flipped off the lights.

"What the ruddy hell—?"

"Shhh! They're coming this way. I'll stall them, you get into bed and cover up." She slipped out of the room before he could say another word.

Ramsey didn't get himself abed and instead stuffed pillows into a mound, made the proper indentations, then stood by the door, listening. He frowned at the ceiling, as yet unable to comprehend how the light appeared and disappeared on command. 'Twas so bright afore, he marveled. Surely the captured fire would burn the place to cinders? Sudden movement beyond the room drew his attention. Mistress Hamilton conversed with the doctor and the authorities, though the men appeared more enraptured with her figure than her words. Any male breathing would, he thought, unable to hear a scrap. He flattened against the wall when one gent moved closer to the glass, peering inside. Ramsey remained still til footsteps receded, then dared a look. After giving a calling card to the lass, the two departed with the doctor.

Ramsey waited, impatient and restless, annoyed he was dependent on Mistress Hamilton to lead him out. Oh, she was a damn fine piece of woman, even if she always looked dower enough to clabber milk, yet 'twere a chilling side to the lass he'd already recognized, and 'twas obvious she wanted naught but to end their association, however thin. Though Ramsey honestly didn't know what he'd do once he was free of this hellish chamber, aught was safer than suffering humiliation on an hourly basis by these white clad creatures of the future.

Ramsey still wanted to go back. To his time. He'd seen enough of this century and didn't care for much of it. Expect mayhaps a little redhead, he corrected with a wry smile, stepping back as the door opened. The woman slipped inside, and he cupped a hand over her mouth, pulling her back against his chest.

"Now we depart, lass, afore I go bleedin' mad."

She nodded, and in the dim light he twisted her til she looked him in the eye. "Ahh, you've a fine temper I see." He grinned. "I do so love a wench with spirit."

She bit his palm, and he released her instantly. "Wench?" she hissed. "Good God, who let you out of your cave?" She rubbed her mouth. "And was holding me hostage absolutely necessary?"

Unaffected, Ram sucked his abused hand. "Nay, 'twas mere curiosity."

"About what?"

He leaned down in her face, cognac-brown eyes brimming with mischief. "Whether or nay you always be looking as if you've supped on a bucketful of lemons?" She glared murderously up at him. "Pray tell, lass, nary a word in your defense?" he teased, then withdrew his pistol, gesturing with the barrel for her to lead.

"Oh, for crying out loud, holster that thing," she said, pushing the barrel aside and quickly retrieving her bag. "You can walk out of here if you want. It just takes some time, a few forms, but you certainly don't need a weapon."

"Then why all the espionage?" he asked as she returned to his side, suddenly distrusting her.

Penny still couldn't believe this guy. "Because *I* want to avoid being seen."

"Have *you* committed a crime?" he whispered close to her ear. She shushed him like a schoolmaster and eased the door open. Poking her head out, she waved for him to follow, and they tiptoed out of the room and down the hall to a door marked *stairs*. The heavy steel closed behind them with such a soft hush, Ramsey paused to glare at it.

"Come on," she whispered, racing down the stairs. Penny always got a weird thrill evading the press like this.

They covered two more flights in record time. Even with his wounded leg, he was right behind her, soundless for such a big man.

"Boy, am I outta shape," she said, winded and leaning against the cement wall.

"Fishing for praise, lass?" he whispered, towering over her and Penny smirked, then opened the door a crack. A clear shot to the car. After digging in her purse for the keys, she inclined her head for him to follow and slipped through the door.

Ramsey trailed like an obedient puppy til she stopped afore a large silver contraption, pushing a key into a lock and turning it.

"Get in," she said, removing the key and striding round the beast.

He looked in horror at the low, shiny wheeled beast, then to her. "In? You want to climb into its belly?"

Penny couldn't be more puzzled. "Yes, and now would be good."

"In God's name, woman, how?"

"The handle," she said over the top of the car and still he hesitated, rapping on the roof and peering into the car. *"Today, Mister O'Keefe."*

A cracking sound drew him around, his gun out, the hammer back, and Penny marveled at the effortless move, then looked where he aimed. Maxwell stood frozen, his camera shudder clicking continuously.

"Damn you, Max."

"You are acquainted with this runt?" Ramsey gestured with the barrel.

"Jesus, what a front page this'll make! Penelope Hamilton flees hospital with her latest lover, Captain Blood!"

In three strides Ramsey was on him, fisting his shirt front and lifting Max off the floor. "If you value your hide, *whelp*,"

Ram said in a tone that could shave ice—"I suggest you beg off those words."

Maxwell looked uncertainly at Penny. "Is he for real?"

Ramsey shoved the barrel beneath the man's chin.

"Yes, I believe so." Humor colored her voice.

"The words, pup, afore I splatter your empty head!"

"Oh, for crying out loud, will you just put him down?"

"Nay." Ramsey didn't take his eyes off the impudent brat. " 'Tis insulted you, he has." Ramsey shook him, making the cameras bang together. "Apologize to the lady!"

"Sorry, Mi—mis H-Hamilton."

He wasn't satisfied, Penny thought, moving around the car. Stopping beside them, she impatiently opened the camera and yanked on the film. Max groaned.

"You can let him go, now, Sir Galahad."

Ramsey abruptly opened his fingers. The photographer dropped to the concrete on his rump as the hollow echo of rapid footsteps came to them.

Penny grabbed Ramsey's arm. "Come on!"

She dragged him to the car, opening his door, his head banging against the metal rim as she shoved him into the leather seat, then sealed him in. Then she was beside him, muttering something about pointless gallantry and turning the key. The silver beast roared and Ram's eyes went wide. People converged outside the coach, shouting her name and questions; small flashes of light blinded him and he turned his face away.

"Seat belt," she said, and he copied her movements, harnessing himself in. She shifted a stick resting atween them, and Ramsey thought he'd be catapulted through the glass when the contraption unexpectedly lurched. Instead he was plastered to the seat, the scenery whizzing past him with amazing speed. His spine numbed with his effort to remain calm, and he swallowed, glancing to her, then to the rushing view before him as they burst from the darkened cave and into the dawn light.

"*Sweet Jesus!*" Ramsey wasn't certain leaving captivity was wise now and dared a look out the rear window. His eyes widened further. God almighty! The building was over six floors high! He looked at Mistress Hamilton. The little witch was bloody close to smiling, rather pleased with herself, it appeared. How on earth she could enjoy this bizarre ride was beyond his comprehension, yet Ramsey willed himself to relax, studying first the panel afore her. A needle moved past a series of numbers within a glass covered dial; approaching fifty, he determined.

She shifted the black stick.

"What does M.P.H. represent?"

Penny glanced at him; his face was extremely pale. "Miles per hour."

"Nay! 'Tis impossible to reach such a speed on land! You lie!"

She looked offended, but kept her eyes on the road. "Why should I lie?" Then added, "Never mind."

She rotated the wheel sharply, and the world passed in a blur. We have struck a pig, he deduced, for the squeal was too sharp to be aught else. Then he realized they were speeding down another street. Again, she moved the stick and the silver carriage sped faster. Ramsey closed his eyes, ordering himself not to be ill. He didn't care for this a'tall. Then they slowed or at least he felt the roaring lessen, and he opened first one eye, then the other.

"You okay?"

He shot her an irritated glance. "I despair to imagine what havoc you might wreak were those reins in your hands, Mistress Hamilton."

"Reins? As in a horse?"

"Aye, and God save me from women drivers," he swore, scowling darkly as a thought suddenly occurred to him. "Why were all those *men* chasing you?"

She ignored his emphasis and said, "They're reporters."

"That offers me no help, woman."

"They report the news." The Jag felt unreasonably small with him in it.

"And our escape—'twas noteworthy?" He received naught but a shrug.

Penny downshifted, stealing a quick look at her passenger. If he didn't know why she was always hounded, she wasn't going to tell him. It was kind of nice talking to someone who wasn't going to run to the papers at the first opportunity.

"Who protects you?" He'd seen none who'd constitute a chaperone or guardian.

"Say again?" It was cute, his playing with the electronic windows.

"Who sees to your safety?" Surely women didn't walk about unescorted.

"*I* do." Penny picked up the car phone and dialed with her thumb.

Ram glowered his disapproval, his gaze glazing over her slim form, the delicate hand wrapped around a thin oblong box. " 'Tis a speck, you are," he scoffed. "Give over now, lass. I'll have the truth."

"It is." Her brows drew down. "How long did you say you were stuck on that island?"

Ramsey's lips twitched. Marooned, was it? 'Twas certainly an enterprising concept.

"Daniel? Miss Hamilton," she said into the box. "My bags arrive? Have we been cleared for take off? Good, I'm about three blocks away. Warm her up."

Ramsey grabbed the box when she made to replace it, depressing the numbered tabs and putting it to his ear as she had. Naught, and he frowned at the box.

"A telephone," she said, enjoying his confusion. Christ. This guy was right out of the dark ages.

Ram silently replaced the box, turning his face away to view the sights beyond the glass. Scarcely dawn, the township appeared blue-gray and he tried to absorb everything passing afore his vision; the bright colored awnings and bold advertisements for food and lodging. The prices stated were an outrage, for a night's lodging equaled the price of his last shipment of pepper! He pressed his face against the glass to see the tops of structures appearing to scrape the clouds, then smothered a snicker over the giant slab of wood with the image of a pirate emblazoned across a ship, beneath his feet the invitation to visit his lair. No sailor worth his salt would don a plumed hat such as that. At least the Scots have done well, he noticed, the McDonald clan owning four taverns thus far.

"What is our destination?" he asked, poking through the glove box. "Since you've taken the choice from me."

"*We* aren't going anywhere. And I'm here." Penny turned the wheel, and the Jaguar slid into the parking slot. She turned off the motor and Ramsey scowled at the abrupt silence, ducking to examine the dashboard. "Goodbye, Mister O'Keefe." He looked up. "It's been an adventure escaping with you." At least he'd kept her mind off Tess, she thought, her smile falling. She extended her hand, and Ramsey grasped it, his eyes colliding with hers as he drew it to his lips, placing a soft kiss to the back. "Oh, please." She wiggled free, shaking her head as she opened the door. "Here, have fun." She tossed him the key and he caught it. "It's rented until tomorrow."

Ramsey fought with the latch til the door sprang open, then climbed out. She was already walking toward a small building. 'Twas no wonder the wench wore breeches; she moved too bloody fast. A man in a small red cap spoke to her, nodded, then disappeared beyond Ram's line of vision. What could she possible want here, he wondered, tossing the key into the carriage and striding after her. Afore he rounded the corner of the building his attention caught on a large box with a glass front. A newspaper, he realized after closer examination. Bending down, he squinted against the sunlight, shielding a corner of the glass to read the date: "June 16, 1989."

Nineteen.

Oh, sweet Mary, Mother of God.

I'm a friggin' antique!

Chapter 8

The hatch opened like a yawning mouth, hydraulics lowering the curved section of fuselage as Penelope approached the silver Lear jet.

"Let's go," she shouted above the whining engines, mounting the steps and ducking inside. Daniel immediately raised the small staircase as soon as she passed, then sealed the hatch. Penny dropped into the lush velour seat, brushing her hair from her face. The loose strands brought her mind immediately back to Ramsey O'Keefe, and she peered out the small thickly glassed window toward the sun bleached terminal. She couldn't see him and suddenly realized that giving him the keys to the Jag wasn't such a hot idea. He was just too innocent about cars.

The jet engines squealed, the wheels rolled.

"Belt up, Miss H.," came over the intercom. "We're cleared."

Absently, Penny strapped herself in, staring out the window.

The aircraft taxied beyond the terminal, and she saw him, hunched over, his dark head bowed between outstretched arms, palms flat on top of a newspaper vending machine. Was he dizzy again?

Abruptly he straightened, wrenching in her direction. His eyes went wide as coins, his gaze clinging to the aircraft. Wind lifted strands of his long hair, whipped at his shirt and coattails as he stood immobile.

He never looked more out of place than he did now, she thought, her heart doing something she couldn't name.

He's alone. And I've abandoned him.

No, I haven't. He's a big boy, she argued. He'll be fine.

But what about his lack of knowledge with the car, his childlike curiosity over the cellular phone. Could he really be *that* out of touch?

Suddenly she punched the intercom. "Stop the plane, Daniel."

"What? Miss H., we're about—"

"Stop, now!"

Penny was out of her seat and at the door, punching controls, sending the steps down before the wheels ground to a halt, cabin pressure releasing into the humid Bahama morning. It hadn't locked in place before she leaned out and shouted, "Mister O'Keefe!"

He peered, squinting against the sun and Penny waved him over, almost laughing at his startled expression when he recognized her.

"Mistress Hamilton?" he mouthed in undisguised awe, moving toward the plane, his pace unhurried. And cautious, if she judged correctly.

"Come on!" She waved impatiently. "We still have tower clearance!"

This has to be the dumbest thing I've done yet, Penny thought. But, she couldn't leave him. Not when he looked so much like a little boy lost at the circus, unable to decide whether or not to find his family or watch the three-ring show. He walked up to the jet, rapped on the wing, the fuselage, then slowly mounted the aluminum steps.

"Will you please move along, Mister O'Keefe. Quickly." When he didn't, continuing to run his hand over the rubber hatch seal, she grabbed his arm and yanked him inside. The copilot secured the door as she directed Ramsey to a seat. Penny pushed the black intercom button.

"Okay, Daniel, let's roll. And Daniel?"

"Yes, Miss H.?"

"Thanks."

"We aim to please, ma'am."

Wheels rolled, the pressure equalized, and Penny looked at Ramsey. As he done with everything else they'd met, he was curiously examining his surroundings, poking at the cushions, feeling the velour interior, jiggling the small table bolted to the floor. It was sort of charming.

"Sit here," she said, switching seats so he was near the window. Like a mother she belted him in, the click bringing his attention from the view outside.

Do all the conveyances of this century require a harness, Ramsey wondered, then briefly glanced outside as the silver bird-ship rattled. The world seemed to race to catch up with them, the noise increasing to a whine.

"What sort is this metal vessel?" His gaze wandered over the inside of the craft.

"A plane. A Lear jet to be exact." He wasn't impressed.

" 'Twill travel the roads such as the silver carriage?"

Penny's brows drew together. "No," she said carefully. "It flies."

Ramsey swallowed, his throat muscles grating like sand. "Tell me 'tis not so, woman. Balloons and birds fly, not metal—" He looked toward the window. "Great Neptune!" He gripped the thin lip beneath the window, knuckles gone white. "We're leavin' the bloody ground!" He pressed his nose to the glass as the Lear jet lifted off the runway, taking them over the tops of bent palm trees and azure hemmed beaches. "Ahh, God almighty," he moaned softly. " 'Tis a sin to tempt this. A bleedin' sin!" Ramsey felt her touch on his arm and vaguely heard his name. He didn't respond. His heart remained wedged in his throat, and he couldn't choke it down.

He was flying.

Sweet Jesus in heaven—flying!

"Mister O'Keefe?"

"Humm." He didn't take his gaze from the scene below.

"You okay?"

She was inquiring after his health, he decided. "Oh, aye, lass, aye." He sank back into the seat, chuckling quietly between rapid breaths.

"I can't believe you've never flown." His hands trembled, she noticed.

Ram closed his eyes, shaking his head. "Never." *Ahh, Tess, you should have warned me, lass.*

"We'll be in Florida in less than two hours."

Ramsey's gaze snapped to hers. He'd not deny the possibility. 'Twas a world far more advanced than he ever imagined. And now he wanted to see all of it. Do everything.

Then he was unconscious.

Penny gasped, feeling his forehead, which was cool, then his pulse, racing like mad. She worried her lower lip for a second, then unbelted herself to get him some water. He hadn't eaten anything solid since—lord, she didn't know when. In the small galley, she searched the latched silver cabinets for cups, then slipped one into the dispenser and punched the button, filling a plastic cocktail glass with ice water. Returning to her seat, she absently set the cup on the stationary table as she checked his pulse again, pleased it had slowed. She was about to release his hand when its sandpaper roughness grazed her skin. She frowned, turning it palm up. Lightly, she ran her fingertip over the unusually thick calluses, the skin bunched and stained dark from hard work. What had he done to survive, she wondered, studying his features as she relaxed into the seat.

Who was this man, really? Where had he come from? And why did he talk like someone out of a fairy tale? Her gaze dropped to the worn grip of the pistol protruding from just inside his coat. He knew how to use it, treated it with a lover's care and a smile tugged at her lips as the image of him holding the antique gun on poor Max burst vividly in her mind. Max would have crapped his jeans if he'd thought it worked. So would I, she knew. Unwillingly her gaze slipped down over his long legs, relaxed and stretched out, nearly touching the next cluster of seats. She remembered how they looked bare;

golden-brown to midthigh, extremely muscular, lightly dusted with dark hair, everything, down to the last detail—much to her annoyance—including the shiny scar that wrapped around his right knee.

He wasn't anything special. Extremely odd, but nothing special. For heaven's sake, the hippie had his head stuck somewhere between the ridiculousness of a knight in shining armor and a little boy playing pirate. Yet he seemed lost, and beyond the constant excitement brightening his eyes, she recognized the loneliness lurking beneath. It matched the one she saw in the mirror.

"Is it me boots that hold such a fascination, lass?" Her gaze shot to his; he was grinning. "Or dare I hope 'tis the man yer interested in?"

She shoved the drink at him, her lips pulling into a tight line. "You passed out."

"Nay." He downed the water, savoring the clear sweet taste as he examined the cup. " 'Twas merely a nap."

"If you insist." A big kid, she thought as he watched the plastic bend and retract.

Ram cast her a side glance, eyes bright and teasing. "Is that worry I hear in your voice?"

"Hardly."

"Ahh, such a sour puss you are, lass," Ramsey said, glancing, then returning his gaze sharply to the view out the window. "Dear God!" He straightened, the sides of the plastic cup splitting in his grip. They rode above the clouds!

"Pretty, isn't it?" she said close to his ear.

"Oh, aye." Montgolfier would never believe this, he thought, trying to slow his breathing as he sat back.

"Are you going to be all right for a minute?"

"I believe I can manage," he answered with a slight scowl, offended by her coddling. She smirked, rising and moving to the opposite side of the flying ship. Ram watched her at leisure, considering whether or not those lush lips were always pinched in a frown as she lifted an oblong box, much like the one in the silver carriage. A telephone, he remembered, deducing she received some sort of response after pushing all those tabs. His gaze clung to her lips, lovely, damned kissable, yet he never met a female with more to smile about, yet rarely took a moment for the simple pleasure.

Blast, if the woman didn't have an elegant reef built around her. Pleasant to look upon, yet dangerously sharp. Anyone with a salt of sense could feel it. 'Twas nary a wonder why she'd no chaperone or protector; those cat-green eyes were more powerful at keeping people at bay than the sting of Toledo steel.

Acquainted with many women in the past, Ram often made a wide berth round such dower females, unwilling to battle their dark secrets for a few moments atween plump thighs. Was that not why you took the leap, old man? For a faceless woman who'd fill the emptiness brought from your world? Ram observed Penelope Hamilton, the stiffness of her carriage, the incredibly beauty of her face and figure, yet a pretty face he'd never had difficulty finding afore, in his century. 'Twas a woman, full of mind and determination, of the independence he recognized in Tess, that he wanted.

Mayhaps 'twas merely the confidence and power she wielded over men and machine that drew him to Penelope Hamilton. 'Twas definitely not her delicious little package that intrigued, for save one instant when he'd clapped a hand over her mouth in the dark, she was the most emotionless wench he'd met. By God, she'd such an *"I can not be conquered, therefore do not bother,"* look in her eyes, Ram was reluctant to strike even further conversation with her. His finest seductive attempts had failed miserably, and he wondered what it would take to win Mistress Penelope Hamilton's cold heart.

Penny tapped her nails against the table surface, then inadvertently met his gaze. Ramsey O'Keefe studied her, meticulously, and though she was certainly used to being scrutinized, she didn't care for the unfamiliar sensations he caused. She wanted to look away, knew she should since she didn't want to give him the wrong idea, but she couldn't. His chocolate eyes seemed to coat and swallow her as she mumbled her credit card number to the operator, unable to break away.

"Hello? Hello? Wainright here. Who is this?"

Penny's attention jolted to the call. "Tony? Hi. It's me."
She shifted away from O'Keefe.

"Where the devil are you, my dear?"

"About thirty thousand feet up."

"Excellent. Hank is just pulling off the exit, I believe. And
a bit too fast." Penny heard Hank give their ETA. "If you can
make that time," Anthony growled, "you're fired!"

"You can't fire him, Anthony. He's my driver."

"You should, my dear. This dinosaur is actually listing to
one side with every turn."

Her lips twitched. Hank could be going forty miles an hour
and Anthony would think it was the Indy 500. "That dinosaur
is worth a fortune, Anthony."

"As if you ever cared," was his reply. The connection crackled and his voice faded.

"Ahh, Tony—" She swallowed, gathering nerve. "I have
a guest with me."

Dead silence. Then, "You can't be serious?" His shocked
voice was enough to make her cringe.

"Amazing, isn't it?" Penny glanced briefly at Ramsey, who
was doing his best to unnerve her with that penetrating stare.
Half twisted toward her, his torso was braced by one elbow on
the chair arm, hands clasped, booted ankles crossed. The stark
outline of his broad thigh against the pale interior held her
attention. Damn those legs.

"Penelope? Penelope?" filtered through the phone. 'Are
you all right?" Ramsey leaned forward slightly, eyes digging
deep into her composure, and Penny bristled, turning away.
"Penelope!" Tony shouted.

"What!" she hissed back.

He tisked into the receiver. "Testy, aren't we? Are you
regretting your gracious invitation?"

Yes, she silently screamed. Yes! But instead she said, "Any
word?"

"I'm sorry, dear. Can't hear—what was—?"

Penny frowned softly. Funny, the connection wasn't fading
on her end. "Have they contacted you?" she repeated.

"The Bahama rescue are—" the connection drifted, then

returned. ''This is ridicu—! Too many build—talk to you—the ground—''

The line went dead, and Penny replaced the phone, quick fear accelerating her heart beat.

Tony knew something.

''Who captains this ship?''

Penny glanced up; he hadn't moved, but his smile was gone. ''What? Oh, a pilot. Daniel.'' She waved toward the front.

''The voice in the grate?'' He pointed to the vented white plate.

''No, yes, the guy that was at the door?'' He looked even more confused. ''Wait a sec.'' What had Tony discovered, she wondered as she punched the intercom. ''Daniel, we're coming up.'' Then she stood, gesturing for him to join her.

Ramsey started to rise, but the harness jerked him back down. Penny's lips twitched and she looked away as he cursed and released the latch. Then he was there, close and towering over her, his dark head grazing the cool beige ceiling. His rough fingertip touched beneath her chin, tilting her face toward his and for one wildly exciting moment she thought he'd actually kiss her.

''Ahh, lass, I would bear the point of a blade if 'twould gain me m'lady's smile.'' The words were softly spoken, sincere, and Penny looked away.

''This way, Mister O'Keefe.'' Oh, why did I do this?

Ramsey sighed, his shoulders drooping as she moved around the partition and rapped on the door. It popped open, revealing Daniel just dropping back into his seat and replacing his headset. Penny ducked, stepping into the cockpit. His blond copilot smiled brightly, pulling his headset to one side as he looked beyond her to Ramsey.

''Daniel, Wes, this is Mister Ramsey O'Keefe.''

Ram nodded absently, his gaze on the magnificent view beyond the glass.

''And believe it or not, he's never seen a plane.''

Both men looked at each other, then their guest.

''I know, crazy, isn't it? How about explaining a little to him?''

"Sure thing, Miss H." Daniel gestured for Ramsey to come closer.

"I'll leave you fellas to this . . . stuff," she said, waving at the mess of dials and switches before turning to leave. The plane hit an air pocket, and she jolted into Ramsey just as he was entering the cockpit.

Straddling the threshold, he caught her about the waist with one arm, steadying her, and Penny's gaze flew to his.

In that brief instant, in the one inescapable swift press of his hard body to hers, he consumed her, his dark eyes probing, reaching inside her chest and squeezing on her heart, his very presence fracturing the shield she'd taken years to perfect. He made her think of warm hands sliding over wet skin, thick soul-stripping kisses and the pleasurable surge of hard slick masculine flesh that had been only a faded empty dream til now. Her insides simmered, hot and dampening, and she dreamed of more.

And Ramsey felt the steaming rush down to his boot heels, searching her liquid-green eyes for some sign she was experiencing the same stirring heat as he. For the space of breath he saw *her,* only her, exquisitely fragile, alluring, and unspeakably needy and it weakened him, unmaned him, an ache like he'd never known afore tearing through him so roughly he felt his bones would snap. His lungs tightened. Her fingers flexed on his coat sleeve, and he tenderly brushed the red strands fanning her cheek, smoothing them behind her ear.

The too intimate gesture jerked her senses back to the interior of the cockpit. "Excuse me," came laced with impatience and Ram immediately lowered his arm and backed up, allowing her to pass. He stared after her for a moment, then turned his attention to the ship's captain.

But not before Daniel stole a covert glance at Wes. Both men couldn't help but notice *that* exchange; it practically left tracks.

Chapter 9

Penny slipped around the partition separating the galley from the cockpit door and sagged against the cool aluminum cabinets. Her pulse throbbed wildly in her throat, hummed in her ears.

She was actually breathless, she realized, closing her eyes.

Oh God.

She felt stripped, as if he'd torn through her soul, saw her ugly secrets and plucked them out one by one for the world to see. It was reckless to let him affect her like this. Ramsey O'Keefe was a dangerous man, different in ways she couldn't name. It wasn't just that he talked oddly and acted like a child in a toy store, but as if he held some intangible power. Over her.

And she had to take it away. And would. She excelled at that; blocking anything and anyone with the strength to hurt her, to venture near enough to discover a weakness and destroy her. It was why—God forgive her—she'd foolishly asked Tess to risk her career. And her life.

Exhaling slowly, Penny rolled around, flipping her hair back over her shoulder as she opened a refrigerated compartment and took out a diet soda. His deep resonant voice filtered to the small alcove outside the cockpit when he asked how the air remained cool. Right out of the dark ages, she thought again, popping the top and draining half of the soda before pressing the cool can to her warm cheek. It didn't help.

Moving to a seat, she dropped into the soft cushion and tried to relax while slowly finishing off the soda. She stared at her hand wrapped tightly around the white aluminum, recalling the brief press of his rock-hard body, still imprinted against hers. And the ridiculous pleasure it gave her. For an unguarded moment the woman in her relished the sweet unexpected burst of passion they'd shared and imagined his kiss, warm and slow and lushly wet. Ramsey didn't seem like a man who'd hurry through anything, if given the chance. She couldn't remember the last time she'd been *really* kissed, except by another actor before a loaded camera, with eighty people watching to see if she got it right.

She cursed Ramsey O'Keefe for making her realize it was too vague and pitifully uneventful to matter. Damn. Her tapered fingers slowly crushed the container, the can's hollow grind scraping against her taut nerves. She pitched it across the aircraft, missing the waste bin.

Damn, damn, *damn.*

Even if she'd invited him along, she would stay clear of him.

Rummaging in the bottom of her handbag for a rubber band and brush, Penny swiftly braided her hair high on her crown. Who did this guy think he was anyway, making her feel as if she had something to hide.

Don't you? a little voice said.

Penny jammed her brush back into her already crammed purse.

"I simply enjoy my privacy, that's all," she said aloud.

You're lying.

"I'm not!"

Then why did you invite him when you want privacy so badly? Why, when he makes you think about what you've missed?

Penny covered her ears.

Finding out it's not such a nice little world you've built, aren't you?

"Oh, shut-up!"

"Is this a frequent affliction, lass?" came softly, amused and as deep as the sea.

Penny's head snapped up, her hands falling to her lap. He was leaning against the galley wall, arms folded over his chest, a teasing smile on his lips. It annoyed the hell out of her. "Had your fill of modern technology, Mister O'Keefe?" She waved toward the cockpit.

His brows furrowed, just noticing she avoided answering any question remotely concerning herself. "Captain Fanelli tells me this ship is yours." The good captain had imparted a great many facts, God love him.

"It is." She didn't care for the way he was staring. "Do you have a problem with that?"

"With women of wealth? Nay." His smiled broadened to a grin. "I've conversed with a few."

Conversed, my ass, she thought, snidely.

He straightened, moving toward her, and Penny's gaze unwillingly dropped to the rolling gait of his hips, those long powerful legs adjusting so easily to the plane's sudden shake through turbulents.

"I once knew a woman who owned an entire fleet, but—"

Her gaze jerked up, eyes sharp and narrowed. "But what?" she prodded, yet had the distinct feeling he was laughing at her.

"The lady reveled in her power, delighted in the comforts her coin provided."

She relaxed back and crossed her legs. "And you're implying?"

Ramsey marveled at her cool delivery. " 'Tis clear that not even this magnificent flying ship brings you a farthing's worth of pleasure."

"This *flying ship* gets me where I want with the least amount of trouble. And that's all I need."

"Is it, lass? I wonder." He leaned down to adjust the twisted collar of her blouse. "What would truly bring you pleasure, Mistress Penelope Hamilton?" His warm fingers lingered at her nape.

Penny stayed perfectly still. "Back off, Mister O'Keefe," she said tightly, resisting the ridiculous urge to nuzzle his callused palm.

Ram's features softened with understanding as he let his hand slowly drop. "I frighten you."

"Believe what you w—"

"Why is that, do you think?" he went on as if she hadn't spoken, his dark eyes briefly sketching her features. "I vow this day to see no harm befalls you, Mistress Hamilton."

The husky timber of his voice made her skin prickle with a gentle tingling and she had the sudden image of clashing broad swords, silver knights, and champions of the heart.

Could you live in my dreams, chase away the demons?

If only he could, she thought fleetingly, then immediately crushed the childish fantasy, disliking what this man did to her carefully guarded emotions, her thoughts, and heaven help her, the sensations she believed—hoped—were dead.

"Find a seat, you two," Daniel's voice blared over the speaker. "And buckle up."

He gazed into those feline-green eyes for a moment, then made to return to his former seat.

"Mister O'Keefe?"

Ramsey turned to see her gesture to the space beside her. He smiled, and her heart did another one of those peculiar flips.

"As much as I'd enjoy the pleasure of your company, lass." He plucked at the folds of his shirt. "I reek of the sea and fear my continued presence would offend you greatly."

Penny nodded as he settled on the opposite side of the craft. For the first time she noticed he was badly in need of a shave and some fresh clothes. She could kick herself for being so insensitive to the barest humane comforts. She had, after all, asked him to join her.

Why, the little voice asked. *Why?*

"How should I know," she hissed and Ramsey glanced over, amused. Penny flushed, looking away.

Tempting fate? the voice needled. *Perhaps you're looking for*—Nothing! Not a damn thing, and especially not in Lancelot O'Keefe. Bringing him along was stupid, and she struggled to remember why she didn't have friends or lovers. Why she *had* to keep her distance.

"Final approach, Ramsey," came over the intercom. "Look out to your left."

The lady had the most peculiar habit of talking to the furniture, Ram thought with a grin, pleased he knew what Captain Fanelli meant. Focusing on the fluffy white moisture rising above them, he fingered the list of books the young captain recommended he read on the subject of flight and aircrafts. Knowledge was power, Ram knew, *feeling* the ship's descent through the clouds. The engine's hum turned to a whine as it had when they ascended, and Ramsey watched the land materialize below. He tried to absorb it all; the jagged white coastline, the roofs of shops and homes with small very blue lakes aside them, all crowded together around the—what had Fanelli called it? The airport, aye. The closer they came to the earth, the more apprehension Ram experienced. Fanelli assured him 'twas safe, this docking of the ship, yet he couldn't control the fear toying with his pulse. The ground rose up to greet them and the abrupt jolt made him suck in his breath. Wing flaps shifted like bird feathers, the massive engines screaming like a wounded eagle in their effort to stop. The bird ship—nay, the airplane, rolled for several hundred feet, turning slightly afore all was still. Only then did he release the air captured in his lungs.

"Welcome to sunny Florida, Ramsey," the pilot drawled over the intercom. "Ninety-two degrees in the shade."

Ramsey glanced at Mistress Hamilton, but she was already out of her seat and moving toward the door. And Ramsey did not mistake the frigid temperature surrounding her now.

"Allow me," Wes said, popping open the seal, then lowering the staircase as the familiar Rolls sped across the asphalt toward them. Miss H. fidgeted impatiently as the hydraulics took their time. The usually unflappable actress actually looked a little flustered, Wes marveled as she flew down the steps.

Ramsey released the harness and left his chair, his hand extended to Wes. " 'Twas an experience I shant soon forget, lad. My thanks."

Wes grinned, shaking his hand vigorously. He liked this guy.

Daniel emerged from the cockpit, smiling. "Leaving us so soon?"

"Aye. I suppose." In truth Ram didn't know what he'd do now and looked outside. A silver-blue carriage stopped afore Mistress Hamilton, the shiny door flinging open. A tall fair-haired man stepped out and every muscle in Ram's body clenched as she threw herself into his open arms, kissing the fellow soundly. A spurt of jealousy tore through him and he gave the tender scene his back.

"Tell me, Captain," Ram said in a tight voice. "How does one moor this vessel?"

Hugging Anthony, Penny darted a look over his shoulder to the jet, thankful Mister O'Keefe remained within the shadowed interior. "I missed you, Tony," she whispered, then stepped back.

It was only two weeks, he thought, his blues eyes inspecting her from head to toe. "You've lost weight, my dear."

"And you're going gray," she returned, then twisted toward the driver as the automatic window lowered on a hum. "Hi, Hank. How's everything?"

Hank smiled brightly, then glared at Wainright. "He's got to be the worst backseat driver in reported history!"

"You exceeded the speed limit three times!" Anthony blasted.

"Hey! We're here, aren't we?"

"Barely."

"For Pete's sake, you two are like bullies in a play yard," Penny said, her smile not quite reaching her eyes.

Hank opened the door and climbed out, muttering something about luggage as he stomped off.

Penny immediately turned to Anthony. "What have you heard?"

Anthony stared into those wide hopeful eyes and hated to break her heart. "They've called off the search. Permanently."

She gasped. "Why? I paid for more rescue teams and—"

"They have a witness, Penelope, a *protected* witness who says he saw her jump off the *Nassau Queen*."

"That's the same news as before and—"

Anthony pressed a finger to her lips, wrapping an arm around her waist. His voice was low and unspeakably sad. "He said she was carried away by a shark."

"Dear God." Tears glistened her eyes, and she hid her face in his shirt front. She couldn't cry, her tears spent days ago. Now it was simply the heartache of the truth sinking in. A shark. It was too horrible to imagine and a long moment passed before she said, "It's my fault, Tony. Mine!" She jerked on his lapels. "If I hadn't been such a coward—"

"Shhh," he murmured against her hair. "Don't beat yourself up over this. Tess wouldn't have wanted that." He swallowed tightly, pushing back his own grief. "You know that as well as I."

Her shoulders drooped even more. "It doesn't help."

"Time will, my dear." He gave her a squeeze and tilted her chin up, placing a kiss on her forehead.

"Nothing will make me feel less guilty about it," she said, accepting his handkerchief and blotting her eyes.

Anthony avoided commenting, knowing she'd have to come to grips with that on her own. "I still can't understand why she jumped in the first place."

"I think I do."

His brow arched questioningly.

"There was something else in that package she stole for me. Apparently worth her life." She stepped away from him, tossing her handbag into the Silver Phantom.

"Any ideas?"

Penny shook her head. "You know Tess. She always took on my problems as if they were hers."

Anthony glanced at the ground, then gazed across the top of the car at the terminal. "Perhaps she wanted to protect you," he murmured softly.

Penelope studied him for a second. "There's something you're not telling."

He chuckled shortly, returning his gaze to her. "It annoys me to no end that I haven't your poker face, my dear."

The jets auxiliary motors suddenly went silent and she folded her arms over her middle, impatient for him to continue. He ran his hand through his lightly-graying hair and exhaled a deep breath, looking anywhere but at her.

"It's all over the papers, her disappearance."

She'd expected that. "And?" she pushed when he stalled.

"And you've been connected to it."

"She was my friend. Our friend. Did you think I'd turn my back on her now?"

"Of course not!" He looked offended. "I simply want you to realize what the police might do."

"The police better realize what *I'll* do. If this witness saw her, then why didn't they hail the captain so she could be rescued? Did *he* want what she was holding and force her over that rail? And if he's such a upstanding witness, why does he need police protection?"

She delivered all of that without so much as raising her voice, the steely texture to her words telling him she wouldn't allow any clue to be overlooked.

"I haven't been privy to that, but as your lawyer—"

"And my friend," she interrupted with a soft smile, apologizing for her insult.

He smiled forgivingly. "I advise you to let them take it as far as they can, then we'll, shall I say, exert pressure."

"You know Sloane is behind this." A statement, not a question.

"If she is, she's destroyed any trail."

He'd been working on it already, she realized, watching his emotions blare across his handsome face. He loved Tess, too. Everyone did and Penny wondered how empty their lives would be without her.

"I must tell you, the oddest thing happened," he said, meeting her gaze. "A man from Lloyds of London arrived on my doorstep, looking for you."

"What did he want?"

"He had a sealed envelope for you. Wouldn't give it over. Said he had to speak with you directly."

"How bizarre. Who was it from?"

"I admit I tried my best courtroom tactics to pluck a bit of information from him, but you know these Brits, tight-lipped and all, yet I did manage to discover that the package was old."

Her forehead scrunched. They both knew she could mark her past no further than twenty-six of her twenty-eight years. If she could she wouldn't have nightmares.

"Over one hundred fifty years old."

Her face was deadpan and Anthony should have realized she wouldn't show the least bit of enthusiasm.

"Tony," she said tiredly. "If it's that old then you know it can't be for me. Or did you forget that I don't even know my real name?"

"Hardly."

"Then who sent it?"

"If I understood correctly." He cleared his throat. "It was from a Blackwell."

Penny turned the name over in her mind. *The* Blackwells? Anthony nodded. "But they're all dead, aren't they?"

"I believe so."

"Then this Lloyds agent must be wrong."

Anthony ignored her obstinate look. "I tried to tell him that, but he said—" He lowered his voice and effected a nasally British accent. " 'My good man, Lloyds of London does not make mistakes.' "

"Brava," she said with a smile.

"Regardless, Bailey came to me because of my talents in archives research. I told you my expertise would be valuable someday," he added smugly. "It seems Mister Bailey, or rather his company, has been holding a similar package, too. For quite some time."

"Go on, Tony." God, with his flair for the dramatic, this was like pulling teeth.

"They've been doing a fair amount of searching for its recipient. Decades, from what I gathered." A strange light came into his eyes, excitement tinting his voice. ''Imagine, my dear, for centuries they've been unable to find *anyone* born with the name Ramsey Malachai Gamaliel O'Keefe.''

Penny straightened, unfolding her arms. No. Her heart skipped an entire beat. It couldn't possibly be *him?* Deep masculine laughter drifted across the sizzling asphalt, and she slowly turned toward the Lear jet.

The broad shouldered stranger appeared in the doorway.

''Tony,'' she managed to whisper, nodding toward the air craft. *''That* is Ramsey O'Keefe.''

Chapter 10

Hank latched the cargo hold and picked up Miss H.'s luggage, then headed toward the car, stopping abruptly when a man he didn't recognize descended the jet stairs.

Sure got funny looking clothes, Hank thought, shifting the bags in his grip. "Who are you and what are you doin' on Miss H.'s plane?"

" 'Tis a sad day when a man cannot greet another with a simple good morn." Ramsey grinned, his gaze briefly shifting over the man's head to Mistress Hamilton.

"You a stowaway?"

Ramsey stiffened, indignant. "You insult me, sir."

Hank's lips twitched. "You can't mean she actually *invited* you?" Hank's skepticism ringed his craggy features.

"That she did."

"Well, I'll be," he marveled, grinning. "Heck, come on." Hank inclined his head toward the car, then lumbered over toward the couple.

Ramsey didn't move. The lass was looking at him as if he'd suddenly sprouted scales and fangs. Then the gentleman aside her turned, his mouth dropping open in a most undignified manner.

'Twas the man Ramsey settled his attention on. Tall and
sandy-haired, he was far older than he first imagined, silver-
gray coloring at his temples, moustache, and neatly trimmed
beard. Yet 'twas the blackened lens of his spectacles that confused him, for they did not seem to hinder his sight, though
Ram could find no reason for walking about like that, other
than the man could not see a'tall and 'twere merely a shield
against, mayhaps, offending others. They made him appear a
bit sinister, although he wore what Ramsey assumed was a
gentleman's attire, the long loose-fitting breeches and coat were
not much different than his own garments. Who was he to her,
he wondered with unreasonable jealousy as the man started
toward him.

Anthony shoved his sunglasses up the bridge of his nose,
taking great pains not to openly gape at O'Keefe's antique
clothing, but the broad cuffs of his coat sleeves, its long flared
hem, the button breeches and worn Jack boots, were too unusual
to go unnoticed.

"Anthony Wainright, Mister O'Keefe." He extended his
hand as Ramsey met the last step.

Ram glared at it for a moment, then accepted, shaking firmly.
Yet as he lowered his arm, Anthony spotted the flint-lock pistol.

Aware of the shift of his gaze, Ramsey casually covered the
stock with his coat, then nodded toward Mistress Hamilton.

"Give the lady my regards," Ram said, moving off in the
opposite direction.

He walked several feet before Anthony gathered his wits.
"You can't go!" The discovery of this man was more than
coincidental, a find like a rare painting. Yet Anthony held
back his excitement, reminding himself there were thirty-seven
O'Keefes in Coral Key's alone.

Ramsey paused, turned. "And who will detain me? You,
Englishman?"

"I'm Welsh," Anthony corrected.

"I see nay difference," Ram scoffed, then continued to walk.

Anthony looked helplessly at Penny.

Yet 'twas her voice that grabbed Ram's attention and made
him stop.

"Come on, you two. It's hot out here."

Both men looked to her. Penelope inclined her head, her arm braced on the top of the open door as Hank stuffed her bags in the trunk.

"Any luggage, Mister O'Keefe?" Anthony asked, recognizing his indecision.

"Nay." For the first time, Ramsey felt out of place in his familiar clothing.

Anthony frowned slightly, yet made no comment, sparing the man's dignity. Penelope hadn't told him anything about Ramsey O'Keefe, other than he'd been fished out of the sea by the Bahama Air Sea Rescue Association while searching for Tess.

"We'll have to rectify that immediately," Anthony said more to himself.

"I need naught from you, English," Ram snarled.

Anthony's lips pressed into a tight line. "Welsh, Mister O'Keefe. Welsh." What had he done to offend this man? "Shall we?" He gestured for Ramsey to accompany him.

Ram had no desire to be where he was obviously not wanted, for her cool rebuff aboard the air plane was unmistakable. She looks as if she regrets ever clapping eyes on me, he thought, then smiled slowly at the underlying challenge. The opportunity to thaw the icy Mistress Hamilton was worth even the company of her Englishman.

"O'Keefe?"

Ramsey nodded curtly, falling in step beside Wainright, trying desperately not to voice the question suddenly torturing his thoughts.

He wouldn't ask. Blast, if he would! He did.

"Are you her husband?"

Anthony's brows shot up and he glanced to the side. "I beg your pardon?"

Ramsey drew on his patience, ashamed of his nagging curiosity. "Are you her mate, man?" He nodded to Penelope.

Anthony's gaze shifted between the pair, and the exchange of uneasy glances were enough to make the Welshman smile.

But he didn't dare, and saw Penny escape into the back seat of her car. Coward.

"I'm merely a friend." With Penny that was as good as it got.

"The woman has no friends," Ram snarled under his breath. "A bleedin' winter wind, the wench is." Lovers, he decided, and hating it.

Wench. The idea of Penelope allowing such a sexist reference made Anthony choke. "She's simply private, Mister O'Keefe," he managed, smothering a laugh. Gad, these two ought to mix like oil and water.

As the men approached, Hank hid a grin he knew his boss wouldn't like and slid behind the wheel. Company, imagine that, he thought as Anthony paused briefly at the door, indicating Ramsey should enter before him.

Ramsey bent a look into the elaborate coach. The lass kept herself tucked in the corner and wouldn't spare him a glance. So, 'twas the way of it, now, he thought, straightening. Ignoring Wainright's puzzled expression, he climbed in beside the driver.

Hank grinned at his passenger, starting the engine as Anthony shut the door behind himself.

"I'm Hank Tanner, Mister—?"

"Captain Ramsey O'Keefe, Mister Tanner." Ram nodded once.

"It's just Hank." A bushy silver brow rose. "Capt'n, huh?"

"Aye," Ram replied absently, busy perusing the rich wood panel before him. Fine craftsmanship, he thought, smoothing a hand familiarly over the polished mahogany. 'Twas like an old friend in this world of metal and machines. "I do hope you can operate this carriage," he cast a glance over his shoulder, "with a mediocum more finesse than your mistress."

Hank snickered softly, and Penny viciously punched a button; a glass divider rose to separate her from that grinning man.

"That wasn't very hospitable, my dear." Anthony tapped the glass and the Silver Phantom Rolls Royce pulled away from the Jet.

"I've been hospitable enough for one day, thank you very much."

"Have you really?" She didn't answer, keeping her face averted as he picked up the phone and dialed. "Penelope, dear, correct me if I'm wrong, but you have literally kidnapped a man who possesses no identification, no funds, with no records of his existence . . . isn't that what the authorities said?" He listened for the pick up.

"Your point, Tony."

"My point is, what are you going to do about it?"

She spared him a brief glance. "Why should I do—?"

He held up his hand, speaking into the receiver. "Grace. Anthony Wainright. Ring up Travis and have him send some men's clothes over to Miss Hamilton's. No, definitely not for me," he said with relish.

Penny smacked his arm without looking.

"I don't know what size. Ahh, about six four or five, two hundred twenty—"

"Two forty, tops," Penny put in, grateful he was helping.

His brow shot up, his smile knowing. "Make it two hundred forty pounds, several variations and *everything,* please. Yes, I'll hold." He tilted the receiver away. "Aren't you a little curious? The clothes, his speech, that he's armed like a museum arsenal."

"Not in the least." Liar.

Up went the hand again. "Yes, Grace. Good. A bonus if he's there within the hour." He hung up, pleased.

"Thanks, Tony."

"It's the least *I* could do."

She winced. He was right, of course.

"How do you suppose he ended up floating in the sea?" Anthony asked.

"I don't know nor do I care." *Who are you fooling?*

"Well, he didn't just fall out of the sky."

"Anthony." Penny sighed, finally turning from the window to look at him. "He was at least ten feet under when they found him."

"Drowning, Penelope?" She nodded. "With no land around?"

"Yes," she said carefully.

"Then how did he get there? Swim? Nearly a hundred miles? And why leave land at all when he could build a fire and wait for the patrols making their regular rounds?"

Together they looked at the back of Ramsey's head.

"I honestly hadn't thought of that." Surprise softened her voice.

"You should." His was smug.

"Why?" Her gaze snapped to him. "I could care less where he came from *or* where he's going."

"He's getting out of the car, that's what he's doing."

Neither had noticed the vehicle slow to a stop, nor the crowd gathered around a tall tree across the busy residential street.

"Oh, this is just great." She lowered the divider. "Hank, what's he up to?"

Hank chuckled. "That Mister O'Keefe saw the kid up in the tree long before I came around the curve."

"For crying out loud, will you please go after him!" Hank was already out of the car before she finished.

Ramsey tilted his head back, shielding his eyes against the sunlight to see the child clinging to the tree trunk nearly at the top.

"It's a good ways up there, Capt'n," Hank said from Ram's side.

"She's naught but a babe," Ram marveled, stripping off his jacket. He quickly removed his pistols and knives, handing them over to the old man, who was busy shrugging toward the carriage.

Penny's lips pulled into a thin line, irritated he'd involved himself, yet captivated as Ramsey sauntered up to the tree and jumped, catching a thick limb and pulling himself up. He scaled with such undeniable ease and agility that Penny could do no more than gape—along with everyone else. He's a damned monkey, she thought, his movements confident, his power to overtake the dangerous distance amazing. He grasped a branch, gained footing on another, and was beside the child in a matter of seconds. Then to aggravate the situation further, he sat on the adjacent limb and proceeded to enjoy the view!

" 'Tis a fair way up, lassie. You must be very strong."

The little black-haired child looked up, and Ramsey's heart did a quick squeeze at those terrified eyes fountaining with tears.

"Are you going to take me to my mama?" she whimpered, hugging the rough trunk. For an instant Ram thought of his son and the dishonor he'd done the innocent.

"Is that what you wish?"

She sniffled and nodded. "Yup."

"The sight is breathtakin'." Ramsey smiled gently as he eased closer, gritting his teeth when the branch threatened to splinter. " 'Tis nay wonder you wanted to come up here."

"Joey made me do it."

"Did he now?" With infinite care, he moved onto the limb below her.

"Yup."

Ram smiled at the child's limited vocabulary. "Well, now. You'll certainly have a fine tale to tell Joey, won't you, sweetling?"

"Yup." The single word held her pride and her fear.

"Shall we join your admirers?"

She looked down, then back to him, chewing on her lower lip. "Mama'll be worried, won't she?"

Ramsey nodded and continued to talk softly to the little girl as he helped her onto his back. She nearly cut off his breath, God love her, with her grip around his neck as they slowly descended. The minute his feet touched solid earth, cheers and applause vibrated from the dense crowd of onlookers as he pulled her from his back and into his arms. She rewarded him with a throat crushing hug, her thin arms trembling. He patted her gently, then handed her over to a woman with outstretched arms.

"Thank you, oh, thank you so much," her mother gushed. Ramsey bowed deeply from the waist, then accepted his possessions from Hank.

"Way to go, Capt'n," Hank said, slapping him on the back. Ramsey merely offered a smile, the older man suddenly reminding him of Duncan McPete. A red carriage as big a bleedin' house screeched to a halt as the pair crossed the avenue. Ramsey paused to watch, then slipped into the coach.

"You climbed darned near fifty feet like it was nothin'!" Hank beamed, restarting the car. "Sure was something!"

"Yes. It was the act of a careless individual."

Ram glanced back over his shoulder at Penelope as the car moved away from the curb. "Pray tell, when has returning a frightened child to the arms of her mother become reckless?"

His words sank beneath her veneer, each syllable pelting a wound long since healed. And Ramsey saw her features pull taut, then slowly softened, the angry lines vanishing.

"I guess—never," she whispered, the corners of her cat-like eyes tilting up, and a smile, barely there, curving her lips. Ram felt the impact like a musket ball to his chest, the hard slam flowering with an unnamed emotion. 'Twas a glimpse into her soul, he saw, yet 'twas nay enough, leaving him thirsty and yearning for more. Then it vanished, her gentle features suddenly carved into cool indifference.

"Yet, if anything went wrong, Mister O'Keefe, you could have been sued because you are not a professional."

"Penelope, dear," Anthony warned softly. Somehow he didn't think O'Keefe would take kindly to her views.

Ramsey arched a brow. "I care not of the legal consequences you speak," he growled. By Triton's will, had he imagined the moment?

"Regardless, *I* could be held responsible. After all, you are in my personal custody—"

"—*Woman!*"

"Well, sort of," she finished lamely, a bit intimidated by his quick rage.

The gall of the little chit, Ram thought. "Madame, I am not an addlepated dolt in need of *your* coddling. Cast meself with a selfish wench, thinks I," he said lowly, his dark glare so intense she recoiled. "Bah!" He backhanded the air. "The devil take the bleedin' lot of you." Ramsey opened the car door. Hank slammed on the brakes, and as if the abrupt stop were nothing, Ramsey climbed out and walked away.

Penny looked to Anthony, who sat back and folded his arms.

"Anthony!" She gestured toward the window. "Do something!"

"You're the one who's ticked him off, my dear." He flicked imaginary lint off his trousers, thinking Ramsey's speech pattern fit him rather nicely. Her helpless gaze shifted to Hank, but he just sniffed the air, throwing the gear shift into park.

Penny sighed. She hadn't meant to anger him. It was just— oh, damn. She shoved open the door and climbed out. "Mister O'Keefe. Wait!"

Ramsey halted, twisting to flip a coin at her. "I am grateful for your aid thus far, Mistress. Good day and good life!" Then he continued on his way.

She chased after him. "Wait, please!"

Ramsey stopped again, but didn't turn around, awaiting her approach and she didn't mistake the canned emotion beneath the rigid set of his wide shoulders, in his belligerent stance. It made her hesitate. He was a formidable man and she'd wounded his pride. Hell, she'd practically taken an axe to it.

"I simply wanted you to understand that you can't interfere without first thinking of what might happen later."

Ramsey turned his gaze on her, and Penny flinched at the disgust in his dark brown eyes. "Naught has changed, I discover. The wealthy see to themselves, and the unfortunate must fend alone."

Her features hardened, her voice low and cutting. "I resent that. You know nothing about me or the life I've lead. I—" She stopped. Why am I explaining myself to this man? "Climbing up after that child was reckless. You both might have been injured."

"Spare me your empty concern, woman." Ramsey started walking, and Penny had to practically run to keep up with his long strides.

"It's not empty, for Pete's sake." She ignored the nasty sound he made and said, "Look, Mister O'Keefe. You could have lost everything, including your life."

Ramsey chuckled meanly. "Call the finest barristers, madame." He flung his arms wide. "For what I am is all that you see afore you."

Penny slowed her step, her gaze glossing over the worn hem of his coat, the thread bare breeches and scarred boots, before she raced to catch up. "That's not the point—"

"*You* would have ridden by," he cut in savagely, glaring at her sideways.

Her posture stiffened. "I probably would have contacted the fire department."

"The child was not ablaze that I could discern."

He wouldn't look at her, and that stung. "Firemen do that sort of thing for a living."

Ramsey stopped abruptly, gazing off into the distance and Penny stared at his profile, waiting. Suddenly, he pounced, his scowl black as midnight, his tall body towering, blocking the sun. "Do you truly enjoy viewing the world from your crystal carriage, princess?" His voice grated with outrage and disappointment and Penny blinked, unreasonably hurt. "Is the distance well beyond scarring your privileged realm?"

Penny swallowed, opening her mouth to defend.

"Nay! Do not speak. For our association is at an end, Mistress Hamilton." He dismissed her with a flick of his hand. "Away with you."

Ramsey left her, alone, in the middle of the street.

She ought to be pleased he was walking out of her life.

But she wasn't.

Chapter 11

"What do you make of the fireworks?" Hank asked as he picked up the coin the captain had tossed and rubbed it against his sleeve.

Anthony leaned against the car, his interest on the pair arguing in the middle of the street. "Certainly does stir up trouble, doesn't he?"

"For who?" Hank grinned. As if he didn't know. "Probably the first man who hasn't taken her lip."

"I consider myself among that group, you know."

"You're management, you have to," Hank explained. "Hell. I figure that guy doesn't know a thing about her, least wise not her *famous* career." His last words he practically sneered.

Anthony chuckled, watching traffic weave around the couple. "That's his advantage. And it appears Mister O'Keefe doesn't give a fig—oh, dear. Look at him, leaving the poor girl like that." Ripping move, he thought, sadistically enjoying her dumbfounded look. Then his smug expression fell. "Damn!"

Hank glanced up from examining the coin, then dashed around the side of the car as Anthony called out a warning to Penelope. It was no use. The crowd of fans were like a swarm of killer bees heading for their queen. Anthony jumped into the Rolls, and Hank burned rubber to get to her first.

At the excited cries and rapid footsteps, Ramsey spun about. Citizens poured from shops and tall glass buildings, waving slips of paper, crying her name with an odd desperation, converging on Penelope til she disappeared amongst the sudden crush of bodies. Ramsey scowled darkly. The lass did not appear to be enjoying the attention, he decided, storming over to the group. Discovering politeness gained him little with this motley collection, Ramsey forced his way between the people, his big body like a rolling bolder as he shouldered a path toward Penelope.

He reached, grabbing her arm and nearly lifting her off her feet, his stinging grip making Penny twist around, ready to deck someone. She looked up, relief sweeping over her as recognition dawned, til she realized that angry glare was directed at her!

"Be gone!" Ram bellowed to the crowd, and the din lessened. "Stand fast, I say, afore I dress the bleedin' lot of you!" The noise died a little more, yet when none obeyed, he made a wide swipe with his arm, clearing a path and propelling her toward the carriage.

Penny stumbled, glaring back over her shoulder, but he simply gave her a push as the carriage screeched to a halt before them. The door burst open and Ramsey clamped a hand on her head, a palm to her back, and shoved her into the rear seat. He turned and walked away.

"Get in!" Anthony shouted, half out of the Rolls.

"I'll stand me own ground, English." Ram took a step.

"Trust me. Get-in!"

The crowd set upon Ramsey with a vengeance, groping, questioning, those damned little black boxes flashing white lights in his eyes, and Ram quickly reassessed the situation; the last thing he wanted was to have his presence well known in this century. Out of sheer self-preservation, he ducked into the back, and the Rolls lurched away afore he shut the door. He dropped into the leather seat with a thump.

"Great Neptune, woman! What is it about you that continually stirs the masses to such a frenzy?"

Hank chuckled to himself, but Anthony made no effort to smother his amusement.

"Shut up, Tony," Penny said, rubbing her scalp.

"Damn me, Penelope, it *is* funny."

"*You* weren't attacked. Lord, I lost some hair this time!" She shook the broken strands to the carpeted floor.

"Does anyone wish to enlighten *me?*" Ramsey demanded.

"She's—"

"Anthony," Penny warned, inspecting her torn pocket.

"—rather popular."

"Pray tell, what for? 'Tis certainly not her sweet temperament!"

Anthony laughed harder, slumping into the seat.

Penelope's eyes narrowed on Ramsey as she said, "Hank! Take-us-home! Now!"

"Yes, ma'am." Hank was grinning.

Ramsey made a low growling sound, disregarding her popularity and focusing his attention on the scenery beyond the window. Though he was back where he started, he could not, in all good conscience, continue in her company, especially to her residence. Nay, not reside under her roof. And to live on her benevolence? His pride would not take the sting and bade him to depart as quickly as possible, to seek his own way. Yet Ram knew naught but a life at sea and was painfully aware that work would be difficult to find in this day of mechanizations. He'd no other choice but to leave.

Ram darted a glance at Penelope.

A prime article of woman, that. And the underlying power of his feelings for the troublesome wench scared him. *That* he could admit, yet disguising them called on a strength he wasn't aware he possessed . . . til now. She intrigued him, beckoned him to look beyond the frame of her face and figure. Though he could not put a name to this odd tugging he experienced since clapping eyes on her, 'twere his brief glimpses of another woman, haunted and needy, secreted beneath a veil of ice that made him regret walking away from her. *Ahh, lass, were you*

*in my time, my century. I would steal you away aboard me
ship til I banished your secrets and discovered your true heart.*

But he was in her time.

They'd gone several miles when Ramsey bid Hank to stop.

"Don't, Hank," Penny ordered, glancing at Anthony.

"Here is adequate, mate."

That Hank looked indecisive annoyed Penny. "Where are
you going, Mister O'Keefe?"

Ram spared her a glance, wanting to end it now. "I must
depart, Mistress, to seek employment, quarters—"

"But you can't go now," she interrupted, that little voice
telling her to stop him any way she could. "Please," she added
softly when her request had no effect and Ramsey thought he'd
come apart with the quiet plea.

"Why, lass?" His blood seemed to freeze on its way to his
heart.

Penny latched onto her first plausible excuse. "Because there
is a man named Bailey looking for you."

The wind instantly left his sails. " 'Tis impossible, Mistress.
I know no such man, nor do I have kin—a'tall," he added
with finality.

Penny knew what that was like. "Your full name is—?"

He folded his arms over his chest, his eyes wary. "Ramsey
Malachi Gamaliel O'Keefe."

"Jesus." Hank put in. "That's embarrassing." Ram glared
over his shoulder. "Sorry, Capt'n."

"He's the one," Anthony confirmed.

"Forgive me, but I am still at a loss as to why I must reside
with," Ram waved, "the three of you."

"No need to get snide, O'Keefe," Anthony said, smiling.
"Bailey has a delivery for you from Lloyds of London."

Though aware of the insurers, Ram was unwilling to believe
such an outlandish tale, for all he knew was gone. It hit him
just then, like a cut to his windpipe, and he turned his face
away. Dane, Tess, his mates, his ship, all naught but dust in
this century. His broad shoulders slumped and he stared at his

boots, aching, solemn. What happened to Dane and Tess? Did they have a good life? Children? Sweet Christ, did they even make it back to the colonies?

Penny and Anthony exchanged concerned looks but 'twas the driver who interrupted his thoughts.

"Hey, Capt'n. Lose this?" Hank handed the coin back over his shoulder to Ramsey and he fingered the disk, his hooded gaze colliding with hers. A faint blush bloomed in her cheeks and she looked away.

"May I see that?" Anthony asked, palm up.

Ramsey shrugged, tossing it to him.

Anthony smoothed a finger over the coin, sending the tinted electric window down and leaning toward the sunlight for a closer examination. "Good God! Is this real?"

" 'Tis naught but a bit of Spanish gold," Ram said absently, his mind on the past; his past.

"Solid gold," Anthony whispered, Penny peering over his shoulder. Anthony looked up. "Do you have any more of these?"

Ram pulled his gaze from the window, his tone dry. "Are you in dire need of funds, English?"

Anthony ignored the dig. "Do you?"

"Aye."

"And is that gold, too?" He pointed to the chains, and Ram nodded curtly. Anthony turned to Penny. "I've got to make a stop. You three go on to the house. I'll catch up." He picked up the phone, briefly glancing at Ramsey as he dialed. "Are you willing to sell this?"

Ramsey folded his arms. Sell gold for more gold, he wondered, then seeing the opportunity to possess a bit of this century's currency, agreed.

"Paul? Wainright, here," Anthony said into the receiver. "Clear the next hour, I'm on my way in. Oh yes, it's important." He hung up, still studying the gold disk.

Penny frowned, her gaze shifting between the crude-edged coin, Mister O'Keefe, and Anthony. She'd never seen him so animated. "What are you up to, Tony?"

He grinned. "I'm not sure, but if I'm right, Mister O'Keefe here is a very rich man."

"You're kidding?" Penny blinked, yet Ramsey scowled, uneffected by the Englishman's excitement.

"Methinks you a dull swift, Wainright." He nodded to the coin. " 'Tis no grand fortune you hold."

"Stop here, Hank. I'll take a cab."

"But we're only a few blocks from the house," Penelope told him.

The car slowed, its wheels spitting pebbles as Hank pulled off to the shoulder. "This can't wait," Anthony said, then addressed Ramsey. "I don't know where you've been, Mister O'Keefe, but gold is over four hundred fifty dollars an ounce. And this," he hefted the coin, "is better than four."

By dollars Ramsey assumed the man meant denominations of money, as in pounds sterling, and if Wainright wanted to spend his day peddling the coin, Ram would not gainsay the matter. He needed money, desperately.

Anthony left the Rolls, yet before shutting the door, he addressed O'Keefe in a voice intended for his ears alone. "I trust you'll see to her safety?" Anthony offered his hand.

Ramsey glanced at Penelope, hesitating, for their argument in the street was unresolved, a wedge atween them still.

"A gentleman's agreement," Anthony coaxed, knowing somehow Ramsey would see it as a matter of honor.

"Aye," Ram answered almost reluctantly and sealed the bond.

"Knew you would." Anthony smiled, then looked at Penny. "Ramsey will see you safely home."

"I don't need his help," Penny called, but he completely ignored her, closing the door and hailing a taxi.

As the carriage pulled away, Ramsey settled back, suddenly delighted by this new turn. His bond of protection and the coin made all the difference, giving him reason to remain where he truly wanted—near her. She looked up from assessing her damaged garments, and he smiled, slow and wicked, not giving a tinker's damn what took the Englishman away, as long as he was gone.

Ramsey's dark gaze slid boldly over her body, her face, afore clashing with hers, and she responded with belligerently folding her arms, repaying the look in kind.

By Triton's will, if 'twas ever a gauntlet lain afore his feet, 'twas in those frosty cat-green eyes.

He arched a brow, incredibly pleased.

Ramsey could never ignore so flagrant a challenge.

Not in his century, nor hers.

Penny tilted her head, gazing across the lush interior of the Rolls Royce. He looked as if he were prepared to wage battle, though she'd no idea what for. He shifted toward her and she flinched. He smiled in return, one of those wide heart stopping grins he gave so easily, then stretched his long legs out, his boots nearly touching her calf. She let her gaze wander from his soles upward, across broad corded thighs straining against his knee pants, over his massive chest to his face.

His brow flicked upward.

"Admiring or taking inventory?"

"Neither. I was wondering how you managed to find yourself one hundred miles from shore."

"Drowning, I believe the surgeon said."

"Mister O'Keefe—"

"—Ramsey."

"Mister O'Keefe," came tight-lipped.

"Aye, lass," he said sweetly.

"Why won't you tell me?"

His features sharpened a little. "For you are, in truth, only feigning interest."

"You'll find I rarely pry into anyone's business, therefore I am interested."

" 'Tis flattered I am, then."

"Don't be. It's mere curiosity."

" 'Tis a shame, for I'd hoped 'twas your desire to know the man and not the circumstances."

Are you willing to do the same for me, she wanted to ask, then suppressed the outrageous idea. She'd no desire to be any more involved than she already was, yet she sensed he read her thoughts, for he turned his attention out the window, dismissing her.

Leaving Penny feeling small and alone and very bitter beneath her familiar cloak of indifference.

And she was finding it an uncomfortable fit.

Chapter 12

Phalon Rothmere slammed the receiver down onto its cradle, making it chime. I'll kill her, he thought, his fury trapped beneath the veneer of refinement and culture.

This time I will kill her.

He punched the button on his desk intercom, drawing in a slow calming breath before he spoke. "Send her in." He stood beside his desk, fingertips of one hand tapping the surface. He glanced down at the newspaper, a strange pain burning through his chest as the French doors opened and a beautiful, exquisitely dressed blond woman strolled into the luxurious room, gliding across the floor like a sloop across glassy waters. Phalon gestured to the chair resting before the ornately carved desk. Elegantly, she slid into the Hipplewhite antique, smoothed her linen skirt, then finally looked up.

"You wanted to see me, Daddy?"

He tossed the folded newspaper in her designer lap. "An associate of yours, I presume?" A rhetorical question. Phalon knew everything before it touched him.

Sloane picked at the paper as if it were contaminated, reading the headline.

"Olympic Gymnast Vanishes; Murder or Mauling?" She

glanced at the first few lines. A shark attack? How convenient. "A Delta sister." Her gaze shifted a fraction beyond him, then back. "As if you didn't know," came bitterly as she flipped the paper onto his desk, unwilling to admit to a thing.

"What possessed you to put my gems in the pouch, Sloane? Tell me, so I might discover how your mind works—finally."

Inwardly, Sloane cringed at her father's controlled tone. "It wasn't my fault your goons didn't catch her." She shoved her long blond curls back over her shoulder, sending a nasty look to the tall man standing in the shadows behind her father. Asshole.

"Your twisted need for a little revenge," he rubbed his forehead, "which I've yet to understand, has cost this family more than you could imagine, young lady."

God, she hated it when he spoke to her like a child. "I honestly think you're overreacting, Daddy. It was just a—"

His hand lashed the air for silence, his patience gone. "What? A prank? Old jealousy, perhaps?" Sloane wanted to hit him then and looked away. "Another one of your petty larks? Like running my yacht so neatly into the pier? Or the insider trading charges with your last lover? Or your gambling?" His tone went suddenly ice smooth, his expression tight with reined anger. "This time, not only is the suspicion of murder annoyingly evident, but I've lost in excess of three million dollars!"

Sloane glanced up; the mention of money always gathered her complete attention, until she realized what her father said. The stones were gone, lost. *Damn, I knew I couldn't depend on those idiots.* What had been so damned difficult? A simple little task: catch Tess in the act of saving her friend's precious career and gain a charge of grand larceny in the bargain. And perhaps shot during her escape. Neat, tidy. God, Tess did exactly as she'd expected!

"Where's Owen?" Briefly she eyed the toe of her Kamali pump.

"How do you think the police gained this much information?" He tapped the newspaper, appearing as if he'd enjoy crucifying her to the antique chair. Phalon knew of the evidence in the packet and saw no profit in blackmailing such a well-respected actress, but it was his man's involvement in this that stunned him. "Owen has been loyal for over ten years, Sloane. How did you get him to betray me? Screw him?"

She stiffened, checking the sheen of her nail polish. "Actually, you should be pleased." Her gaze flew to his, years of being ignored icing her tone. "Betrayal has been a well-honed art in this clan for centuries, hasn't it, Daddy?"

Phalon's expression darkened, his pale-blue eyes narrowing to mere slits, and the satisfaction of wounding him made her reckless.

"And millions? Really?" She snorted unbecomingly. "For aquamarines, topaz, and a few rather dull amethysts?"

"Sloane," he paused til she looked at him. "They were *all* diamonds. Natural colored diamonds." His tone was precise and biting and her tan paled with every word. "With over a dozen rare *flawless* pink marquis. Family heirlooms," he added quietly.

Sloane stood, pacing. Heirlooms. The money came second, for she knew what family heritage meant to him. He was obsessed with having the perfect ancestors, the perfect lineage.

The perfect daughter.

And she wasn't. Wasn't the male heir he wanted, nor quiet dignity like Penelope. And she wasn't the never-forgotten champion who stole the heart of a nation.

She wasn't anyone.

Because of them. Tess Renfrew was nothing but a slip of vulgar white trash and Sloane hated her, hated her how her achievements made Sloane's life miserable. Hated how her father always compared her to Tess. He didn't care that she'd increased profit of their garment factory thirty percent, never complimented her on all the opportunities her chic parties brought him. What would he say if he knew she'd slept with that weasel of a councilman to sway votes he needed for zoning. I ought to tell him, she thought, just to make him realize he isn't as powerful as he believes.

She had Penelope Hamilton trapped, didn't she?

Sloane smiled suddenly, sly and quite pleased. Well, Penelope will get her due, and then the world will know what the squeaky clean actress is really hiding. And Tess will go down with her. Sloane almost laughed aloud. If she hasn't already twenty leagues under water.

"I'm cutting you off, Sloane. Completely."

She whirled about, horrified. "You can't!"

His dark look dared her to defy him. "Bailing you out is a strain on the family treasury." A few years without her frivolous spending should compensate for his losses, he decided. At least they didn't know about the stones yet. Bailing Owen out of jail was impossible; the connection could be traced and Phalon was counting on a promise of money to keep him quiet before he had to take drastic measures. Owen was a good man and Phalon made the mistake of trusting his shallow tramp of a daughter with family secrets.

Phalon snapped his fingers, gesturing toward his daughter. The thick shadow came into view.

"Daddy?" Her confused gaze shifted between the advancing man and her father, fear yanking at her stomach as Larson reached. "Don't you dare touch me!" She slapped his hands away, backing up, but the huge man latched onto her arm, yanking her purse til the beaded strap broke. Gold spheres scattered across the floor like a fistful of tacks as he tossed it to his boss. "All you had to do was ask," she said with false bravado.

Phalon dropped into his chair and dumped the contents on his desk. He sifted through the feminine paraphernalia to find her wallet, extracting money, credit cards, account numbers. All she carried for easy access to his money. Family money.

"Let go of me!" She struggled, prying at the bruising fingers circling her arm.

"Our name is connected to this . . . mess, because of you." Phalon looked up, meeting his daughter's gaze before nodding to his man, Larson. Larson slapped Sloane across the face. She stumbled back, more from the shock, than the stinging pain. "Daddy?" Her heel caught on the carpet, and she twisted her ankle, then righted herself. "What's this going to prove?"

"Maybe you'll remember that what you do reflects on me." Phalon swung the leather chair around, ignoring her calls as

Larson slid his arm around her slim waist, pulling her flush against his body. He smiled, gazing into her eyes with the tenderness of a lover, and her lips curved, relief sweeping her, an instant before his fist slammed into her side. She moaned and he struck her again, executing the beating like a surgeon, striking areas that would cause the greatest pain, yet leave the damage invisible to the public. And all the while gazing into her eyes, his mouth inches from hers, a near kiss.

Sloane refused to scream, refused to look away. It would give either man too much satisfaction. Pain burned through her battered kidneys, and she felt a rib bone fracture beneath his fist. Hot tears blurred her vision and she swallowed back the sob swimming up her throat.

Phalon swung the chair back around. "That's sufficient." His voice cut through her pain like a douse of alcohol.

Larson still held her close, his hand coming up to gently stroke across her cheek. She spit in his face and he smiled, thin and arrogant as he reached inside his Armani jacket, snapped out a monogrammed handkerchief and dabbed the spittle from his cheek. Sloane slipped into unconsciousness.

"Touching," Phalon muttered, tossing the useless purse at Larson. "Get her out of here."

Larson gathered her in his arms like a knight collecting his bride and disappeared through a passage hidden within the paneled wall.

Phalon Rothmere steepled his fingers, tapping them against his lips, his gaze on the newspaper and the grainy photo of the beautiful black-haired woman beneath the headline. It was a shame. Tess Renfrew, a nobody from nowhere. From the moment he'd first seen her photograph in the newspapers, when she was no more than ten or twelve, Phalon had recognized her underlying strength, her resilience. And when he met her years ago at some ridiculous sorority function of Sloane's, he'd learned just how far she'd elevated herself from her unfortunate beginnings.

She'd fascinated him, her vitality.

Leather creaked as Phalon slowly swung the chair around and studied the antique painting hanging on the wall above him. WOMAN IN GREEN marked the brass plate at the base of the frame. Dark hair flowing about her pale shoulders, she was shrouded in a deep-green gown, gentle waves and the ocean's mist swirling about her bare feet. White sand coated her dress hem and a delicate pair of green slippers dangled from her fingertips, as if she cared less if she lost them during her walk. His gaze honed in on the face, her expression forlorn, yet prepared for a challenge.

He flicked a brief glance at the newspaper photo, comparing it to the painting.

The resemblance was uncanny, her energy and sensuality captured lovingly in every stroke of the brush, held motionless, like a guardian, for two hundred years.

Chapter 13

'Twas a majestic home, bespeaking of wealth and grandeur, two floors, and stretching a bloody block; gabeled roof, a railed porch rambling to the right, stables off to the left of the estate, a gated carriage house, yet what arrested him was the ten-foot white stone wall surrounding the grounds, the spears of iron mounted along the edge deterring visitors. A friggin' prison, he thought, comforted by the scent and sound of the sea beyond the house.

As they mounted the porch steps a woman threw open the door and Penelope launched into her open arms, hugging tightly. Ramsey stepped back, watching the tenderness shared atween, the way Penelope consoled when he suddenly recalled she'd been in the tropics searching the sea for her lost friend. *Grief shared, lessens,* he thought as she glanced back, obviously discomfited that he'd witnessed the tender scene and gesturing for him to join her.

It struck him then that the older woman wearing the apron with the words: OUT OF BODY, BACK IN FIVE MINUTES, printed on the starch white, was most likely her mother. Or mayhaps the housekeeper?

"Is Travis here yet?" Penelope asked the instant she was inside.

"Came nearly a half hour ago." Margaret tossed her thumb toward the winding staircase as she held open the door. "Dumped a rack of stuff off in the green room, along with a dozen bags and boxes, then left."

The housekeeper, Ram decided.

"Did Anthony call?" Penny said, setting the alarms.

Margaret shook her head, her gaze focused on Ramsey.

Ramsey peered over Penelope's shoulder, closely inspecting the numbered switches. A black line illuminated with a glowing red, printed out her choices, then disappeared. Fascinating.

Penny glanced to the side. God, he looked ready to drop. "It's an alarm system and will go off if there are any intruders."

Ram frowned. "Off? As in take to the sky?"

She forced herself not to laugh. "No, just make loud noises and signal the police if anyone tries to break in." His ignorance of things she took for granted, was, in its own way, charming her socks off, and she really didn't mind playing teacher. He took his promise to Tony seriously, going out of his way to see her well-protected, even checking the locks on the gate and inspecting the immediate grounds. Although it wasn't necessary, Penny was touched. She hadn't given him any reason to be so concerned.

Ram nodded, pleased she'd explained as she slid a panel over the switches, hiding them from view. Clever, he thought and together they turned toward the gray-haired woman standing in the foyer. Hank clomped past, burdened with luggage, not bothering to speak as he headed up the stairs.

"Margaret O'Hallaran, this is Mister Ramsey O'Keefe," Penny said, dumping her purse on the small table behind Margaret. "He'll be with us for a while." Margaret, bless her, didn't show the slightest fraction of surprise. "Would you show him to the green room so he can clean up and rest?"

"Sure." So, this is who those clothes are for, Margaret realized, looking Ramsey up and down with undisguised interest. Well, ain't this a kick. A man in the house. "He fresh from a movie set or something?'' Margaret asked, inclining her head toward Ramsey.

Penny glanced at him, her features softening. ''As a matter of fact, those are his clothes.'' A strange smugness marked her tone.

''Go on with you now! The gun and knives too?''

''It's impolite not to address a person directly, Margaret,'' Penny said, her heart tripping when he winked at her.

Folding his arms over his chest, Ramsey leaned indolently against the wall, grinning when Margaret's inspection finally made it back to his face. He returned the same scrutiny, then stepped forward and grasped her hand.

'' 'Tis a grand pleasure, Mistress O'Hallaran. Succor to me parched soul to meet a true Irish Rose.'' Ramsey bowed, drawing her hand to his lips for a kiss.

Margaret turned her head slowly toward Penny. ''He rehearsin' or something?'' Penny shook her head, and just as slowly Margaret looked back to Ramsey. She snatched back her hand. ''Well, that's got to be the purest pile of *blarney* I've ever heard, Mister O'Keefe. And I ain't fallen for it.''

Ramsey tried to look wounded. ''Ahh, you cut me weary heart, Meggie lass.'' He grasped her hand again, tucking it into the crook of his arm. ''And 'tis such a far far way I've traveled.'' Chuckling to himself, Ramsey steered her across the tiled foyer toward the elegant winding staircase.

''That a fact?'' she muttered, her brows screwed in confusion.

''Further than you could imagine, lass.''

''Got a lot of parched souls and weary hearts where you're from?''

Ramsey threw back his head and laughed, and Margaret smiled at the rich man-sound peeling through the house. ''Aye, Meggie. And 'twas kind of Mistress Hamilton to offer me lodgin', was it not?'' He leaned close enough to whisper in her ear. ''Yet I am not such a dolt about domestic matters that I cannot see 'tis you who supervises this spotless mansion.'' Margaret blushed girlishly. ''Is it this way to the green room?'' He gestured ahead, seeing as he was leading her along. Margaret nodded slowly, then glanced over her shoulder at Penelope. "So tell me, Meggie rose, where have you kin?"

Penny nearly laughed at Margaret's bewildered look. She was like a sorority house mother and that he'd made it past her, or rather *around* her good graces, was a feat and a half. Bet he could charm the habit off a nun. After Tony left them, she and Mister O'Keefe traveled the short distance chatting amiably, not asking anything personal and sticking mostly to the history of her Victorian house. He'd been stunned at the size, which was odd, because her home was modest compared to her neighbors. Very modest. Several feet behind them, Penny followed, her attention snagged on the broad width of his shoulders and those long muscled legs. You're in for it now, Penny told herself. He's in your house, in your private world, and you haven't the faintest idea how to get him out.

Live dangerously, a voice said.

"I'm done with danger," she muttered under her breath and looked up to see Ramsey glancing over his shoulder at her, an amused smile on his lips. I have to quit doing that, she thought as Margaret pushed open the guest room door and ushered him inside.

"Everything's there for you, Mister O'Keefe." Margaret waved to the interior and Ram smiled his appreciation. "If you need anything else, sir, just give me a shout."

He pulled her hand from his arm, brushing his lips across her knuckles. "I beg you, Meggie, call me Ramsey. Naught a soul I've met will." His gaze darted meaningfully to Penelope.

She nudged him with her elbow, smiling. "You're a card, Ramsey, a real hot ticket." She hadn't let anyone call her Meggie since she was a girl. "You hungry?"

Ram's mouth watered at the mere mention of food. "Famished, madame," he said with feeling. "Are you as fine a cook as you are a housekeeper?"

"The best," Penelope said from behind Margaret.

The older woman beamed. This giant of a man was a meat and potatoes guy, she decided immediately. "Real cooking," Margaret said to the ceiling, giving thanks for the opportunity, then heading toward the door. "Oh—" She paused. "Travis left this." She withdrew an invoice sheet from her apron pocket. "It's the bill for those." She inclined her head to the black and gold embossed boxes and bags and the rack of men's clothes.

Penny reached, but Ramsey was swift, plucking the slip and quickly stuffing it in his pocket. "Accept not a farthing from Wainright," he said to Penelope. "Is that understood?" Ram loomed over her, his expression set to take only aye for an answer, and Penny felt small and delicate with absolutely no will power when he was this near. "Understood, Penelope?" Her name tumbled from his lips like a soft caress, smoothing down her shoulders.

Holding his gaze, Penny nodded obediently.

"Guess that clarifies exactly *who* the customer is, doesn't it?" Margaret whispered on a smile, leaving without their notice.

The door closed softly, the guest room suddenly too small and intimate for all they'd been through together. Ramsey's gaze sketched her upturned face, waiting for her wall of ice to rise atween them. When it didn't, he stole the opportunity of privacy.

"Will you accept my apology for my harshness in the street?" He was mortally ashamed that he'd spoken to her so rudely. She'd already done much on his behalf.

"Only if you accept mine," came in a strained whisper.

His smile was faint and soft, not one of those blinding grins that sent her insides dancing, but a tender, incredibly masculine curve of his lips. It left her utterly breathless, melting her knees, and she didn't step back when he grasped her shoulders with a gentle hold. Before she could wish otherwise, he pressed his lips to her forehead.

Penny closed her eyes, swaying toward him, yet even the simple, almost brotherly kiss made her senses shift and twist. His lips touched her cheek, the corner of her mouth and she felt a shiver pass up from her toes. He was dangerous just *being* Ramsey, for there was nothing sibling-like about what he made her feel.

He met her gaze, rubbing her arms. "Will you be calling me Ramsey, now that we've shared a kiss?"

But that wasn't enough, she wanted to say and the reckless thought jerked her from his grasp. Ramsey sighed, his broad shoulders drooping. He sensed the chill and cursed it. She erected that shield too handily for his liking and as she turned toward the door, Ramsey dropped onto the bed and pulled off a boot, tossing it to the floor. Penny reached for the knob, glancing back over her shoulder for a last look.

He tugged at the second boot, sluggishly letting it fall to the dark green carpet, and she noticed blood staining his bandaged leg wound. Running a hand over his face and through his hair, he rotated his head on his neck, then let it drop forward. A bolt of sympathy shot through her, blending with admiration for the mysteriously uncommon Ramsey O'Keefe. After all he'd suffered, this throwback from the dark ages had selfishly saved a child, rescued her from crazed fans, gained a friend in Tony and Hank, and disarmed the usually stern Margaret Brigette O'Hallaran into letting him call her Meggie. Lord, the man had been legally dead two days ago! Ever since she was a kid on the streets, she didn't think there were any *really* courageous men left in this world. Til now. And whether Penny wanted it or not, Robinson Crusoe was here, and she admitted, finally, that he was the most intriguing distraction for her grief.

"Mister O'Ke—ah, Ramsey?" He looked up sharply, startled to see her still standing in the doorway. "No, don't get up," she said when he struggled to rise. "I just, ah, wanted, ah . . ." Penny glanced to the side. What did she want? That his stay must be temporary? That just to look into his soothing dark eyes made her forget why she chose to isolate herself? Or to ask him for another more intimate kiss because the first left her burning as if she'd ignite her lingerie?

Penny blinked.

Oh, God. Where did *that* come from?

She met his gaze. "Welcome to my home, Ramsey." She left, closing the door and Ramsey smiled tiredly.

Ahh, yer softenin' to me, lass, he thought, pleased as he gathered the strength to pull himself off the bed. He found the

privy, staring in amazement at the huge room. He'd ceased
asking questions about modern inventions, no longer wishing
to appear the dolt and needing to discover such on his own.
He tested the wood and brass handles over the stationary basin,
smiling as hot water—*hot water* spewed from the spicket. He
played, filling and emptying the basin, pleased. Ram turned,
staring down at the dark green bowl anchored to the floor. A
chamber pot, he deduced, lifting the circular lid, then depressing
the brass handle, pleased it could be emptied without the need
to—well, 'twas a task no one cared for and as far as advance-
ment was concerned, Ramsey considered this one monumental.

In the corner on a dais, tucked in an alcove, lay a tub set
flush with the floor, beyond it, potted foliage rested afore a
three-sided window, offering a magnificent view of the sea,
waves crashing gently on the pearl-white shore. 'Twas tranquil,
he thought, moving to the small green tiled room with a clear
glass door. Inside, high on two walls were cones punctured
with hundreds of tiny holes and below them, huge crystal knobs.
He studied the track and frame, much like the aft windows
of his ship, then slid the door back, turned a knob and was
immediately drenched with ice cold water.

"Neptune's balls," he hissed softly, twisting to find a towel
and catching his reflection in the wide silver glass above the
basin. Bracing his hands on the smooth counter, Ram stared
at his image. Great saints, but he looked awful, bleedin' night-
marish, and to know Penelope had seen him so unkempt, embarrassed him. His clothing was salt stained, his sleeve torn at the
shoulder. Well, 'twas not his finest garments he wore aboard
ship, he reminded, yet with little compensation. He rubbed a
hand over his jaw, the dark shadow of whiskers making him
look sinister. His eyes were bloodshot from lack of sleep, and
he'd lost a bit of flesh it appeared. He caught a whiff of odor
and sniffed at his garments. Oh good God! 'Twas a wonder
the lady didn't swoon from the foul vapors.

Ramsey quickly investigated the drawers and cabinets, finding them well-stocked with the thickest of towels, cakes of
scented soaps, and what he assumed was a shaving razor, though
the tiny flimsy t-shaped contraption could hardly stand his

beard. His cabin boy took a strop to his own blade frequently to scrape but a day's worth from Ram's chin. He discovered containers marked *toothpaste, shampoo, shave cream,* and God love inventors, *deodorant* and after reading the instructions, understood their use. He glanced at his reflection and vanity took hold. Stripping quickly, he checked his leg wound, discarding the soiled wrappings afore stepping into the rain chamber. He indulged in the abundance of free flowing hot water til his fingers wrinkled, then with a towel wrapped around his hips, he attempted to shave. Unpracticed at handling the small razor left him with a jaw nicked like a pubescent schoolboy's and other than soap, the only familiar item in the cabinet was a toothbrush. His own was fashioned of teakwood, a gift from a captain who'd sailed the Orient, and no doubt still rested on the commode in his cabin. About to apply paste to the brush, Ram suddenly wondered if Mister Cameron had sunk his frigate. The young pup had not gained the air of authority it took to captain *Triton's Will* yet. Nay—to *have been* captain— was—is—God save me from such thoughts, he cursed, squeezing the tube and squirting paste on the mirror.

Several moments later he left the bathing room, a rolling cloud of mist following in his wake and Ramsey enjoyed the shock of cool air hitting his warm bare skin. He paused, glancing around the room when he noticed the drawn drapes, dimmed lights, and the tray resting on the foot of the bed. Meggie, you sweet wench, he thought, toweling his hair dry with one hand and sampling the fare with the other; generous roasted beef sandwiches, tart dilled pickles, fried slivers of potatoes that crunched and tasted so light Ramsey consumed the pile afore he realized it. He held up a tall fluted glass, examining the liquid in the dim light; the unmistakable aroma of ale made him groan with anticipation. He sipped. Rather weak, he thought, swiftly downing the iced pint, surprised he enjoyed the cooled spirits. Plunking the glass down on the tray, Ramsey patted his stomach. Meggie will be pleased he'd left naught but crumbs, he thought, setting the tray aside and falling back onto the bed. Ahh, God, 'twas the sweetest heaven. Used to a damp straw bedding, Ramsey buried his face in the fragrant spread. I be likin' your century, Penelope, he thought, then, like a tired child crawling into bed, he dragged the covers down and slid beneath the cool green sheets.

Nearly a dozen hours later, the door opened, at first a crack, then further. Penny poked her head around the wood, smiling when she spied the barren tray in the soft bedroom light. Good boy, she thought, making a beeline for it, her blue satin pajamas shimmering. She didn't even get close, suddenly freezing in her steps. He lay cross ways on the bed, facedown, one arm dangling over the edge, the dark sheet wrapped snugly around his lean hips and legs. A bare calf peeked out from beneath the downy pile. What did he do to keep in such spectacular condition, she wondered, her eyes traveling upward. Her gaze halted sharply on the area where his nut-brown skin faded, low on his spine. Shiny crisscross slashes marred the muscled perfection. Dear Lord. She'd forgotten. Slowly Penny stepped closer, hesitantly extending her arm. Her fingers shook.

Oh Ramsey.

Her vision blurred as she imagined the excruciating pain he must have suffered to have so many scars. Leaning over him, she allowed her fingertips to graze the smooth, healed wounds.

Penny suddenly found herself thrown flat on her back, on the bed, his solid weight crushing the breath from her lungs. Something cold and hard ground beneath her chin, forcing her head back, and in the darkness—she heard the distinct click of a pistol hammer.

Chapter 14

"Care to die?" Deadly cold and full of positive intent.

"R—Ramsey," she whispered. "It's me, Penelope."

He immediately pointed the barrel to the ceiling, his sleepy eyes focusing on her face. Cautiously, he eased the hammer down, a muscle flexing in his jaw as he slowly set the pistol on the night stand beyond her head.

The air hummed with rushing adrenalin and Penny swallowed.

Abruptly Ramsey buried his face in the rumpled pillow beside her head.

Penny didn't dare move. "Was that thing really loaded?"

"Silence, woman!" Muffled, but clear—and extremely angry. Suddenly he reared back, grabbing her by the shoulders. "You little half-wit!" He gave her a quick, hard shake. "I might have killed you!"

Before Penny could retort, he rolled off her and sat up, hunter-green fabric pooling around his bare hips.

"Sweet mother of God!" he rasped, pushing trembling fingers through his hair. Slowly Penny shifted upright, acutely aware of the fury working through him, crawling up his spine and flexing his muscles. He didn't move, his stillness poised on some undefinable threshold. And she flinched when he suddenly snapped a look back over his shoulder, dark eyes like chips of blackened amber.

Ramsey's gaze rapidly sketched her features, easily reading her fear, her uncertainty. He ached to quell it, for it mirrored his own. I could have so easily killed her, he thought again. The woman had no notion of how handily the unstable weapon could have exploded in her lovely face.

"I better go," she said uneasily and made to leave the bed, but Ramsey reached for her, grasping her arms and dragging her across the bed and onto his lap.

He stared into wide green eyes. "By God, I would rather die than harm you."

"I—I'm sorry," she whispered on a trembling breath, her hand coming up to touch his jaw. "I honestly didn't mean to scare you like that."

His fingers flexed on her arms, his lung working.

"Ramsey?"

Temptation rode him, and his name on her lips, the tenderness in her eyes, spirited through him as seductively as if she'd come to him baring herself for his favor. 'Twas unwise to voice his thoughts, for the lass was vulnerable and harbored a chilling independence as if 'twere her birth right, yet he wanted to taste her, *needed* to, just once, if only to assure himself 'twas not his imagination brewing this tension atween them.

He drew her suddenly closer, his mouth hovering a breath above hers, and Penny inhaled, her eyes flaring at the jolt of imaginary sparks crackling between them. That he wouldn't speak drove her wild with an unfamiliar stirring, a quickening heat consuming her blood. She could feel her pulse race, her skin flush. He'd never looked at her quite like that before.

And a tingling raced up the back of her thighs.

The charged air thickened, and when her tongue nervously moistened her lips, he groaned and crushed her mouth beneath his, swallowing her startled gasp. She was totally unprepared for the onslaught, of wicked heat and man, as his mouth rolled savagely across hers, licking, tasting, his head twisting maddeningly back and forth, and a dark sound rumbled in his chest when she answered the power, matching and mating with his mouth.

It scared her, this feverishness racing along her bloodstream, a greedy throbbing for his touch, yet her small hands gripped his biceps, groping up to clasp his head, her movements leaving her open to his attention. Recklessly, she wanted it. And it was an excruciating instant before he touched her, shaping her breasts til she trembled, thumbs circling her nipples, and Ramsey felt her hungry whimper against his mouth, felt her thrust into his palms. He flipped the satin covered buttons free, spreading the fabric, his hands smoothing over her lush naked swells afore sweeping around to pull her tightly to his bare chest.

The contact was galvanizing, her mouth and tongue sliding ravenously across his in seethingly erotic strokes. He wanted to taste and touch and know all of her, yet could feel the urgency in her, uncapped, impatient. He shifted, stretching her across the support of his arm afore he bent to her plump nipple. He took tender flesh into his mouth and Penny cried out softly, plowing her fingers into his hair as Ramsey laved and sucked, his free hand sliding luxuriously over the satin covered flesh of her hip, her thigh, seeking her tender center. She opened for him, muscles tense with anticipation, hovering on the pulse of need.

He rubbed and Penny clung to his neck, squirming against his touch, breathless for more, now, and he sensed it, shoving the silken fabric down over her hips, her buttocks, frantic to give her what her body begged for as he drew the satin free of her limbs. His hand scrubbed back up the muscled slope of her thigh, her skin jumping at his touch as he lowered her to the bed, his fingers curling around her knee and drawing it over his thigh.

"Share this with me," he murmured into her mouth, kissing her, holding her snugly, his hand sliding atween her thighs. He heard her breath catch as he cupped her, the heel of his hand rubbing gently afore he parted and probed, sinking a finger inside.

She arched like a bow. "Oh God," she moaned and he withdrew and pushed, again and again, yanking the strings of her desire with delicate strokes. She wrapped her arms around his neck, a tight sound escaping her throat, and he spoke softly.

"I want to taste you." His thumb circled lightly around the bead of her sex. "Here."

She whimpered, fighting her pleasure. He could feel it in the stiffness of her body, the way she clawed him, nearly climbing up his chest.

"Release yourself, Penelope. Ride the wave," he said into her ear, then kissed her damp mouth, lusciously deep and long. Her hips rocked and he introduced a second finger, plunging, retreating, gaining tempo. Slick feminine muscles grabbed and pulsed.

"Look at me," he said and she tilted her head back. His gaze searched hers, his entire body quaking. "Let me feel it sweep you." He held her tightly against his chest, gazing into her smoky-green eyes as he stroked the sensitive core of her, her slim body like liquid rhythm, undulating to the quick tempo of her passion. Her hopeful eyes held him prisoner, a trap far stronger than her body. "Aye, lass," he coaxed, feeling her climb as if he were sheathed inside her.

Suddenly she went taut, feminine muscles convulsing around his touch, hips grinding, fingertips digging into his skin. A fractured rasp sanded in her throat. She trembled, her soft shudders coating him like steaming velvet, afore she closed her eyes and dissolved against him.

Ramsey held her, without motion, the image of her exquisite climax repeating in his mind. 'Twould be an eternity afore he tired of the sight, he thought, and just as her breathing returned to some semblance of normality, she abruptly leaned back.

Quick little gasps puffed the hair covering her face and mouth, and she brushed at the tangled mass, searching his features.

He smiled, crooked and pleased and as if she were made of glass, he rained painfully sweet kisses over her cheek, her eyes, lightly brushing her mouth.

"Ahh, lass," he said after a moment, caressing her bare legs. "Has no one warned you 'tis dangerous to sneak into a gentleman's bed chambers?" God, she was exquisite, he thought, all rosy and freshly ravished. He leaned in for a kiss, the strength of his arousal pressing warmly against her thigh. She jerked back, the fear in her eyes making him uneasy. "What think you, lass?" He tried to keep his features impassive, but something was very wrong.

"Oh God, Ramsey." Her eyes beseeched him. "I can't do this. I'm sorry." She pushed him back with little effort and left the bed.

He reached, catching her hand. She tugged, refusing to look at him.

"I would not take from you what you are not willing to give, Penelope." She lifted her gaze to his. "Never."

His sincerity stuck her like a mortal blow. "I know," she moaned miserably. "I don't mean to be selfish, but . . ." her lip quivered, the sight tearing through his heart. "I'm sorry." She pulled free, rushing from the room.

Ramsey sighed, frowning. Was her fear that he was left unsatisfied and might demand she fulfill him or was she ashamed that she'd allowed him the intimate liberty and knew she enjoyed it? The former did not speak well of her opinion, yet even as he glanced around at the sensual debris of tumbled bedcovers and satin trousers, Ram knew her lush response would haunt him more this night than the fierce throbbing in his groin.

He slumped down on one elbow, then gave up and fell onto his back, studying the swirled ceiling. Run and hide all you wish, lady heart, for I've discovered your weakness. Ram snatched a pillow hovering on the edge of the mattress and stuffed it beneath his head, extraordinarily pleased that weakness was him.

Chapter 15

An hour later at the far end of the hall across from his chamber, Ramsey grasped the painted crystal knob and tugged. The door, cleverly disguised by wallpaper, gave a little, the top sticking. He thumped it with his fist and pulled, opening it quietly and discovering what he assumed; a servant's staircase, narrow, steep, and rarely used, if the musty odor was any indication.

Ramsey slowly descended, having given up tempting sleep this night. His mind refused to rest, except on Penelope and her wild run from his arms. Mayhaps she wasn't as discomforted as he suspected, and she'd simply cast the entire moment to the unpredictability of fate, dismissing the whole affair. *That* did not sit well in his belly and he paused on the staircase, recognizing that in his thirty-three years, he'd likely put a few women on the receiving end of these uncomfortable feelings.

Tess had teased him mercilessly that he always thought first with the contents of his breeches, and mayhaps this uneasiness was well-deserved, for although he was learned in loving a body, what knew he of gently couching a lady's heart? And one too terrified to accept aught beyond passion?

Penelope did more than excite him or send up a challenge

with her independence; she made him dream and ache for things he'd no right to lay claim. He may lay possession to her body up there in his chamber, but in no way did he possess more.

His bare foot met the last step and his attention caught on a polished wood and brass sconce, much like the one on his frigate, its candle untouched. 'Twas for decoration, he decided, for he'd already taken apart the switch in his chamber to discover the source of instant light, unsuccessfully, only to find it naught but a confusing mess of wires. Dismissing it, he shouldered open the lower door. It gave without a sound and after sealing away a bit of his century, he headed left, toward the pale light spilling softly into the hall, radiating like a beacon. He hoped 'twas the galley.

Not knowing if he would be intruding on someone's privacy he peered around the door jam. He smiled. Beneath the dim light, Penelope sat afore the dining table, her knees drawn up to her chin, a plush black velvet robe scarcely catching at her shoulders. She held a container in one hand and a spoon in the other, steadily shoving a soft confection into her lovely little mouth. She flicked damp hair out of her way, to more important matters it appeared—to dip the spoon into another bucket, then a plate, pausing only to sample, savor, then on to the next platter or bowl. She was like a child foraging the cupboards.

"Ah—ha, nourishment."

She jolted at the sound of his voice, staring up at him with wide eyes, the spoon protruding freely from her mouth. Ramsey tried not to laugh.

Penny grasped the spoon and turned away, leaning over the table to scoop up a dollop of soft cheesecake, taste, then switch to a fork and spear a chunk of smoked salmon.

"May I join you?"

Penny shrugged, not trusting herself to answer. She ought to be embarrassed, or at least, feeling a little guilty after spontaneously-combusting all over the man, then running like a scared virgin. God, he must think she was nothing but a tease. And his formidable presence was enough to make her want to climb into a hole and yank it in after her. Yet another part of her wanted to drag him inside with her. The part she left upstairs, in his arms, yet she couldn't, for to give up any more of herself to a man she scarcely knew, especially this man, left her weak. And weakness left her open for hurt. He was a temptation she couldn't afford. And it scared her. No, *he* scared her; his natural sensuality, his archaic mannerisms, his sudden odd appearance into her life. And worse, this uncontrollable power they shared. Did it bulldoze him as hard as it did her, she wondered, stealing a look as he sauntered closer. Why did he have to look so unaffected, the swine? And out of the corner of her eye she saw him briefly hesitate, and Ramsey let his senses take his fill of her.

God almighty, just to look at this woman drove a bone-quaking desire through his bloodstream. Ahh lass, have you a notion of what you've done to me, Ram wondered, grasping the back of a chair and positioning it right beside her, close enough to catch the scent of her freshly-washed skin as he slid into the tuffed seat. 'Twas his first occasion look upon her face unfettered by powders and paints and he adored the stark contrast of auburn brows and lashes against the pale creamy gold of her skin. He wanted to kiss every inch of it and as if by command, the black velvet robe slipped off her shoulders, exposing the gentle swells above her breasts. *She* was too busy eating to notice, but a voice in his head cautioned him to tred carefully with this woman.

He leaned closer. "What has captured your interest, love?"

A tremor shot through her at the endearment, and Penny looked to see what he meant.

"Ice cream." She held out the little pink bucket.

He peered skeptically atween her and the brownish swirled concoction.

Her brows rose. "Never had any?"

Ramsey picked up a spoon and scooped out a healthy portion. "There are a great many things I've yet to experience, lass," he said, wiggling his brows and looking her over afore he shoved the spoon into his mouth. His eyes instantly rounded, and he held the ice cream in his mouth afore deciding to swallow. "Delicious. Chocolate." He dipped again.

"Not just chocolate, Ramsey. Rocky Road." She handed

over the tub, then picked up the cheesecake. She ate, covertly
scrutinizing the man beside her. God, he was sexy. Long chestnut-brown hair draped his shoulders. A little trim and he'd be
even more devastating. God, like you need to add to your
distractions, she thought, her gaze skimming the dark gray silk
hugging his broad shoulders, the crimson trimmed robe gapping
open to the loosely-sashed waist, giving her a view of the
skimpy drawstring holding up matching silk trousers. Great
chest, tanned, defined, the center sprinkled with bronze curls
and inviting her touch. She licked the back of the spoon, silent
as he finished off the ice cream, then studied the treats. His
gaze turned to the remnants of the cheesecake.

"No. It's mine." She held it out of his reach. "You try
something else." She waved at the table.

"I want that."

Penny could help but smile as he rose up slowly, his spoon
poised for attack and she twisted away, protecting her treasure.
Ramsey nuzzled the skin of her bare shoulder, his lips marking
a moist path toward her breast. The plate *clunked* to the table,
and she turned into his touch.

Suddenly he dropped into his chair and dug his spoon into
the cake, shoving the sweet morsel into his grinning mouth.

"That's unfair tactics." Embarrassment flamed her cheeks.

"Defenses are stormed—" he leaned closer, his gaze sliding
luxuriously over her skin—"through the most vulnerable spot,
Penelope."

He made her sound like a castle. And when he tried to kiss
her shoulder, she yanked up the robe, pinning him with a
challenging glance.

Ramsey sank back into the chair, smothering a chuckle.
Patience man, he warned himself, taking another bite of cake.

"Such an odd combination, your dining habits." He waved
at the assortment of plates and bowls, then sampled a bit of
warm cream covered noodles.

"I know." She yawned hugely. "I always midnight graze
when I'm ups—" She clamped her lips shut as his gaze sharpened on her.

"Why are you upset?" he said after he'd swallowed.

"I'm not."

He scowled, dark eyes intense. "Do not attempt to deceive to me, madame." He speared some salmon. "I'll not stand for it."

"Is that so?"

He chewed slowly, his gaze searching her features, recognizing her cool cloak and aching to strip her of it.

"Never consider that I am a fellow easily pitched a keg of fob and gamon, Penelope."

"Pitched a keg of *what?*"

He hesitated, redefining the phrase. "Lies," he said crisply.

"Neither am I. So why won't you tell me where you came from?"

"Lexington." His fork came back to the cheesecake.

"A far cry from the Bahamas, Ramsey," it was her turn to warn. "How did you get into the ocean?"

"I swam," he said, then shoved a large hunk into his mouth.

"Now *you're* lying."

Ramsey didn't want to hide the truth from her, but she would not accept it. Good God, he scarcely did, a cold shiver running over his back every time he realized exactly where he was. But Penelope was unprepared for him in her life, and to spout of his leap through time would surely have her calling upon the constabulary to cart him away. And he was not prepared to leave her company just yet. Mayhaps never.

"Does it matter from whence I've come?" came softly as he swiped a napkin across his lips and met her gaze. "If I'd said I'd fallen from the sky and into your world, would it matter?" He leaned closer. "If I say aye, I was shipwrecked or abandoned, or a victim of a mutinous crew," he waved as if 'twere the most outlandish scenario, "would it change the moments spent in each other's arms?"

He had the most sincere gentle eyes, she thought. She didn't want anyone to know where she'd come from, so why was she badgering him? And the notions he recited were too ridiculous to consider.

"No," she finally said.

"Are you certain?" He jammed the spoon into some unidentifiable mass. "You took a bit of time." Ram tasted. His chewing stopped before it really started and he mumbled around the
food, "What in God's creation was that?"

Penny's gaze shifted briefly to the plate. "What?" She
smiled devilishly. "Need more salt?" His eyes pleaded for
mercy. "It's pickled pig brains." He moaned helplessly, glancing frantically for a place to spit and she held up a paper napkin.

Ramsey spat the gray matter into the paper, glaring at her,
his chair scraping back as he stood, then sprinted to the sink.
Her giggle filled the kitchen and his hands hovered in frustration
afore he recalled how to release the water and drank straight
from the faucet. "Bah!" He rinsed his mouth. "You enjoy
consuming animal organs?"

"It's an acquired taste."

"If I must acquire the palate, I shall forego the challenge,
I'm thinking."

"More for me, then." She spooned the slimy stuff, holding
it up to her lips. Ramsey waited, shutting off the flow of water.
She smiled, dropping the silverware into the bowl and pushing
it aside. "Just kidding. Hank's the one who loves it."

Ramsey shuddered and began cleaning up the mess. He
paused in covering a dish of fudge. "Are you finished, ah . . .
grazing?" he said after some thought.

"Yes." Penny yawned again, propping her head in her palm.
"You don't have to do that. It's my mess."

Ramsey didn't tell her he needed something to occupy himself afore he carried her off to his bed. He searched the galley
cupboards, opening a pair of tall silver doors, amazed to discover the box quite cool and filled with food and drink. Like
the conditioned air, he deduced, touching the smooth chilled
walls. He deposited the plates and bowls on the shelves, gritting
his teeth against the urge to investigate the room full of
machines. He'd have to examine them whilst none could come
upon him, he thought, stealing a peek inside a box full of racked
and soiled dishes. When he turned back for the last of it, she

was slumped forward, her fingertips stuck in the blueberry cheesecake.

Ramsey smiled, coming over to her and wiping off her hand, then gathering her in his arms. She snuggled into his embrace, looping her arms round his neck, the motion so natural Ramsey's heart split a little. He pressed a kiss to the top of her head, then carried her upstairs, pausing on the landing, confused. He'd never seen her enter or leave any one of the doors lining the balcony railing to his right and his chambers were at the far end, the servants case across. His gaze moved left and he immediately headed straight for the door left ajar, shouldering his way inside. Instantly he knew this chamber was hers. Though the decor was surprisingly vivid; deep blue-green, accented with pale dove gray, 'twas the epitome of femininity; plush with downy spreads and ruffled pillows, softly draped windows, velvet settees and chairs. And an absolute disaster.

Ramsey negotiated his way around piles of clothes, shoes, reticules, and soiled towels, gently depositing her in the center of her bed. His gaze scanned the drape of teal mesh netting hanging from the ceiling in tiers like a sultan's *harem* to the woman lying abed. She is not as she seems, he thought, tucking her bare legs beneath the striped coverlet. She murmured incoherently, curling on her side and cramming a pillow beneath her cheek. He brushed her hair from her face, then looked around the room.

On the far side of the room was a large black box with a dark glass front, beneath it another, much smaller yet thinner box and on a shelf below were what appeared to be books, but from the distance Ram couldn't be certain. Afore the whole box-housing were empty bowls and glasses, stacks of papers and writing instruments. The entire area confused him and he dismissed it, his gaze skimming over the jumble of pots and jars on her vanity, a scarf and something he couldn't identify twisted around the chair legs. Garments were strewn over the back of the gray settee and across the top of her dressing room door. Another hurricane in there, he decided, scanning her chaos of her bathing chamber. Ramsey shook his head, returning his gaze to her.

'Twas a unexpected contrast to the controlled woman he met three days ago.

Aye, love, and what else will I unravel about you afore you show me your heart again? He bent and kissed her lips, a soft press meant to send her into gentle dreams.

It didn't.

Chapter 16

The coffeemaker sputtered, sending the aroma of a rich Colombian blend throughout the spacious kitchen as Margaret O'Hallaran pulled out more appliances, pans, and food to prepare breakfast. A man's breakfast, she thought with satisfaction, her sneakers squeaking as she stepped. While bacon sizzled, she popped a dozen muffins into the oven, then cracked two eggs into the hot skillet, smiled, added a third, then sent the bread down into the toaster as she reached to pull the butter close.

"Good morning, Margaret." Penny tied her hair back, then stepped fully into the kitchen. "Aren't you the happy little chef." She pecked a kiss to Margaret's cheek.

"Ain't it grand, Miss H.," Margaret beamed as she moved around the cooking island to set the table. She worked like a precision time piece, laying out the service perfectly from her position. "He's out on the sundeck, if you were wondering." Margaret looked up to catch her reaction. Yup, just as I thought. That look was enough to fry his eggs.

Penny gazed out the wide glass doors, focusing on the far end of the screen covered deck, beyond the pool, to where Ramsey sat in the heat of the early morning sun, beside the umbrella covered table. He was shirtless, a stack of books beside him on the surface and one on his lap, sipping water while he read. He seemed to marvel more at the paper and book, she thought, than what was printed in them.

"He was up before me and Hank," Margaret said, sliding the eggs onto a plate, then setting the dish on the back of the range to keep warm. She checked her muffins. "And I saw the sunrise."

Did he ever go back to sleep, Penny wondered, moving to the counter and pouring herself a cup of coffee. She sipped, strolling to the glass doors again.

"Tell him chow's almost ready, will you, honey?"

Penny nodded, slid back the glass and stepped out. Heat and humidity buffeted her cool skin and she smoothed the folds of her yellow sundress, then closed the door, walking slowly toward him, negotiating around potted plants and a wicker sofa. His large muscled frame was partially shrouded by a group of potted fig and palm trees and she stopped just short of his line of vision, studying him. His hair wasn't tied back and she decided she liked it, amongst other things. Like the droplets of sweat trickling down the center of his broad chest and the way he sat negligently in the chair, his jean covered legs stretched out before him.

She'd never met a man who was quite so—*masculine,* even though she knew several men who made Ramsey O'Keefe look like chopped liver. So what was so appealing about this particular man?

Last night flashed in her mind with amazing clarity; the terror in his eyes when he thought he might have hurt her, his kiss, his cherishing words and sensual touch. Her spine tingled with the blazing memory, and though it had been a while since she'd made love—*You never experienced anything so unselfishly giving as that,* her conscious interrupted and her skin flushed. No, she admitted. Never.

Yet even when she found herself tucked in bed, still wearing her robe, she tried to marshal her familiar remoteness, the detachment that came so easily in the past, demanding she

sever herself from him and this unusual situation. Now, before
it was too late.

She tried. God, how she tried. But even as she remembered
her reasons for keeping distance, his blinding smiles and teasing
crept into her mind. His kid in the candy shop attitude destroyed
any notion that he'd think of her as less than his equal and his
tender concern for a stranded child, and even her own safety,
touched her in spots she didn't want anyone to reach. But he
had. Suddenly she felt as if she were intruding on his privacy
when he closed the book, setting it aside as he pinched the
bridge of his nose. He leaned forward, bracing his elbows on
his knees and digging at his eyes with the heels of his palms,
a slip of paper caught lightly between two fingers. Something
wasn't right.

"Ramsey?" He sat upright, yet refused to met her gaze.
"Are you okay?"

"I am fit, aye."

Apprehension curled in her stomach. His voice sounded
strained and why wouldn't he look at her? Penny moved close,
and he shifted further away, his long hair shielding his face.
The knot twisted tighter and a part of her warned that this was
bound to happen if she opened herself up to anyone again. But
still, she came to him, worry creasing her features.

Ramsey tried to compose himself, keeping his gaze on the
narrow pier and boathouse beyond as he stuffed the tailor's
receipt in his pocket. Unable to sleep, he'd studied the history
books since dawn, stunned to discover his country battled the
British again in 1812 and horrified to know the colonies had
waged war amongst themselves fifty years later. The notion
sickened the Continental Marine, especially after witnessing so
many perish in the revolution. God almighty, we actually killed
our own people! Ramsey struggled with the knowledge of a
war dividing a country he'd fought to bind together and tried
to imagine cutting Dane down for merely having a different
opinion. He couldn't, thank God. Ram glanced at the book
titled, *Jane's Fighting Ships,* and his spirits plummeted further.
His profession was utterly useless in this century; ships were
no longer sailed by celestial calculations, wind speed and the

skill of a seasoned sailor, but by machines measured in horse-power, steered by bloody *computerized* rudders and throttle controls and something called RADAR.

The vessels Ramsey had mastered were for mere pleasure now, and smaller than a bleedin' sloop! My God, how was he to pay his bills now? A reasonable man, Ramsey considered the cost of garments and lodging would have increased over the years, but sweet Christ, sixty-five dollars for a pair of well-worn breeches? 'Twas friggin' near a boatswain's yearly wage!

A glassy *clink* made him look toward the source. His gaze turned sharply from the delicate hand retreating from the steaming cup to the woman kneeling afore him.

Ramsey looked at the deck and the motion smacked of cow-ardice. "I beg of you, lass, leave me in peace."

Her heart shifted at the quiet plea. She never thought to see him like this. "Talk to me, Ramsey."

A muscle worked in his jaw. "I cannot." He still wouldn't meet her gaze.

"It can't be that bad."

He scoffed. "You would not understand, Penelope. Please, trust me in this." To bring her into his troubles was dishonorable and damned complicated.

"Come on." She ducked, trying to catch his gaze and he slowly tilted his head to look at her. Penny quickly schooled her features. God, he looked so . . . defeated. "Let me help. I can see you're upset."

He shocked her with a quick lop-sided grin. "Are you admitting that after one evening of showering me with your unspeakable passion, you can make that deduction?" God almighty, but she was worth any anguish.

Penny blushed to the roots of her hair, failing miserably to ignore those dark eyes that gleamed, a bit smugly, with the memory of her spread naked and eager beneath his skilled touch. Why was he so pleased about last night when she'd left him suffering? "Try to behave yourself."

" 'Tis not in me nature," he said with a half smile, his silky tone speaking volumes as his gaze caressed her bare shoulders. Her yellow skirt fluffed around her like the creamy petals of a buttercup, and Ramsey was pleased a night of loving left her radiant and glowing and unbelievably relaxed. He'd have to remember that.

"I didn't mean anything by it."

He leaned closer. "I did," he said and she inhaled sharply, suddenly brushing his hair back off his shoulder. Several thin red lines streaked his skin. Her nails, she realized, her face darkening with embarrassment.

" 'Tis a bit like being branded," he teased, and her gaze flew to his, yet before she could apologize he asked, "Will you sneak into my rooms and again bestow—"

She clamped her hand over his mouth. "Please. Don't say it. I asked for that." His eyes gleamed with laughter. "And I wasn't sneaking." Her gag still in place, he arched a brow in doubt. "I want you to know I don't do that sort of thing. Ever. At all!" She stared at a spot beyond him, frowning. "That was really so unlike me."

He peeled away her hand. "What *is* like you, Penelope? The wild cat I ensnared last eve?" Her skin pinkened, his husky tone sending goose flesh down her back. "Or, my icy princess, confident and in control of her kingdom? Or was it, mayhaps, the teasing lass who fed me comfits and pig's brains at two in the morn?" He drew her hand to his mouth, dropping moist kisses to her palm, the inside of her wrist, his softly spoken words warming her damp skin. "I confess I prefer all three, especially the tempestuous siren who marked me with the heat of her passion."

She made a pained sound, an ache blossoming in her chest, her need of him hungry to be fed, yet knew she shouldn't allow this to go further. "Ramsey, don't." She tried to pull free.

He wouldn't let her. "Do not what? Want you in my arms again? Want to feel your body rejoice in my touch?" He inhaled through clenched teeth, his mind and groin recalling her every nuance with restless clarity. " 'Twill not happen. For once tasted," came low and haunting, "I crave more." Dark eyes caressed her face, her bare shoulders. "By God, Penelope," he rasped. "Even the woman-scent of you lingered to torment me in my dreams."

Penny swallowed, unsure, yet greedy for more. No one had ever spoken to her like that, as if he'd come apart at the seams. "That shouldn't have happened and I'm sor—"

"Shh," he hushed. "Do not apologize." A gentle warning edged to his tone. "For I do not seek it. And 'tis beyond our control." Her look said otherwise and he asked, "Are you ashamed of what we shared?"

Shared. She couldn't remember the last time she let herself share anything with a man. "No." She wasn't, would never be. God, last night in his arms felt so right it scared her. "I don't understand you, Ramsey. Any other man would be laying on the guilt for me leaving like that."

His thumb made a slow circle over the back of her hand, not a hint of smugness in his tone when he said, "I will wage that I am not a'tall like any man you've known."

That was certainly an understatement. "I haven't *known* many," came tightly and he smiled. "But I can't give you what you want." Her manner implied the sexual.

"Again you assume to know what I desire." His expression softened, turning devilish. "And 'tis not the first time a lass has run from me bed satisfied."

She sat back on her calves, trying to think of something clever to deflate that puffed ego, but, "Oh really?" was sorely lacking.

"What is this?" Brows high, he tilted his head, offering his ear. " 'Tis jealousy I hear?"

She cleared her throat. "Why are you reading these?" She waved at the stack of books, noticing an open, well-thumbed dictionary.

His smile widened at her avoidance. "One studies a subject thoroughly to diminish one's ignorance, lass," Ramsey said as his gaze drifted over her features, her slim bare throat and shoulders, down across the plump swells of her breasts filling the heart shaped bodice. Was it proper for women of this century to reveal so much skin?

"Is that so?" Penny swallowed, damning her swift reaction to him and dragging her gaze from his. She inspected the titles; *U.S. History, Military Warfare, The Marines of the Frigate*

Navy, On This Day in America, A Timetable of Inventions and Discoveries. "What did you find that you didn't already know?"

Unable to answer without sounding like a candidate for Bedlam, nor resist the feminine temptation perched afore him, Ramsey grasped her about the waist, pulling her closer. A change of subject was at hand.

"Good morn, Penelope," he whispered, intimate-soft and deep, and her questions vanished beneath the onslaught of his alluring sensuality.

"Think so?" There goes that tingling again, she thought.

"Aye. Dare I hope for a kiss to begin me day?" he murmured, his head descending.

Penny knew she should push him away, knew she ought to remind him he was assuming too much and best forget what came before now, but as his lips covered hers, her resistance wilted under the hot morning sun. His kiss was erotically slow, a gentle wakening of the desire they shared last night. And he wasn't going to let her forget even a moment, humming his pleasure as her hands slid up his damp chest to wind around his neck. Her fingers played in his hair and he gathered her tightly to him, biceps flexing as he held her off the wood deck, snug atween his thighs. His lips toyed with hers until they were moist and swollen, and he held her tighter, his masculine strength pressing against her.

"Ramsey." Breathless, hesitant.

"I'm hungry, lass."

Penny smiled teasingly. "Margaret said breakfast was ready." Heck, she thought sluggishly, it ought to be charred to a crisp by now.

He chuckled, hoisting her onto his lap and holding her there when she was wont to wiggle free. "Nay, do not think to leave me now," he brushed his lips below her ear, her throat, "for I seek more delectable nourishment."

Penny tilted her head for better access, trying to sound defiant. "And what you want is all that matters, right?"

"Nay, you've only but to ask." His voice was filled with dark promise. "And I will attend to your *every* pleasure." She moaned, sinking into his embrace and Ramsey breathed deeply, fighting the urge to slide his hands beneath the folds of her indecently short day gown and dragged the ribbon from her hair. Deep red hair spilled over one shoulder and his gaze absorbed all of her in one heady sweep. "By Triton's will, you are a beautiful creature, lady heart."

He said it with such emotion Penny knew he didn't give the compliment often. She didn't wonder over the nickname either. She couldn't. He was kissing her again and doing it to absolute perfection.

Like a lover with a hundred years of experience.

Before the musical doorbell completed its chime, Anthony Wainright pushed open the front door. "I must be in the wrong house. Is that bacon I smell?" Anthony breezed inside, giving Margaret a peck on the cheek as he passed. "Is she up yet?"

"Oh, yeah, she's awake, all right."

Anthony stopped, recognizing the humor in her voice and turned to look at the housekeeper.

With a secretive smile, Margaret inclined her head toward the kitchen as she shut the door. Anthony headed in that direction, halting at the entrance, his gaze skimming over the obscene meal laid out, then around the room. No Penny. Movement beyond the glass doors caught his attention and his eyes rounded when he realized what he was seeing.

Anthony couldn't believe it. Yes, he could. No, he corrected. He could not. Not Penelope Hamilton, ice queen of Hollywood, in the arms of Ramsey O'Keefe!

"What's been going on here?" Penelope appeared thoroughly engrossed, enjoying Ramsey as much as he was enjoying her. Anthony felt like the voyeur in the worst way.

"You tell me, Mr. Wainright." Margaret poured orange juice into an iced glass.

Anthony cast her a side glance as he said, "How should I know? They were at each other's throats when I left them."

"Well, they're heavy into *kissing* each other's throats now."

He brought his gaze back to the couple. "Yes. I can see

that.'' Well, it seems they've gotten well past *Mister* O'Keefe and *Mistress* Hamilton, Anthony thought, moving away from the glass doors and sloshing coffee into a mug. This was good, he decided, very good.

"How 'bout you going out there and telling them breakfast is ready?"

"Me?" Anthony squawked, the mug halfway to his lips. "I couldn't possibly—'' Then he smiled, suddenly seeing the merits of the situation. "Do you really think we should interrupt them?"

"Heck, yes! My cooking's going to waste!''

With mug in hand, Anthony slid back the glass door loud enough to startle the pair and an evil satisfaction slithered over him as they abruptly separated. Ramsey set Penny to her feet, then stood, reaching for his shirt, turning his back as he stuffed the tails in his jeans. Penny was already heading toward him. Damn me, cheated out of a little torture, he thought with a secret grin.

"Don't say a word, Tony.'' She kept walking.

"I wasn't. Honest.'' The innocent face lost much when his lips twitched.

"Like hell.'' She entered the house.

"Ramsey!'' Anthony called. "Good to see you well rested.''

Ramsey's eyes narrowed as he came forward and shook Wainright's offered hand. Ram was angry at himself, less for stealing a kiss and more for placing Penelope in such a compromising position afore the Englishman. Would he have to duel for the lady? Though Penelope did have a certain attachment to the man, Ramsey would respect her judgment. For now.

"Come on and eat before Margaret explodes.'' Anthony urged him over the threshold. "She's never cooked so much food, and mind you, you're expected to clean your plate.''

When Ramsey stepped inside, Penny was already standing on the far side of the polished butcher's block table, admiring the fit of his white button front shirt, band collar, cotton and clinging. His sleeves were rolled back, exposing thick tanned forearms, and the button-fly jeans did absolutely nothing to hide the fact that he was a healthy man.

If the woman did not cease her staring, Ram thought, his body would betray him, right here in the galley for all to see. And he could not be accountable for his revenge. Needing a distraction, he inhaled deeply, his grin wide and pleased.

"Ahh, Meggie, me rose. What have you done?"

"Park it there, Ramsey," she said, pointing to a chair as she set a full plate before him. Anthony sat and helped himself.

Ramsey slid the napkin to his lap as he picked up the fork. He was famished, the *midnight grazing* only wetting his appetite for more substantial stores. And he did justice to Margaret's efforts, slavering butter on muffins, dunking toast in his eggs and chomping into bacon. And Penny didn't think she'd seen anyone devour so much food in one sitting, then considered how many calories it must take to maintain two hundred-forty-some pounds of man.

"You never smile like that when I eat," Penny said to Margaret, slipping into a chair and placing a muffin on her plate.

"You don't eat enough to keep a bird alive and it's all the wrong stuff." She inclined her head toward Ramsey. "And I've waited a long time for this," the housekeeper said pointedly as she warmed Penny's coffee.

Penny frowned, catching the hidden meaning and wanting to blunt Margaret's parental hopes.

Half his meal finished, Ramsey finally came up for air, leaned back and drained the tall glass of juice without stopping. "Meggie O'Hallaran, you're a wizard." He plunked the glass down. "My own cook could not have presented so fine a fare." He patted his stomach and Margaret glowed, freshening his coffee while making a face at Penelope. Ramsey continued eating.

"Your cook?" Penny piped in. "You had a cook?"

Ramsey glanced up, seeing three pairs of eyes trained on him. He removed the fork from his mouth and slowed his chewing. "Aye." Ram swallowed. "On my ship."

"If you had a ship, how come you were floating in the middle of the Atlantic? No, let me rephrase that," Penny said, "*drowning* in the Atlantic?"

"She sailed without me." Ramsey forked a chunk of egg

and shoved it into his mouth. 'Twas not a lie, he reasoned, *Triton's Will* did sail without him prior to the encounter with Phillip, and Dane's *Sea Witch* was left behind, in 1789.

"I thought you were marooned or something."

Ramsey smiled roguishly. "I believe we've addressed this subject afore."

"And you still haven't explained—" The doorbell chimed and Penny's frown deepened. "How come the alarms didn't go off?"

Ramsey dropped the fork, swiped his lips with a napkin and left his chair afore Anthony said, "I left the gate open and shut off the alarms."

Ramsey froze, then rounded on him. "You *what?*"

Jesus, Anthony thought as he slowly stood. If looks could kill.

"Have you forgotten the lady was nearly molested in the center of the village only yestermorn!" He clenched his fist, itching to throttle the Englishman and Penny recognized the canned fury. Like last night, a voice reminded.

She came to his side. "Ramsey, take it easy." She touched his bare forearm. "Tony's not a fool and crazed fans rarely have the nerve to approach the front door." He covered her hand, the hot wind immediately leaving him.

"It must be the coin dealer I contracted," Anthony said, marveling at the quick change.

Ramsey saw naught beyond the breech of decorum, and the eighteenth century man reacted naturally. "Regardless of your case, a gentleman does not call upon a lady's home without prior notice. Implore this coin vender to return at a decent hour and mayhaps they shall be received."

"Well, aren't you the lord and master," she said tightly, her look warning that last night didn't give him the right to rule.

He arched a brow, very aware of her censure. He chose to ignore it. "You often take callers at this hour?" A wealth of suspicious jealousy colored his tone and Penny experienced a quick flash of girlish pleasure.

"No, but—"

"She don't take *callers* at *any* hour," Margaret muttered, meant to be heard and Penny shot her a quelling glance.

"The coin *vender* is a lady," Anthony said, Ramsey's anti-quated attitude glaring like a beacon. "I asked her to come here." He headed for the front door and Ram followed, guiding Penelope afore him with a hand at the small of her back.

"Do you trust me enough to let me handle this?" Anthony grasped the knob.

Ramsey's gaze collided with Penelope's, and she nodded minutely. Ram agreed with a terse, "Aye," suddenly wishing he was armed as Anthony threw open the door.

"Who are you?" Penelope said, expecting a woman and finding a portly man in a three-piece suit, complete with watch fob and huffing like a steam engine.

"Bailey," Anthony whispered.

"Miss Penelope Hamilton?" he said to her, mopping his upper lip with a handkerchief.

Penny stepped forward, nodding, and Ramsey was there, beside her, like a hungry lion ready to pounce, yet Bailey disregarded him and addressed Penelope.

"Sebastian Bailey, Lloyds of London." He offered his card, shifting his briefcase to his other hand. "Good morning, Mister Wainright," he regarded and Anthony nodded, preoccupied, his gaze flipping from Ramsey to the Lloyd's agent.

"I told Tony yesterday this was a mistake." She returned the card but he wouldn't accept it. "And for reasons I won't divulge, I'm positive this acquisition isn't for me."

Ramsey studied her, curious over her certainty, and the sudden chill about her.

Bailey looked insulted. "I assure you, Miss Hamilton, Lloyds of London does *not* make mistakes. We've been waiting a long time to bestow—" His words faded, Wainright's stunned expression drawing their attention.

"Tony? You okay?" His Adam's apple was bobbing hard enough to make his necktie move.

"Oh my God." His gaze shifted from Bailey to Ramsey and back, excitement racing through his blood. He'd suppressed the thrilling possibility that Ramsey was *the* Ramsey O'Keefe when Penny first mentioned him, for his own sanity and a bit of investigation, but the time had come, he thought, for discovery. "Mister Bailey, this man," he gestured to Ramsey—"is named Ramsey O'Keefe."

The Lloyds agent stared up at the tallest gentleman, his bulging satchel slipping from his lax fingers and crashing to the floor.

"O—O'Keefe?"

Ram frowned. The man had suddenly gone dangerously pale. "Aye. Captain Ramsey O'Keefe." Ram bowed slightly at the waist, then watched as the cultured Englishman staggered back, his legs wobbling like a marionette suddenly without a master.

Chapter 17

"Weak stock, the English," Ram muttered, grabbing Bailey by the shirt front afore he hit the deck.

Bailey straightened instantly, looking surprisingly composed and business-like for a man so out of sorts a moment ago.

"So sorry." His cheeks pinkened. "Not my usual reaction, you know."

"Nay, I do not."

"Yes, well, ah, I suppose so." The faxed report was true. Lloyds routinely searched medical, tax, and police records for beneficiaries and when the British consulate in the Bahamas contacted him yesterday, offering up *that* name, Sebastian Bailey was prepared to fly to the Bahamas this morning to verify the existence of one Ramsey M. G. O'Keefe. Yet just before his departure he'd received word that his suspect had vanished. Silently he admitted he was utterly destroyed at having come so close, then lose the man. But to find him here, with Miss Hamilton, was an opportunity he never imagined having again.

"Exactly what business do you have with Ramsey?" Anthony said into the silence, unmistakably curious.

"I'm not a liberty to discuss it, until I have absolute proof." Bailey gazed up at Ramsey with something a kin to awe, yet the recipient regarded him with little more than annoyance and Penny wondered why he disliked the British with such distinction.

"Proof of what?" His arms akimbo, Ramsey gaze ripped over Bailey from head to foot.

But Sebastian wasn't shaken. He'd a job to do. "That you are in fact, *the* Ramsey O'Keefe my company seeks?"

Ram severely doubted he was and dismissed the little man as a car sped up the drive, skidding to a halt. They watched a tall slender woman exit the dark BMW with the grace of a dancer.

"Miss Clarissa Two Leaf," Anthony announced, his bearded face splitting into a smile. "I'm afraid your business will have to wait," he said to Bailey. "She has an appointment."

"Certainly." Bailey understood professional courtesy. He was after all, not expected. "Might I use your phone?" he said to Penelope, glancing briefly at Ramsey. "If Mister O'Keefe is our client, I need to courier some documents from my hotel."

Penny nodded, though she thought this all a huge waste of time.

The woman, distinctively native American Indian and wearing tortoiseshell glasses that continually slipped down her nose, met the porch landing, her gaze going immediately to the familiar. "Mister Wainright." She nodded cordially, shoved the glasses, then tucked a stray lock of hair back into the sleek twist as she moved inside.

She's lovely, Penny thought as they made introductions, then could have kicked herself for jealously glancing at Ramsey. If she'd expected to find his gaze on Ms. Two Leaf, she was dead wrong. God, she thought with a touch of apprehension. What have I done to deserve that look?

He'd recognized the change in her, like the shifting of cloth, the instant Bailey appeared on the door step, increasing with the second visitor. She was reserved, ill at ease with the people filling her home. Her posture was rigid, her stare hooded, and his scowl showed his dislike, but when she met his gaze, employing to understand his harsh expression, Ramsey could do naught but smile reassuringly and come to her side. Though she didn't touch him afore strangers, Ram felt her body soften. And he rejoiced in it.

"Call for Meggie," he whispered in her ear and she jabbed the intercom, buzzing the housekeeper and offering coffee and breakfast to the guests. Margaret's squeaking sneakers marked time on the tiled floor as she led Bailey and Two Leaf to the kitchen.

Penny spared a tight glance at Anthony.

"Don't say it. You're just upset over not being consulted til the last minute." Anthony kissed her cheek, then turned her toward the kitchen. "Try to remember Bailey is here to see you, dear, and go play the star for the public." She didn't move. "This is for Ramsey, too, you know," he whispered unfairly, giving her a little push.

Penny stole a glance at Ramsey, who didn't look the least bit ruffled by the early morning intrusion and was staring at her as if searching beneath her clothes, her skin. Yet, just to have him look at her so intensely gave her a deliciously maddening thrill. Flipping her hair over her shoulder, she headed toward the kitchen, moving across the floor in her best Cadillac walk. Hell. If he was going to look . . .

Ramsey's lips quirked, his gaze following her smoothly shifting hips, those gloriously sleek bare legs, very aware 'twas a stride fashioned for his pleasure, God love her. "You called her a star," Ram said when she was gone. "Give over, English. What mean you by such a remark?"

Anthony grinned. "Welsh, Ramsey, Welsh, and you know, famous person, a celebrity." Ramsey's features deepened to a scowl. "Penelope is an actress, Ramsey. One of America's finest."

Ram's eyes flared, then drew down to mere slits. He had witnessed plays and operas and considered actors pretentious little weasels out to satisfy their own vanity, and no better than sodomites and bawdy house dancers. And Penelope was neither pretentious, nor vain. 'Twas ludicrous to imagine her performing for money. Surely not.

Deep into his own thoughts, he followed Anthony off to the right, down a short hall and into a paneled room. Polished wood, old oxblood leather, and the scent of beeswax instantly surrounded Ramsey, familiar, comforting. It reminded him of his cabin.

Anthony shut the door and went to the desk, resting his hip on the edge. "What's the matter, Ramsey? You look confused."

"Is Penelope a widow?" Ramsey dropped into a winged-back chair, the leather creaking as he crossed his legs at the ankle.

"No," Anthony said, taken aback. "Why do you ask?"

"This home. Her wealth. 'Twas earned by this—this *acting* profession?" His tone disapproved, the words souring in his mouth.

"Sure. Her last film grossed over one hundred million."

Ram straightened in the chair. "Pounds sterling?"

"No. Dollars."

Ram stared, unfocused, his heart racing as he recalled the almanac he'd read this morn and converted pounds to dollars. He lost count, finally lifting his gaze to ask, "What—God forgive me for asking this—is a film?" His voice was faint, his breathing labored.

"A movie, cinematography. A moving picture," Anthony added carefully when Ramsey continued to stare at him.

Paintings that moved? Ram forced himself to calm down and consider the progress of inventions. Hadn't he read only this morn of a camera instrument that froze images on paper? Hadn't he seen the proof in those books? " 'Tis no matter," he finally decided, dismissing the matter in lieu of a headache. "I imagine I will discover such in due time."

"Good God, Ramsey, where have you been all your life?"

Ram flashed him a grin. Cutting your ancestors to ribbons he wanted to say, but instead changed the subject. "Mistress Two Leaf. Rather unusual name."

Anthony frowned a moment longer, then a secretive smile curved his lips. "She has some information you'll be pleased to hear. And it's best that we deal with her first." Although it galled him not to drag Bailey in here and demand answers, Anthony punched the desk intercom. "Margaret, will you ask Ms. Two Leaf to join us?" A moment later Margaret opened the door, allowing the woman to enter. Ramsey leapt to his feet.

"Mister O'Keefe," she said, extending her hand. "It's a pleasure."

" 'Tis mine, m'lady." Ramsey placed a soft kiss to the back of her hand and she blushed, drawing back in time to shove her glasses back up and offer a tiny smile.

"Well, yes, ahh—" He was not what she expected, Clarissa thought, wishing she'd dressed a bit more femininely as she set her briefcase on the desk, flipped the locks and pried it open. "Mister Wainright allowed me the opportunity to study and analyze your coin at length." She produced the gold coin, laying it on a blue velvet tray, then with a flourish, set notarized documents beside it. "I'd love to know where you got this."

Ramsey folded his arms over his chest, eyeing the wench from head to foot. Why was everyone so interested in this bit of gold? " 'Twas the payment of a bet."

Delicate black brows rose above the glass frames. "Really? Well, I can attest that you certainly are the winner. This coin is better than eight hundred eighty-five-fine, nearly nine hundred eighty-five, contains hardly any copper, and the mint stamping process is the first of its kind. I'd say it was over two hundred seventy-five years old from my tests. These," she tapped the documents with a manicured fingernail, "are certifications of authenticity."

"Authenticity as to what?" Anthony put in, smiling at Ramsey.

She looked at Anthony. "The coin is a Spanish doubloon, Mister Wainright, and because of its excellent condition and stamping, far better than anything found on the Atocia," she added smugly. "Its worth is frankly, priceless."

Ramsey's gaze shifted to the coin before he turned away and dropped into a chair and reasoning that if Penelope trusted Wainright and he this woman, Ramsey would allow him to proceed as he wished. He had nothing to lose and he was desperate for money. But the Atocia? She sank in the Matecumbes in 1622. How had anyone been able to recover her cargo?

''And the sale of it?'' Anthony prodded, enjoying every second of this.

''As per our company, I must ask if you're absolutely certain you want to, Mister O'Keefe?''

Staring at the tips of his new soft soled shoes, Ramsey stroked an imaginary moustache with his thumb and forefinger. ''Aye.''

Her eyes sparkled with excitement. ''I completed your instructions this morning, Mister Wainright.'' She fished in her briefcase. ''A private auction, sealed bids. I took the liberty of alerting only buyers who could afford such a relic and the bids were air expressed in early this morning.'' She held out a pair of envelopes. ''These were the two highest offers.''

Ramsey accepted the missives, flipped open the first and read. His eyes rounded and he straightened abruptly. ''Sweet Neptune's mother! You cannot be serious!''

''As you can see they were very competitive bids. It's an extremely rare find, Mister O'Keefe.''

Ramsey tore open the second envelope and could do no more than shake his head.

Anthony chuckled softly. The look on the man's face was worth his efforts.

''Do you accept?'' she asked politely.

''Aye,'' he whispered, then a little louder as he came to his feet and handed the paper to Wainright.

''Well, well, Ramsey,'' Anthony said with as much dignity as he could muster. ''How does it feel to be *that* rich?''

God bless the twentieth century, Ram thought, then burst out laughing. Miss Two Leaf smiled, shoved back her glasses, then held out another envelope. Ram looked puzzled.

''I anticipated that you'd accept and my company has authorized me to deliver a cashier's check in that amount. Less the commission, of course.'' Ramsey slowly accepted the draft, numbly signing the receipt. The man's shock was a job perk she didn't encounter often, like finding a lost heir or something. ''A true pleasure doing business with you, gentlemen.'' The transaction completed, Miss Two Leaf slipped the coin into a velvet bag, took back the documents and deposited it all in her briefcase. After a snap of the locks she shook their hands, then quickly headed for the door. She paused, her hand on the knob. "If you have any other rare coins, Mister O'Keefe—" Ramsey dragged his stunned gaze from the check to her—"I can verify those also, and if you decide to sell, well, you know where to contact me."

There was a message in that last bit, Anthony thought as he walked her to the front door. He returned to find Ramsey in the center of the room still, staring at the check. "Amazing, isn't it?"

"Aye." Ramsey looked up. "An hour ago I was a bleedin' pauper and now—" He waved the draft. Anthony smiled, pleased he'd eased Ramsey's fears, then moved to a credenza beyond the desk, unaware that Ramsey studied him as the Welshman splashed golden liquor into two short glasses.

Anthony faced him, the small crystals cupped in one hand, yet stilled when he saw the judging look on Ramsey's face.

"Why have you done this for me, Wainright? You owe me naught."

"Because, Ramsey—" Anthony offered a glass. "Whether you like it or not, we are friends."

The corners of Ramsey's eyes crinkled as he said, "The Fins have no words for 'you *will* trust me,' but say, rather 'you *are* trusting me.' Are you certain you are not Finnish?"

"God, I hope not. You have enough trouble remembering I'm Welsh."

Ramsey extended his hand and Anthony shook it firmly. "My thanks, Antony. Only this morn—" Ram dug in his pocket—"I was wondering what dishonorable profession I must undertake to square this." He waved the tailor's bill.

"Small change," Anthony said, then heaved a deep sigh. "Prepare yourself, though. Dealing with Lloyds of London isn't going to be this easy."

Ramsey bowed shortly. "I accept the challenge, Welshman," he said and in unison they tossed back the whiskey.

It ought to be a healthy one, Anthony thought. Lloyds of London was legendary. Its beginnings in insuring ships and cargo, Lloyds was now the world's most prestigious insurance brokers, called upon to verify the value and authenticity of documents, paintings, artifacts, even people and certain body parts, for insurance, estate claims, and museums. They prided on being the most reputable and forthright, for well over two hundred years. And Anthony couldn't imagine them being incorrect on this delivery for Penny. Damn me, she was going to be hurt by this, he just knew it. The best detectives in this country couldn't find out who Penelope Hamilton really was, and he didn't blame her for her skepticism over a one hundred and fifty-year-old inheritance she didn't deserve. But as to Ramsey and his involvement; so far he was only a name to them and as Anthony punched the intercom button, he could hardly wait to witness the verification Lloyds needed for their records.

Penny opened the door to the study without knocking, Sebastian Bailey trailing obediently. She stopped short when she saw Ramsey. Good God, the man's smile bordered on brilliant. His right shoulder was braced against the mantel, arms folded over his broad chest, his position giving his lean hips at a deep slant with his weight resting on one leg. The casually seductive picture strained her ability to walk smoothly toward him. But she did, just because he knew he was aware of his effect on her, damn him.

"Twenty-year-old scotch at nine in the morning, gentlemen?" she murmured, taking the empty glass and handing it to Tony, who looked as if he'd bust a gut any second. "I gather by that smile, your meeting was a success?"

"Oh, aye," Ram said, his gaze shifting briefly to Wainright. Anthony chuckled knowingly, gesturing to the high-back leather chair behind the desk for Bailey. The Lloyds agent immediately laid his briefcase and an enormous courier sealed package on the surface and began preparing his papers.

Penny glanced between Ramsey and Tony. Though the coin was obviously worth mega bucks, she wanted to kick either one for keeping the details secret. Male bonding, she supposed, sliding elegantly into one of the chairs positioned before the desk. She looked at Ram, nodding to the unoccupied seat beside her.

Ramsey slowly shook his head, his gaze skimming her in

one lush sweep. "I want to look at you," he said for her ears alone and she flushed. A rare occasion he knew, just as he was aware of the sappy smile smeared across his face. He couldn't help it. In the space of a quarter hour, his worries were wiped clean and he'd set his cap on a new, much more intriguing goal.

And the look in his eyes, the quick darkening to nearly black, struck Penny oddly, almost threateningly, like vulnerable prey before a practiced hunter. Something was different. The hopeless despair she'd witnessed in his eyes when she'd first spied him on the sundeck earlier was gone, and she could actually feel the ease of his burdens, as if he'd shed a heavy coat. The money, she realized. That she could sense this about him amazed her. And warned her. He's getting too close, she thought, and though the consequences would destroy them both, she never enjoyed a man's company like she did his. Men in her past had always had an ulterior motive, a script they wanted her to read, a bigger slice of the gross, a ride on their association. But not him, not Ramsey. He was honest, private and cared less about the world beyond the moment. To the best of her knowledge he still didn't know about that part of her life and she wanted to keep it that way. This worry over what he might think was unfamiliar and she wasn't certain she was prepared for all that dark stare implied. She needed time, yet already realized after the stolen kisses and teasing this morning, that, when Ramsey O'Keefe wanted, he was not a patient man.

And in her eyes Ram saw first wariness, confusion, then a touch of fear, yet a deeper instinct told him Penelope Hamilton had wounds far harsher than the scars marring his back. She was an actress, schooled in the art of assuming an artificial demeanor, and she used the talent when it suited her purposes, a shelter, yet the longer he knew her, the more of her true self he unearthed from beneath her pretty package. He wanted all of this, a complicated woman, and 'twould take a strong and patient man to weather the journey into her trust. Fate and time, he realized, had given him the challenge of his heart.

Oblivious to the exchange, Sebastian Bailey stared at O'Keefe, his heart pounding wildly, and he wasn't certain the

ancient muscle could take the excitement if this man was truly
the one his company had been looking for—since 1789.

Bailey dragged his gaze to the envelopes he held. Only two
other Lloyds agents knew about these particular deliveries and
only four before him. The handing over of the Blackwell assign-
ment was a reverent duty, like the passing of a torch or a family
sword to a new heir. Yet it was also a well-worn joke; one
would sooner see hell freeze than live long enough to bestow
the Blackwell legacy on Ramsey O'Keefe. The contents of both
claims had always been sealed and since 1955, Sebastian had
been the keeper. Until today. His hands shook as he set the
letters on the polished surface and cleared his throat.

"I will dispense with my business with Miss Hamilton first,
if you don't mind." Without waiting, he slid one envelope
across the desk. Penny reached for it slowly. Her hands trembled. She didn't take it.

Ramsey straightened, frowning atween the aged missive and
her. "Penelope?" Her cool composure slipped, as if she'd
crumbled into dust at the slightest touch.

Sebastian's heart went out to the woman, knowing she'd
recently lost a dear friend and couldn't possibly be prepared
for his intrusion. "Lloyds has been holding this since the 1830s,
Miss Hamilton, though I've yet to fathom the circumstances
behind it." The benefactors' instructions were specific; a single
letter to be opened on June 16 of this year, oddly three days
after the gymnast disappeared, its contents followed in detail.
Bailey had done just that, despite his surprise at finding a one
hundred fifty-eight-year-old piece of wax sealed paper to be
given to this particular woman. "Did your family know the
Blackwells?"

Ramsey felt his legs buckle beneath him and he grabbed the
back of her chair for support. His breath locked as he waited
for her to answer.

"No." Penny jerked her hand back. "They didn't."

"How odd," Bailey said, flipping open a broad leather bound
book. The dingy paper crackled with age as he turned to a
marked page, running his finger down the script. "Our records,
even back then, were very precise. Yes, T. Blackwell, cosigned

by D. Blackwell. The delivery was very specific." God, even the faded address was correct. He looked at her over the rim of his glasses. "Has your family lived in this house long?"

"I bought it, ten years ago." She didn't want to go through this, not again, not the questions and heartache. Lloyds was wrong. She was no one, really. Penelope Hamilton was someone she made up to wear. And locked herself inside.

Sebastian nodded, sliding the ledger toward her as he held out a pen. Her vision blurred as she lifted from the chair enough to pen her signature and accept the envelope, then dropped into the leather seat. She stared at the aged paper, trembling.

Her name was neatly scripted across the outside.

"Penny?" Anthony called softly, taking a step, his gaze bouncing between Penelope to Ramsey. What the hell was going on? Penny was on the verge of a scream, he was sure, and Ramsey, my God, the man was positively ashen.

"It's Tess's handwriting," came in a strangled murmur. She'd recognize it anywhere.

Please, no. *No!*

Her fingers tightened, and she wanted so desperately for this to be a joke, a horrible mix-up, the crushing reminder of what she'd done to Tess almost too much to bear. "This is impossible," she hissed, staring at the folded parchment. "She couldn't have sent this." Then open it, she reasoned sanely, and broke the Lloyds wax seal, peering inside. She frowned, lifting out a strip of black grosgrain ribbon. From the end, a single antique skeleton key twisted and turned in the lamp light.

She looked up, totally confused. "Mister Bailey?"

"A crate will be delivered to you this evening," he read from his instructions. "I imagine its contents has something to do with that." He nodded to the key. Sebastian Bailey had seen the crate only once when he assumed the *torch,* to be certain all was intact. More than he knew was wise, he wanted to see inside these acquisitions, but that was a specification of the bequeathal; no one but Penelope Hamilton and Ramsey O'Keefe were privy to their contents.

Suddenly Bailey's eyes shifted up and to the left of her, and Penny, following his gaze, twisted in her chair to look up at

Ramsey. Her heart collapsed at his stricken expression. He wasn't seeing her, his stare blank, his hand bloodless where he gripped the chair back. He looked as if the life were ripped from him.

"My God, Ramsey, what is it?"

No answer. Penny glanced to Tony, yet he responded with a shake of his head, warning her back, and she felt helpless. He's miles away from here, she thought, staring into his empty eyes and Ramsey felt trapped, his world blunted by unexpected pain.

They were dead. All of them; Dane, Tess, Duncan, Cameron, his mates. It scraped at a rawness inside Ramsey, a realization he'd pushed aside to immediate survival. But his time had found him, making him remember and want and mourn. All that was of the Continental Marine was naught but bones and decaying ash, his life, his past, erased. He felt abandoned. 'Twas childish he knew, for the choice to leap was his own, yet whilst he gloried that Dane and Tess had not forgotten him, he cursed them for renting the wounds of memory. By God, he needed to know what happened to them! Although Tess had a notion that he'd travel forward through the curtain of time, what could they have possibly endowed to him? Aught he left behind was of little consequence, yet they'd gone to such pains to see *something* delivered into his hands.

Ramsey heard the whisper of his name and blinked, turning his head and finding Penelope standing a few inches away, her lovely green eyes etched with confusion. 'Twas Tess she had been searching for in the Caribbean, Tess she mourned. Ahh, love, do not grieve, he wanted to tell her. Tess lived like no other. She lived only for love.

But Penelope wouldn't believe 'twas so, not until she realized *her* Tess was the Lloyds of London Blackwell.

By the blood of Triton, he wished he could tell her the whole of it, but she would never accept that he'd traveled two hundred years forward in time—not until she believed Tess had traveled backwards. As his gaze roamed her features, he was impatient for her to recognize the twist of fate that brought him to her.

Tess stole for her, he remembered suddenly. Ah, love, what

was so horrible that you allowed her to risk her life? Merciful Jesus, what guilt she must be suffering over Tess's disappearance, he sympathized, and searched his memory for Tess's exact words the day she confessed to being a midnight thief.

Sloane was about to give some damaging material on my friend Penny to the newspapers. Pen asked me to get it back. It was hers anyway. Hell, Sloane even told me where to find the packet. Incriminating material. Blackmail. And 'twas staged. Tess was meant to be caught in the act and killed. Ramsey didn't believe for a moment that Penelope had anything to do with the threat to Tess's life, but was she even aware that the evidence against her was packaged with a cache of rare colored diamonds?

"Why are you looking at me like that?"

He heard the fear in her tone and forced the tension from his features, smiling broadly. "I cannot help it, love. 'Tis the way God made me mug."

Her body relaxed and without thought he slid his arm about her waist. He pressed a tender-sweet kiss to her startled lips.

I have traveled to Tess's century, he realized with tremendous pleasure. And in his arms was the dearest person in her life, save Dane.

Chapter 18

Penny wasn't fooled by that blinding smile, and her frown said as much. "What happened to you just then?"

"I realized my good fortune, lass."

Off to the right Anthony snickered, yet the sadness she'd seen in Ramsey's eyes was unmistakable and she tried to recall their last moments of conversation and discover the source.

He didn't give her the chance and over the top of her head spoke to Bailey. "Blackwell?" Ram said, while urging her into her seat. "As in the *Coral Key* Blackwells?" Ram thought to play with the little knowledge he possessed to get out of this situation, for he could not easily explain away his shock.

Penny was still frowning at him when he settled into the seat aside her and casually enfolded her hand. The motion was presumptuous on his part, she thought, staring down at their clasped hands, thinking that it felt natural but looked startlingly foreign. She never allowed anyone to touch her as much as she had him, yet as she decided he was taking too much for granted, the warmth of his palm seeped into her skin.

Nothing should feel this comforting, she thought, threading her fingers with his. And cursing her vulnerability.

"The Blackwells started this town a couple hundred years

ago, right?'' Anthony said into her thoughts. ''I understood they were all deceased.''

Inwardly Ramsey flinched.

''Apparently not,'' Penny said. ''How else would all this,'' she gestured between the papers and the key she held, ''be delivered if the premium hadn't been maintained?'' She sank deeper into the chair, the black ribbon wrapped around her index finger. ''I don't know these people,'' she pointed out again. ''Why would they leave a crate for me?''

Bailey met her confused gaze, helpless himself, for he'd no clue as to how or why the Blackwells endowed a stranger not yet born when the claim was set. Regardless, he could neither reveal that the benefactor had seen to the provision of funds, at eighteenth century rates held in trust, in anticipation of the extinction of the Blackwell clan. Which was apparently the case now.

''I'm forbidden to speak on the matter. Explicit orders, you know.'' He dismissed any further questions as he addressed Ramsey. ''Your full name, sir?''

''Ramsey Malachai Gamaliel O'Keefe.''

Bailey's pale eyes flared and he glanced down at the antique ledger. ''And you were born where?''

''Lexington, Massachusetts.''

Sebastian Bailey stood, tugging at his vest. ''I must ask all but Mister O'Keefe to leave now.''

''Damn me,'' Anthony muttered, exiting the room like a freshly-punished child. ''Rats.''

Ramsey offered no protest, though Penelope stood immediately to leave. She looked a bit offended, he realized, coming to his feet afore her. Yet to allow her to witness aught Bailey possessed, which no doubt was a least two hundred years old, would only serve to confuse her. Ram knew he must conceal this *transaction* from her, til she at least, opened the crate from Tess.

''I have my orders. Please, Miss Hamilton.'' The last was business-like terse.

And still Penny hesitated, the envelope and key clenched in her fist as she stole a glance at the wax sealed envelopes on the desk. Old, like hers, yet she couldn't make any further comparison because they were turned face down.

She met Ramsey's gaze, searching. Who was this man? He had no identification, no records, and according to Tony's data search, Ramsey O'Keefe did not exist, never had. But he was here, eager to proceed with business and throwing a wrench in her life. She supposed she should forget her curiosity. But the way he talked, his gallant behavior, the way he arrived in her life, kept her mind turning back to who he *really* was.

I have laid in your arms and still you are a stranger to me.

If he could not prove who he was, then how can Lloyds of London fulfill its obviously strict obligations? And was his endowment from a mysterious Blackwell, too, she wondered, finally turning away, though no one had so much as implied it. As she grasped the door knob, the brittle vellum slipped from her fingers and she bent to retrieve it, her gaze locking on the handwriting again, precise, even. Tess's. A chill climbed her spine, even as she denied the crazy notion, and she looked inside the seldom used study, her gaze meeting Ramsey's dark sable eyes across the room.

Will Tess ever be dead to me as long as you are near?

Ramsey held her gaze as she gently closed the door, yet he continued to stare at the sealed wood as Bailey came around the desk and grasped his hand, shaking it firmly.

"I cannot tell you how pleased I am to finally meet you," he gushed, then managed to contain his excitement. "Please." He indicated the chair, then moved behind the desk, dropping into his own.

Ramsey was still trying to fathom the look in Penelope's eyes as he took his seat, resting his ankle across his knee. "What have you for me, man?"

Bailey broke open the first sealed envelope and slipped the document free. He read, the quiet making Ramsey fidget.

"Remove your shirt, please," he said without looking up.

"Surely you cannot be serious?"

Sebastian peered over the rim of his glasses. "Forgive me, sir, but I've orders to match a description."

Angrily, Ramsey flipped the buttons of his shirt, then stood and stripped it from his torso.

Bailey was amazed at the sheer size of the man while he silently marked off the man's hair and eye color, two thin slashing scars on his arm, plus a neat smooth circle on his shoulder, as his detailed list indicated. "Turn around, please."

Ram ground his teeth. 'Twas bleedin' humiliating and he knew what the man was searching for, yet remained motionless, damning Dane to the pits of hell, for his mates were the only people, save Penelope, who knew of these old wounds.

Up until this moment Sebastian never expected anything so horrifying would mark the man. His gaze moved over the pale crisscross slashes at the base of his spine to Ramsey's upper right shoulder. Sebastian rose up slightly, squinting to see the jagged star-shaped flesh.

"Thank you, Mister O'Keefe, you may dress."

Ram did, quickly, his eyes narrow as he stuffed the shirt tail in his trousers, then dropped into the chair.

Sebastian noticed the banked anger and felt obliged to say, "I apologize for all the cloak and dagger, but the benefactors insisted. Since this," he cracked the wax stamp, "is the second of three, I'm obligated to inform you that if you answer incorrectly to any of the questions, I will stop and say no more."

Ramsey nodded, anticipation making his palms sweat. He didn't doubt for a moment that Tess had enjoyed preparing this. Had. Swift pain scored through his chest again and he stared numbly at the desk littered with papers. This is all he would have of his friends, his past, save the coins and the possession he'd taken through the barrier of time.

Oblivious, Bailey unfolded the parchment. He couldn't possibly know these, he thought, then read again. "What was the name of the American ship anchored in the Caribbean harbor on the night of June 30, 1789?"

"The *Barstow,*" Ram said almost absently. "A captured American sloop."

Sebastian inhaled sharply, his gaze flashing up.

"Who sat to the right of Captain Blackwell at dinner the previous evening?" His tone dared him to fail.

Ram's eyes narrowed in concentration, imagining the set table aboard the *Sea Witch*. "First mate to the *Triton's Will*, David Cameron." He would be captain now—then—ahh, bloody hell! Ram shifted in his seat and Bailey studied him for a moment before proceeding.

"Who captained the warship *Chatam?*"

Ram's lips twisted in a cruel smile. "Bennet." The one word held a wealth of revulsion.

Sebastian dropped the paper and sat back, withdrawing a handkerchief and blotting his upper lip. He still couldn't believe it.

"Is there a problem, man?"

"No, no." He tugged at his neck tie. "But I confess, Mister O'Keefe, I never imagined to open these letters, at least not in my lifetime." Was he a relative? The Blackwells arranged this elaborate delivery, yet if it had been some eccentric notion to make certain a relative kept family possessions, that didn't explain how O'Keefe knew those answers. Unless the letters were copied and he knew them for an heirloom he might possess. How could anyone, two hundred years ago, know he would be here to accept it? And the physical description was far too accurate to be explainable. Sebastian knew, without a doubt, that the contents of those letters had never been opened. In fact, they hadn't been out of their original strong box until the British consulate phoned him yesterday. More confused than he'd been in years, Bailey reached for the third envelope and broke the seal.

"Where did you meet—" Sebastian's gaze shifted rapidly between the letter and the man, then back.

"Continue, Mister Bailey," Ram said softly, encouragingly. "We have come too far to hesitate now."

"Where did you meet Captain Dane Blackwell?"

Ram's lips twitched with the memory. "I believe 'twas during an altercation in a tavern."

"It says here a barroom brawl."

Ram quirked a brow, waiting for the man to adjust his thinking.

"Oh, yes, I see." Which Blackwell was this, Sebastian wanted to ask, but instead did his job and read on.

"What gift did Captain and Mistress Blackwell receive on the evening after their wedding?"

Ram's lips curved with memory. "A painting, a portrait of Mistress Blackwell walking on the beach."

Bailey tossed the parchment aside, sagging into the chair. Word for word, as if he'd written it himself. Incredible. Sebastian stood and after flipping the pages to the beginning of the worn ledger, he indicated with a shaking finger where Ramsey was to sign. Ram accepted the writing instrument, pausing to examine the gold cylinder, twisting the middle as English had done, amazed at the instrument's smooth stroke, devoid of odor and splatter as he penned his name. Sebastian compared it to a scrap of paper enclosed in his instructions, and Ramsey recognized 'twas a part of his ship's log, afore the Englishman stowed it in his ledger. Bailey unlocked the courier's case and withdrew a broad leather box, setting it on the desk. A moment later he added a misshapen parcel wrapped in oiled animal skin and secured with rigging twine.

Ram's heart thudded frantically as he slowly unfolded from the chair. The box and hide were achingly familiar, as if he'd laid his hands upon the like only days afore. He approached the desk, smoothing his fingertips over the worn leather, then the thin gold plate engraved with the initials R.M.G.O. These were his. *His.*

The Lloyds agent was already collecting up his papers. "If I may ask, Mister O'Keefe—" Bailey shuffled and stuffed, then snapped the case closed and looked up—"Who are you exactly?"

Ram's brows furrowed. "I understood this inquisition was to establish just that."

"It only verified that you are who you say you are, but not how you knew those answers. No one could have possibly known them." No one living, Sebastian added silently, feeling goose flesh rise on his neck.

Ramsey inhaled deeply, looking the man in the eye. He could offer naught but the truth, and in a deadpan voice said, "I am captain of *Triton's Will,* an American privateer frigate owned by Dane Blackwell and under the command of President George Washington.''

Bailey's eyes rounded as Ramsey spoke. ''Wha—what are you saying?''

''I am a Continental Marine, sir, who has traveled from here—'' he tapped the leather chest—''to here.'' He gestured to the room, the motion encompassing this house, this century.

Bailey stared at him a moment longer, his critical gaze narrowing a fraction. ''I may retire in peace,'' he muttered dryly, then strode to the door, believing the man would not offer a reasonable explanation. If there was one.

Her hand raised to knock, Penny froze, wishing she'd heard the entire conversation. *A Continental Marine.* What bunk! Yet even as she decided Ramsey was teasing the agent, she experienced a niggling doubt. He sounded so confident. But Marines were shaved heads with attitudes, like Tess's dad and Hank. And where was this unmentionable place he'd traveled from, she wondered, lowering her arm and moving back down the hall as the doorknob rattled.

Leaving the box and bundle untouched, Ram escorted the Lloyds agent to the front door, only too aware that Penelope was nowhere in sight.

''Give my regards to Miss Hamilton,'' Bailey said. ''And please, apologize on my behalf for intruding on her grief.''

Ram nodded sagely, wishing he could give her the peace she needed.

''Good day to you, Captain O'Keefe.''

''My thanks, Mister Bailey.'' Ram bowed and the Lloyds agent smiled, imagining him in frock coat and knee britches. After what he just went through, he was ready to believe anything.

Ramsey closed the door after him and released a heavy sigh,

mashing a hand over his face. When he turned away he found Antony watching him, a half-eaten sandwich in his hand.

"You're not going to answer a single question, are you?"

"Nay, my friend. I fear I cannot."

The two men stared for a moment, then Anthony smiled, "Well then, let's go deposit that check, I'm bored." Anthony finished off the last of his sandwich, dusting his fingertips. "I'll bring my car around."

Ramsey strode back to the study, halting in the doorway when he saw Penelope curled in the chair behind the desk, staring at his possessions.

He frowned. " 'Twas rude, Penelope, not to see the man out."

She didn't look up. "Don't scold me, Ramsey. I'm not a child." Her tone was clipped, and as he moved closer he noticed her stare lay somewhere beyond the box and bundle, her fingers manipulating the key over and over. The movement was frantic, tensing. Guilt tore at him that he couldn't help her find answers yet.

"Mister Bailey offered his condolences at your loss." She winced, gripping the key. "Your grief . . . 'twill ease in time, love."

Her gaze snapped up. "What do *you* know of what I feel? My best friend, my *only* friend is gone, dead, drowned, eaten by sharks. God, I'll never know." She inhaled a deep breath. "But I've accepted it, damnit. Now why won't anyone let me bury her!"

"Nary a soul says you cannot."

"Oh yes there is," she said defiantly. "You, the damn Blackwells and their mysterious crate." She came to her feet. "Well, it can stay locked up another hundred years for all I care." She flipped the key onto the surface, then rounded the desk, heading toward the door. "I hate them for this."

Ram lurched and grabbed her hand, but she didn't spare him a glance, twisting out of his grip and leaving the study.

He didn't follow, giving her the solitude she demanded without words.

* * *

"A woman does not jump off a crowded cruise liner without witnesses," Penny said into the phone. "The police will question every staff member and guest, Captain. The cruise line is held responsible and do not doubt that I will discover why you allowed a passenger to jump off your ship, then left her in shark infested waters to die." A pause, and though her body shook with suppressed anger, her voice was measured, icy. "Really? How convenient. Make the ensign available to the police, Bahamas and U.S." She hung up without further comment, then folded her arms across her middle, staring at the floor. Control, she told herself, don't lose it now.

When she finally regained control and looked up, she saw Ramsey, walking away.

Anthony maneuvered his Mercedes down a quiet road lined with palmetto and oranges trees, their branches hovering over the pavement, offering shade to the blaring sun. Beside him Ramsey was content to watch the scenery pass before him, though he knew he was furious, his pride bruised. They'd spent the past two hours at Anthony's bank, trying to cash Ramsey's check. It was impossible and Anthony should have seen this coming. For without identification, Ramsey couldn't prove who he was and open an account. The matter was at the bank's discretion and before they suggested he call Penelope and humiliate Ramsey further, Anthony cosigned on a signature account, which meant Ramsey couldn't get to his own money without his presence and signature.

Personally, Anthony thought he would have blown his stack long ago, though when Ramsey finally handed over the cashier's check, the look on their faces as they realized how much revenue his accounts would bring to the bank was damned comical. They were apologizing all over themselves and Ramsey's glacial dismissal of the bank president was a study in final retribution.

Penelope couldn't have done better.

Damn but the man was a mystery, complete and absolute,

his manner, that he addressed him as Antony instead of Anthony, and he'd yet to understand exactly where Ramsey had been all these years and why he kept it a secret. He wanted to ask about what Lloyds had to say, and give him, but even after enjoying a beer at his favorite pub, Ramsey had not offered an explanation. Though he had his suspicions.

Anthony almost laughed aloud when he recalled the pub, and the women nearly fighting to fill the empty seats at their table. That seemed to shock Ramsey, though he was polite, buying a round, charming them all with his strange speech and chivalrous manners. But he accepted no offers, though Anthony knew he must have a pocketful of match books inscribed with names and numbers. His impatience to see Penelope was clear, and he wondered if the girl knew just how faithful this man was being to her, when he'd no reason. And what would the papers say when sources learned that Ramsey was living with Penelope, although Ramsey never mentioned it. He hated to think of the mess they'd make of what little pleasure the woman had had in years.

Suddenly Ram leaned forward, staring ahead with obvious intent. "Rein in, Antony, if you please."

"Rein what? Oh, stop. Certainly." Tony braked slowly and they came to a stop before a spiked iron gate.

"Bloody friggin' hell!" Ram muttered, his gaze on the name-plate suspended on the gate. His eyes shifted to the stately home beyond the stone confines, then back to the plate. He sank into the plush seat and mashed his hand over his face.

"Is there a problem?" Anthony said. Ramsey looked as if he might be ill.

"Is this not the Blackwell home?"

Anthony squinted, leaning forward to see. "I believe it was, yes," he said, throwing the gear into park. "There was some scandal about twenty-odd years back, you know. Over the sale as I recall. The Blackwells claimed they were bilked out of their ancestral home, though nothing was ever proven."

Ramsey lifted his head, his heart aching as he stared at the house, memories flooding him. 'Twas Dane's home. Ram had been inside, in nearly every room. From his position he could see the bed chamber where he'd slept on his visits. This house had been a refuge for him, a safe harbor when he felt alone. Until Phillip Rothmere had touched its occupants. Now, it appeared, his cruel fingers could stretch across two hundred years, for the proud name of Blackwell had been replaced with the elaborate scroll of Rothmere.

Chapter 19

God, she hated losing control.

Swiping at her eyes, she sniffled, then slanted a quick look around the edge of the unused boathouse, hoping no one saw her like this. Staring at her bare toes, she kicked at the water, the waves splashing lightly against the pier. Who did the Blackwells think they were, playing this game and disrupting her life with their secrets? Who did they get to write just like Tess; even the little check marks dotting the i's were the same. If the writing hadn't been so close to Tess's she would have accepted the key without a fuss, opened the crate and returned the contents to the family. But there weren't any Blackwells left. A shame, she thought as she sanded the key between her palms, a chill running swiftly over her arms.

And where did Ramsey go in such a hurry? *Avoiding you* she thought ruefully, not blaming him for leaving so abruptly after the way she'd treated him. None of her torment was his fault. Well, some of it was. And the sight of the leather box, bearing his initials, made her increasingly uneasy. The temptation to look challenged her, yet she left the study, retrieving the key and respecting his privacy. But that didn't stop her mind from wondering who'd left him those things and whether or not his gifts were as old as hers. Had an ancestor endowed the package? For they couldn't possibly be his. But his words spoken to Bailey kept ringing in her head, sure and proud. A Continental Marine. Was he insane? Questions that desperately needed answers tormented her, but she was afraid to find the truth, afraid Ramsey might be something he wasn't. Aside from overbearing, arrogant and a bit pompous, she thought with a smile.

"Penny?"

Startled, she twisted around, shoving the key into her skirt pocket.

"You ought not be out in the sun so long?" Margaret shielded her eyes as she peered closer, inspecting Penelope's skin for a burn. "You put on any sunscreen?"

The actress smiled. "Careful, Margaret, your mother hen feathers are ruffling." Penny climbed to her feet, her heeled sandals dangling from her fingertips.

"Well, somebody has to look after you. You don't eat right unless I make you. You stay alone far too often for a woman your age, and God knows you're a lousy housekeeper."

Penny grasped Margaret's arm and brushed a quick kiss to her cheek. "And I love you dearly for it," she whispered.

Margaret's eyes widened, then misted with tears. She'd known it all these years, of course, but the girl had never come out and said so before now. Oh, she'd shown it often enough, by paying her a ridiculous fortune in wages, giving her time off whenever she wanted and furnishing her with a trip anywhere in the world each Christmas and birthday. But to hear it was enough to make the old woman weep with joy.

Penny smiled gently. "Hey, none of this, Meggie me rose." She dabbed at the lone tear with the hem of Margaret's apron, then looped her arm through the housekeeper's, guiding her off the narrow pier. "Did you come out just to check on the condition of my skin or did you just miss me?"

"Customs is here. Front hall."

She'd heard the bell, but hoped it was Ramsey.

"Great. Just what I need, more strange people in my house."

"It has been a day, hasn't it?"

Penny glanced to her side as she opened the pool screen door. "You want details, huh?"

"No, not really." Her tone wasn't the least bit convincing.

"To be honest, I don't have any. Just this." She showed her the key.

"Ain't that a kick. What's it open?"

Penny shrugged, stepping into the coolness of the house. "Haven't the foggiest, but a crate will be delivered this afternoon, so be on the look out, will you?"

"Sure. Who from?"

"The Blackwells think they owe me something."

Margaret's features slackened. "*The* Blackwells?"

"I know, bizarre," she said, pausing to dust the sand off her feet and slip on her shoes. She and Margaret headed to the front hall and found two dark haired men, dressed in somber suits and still wearing their mirrored sunglasses. Secret Service wanna be's, she thought, her lips twitching.

"Identification?" she said coolly, and they flashed her the familiar I.D.s. She compared picture to face, then said, "This way, gentlemen," and headed for the stairs.

They'd come for her luggage, or rather, the inspection for contraband, and the convenience was a perk of her celebrity status she didn't mind. Airport managers didn't care for the security threat and chaos her presence caused and she wanted privacy, at all costs. Customs placed a thick plastic seal on her luggage locks in the Bahamas, heat crimped so it couldn't easily be removed. Then customs in the U.S. cut it off, did their inspection and she didn't have to wait around in the airport and suffer the humiliation of having her dirty lingerie displayed to every camera, fan or official who wanted a peek. She met the landing, rounding the rail to the right and stopping before the second bedroom after Ramsey's. She flung open the door and gestured to the designer luggage stacked on the brass bed.

"Inspect away. I'll be back to sign the papers in a minute," she said, then backtracked down the balcony hall and across to her rooms. She didn't like watching the inspection. It was kind of like not looking your gynecologist in the face during an exam. You just wanted it overwith as quickly as possible, no reminders.

She took the time to rinse the sea salt from her skin and brush her hair, barretting it high off her neck, then made an effort to pick up her bedroom. But it was definitely a three-man job. Well, at least I can take the dirty dishes downstairs, she thought, and left, balancing a stack. A ripping sound caught her attention and she paused at the landing. What in the world, she thought, heading quickly for the guest room.

Penny froze in the doorway as customs agents wielded silver switchblades, destroying her luggage with a vengeance. She dropped the dishes. "What the hell do you think—!"

One man grabbed her arm, dragging her into the room and slamming her against the wall. He pressed his blade tip to her throat.

"Where are they?" he demanded.

"Where's what?" Penny didn't dare swallow.

He nudged the blade, a sharp sting answering the motion. Her blood colored the silver point.

"Give them to me or I'll cut you so bad no one will want you!"

"I'm afraid I don't know what you're talking about." Her tone was even, unaffected and she could see it angered him.

Behind them, the other man tossed a tattered case on the floor. "Nothin'," he sneered.

Her assailant's body mashed her against the papered wall, his face close, his breath smelling of peaches as he gave the knife a short quick dig.

Penny inhaled sharply. "I *don't* have what you want," she bit out precisely. "I swear!" A wet warmth trickled down her throat to her chest.

In the next heartbeat she heard rapid footsteps, her gaze shifting toward the door, yet before she could make him a soprano, he abruptly backed up and backhanded her across the face, the blow sending her to the floor.

At the sound of weight hitting the upper deck, Ramsey bolted, overtaking the staircase in time to see a dark figure pass through the old servant's door. His gaze swept the area.

"Penelope!" Harsh, tormented.

"In here," she called. He leapt the railed balcony and found her on the carpeted floor, struggling to sit up. His eyes lit on the stream of blood dripping down her chest and staining her dress.

"Sweet Jesus!" He slid to his knees, gripping her shoulders, inspecting her wounds.

"I'm fine, really," she managed, swiping at the blood on her lip, then smoothing her fingertips beneath her chin.

"I'll kill them!"

Penny looked up sharply, stunned by the fury glinting in his dark eyes.

"I swear, with me bleedin' hands, *I'll kill them!*"

He started to rise.

"Ramsey, no! No!" Penny grabbed his shirt sleeve, her bloody fingers slipping across the fabric as he took off toward the hidden staircase. "Ramsey!" she screamed, but he was gone. Tony was there, helping her to her feet. "Call the police. They were armed." Then she headed to the old staircase, hoping Ramsey realized it.

Ramsey met the last step, wove his way through the butler's pantry, then burst out the back door and saw two men running across the short stretch of beach. He gave chase, kicking up sand as his powerful legs overtook the separation. He heard a roaring sound, the bubbling churn of water as his feet met the pier and the first man jumped into a small boat. With a growl of rage, Ramsey dove for the second bastard's legs, knocking him to the wood deck. Ram dragged him back by the waist band, hoisting him to his feet as he sent his square fist into a too pretty face. The man's nose shifted under the meaty blow. The intruder retaliated, ramming his knee into Ramsey's stomach. He folded over, yet afore the other could do damage to his mug, Ram rolled away and leapt to his feet, fists singing. Jab, right cross, upper jab to the chin. Ramsey sought to deliver him to Satan, the swift combination offering no mercy and her attacker stumbled back on rubbery legs. Ram grasped the man's shirt front and drew his arm back.

A sharp crack made him freeze.

Gunfire was a sound Ramsey never forgot. He threw his hands up, and the beaten man staggered, knees buckling, then straightened, swiping at his bleeding nose afore scrambling over the edge of the pier and into the boat; a third man stood at the stern and fired two more shots into the pier at Ram's feet to keep him where he stood.

Ramsey remained motionless, grinding his teeth to powder as the small boat banked on a curve of white foam and peeled away from the shore, his gaze on the weapons still trained on his heart.

Penny ran across the sand, stopping short when he slashed the air for her to stay back. He looked as if he'd explode, she thought, his fists clenching repeatedly, vibrating up to his shoulders and bunching his fury. She hesitated, inching closer. Ramsey looked at her, extending his arm, and she flew to him, clinging as he drew her tightly against his side and pressed his lips to the top of her head. His quick breath warmed her hair and she tightened her grip around his waist, the sound of the gunshots ringing through her mind again and again.

Penny didn't think she'd ever been that scared before.

"Who do you know that would do such a thing?"

Penny tilted her head back. He was staring at the sea, a dark challenge in his eyes. "What makes you think someone *I know* did this?"

" 'Twas well planned, Penelope, and those men," he nodded to the returning wake, "knew the lay of your house." He met her gaze. "Intimately."

Chapter 20

On the staircase, Ram hovered behind a whey-faced lad as he powdered the wood rail.

"Any idea of what they were looking for?" Det. Dave Downing called up the curving flight from his position at the foot.

"Aside from coin or jewelry?" Only Ram's eyes shifted, pinning the detective. "Nay."

But he suspected, for the attackers were specific in their intent, following her pattern and taking pains to disguise themselves for a first look at the suitcases sealed in the islands, assuming she brought their prize with her.

'Twas the diamonds the bastard's sought. He was certain of it. For they'd come from this century. Tess claimed 'twas so, afore a stunned group of Marines, Dane amongst them, confessing how she'd come by the cache of rare colored diamonds whilst stealing back blackmail for Penelope. In this century.

Whose game was Penelope caught atween now? He could not honestly point the finger at a Rothmere, for the vengeance of Phillip died a fiery death in 1789. Who then, was tempting discovery by seeking out Penelope? How far were these people willing to go, and what retribution would befall her, for the stones were lost atween the barriers of time and space. But only he knew that. And he was determined to get to the root of it, yet he did not trust the constabulary to apprehend the culprits. For without the knowledge of the diamonds existence, they'd no connection to investigate. And he could not offer the information.

Ramsey felt trapped.

"Excuse me, Captain O'Keefe."

Ram shifted position, allowing a young uniformed officer better access to the banister, observing over the lad's shoulder as he *dusted for fingerprints,* an amazing process he was assured would be indisputable, for no two were alike. The procedure posed no threat to Ramsey, for one's prints had to have been recorded first, he was told, and since Ram did not exist, by the records of this time, he dismissed the concern.

The officer held the clear strip up to the light, pointing to the print. "That could be our man."

Ram squinted. " 'Tis doubtful, lad." The officer glanced to the side, frowning questioningly. " 'Tis mine." Ram held up his hand, wiggling his index finger to show the scarcely healed cut dividing the tip.

The lad compared the two and sighed, disappointed, yet continued methodically in his work.

"And I believe they were gloved."

"Damn it!" Downing gave the bannister an angry shove. "Why didn't you say that before?"

Ramsey descended the remaining steps, stopping afore the dark haired detective. "You did not ask." Nor, at the time, did he consider it mattered.

Downing's gaze narrowed suspiciously as customs officials passed with the tattered suitcases. "What type of gun did they use?" He followed O'Keefe across the foyer.

" 'Twas unfamiliar," Ram said truthfully.

"Anything like this one?" Downing opened his coat, withdrawing his gun and Ram paused, turned, fascinated as the detective emptied the bullets afore handing the weapon over for inspection.

Fine workmanship, Ram thought, smoothing his fingers

across the barrel, then testing the weapon's balance. "Nay, 'twas no wider than a book, as one piece, naught like this." He gestured to the fat chamber and molded stock, then handed it back and kept going.

Downing reholstered his gun, then scribbled a few notes before asking, "Can you describe them again?"

Ramsey stopped in the center of the front hall, rolling his head on his neck.

"I have done this, man, twice afore." Tired, annoyed.

"Maybe something else will jog your memory."

He glanced over his shoulder. "Me memory is fine."

"How do you get around without identification?"

"At present, I've no place to *get round* to." 'Twas a fair day when a man's word was his bond, he thought, and considered offering the police officer a bribe just to shut him up, but he recognized 'twould not be as well received in this century as 'twas in his. Yet he was certain they were suspicious, of him and his presence in Penelope's home. His evasiveness would take him only so far.

"Did O'Keefe hit you?"

Ramsey spun on his heels, his gaze sharpening on the slim blond detective.

"Of course not," Penny said, lowering the ice pack from her jaw, her thinning gaze giving her the look of a tigress on the hunt. "What are you getting at?" This was the third time the Don Johnson reject had insinuated something with his questions.

"I think you came back from the islands and O'Keefe was jealous, ripped up your suit cases and then knocked you around when he didn't find anything to confirm his suspicions."

"And four eye-witnesses and two slugs in my pier brought you to this conclusion?" Penny wasn't about to tell Detective Pete Mathers she'd met Ramsey only four days ago and he'd been with her ever since.

"And be assured," Ramsey added, strolling into the large parlor. "If I were so dishonorable as to beat a woman," he looked Mathers in the eye as he passed—"she would be dead."

Penny glanced down at his broad fists, remembering how

gentle those hands were on her body and knew he could never do what the detective implied.

"You have a solid alibi, Ramsey, and don't have to explain anything," Anthony cut in softly, then shifted his gaze to Mathers. "Unless you're going to continue harassing a witness?"

"Lawyers," Mathers muttered, then focused on Penny as if he'd never slandered Ramsey. "O'Keefe says the old door was stuck *last night.*" His tone rode on the snide and Penny decided it was best to ignore it. "I need the names of anyone who knew it existed." His pen was primed to write on a little note pad and Penny could see that list plastered on the front page of the *Interrogator* already.

"I don't see how that will help, since this—"

"Let me decide that, all right?" Mathers snapped rudely.

Suddenly Ramsey forced himself atween Penelope and the detective, towering over the blond man, his dark eyes flashing with outrage. "You will curtail your insolence toward Mistress Hamilton, afore I teach you a few lessons in proper manners," came in a low snarl. The man had no decency, Ram decided, or the puny turd would not presents himself in public, afore a lady, with an unshaven face.

"You threatening me, Mister O'Keefe?" he said suspiciously and his partner glanced up from questioning Margaret, his gaze sharpening on Mathers.

Ram's lips twisted into a cruel smile, his tone forming icicles. "I do not threaten, *whelp.*" Ram tolerated no insubordinance aboard his ship, nor would he in his lady's house.

"Excuse me," Penny stressed, edging around his big body when he refused to budge. She glanced up at Ramsey. "Do you always have to flex and growl," she murmured under her breath, then faced the detective. "The good cop, bad cop, isn't working, Mathers. Give it up and quit wasting my time." She snatched the pad and pen from his hand, scribbling a list of a half dozen names.

Ram noticed Tess was not on it.

She crossed a *t* and handed back the pad and pen. "And if you'd done a little *detecting,* you'd know the plans of this house are public record. It's a historical landmark. Anyone could have known of the old servant's staircase." Penny enjoyed his embarrassed flush. "And I'd better not find that publicized," she warned, nodding to the list.

Ramsey glanced to the side, his brows drawn close in a frown. "What say you, lass? Surely those names would be of no interest?"

"The public is interested in what she eats in as much as—" Mathers met Ramsey's gaze—"who she sleeps with."

Ram exploded and slapped a hand to the man's chest, grabbing a fistful of the shirt and hauling him up to meet his face, his low snarl enough to make Penny cringe.

"Let him go, Ramsey." She was saying that an awful lot to this man. He looked indecisively at her, then released him, abruptly, and the officer staggered back.

"Try that again—" Mathers adjusted his shirt. "And you'll be up on charges, pal."

Ram leaned down, filling his vision. "I suggest you debark afore I make you a grin in a glass, *mate.*"

"And I think we've answered enough questions." Her tone brooked no argument as she folded her arms over her middle and leveled a quick keep-out-of-it glance at Ramsey.

"Quite enough," Anthony added, holding out his business card between two fingers. Mathers took it, shoving it into his coat pocket without so much as a glance as hand radio static drew his attention.

"We're through here," Downing said from the doorway as police officers emerged from all areas of the house, lugging cases, footprint casts and spent bullets.

Ramsey followed on their heels, opening the door only to find two men on the stoop, a large crate atween them. He muttered a curse, glancing at Penny.

She was still as a statue.

"What's this?" Mathers grabbed the clipboard from one man, who promptly took it back.

"'Tis none of your concern, man, now begone." Ram clapped a hand to the detective's shoulder, the motion appearing almost affectionate even as he propelled him out the doorway. His partner murmured apologetically to Penelope, then followed suit. Ramsey threw open the second French door, gesturing for the men to bring the crate inside.

"Upstairs, please," Penelope said more to her feet, gesturing distractedly toward the staircase.

"I'm sorry, ma'am, but we have orders to uncrate it before witnesses. You must break the first seals."

Penelope smoothed the spot between her brows and nodded. With his body, Ramsey barred the constable a view of the crate and shut the doors with more force than necessary.

Penny stared at the crate wrapped in heavy sailcloth, stitched and oiled. A specially made casing of the period likely to insure against decomposition over the years, she thought, then glanced around the foyer at the expectant faces, Tony's especially. She took a slow breath and came forward, snapping the two large wax seals. The men in starched gray jumpsuits immediately cut away the oiled sail cloth, then put crowbars to the crate, separating the wood with a splintering crack, breaking the black wax seals on the seams, each emblazoned with a scrolled *L.L.* Penny stood perfectly still, yet the hairs on the back of her neck swirled, the skin tightening as the last of the slats were removed.

"My God." She sagged against the papered wall, staring at the antique trunk.

Her name was clearly etched across a broad gold plate on the front above a simple padlock. The sight of it made her ill.

"Magnificent," Tony murmured, moving closer, his fingers rasping beneath his bearded chin as he studied the piece with a curator's eye.

Ramsey bent and examined the sea chest, its familiar structure, the leather hinges tight and smooth, its brass latches still bright with newness, untainted by moisture. His gaze shifted to Penelope. She was signing the receipt, nodding to whate'er Antony was saying, yet even from his position Ram could see her hand tremble.

"Second room on the left," she instructed the delivery men in a fading whisper as Anthony offered identification and wrote his name beneath hers.

"Nay, lass." Ram waved the men back, standing the chest on

its side, the contents shifting audibly. " 'Twill be me pleasure.'' With his back to it, he squatted, dipping his hand over his shoulder to grasp the leather handle.

"Ramsey, it's their job,'' she said before he injured himself. He ignored her, positioning his free hand beneath the crafted oak chest and with a grunt, hefted it on his back. Penny's brows shot up as he straightened.

He looked at her. "I'll not have another stranger above stairs,'' he said, then crossed the foyer to the staircase with a swiftness no one could match.

"You'll not—?'' She smiled tightly at the delivery men, murmured, "Excuse me,'' then followed the chauvinistic over-bearing man in tight jeans up the stairs.

"You'll not allow anyone above stairs?''

"Aye." He turned into her rooms.

"Have you forgotten this is *my* house?''

" 'Twould be difficult not to, lass.'' Ram deposited the seachest on her bedchamber floor and faced her.

"Then quit acting like it. And while we're on the subject, I certainly don't need you to butt your muscles in every time you think I'm might be offended.'' He quirked a brow, working a kink out of his tricep. "I've been handling guys like Mathers for years. I don't need your protection.''

"Certainly m'lady,'' he mocked, "for you've proven 'tis so—'' he fingered her bruised jaw—"dealing with your attack-ers with such superior efforts.''

She shoved his hand away. "I was taken off guard.''

"Mayhaps.'' Her blood stained dress reminded him how incapable he felt to protect her in this century. "But what of next time?''

"There won't be one.''

Ram scoffed. "They did not find whate'er they sought, woman.'' He loomed over her, arms akimbo, his eyes unyield-ing. "Do not believe my presence in *your* home will deter another attempt.''

"Well, the police are on it now, so you needn't feel—''

"By Triton's will, you are a stubborn wench!''

"Wench!" She stepped closer, nose to nose. "Listen,

Neandrathal man, don't you dare assume that you can just take—''

"I dare all I please," he cut in savagely. "For you are too blind to see these bastards knew more than the lay of your house, they knew your habits!" If a time-traveler could be lost in this century, one of their own could vanish forever. "And that imbecile will never find them!''

"That doesn't change the fact that I don't need *you* to be my watch dog!''

Ramsey wanted to shake her. She was too bloody independent for her own good, and she'd walk into a nest of trouble again if he wasn't careful.

"You are innocent to this, Penelope." His voice was edged, warning of the coming explosion. "And by the Gods, I will protect what *is mine!*''

"I'm not yours!" burst from her lips. "I'm not!''

Ram smothered the sting of her denial and said, "You were every bit as such last night.''

She inhaled, eyes bright, posture stiff. "Of all the pompous, egotistical, self-indulgent—!''

His arm shot around her waist, jerking her against his body, his lips descending upon hers with a crushing force, molding, shaping hers, his tongue prying open her teeth afore plunging inside. She shoved at his chest, twisting, and his mouth followed hers, his muscled leg insinuating atween her thighs. His hand dove down her spine, pressing her tighter to his length and in that fraction of time, she gave up.

And she sank into him, gripping his shoulders, raking her fingers through his hair. She answered him, reveled in him, for his touch bore the same soul-stripping fire as the evening before, taking her beyond sex and pleasure and into a plane of greedy passion and an unrelenting hunger she knew she'd never satisfy without him.

And she hated it. For her want had nothing to do with the strength surrounding her now, or his masculine instinct to protect her like some guardian angel, but from her weakness, her inability to resist only *this man,* and keep him from the ugliness that would eventually rear and destroy this spark of life they shared. It would happen. She could feel it. Like an ache in her bones. And just as she sensed the old trunk lying near, she sensed a rushing tide she couldn't stop. It made her want to run. And selfishly she wanted Ramsey with her.

His kiss suddenly gentled, soothed, and slowly, with the tenderness of homage, he drew back.

"Why did you do that?" Breathless, blinking.

He quirked a smile. "You had that look about you."

A tapered brow arched smoothly, at touch chilly. "And that was?"

"Kiss me, Ramsey," he said dramatically. "Afore I say aught I'll regret."

Her lips twitched. "Oh, really?"

"Ah, there 'tis again," he said, then kissed her, a wild slide of lips and tongues, possessive, sassy and far too enticing to let it continue. Or he'd take her to his bed, if just to prove 'twas where she was true to her heart—and him.

"Have you the key?" he murmured against her lips, adoring her dreamy expression.

"Huh?" Slowly she opened her eyes.

"The key." He glanced meaningfully at the trunk. "Do you not wish to open it?"

Her gaze locked on the gold name plate. "No!" came quick and sharp as she pushed out of his arms, then softer, embarrassed, "No, thanks anyway."

He searched her face. "Are you not curious? Frankly Penelope, 'tis chewing me insides." He tapped the trunk with his foot.

She smiled weakly. "Mine too, but I don't think I'm ready to see what's in there."

Ram's chest tightened and he tamped down the urge to solve the puzzle for her now and be done with it. She looked unbelievably fragile, like a jade kitten he'd once seen, exquisite, smooth and hard on the surface, yet with little pressure the crush of his hand would crumble her into powder.

"The gift has waited this long, I daresay 'twill wait til you wish to unwrap it." Her shoulders sagged and he realized how much the damned thing terrified her. What secrets did she believe were inside an old chest that could possibly harm her?

As she tiredly scrubbed her hands over her face, he wondered if he'd the strength to watch her agonize over it afore she opened the trunk.

Penny caught her breath when he bent and slid his arm behind her knees, lifting her in his arms and moving toward the bed.

"Put me down, Ramsey . . . or is this your way of telling me you're horny?"

He blinked owlishly, utterly shocked. "Cheeky *wench,*" he said on a huge grin, then dumped her unceremoniously on the mattress. Penny bounced, shoving hair from her view and glaring at him. It had no effect and with a broad finger, he pushed up her chin, checking the knife wound. 'Twas smaller than he first realized and could wait to be properly tended.

"Sleep," he ordered, then slipped off her sandals.

She propped herself on her elbows. "I'm not tired."

He pushed her back down. "You are an exceedingly poor liar, Penelope." She opened her mouth to argue and he warned, " 'Twould be unwise to defy me."

"God, you're a bully."

"I'm not accustomed to being disobeyed." Firm, but apologetic.

From her vantage point he looked like a giant addressing his underlings. "I'll just bet," she said and watched him turn to leave.

Ram paused, looking over his shoulder; feline-green eyes regarded him with an odd intensity. Abruptly, he turned back and ducked beneath the netting, bracing his palms against the mattress on either side of her. She lay still, her eyes glassy, cat-like, her rounded breasts swelling with each erratic breath, threatening to spill from the snug confinement. She licked her lips and the unspoken invitation drew him closer. He wanted to assure her, keep her safe from demons and dragons out to harm her and as her expectant gaze locked with his, he slowly lowered his head, brushing his mouth to hers. Her purring sigh teased his lips and the fire quickly sparked atween them. He increased the pressure, his chest hovering a fraction over hers as his warm lips rolled back and forth, imploring her to give over the honeyed sweetness. Velvety heat seared through Penelope, sliding richly over her skin and tingling her toes. Last night blossomed in her mind, their scorching passion, her brushfire lust and the freedom she found in his arms. And she arched slightly, a subtle plea, her hands hesitating to grasp his shoulders and pull him down, her body screaming to feel his weight, but he drew back, smiling when it took her a moment to open her eyes.

"I promise, Penelope," he whispered, brushing the pad of his thumb across her lips, "you've naught to fear."

Penny blinked. Except you, she thought, her insides quivering from the power he wielded with a single kiss. He straightened and quietly left her bedroom, sealing the door behind him.

Chapter 21

Ramsey stood outside Penelope's door, grinding his teeth, debating whether or not to reenter the chamber and satisfy the mounting hunger she created in him. God, he wanted to make love to her. Right now. Again and again, wild and passionate and devouring until she begged him to cease, and then he'd refuse, taking her to that lush peak once more and savoring her breathless cries of pleasure.

God.

He was erect.

He was sweating.

Sweet Christ, he had to cease pondering over such images. 'Tis bloody unnatural, he thought. Shoving his hands in his pockets to disguise his state lest someone come upon him, Ramsey twisted around and leaned back against the adjacent wall.

He smothered his vivid imagination, recalling the day's events and the consequences. He'd more important matters to contend with now, he reminded, to be selfish of his own. He heard the clink of crockery and straightened, seeking out the source. He found Margaret on her knees, collecting up the shattered dishes into her apron.

She sniffled, her tiny sob catching him in the gut.

"Aw, Meggie me rose," Ram soothed, bending. She wouldn't look at him and he tipped her chin up. Her face was streaked with tears.

"I'm being silly I know, but when I heard her scream and those gun shots," her voice broke with tears, "I swear my heart dropped to my toes."

He pulled her to her feet and she nestled the broken dishes carefully. "I don't think they truly meant to hurt her, Meggie."

She reared back. "For the love of Mike, Ramsey, they tried to kill you!"

" 'Twas merely a warning." His calm voice soothed.

"Maybe," she said, yet wasn't convinced. "But after losing our little Tess, I can't help worrying." Her lip quivered.

"Ahh, lassie, you love her so, don't you?"

Margaret nodded, leaning against him as they left the guest room. "She's all I've got," Margaret murmured and Ramsey withdrew a handkerchief and blotted her wet cheeks. Did Penelope realize how much love surrounded her?

"How long have you known Penelope?"

Margaret glanced at Penny's closed door, then at Ramsey. "I practically raised her."

His features tightened. Though 'twas common in his century for servants to tend to children, somehow he imagined 'twould be different now.

"I can't tell you anymore, 'cause I promised, but let's just say Penelope has a right to be . . . unresponsive to relationships." She stared up at him for a moment, then finally smiled. "She's a bit reclusive, if you haven't noticed."

"I have."

"But she needs you. You're good for her. Even if she'd rather die than admit it."

"Are you saying you're rather fond of me, Meggie?" He grasped her free hand, bending over it for a kiss.

"Go on with you now," she said, pulling free. "You're sort of hard not to like, Ramsey O'Keefe." Straightening her shoulders, Margaret headed off, then paused, casting a backwards glance at the big man. "I don't suppose you dirtied up that room enough for me to have something to do?'' She nodded beyond to his bedchamber.

"I've taken care of meself for years and see no reason to cease now."

"I 'spected as much," she said, disappointed. Ram's shoulders shook with silent laughter as he watched her ascend the staircase, muttering about insensitive police leaving her enough dust to clean up til Sunday.

Ram turned into his quarters, suddenly exhausted. He sat down on the bed, then fell back, throwing one arm out. His knuckles smacked the side of the strong box and he winced, coming upright, pulling the chest close. Upon finding it locked, went to his frock coat, digging in the pocket. He returned with a small key suspended on a strip of leather, inserting it into the lock. Taking a deep breath afore he turned the key, he flipped the latch, his smile pleased and reminiscent as he settled comfortably on the mattress.

Braced within the molded shelf of the box was his sextant and a gold and silver astrolabe, gifts from his father, to chart his courses home, his sire had said. And though he'd never mentioned it, Ram knew Father had sold his finest horse to purchase the expensive instruments. His hand dipped inside the box, coming back with a silhouette of his mother. He smoothed a thumb over the artfully-cut black paper, his mind filling with sweet memories; her softly accented voice, the scent of lilacs, and her love of music. His throat burned. His gaze fell on a locket, small, unadorned and tucked in the corner of the molded velvet. He didn't touch it, couldn't, for he knew hidden within the folded gold was a wisp of downy brown hair, new, still scented with innocence. A lump thickened in his throat, shame and outrage simmering beneath the surface. He smothered it, suddenly overturning the chest on the coverlet and separating the items. Picking up his signet ring, he briefly studied the etched gold before slipping it on his middle finger. A sparkle caught his immediate attention and he grasped the end of a gold chain, holding it high in the air. He frowned as the beautiful dark pink pear-shaped diamond twisted and turned in the fading twilight, the gem's brilliance winking in soft rainbow patterns across the wall. His features suddenly stretched taut. 'Twas one of the stolen diamonds, he realized. Yet why would Dane put such a valuable piece within?

There were random items remaining on the bed, bits of his past he prized and though he'd seen them a month ago, it felt like years since he'd looked upon his possessions; his jackknife, the date of his first voyage carved into the worn handle grip, his divider, protractor, and reflecting quadrant, a pearl encrusted jabot pin once belonging to his grandfather—the only item his father refused to sell when they were nearly penniless—and a pressed sprig of red paintbrush tucked in oiled paper. His younger sister had picked that for him—the day afore she was killed by a British bullet.

Ramsey carefully placed his possessions back in the chest and leaving it open, pulled the bundle close, untied the hide straps and unfolded the soft skin. A creased paper addressed to him lay on the top and he immediately recognized the dark fluid script to be Dane's. Quickly he broke the seal, unfolded the parchment and read.

> *My dear friend,*
> *Tess and I pray this finds you hail and hearty. I must first write the words I could not say to you afore. Thank you, my friend, for allowing me to keep her here with me. Your sacrifice is the greatest gift of your heart. You will never be forgotten, this I swear. Since we had no indication of what century you would arrive in (Gad, I cannot believe I am actually penning such a notion), we could only hope 'tis the future, for your sake. This I envy you, Ram, for my wife speaks of the wonders only if I press her. She wishes to live in my time, and I admire her for that. I will confess to you that she has set Coral Keys society on their rumps with her bold talk and the vitality she radiates. I honestly believe 'twas her smile that coaxed Father from the grips of his despair over Desiree. She cajoled him into riding again beneath the guise of lessons for herself. Oh, how I love the little sneak.*

'Twas her doing, this package. She cares deeply for
you, my friend, and wept for days at the loss of your
presence. Tess wishes this to be placed in the hands of
Lloyds of London as quickly as possible, that it may find
you when you need it most. She is tormented with the
knowledge that you will be alone and eased her anguish
by providing you with your favored possessions. She
insists (and you above of all souls can attest to how
accomplished she is at that task) we must warn you that
our world's progress has wrought conveniences and dan-
gers you must understand. I shall let her explain and bid
you fare well, Ram, and God speed.

Dane

Ramsey blinked rapidly, then pinched the bridge of his nose.
He would miss them forever, he thought, and set his cap to
discover their legacy. And how it had died. He pulled a small
tapestry-covered book from the stack and slowly opened it,
reading Tess's neatly penned words. He threw his head back
and laughed when she scolded him for jumping ship and in
short words told him not to attempt to bed every wench who
looked in his direction. His lips curved in a tender smile with
the memory of Tess's quick set down, slicing his seductive
tactics to ribbons. Suddenly he considered himself fortunate
not to be the recipient of her sharp tongue. What would she
think if she knew of the relationship he'd struck with Penelope?

Ramsey read of disease and automatic guns, of medicinal
advances, drug dealers, women's rights, whose progress amazed
him, and mostly she stressed not trusting his secret to anyone.

Then she mentioned Penelope. And he swore his heart
stopped.

If you should actually arrive in my century, consider
contacting her. I'll admit that Pen is rather cool to anyone
she doesn't know (and some she does) but that's upbring-
ing. Have a little patience. I know why you went, Ramsey,
and you can't devote yourself to looking for the perfect
mate. It grows as it did between Dane and I. We were

*forced friends. We had no other choice, stuck out in the
middle of the ocean together. You have the advantage.
You know you have traveled through time. I had to wait
until a man was killed at my feet before I understood.*

He read on, taking comfort in her words and wishing she'd
tell him more about Penelope. He reached for another journal,
the motion sending his spyglass to the floor with a soft thump.
Retrieving it, he opened the brass and black leather scope and
sighted out the window. Rising slowly Ram moved closer to
the glass; for several moments he studied the horizon, focusing
on a small boat, its single occupant tugging a net up over the
port side. Suddenly he yearned for the sea, the rolling list of
a deck 'neath his feet, the bracing wind stinging his cheeks.
And the rotten food, foul water, and cramped quarters, a little
voice niggled. He lowered the scope and dropped his head
forward. The restlessness he recognized. 'Twas the same as
when he'd been in port for any length. Ramsey needed to work.

A knock sounded and Ramsey hailed them enter as he
snapped the scope shut.

Anthony poked his head into the room.

"Am I interrupting?"

"Nay." As Anthony stepped inside, Ramsey's eyes darted
to his possessions and he cursed his thoughtlessness.

Anthony's gaze fell to the objects on the bed, the open chest
and the pile of letters and books. He turned a jaundice eye to
Ram, yet when no explanation was forthcoming he said, "I'm
leaving."

Ram bowed slightly. "Good day to you, then."

"No, you've misunderstood," Anthony said on a short
chuckle, his gaze darting to the items strewn across the green
comforter. "I'm leaving the country in the morning."

Ram's brows shot up into his forehead.

"I've some business to take care of, ah—" His gaze shifted
to the bed again, then back to Ram. "Ah, people to see, contracts
to sign, you know, clients to pamper." His gaze strayed again
and he burst with, "My God, Ramsey, is that an astrolabe?"
Anthony walked swiftly to the bed, gingerly picking up the

instrument. "Damn me, it is!" He examined it, dipping into his pocket for his glasses and putting them on before taking a closer look. "Magnificent." He turned it over on his palm. "Is this really made of gold and silver?"

Ram nodded once, desperately searching for a plausible excuse to offer. Obviously the like was no longer common in this century.

"May I?" Anthony indicated the sextant. Ramsey couldn't deny the request without reason and handed it over.

Anthony studied the antique instrument. It was in excellent condition, well-oiled and dust free, and he marveled at the hand-bored markings. Turning it bottom side up, his eyes flared a fraction at the name scrolled in gold filagree across the thin base.

His gaze shifted to Ramsey. "I suppose you'll tell me this R. M. G. O'Keefe is an ancestor of yours?"

Ramsey gave him a tolerant look and without a word, took back the sextant, replaced it in the box and snapped the lid shut.

"Come on, Ramsey. Give over. The inscription is too remarkable to be a coincidence." Everything about this man spoke far deeper than a stroke of luck.

"I beg you, do not ask, Antony, for I can offer you naught that will satisfy your questions." With his back to him, Ram gathered the papers in a pile.

"Try me, Ram. I'm not such a hard sort."

Ramsey stilled, darting a glance at his new friend. "Nay, I cannot."

Anthony's gaze searched the stack of books and papers for an explanation. For an instant he thought he recognized the handwriting on the outside of one envelope but Ramsey tossed the oiled hide over the entire mess before he could decide.

Ram faced Anthony. He was not ready to trust his secret to anyone, not yet. "I thank you for your concern," he said, not unkindly. "Is there aught I might do for you whilst you're traveling?"

Anthony blinked, taken back. "Well, ah, no, then again," he said slowly, "you could stay here. With Penelope."

Frowning, Ramsey turned away. Moving to the window, he braced his forearm on the upper frame and watched the sea. "I had planned to find quarters of my own as soon as possible." He could not go on living in her home, not when he could afford one of his own. Regardless that they were, for proprieties sake, well chaperoned, 'twas improper. And by God, he could not disregard the absurd feeling of being *kept*. Yet leaving her could be deadly, he reasoned.

"Why?"

Ram shot him a level look. "I know that even without the aid of those spectacles, you are not totally blind."

"Well, no." Anthony smoothed his moustache, clearing his throat. "I'd have to be not to notice."

"You are angry?"

"Should I be?"

Ram turned from the window, running a hand through his hair before he spoke, "I do not understand the relationship atween you and the lady, Antony. Forgive me if I've intruded on your claim—"

"Whoa! Wait a sec. I don't have any claim on her, Ramsey. *Nobody* lays claim to that woman and I'd think after today you'd know that." It was more than a friendly warning, then he paused, looking thoughtful. "Is this why you disliked me so much at first?"

"Aye."

"I love her," Anthony said, and Ram's gaze snapped up from where he'd been studying the carpet fibers. "Like a sister or a daughter, I should say." Anthony rubbed his bearded chin. "God knows I'm old enough to be her father. Does that ease your mind?"

"My mind was not troubled over the matter, Welshman."

"Confident, aren't we?"

Ramsey simply folded his arms over his chest, his eyes hooded.

"That attitude will get you in trouble, O'Keefe, beware."

"When I need your advice, Welshman, I shall beat a hasty path *from* your doorstep."

Anthony threw back his shoulders. "I do believe I've been insulted."

Ram fished in his pocket and tossed a handful of matchbooks on the bed, then slanted a look at Anthony, arching a brow.

"Point taken, old man," he said on a conceding laugh, knowing each contained a woman's name and number. "You've also proven yourself capable of protecting her, if anything, from herself. And I'll tell you right now, she won't allow another stranger in this house, not even the mailman, nor will she ever concede to hiring a bodyguard."

"Your point?"

"That cut on her throat and those shots taken at you are attempted murder in the eyes of the law. Whoever's behind this won't go away." He seemed to be muscling up his words, Ram thought, afore he said, "That's why I want to hire you."

Ram looked stunned. "I beg your pardon?"

"As her bodyguard, of course."

"You've no need to pay me to see her safe. This I've promised her."

"You'll stay then?" Anthony had a lesser, though ulterior, motive. He didn't want Ramsey to disappear before he figured out the mystery of his arrival.

Ram nodded, extending his hand. "I shall do my utmost to see she enjoys herself, Welshman." Ramsey smiled, slow and male arrogant.

"I'm counting on that." Anthony left, satisfied with Ramsey's promise, yet he hadn't met the top step when Ramsey hailed him. Anthony paused, waiting until he met him at the landing.

"You know her friends, mate," he said lowly, not wanting Penny to know he was prying into her life. "Are you aware of a person by the name of Sloane?"

Anthony's features tightened. How did he know about that mess? "A college sorority sister. Didn't get along at all, though."

Ram scowled, awaiting an explanation.

"See, when Penny entered college, mainly to be with Tess, she already won an Oscar for her first film." This meant nothing to Ramsey, Anthony realized and speculated again, where this man has been for the last thirty some years. "That honor rubbed a few of the local society types the wrong way. Especially Sloane. But Tess was always her final target. Always." His shoulders moved uneasily and Ram recognized his banked anger. "I never understood. I mean, why Tess?"

Ramsey could offer no help. "And the woman's sir name?"

"Rothmere," Anthony answered, then winced when Ramsey blackened the air with a string of curses, and could do no more than stare as Ram spun about, vanishing into his rooms.

Chapter 22

"What is it that you do for Penelope, Welshman, that she allows you free rein in her galley at this late hour?"

Anthony twisted around, startled, then smiled. "Hey, I selected the wallpaper, that at least should get me an open invitation, you know."

Ram chuckled to himself as he went to the tall cooling box, opening the door and removing a platter filled with cold meats and fruit Meggie said she'd left for him.

"I was tempted to eat that." Anthony gestured to the platter as Ramsey searched the cabinets for bread. Anthony hopped up and opened a drawer, pulling out a loaf, then went to the refrigerator, coming back to the table with mayonnaise, mustard, lettuce, and tomato to add to the feast.

After reading the bread label and reminding himself to look up calorie in his dictionary, Ramsey studied the samplings. "You have not answered my question, Antony, and I thought you were leaving tonight?" Ramsey slapped a huge portion of roast beef and cheese on a slice of bread, folded it over and chomped into the sandwich.

"In a hurry to get rid of me?" Anthony relaxed into his chair again.

Ram's lips stretched into a slow smile. "Shall I show you the door?"

"Not yet. After a night like we had, I was just trying to gather the strength to drive to my hotel."

Ram frowned. "She has not offered you lodging here?" Despite the circumstances, Ramsey didn't think Penelope was being intentionally rude.

"Don't want to. Penny's a horrible grouch in the morning—" Ram's eyes narrowed at the implication—"and I prefer room service to this." He gestured to the platter as Ramsey joined him at the table. "And to appease your curiosity, Penelope is one of my clients."

"Clients?" Ram settled into a chair, looking Antony over afore he said, "You're a barrister?"

Anthony's brows knitted, then smoothed out. He then smiled. "A lawyer, yes," he said as he neatly folded the newspaper and studied a headline. "Though I admit Penelope's career has kept me busy and well paid."

Ramsey's sandwich paused on the way to his lips, his eyes glittering with quick anger. "Explain that statement, Welshman, afore I call you out."

Anthony peered over the edge of the newspaper and smiled. "No need to get your feathers in a tuff. I advise, financially and professionally, five actors, two writers, and one extremely temperamental singer. Have for years, though Penelope rarely rings me up to consult on scripts anymore." He shrugged. "I'm retained for a fee. If she doesn't work, I don't get paid."

Ramsey scowled darkly and with a disgusted snort, tossed the sandwich aside. "Yer naught but a bloody pimp."

Anthony's eyes brightened, crunching the paper as he lowered his arms to the table. "I think you should rethink that, Ramsey."

The air rang with a silent duel, charged, afore Ramsey's shoulders drooped. God, would he ever understand the ways of this century? "Forgive me, Antony." He waited for acceptance, then said, "But I find it difficult to believe Penelope is an actress."

It was clear he thought the whole idea distasteful and that

bothered Anthony, for he alone saw something grand growing between Penny and this man. "Maybe you should see her do it before you judge."

Ram scoffed. "She'll not perform for me."

Anthony's smile was patient. "You can watch it on video tape."

Ramsey's head pounded with confusion. " 'Tis a question I'm certain to regret but, what the ruddy hell is a vee-dee-oh tape?" Anthony opened his mouth, laughter no doubt about to spill forth and Ram put up a hand. "I beg you, Welshman. Spare me the humiliation and do not make light of my ignorance."

Anthony fought to keep the chuckle painless and crooked a finger at Ram. "Come on. Class is in session," he said, leaving his chair. Ramsey grabbed up his sandwich, following. They passed the study, rounded a corner and crossed the threshold of a room Ramsey hadn't seen afore. 'Twas decorated in thin red and white striped wall paper, red boarded walls and white sofas, chairs, and tables, liberally doused with red sleek-edged pillows. 'Twas cheerful, Ram thought. On the far wall opposite them were two floor to ceiling windows, atween them a tall white armoire. Anthony strode immediately to the cabinet and touched the center. It magically sprang open and he spread the doors wide. Inside were several black boxes of random sizes, larger versions of the ones in Penelope's room and Ram advanced for a closer inspection, finishing off the last of his sandwich.

Anthony glanced to his side. "You've never seen a T.V., have you?"

Ram shook his head, chewing, bending to examine the books on the bottom, astonished to find the bindings false, the contents yielding a thin black box with wheels of—he didn't know what it was. Straightening, he read the title: *Terminator.*

"That's a video tape. And you play it through this, a television." Anthony pointed the control at the screen and depressed a button.

Ramsey jolted, stumbling back, the tape flying from his grip as he fell over the low table when the box front lit up with dancing raisins.

"Sweet Jesus!"

Anthony folded over with laughter and Ramsey sent him a disgusted glare, then dusted himself off, his gaze riveted to the images moving beneath glass. The raisins, which appeared more like clumps of sheep dung, sang about hearing it through the grape vine, then a bowl of some flaked substance dotted with wiggling bugs spun onto the image. Fascinating.

Anthony felt a bizarre mix of confusion and a peculiar delight. To introduce someone to the world of television and video wasn't a normal occurrence, and he'd bet a million that there wasn't a man around who could say he hadn't, at least, heard of it. Yet it was clear that more than just T.V. was new to Ramsey.

Briefly Anthony explained the process of television as best he could, but he found his explanations lacking when Ramsey pressed him for every detail, wanting to know more and more.

"Good Lord, Ramsey, I'll get you a book on it if you want."

Ram nodded, busy watching the glass change from raisins to a beautiful woman walking on the beach and talking of— Ram flushed and looked away. How could this television speak to decent folk of a woman's monthlies as if 'twere comfortable conversation!

Anthony arched a gray brow in Ramsey's direction, noting the dull red flush climbing the back of his neck. "You're not alone, Ram. Most men don't care for those commercials either." Gad, Anthony thought, wait until he sees one for jock itch. "Here, sit." Anthony pushed Ram into a chair and handed him the controls, then went down on one knee, running his finger across the titles. Withdrawing one, he popped open the case and slid it into the VCR, explaining as he went.

The screen, as Anthony referred, went black, then brightened with the Universal introduction, which Anthony instructed Ram to fast forward. Carefully Ramsey depressed the button and watched the images advance with amazing speed. Anthony showed him how to pause, stop, rewind, and slow motion the tape and Ramsey enjoyed playing with the control so much that Anthony threatened to take the new toy. Then the title came into focus, *Habits of Nature,* starring Penelope Hamilton.

Ramsey sucked in his breath, leaning forward. He punched buttons, frantically seeking the one that would still the tape, then studied the image of Penelope's face, ten times its size. God, she looked so demure and innocent. 'Twas as if he could reach out and draw her forth and into his arms. He continued the tape.

Anthony plunked down on the couch and Ram glanced to the side. "I was under the impression you were leaving."

"I haven't seen the final of this one. It's just recently come out in video."

"How else does one view such a thing?"

"In a theatre, Ramsey, with a screen that's a hundred times as big as that thirty-five inch thing."

Ram brought his gaze back to the screen and suddenly understood that Penelope's profession entailed more than plays, and he wondered if she'd performed on stage a'tall. Then he asked.

"Sure, that's how she started in the business, summer stock. Working her way up like everyone else, costumer, chorus, extras, until she got her first major role in *Dead Orchids*. She's been busy ever since. It's in there somewhere." He waved at the base of the cabinet. "That's three deep of tapes. Penelope likes watching movies." His lips thinned. "Alone, unfortunately."

Ramsey paused the screen to ask, "How did you meet her, Antony?" The question nagged at him since the moment he'd met the Welshman.

Anthony smiled with the memory of the gum snapping sixteen-year-old who looked as if she'd ridden with the Hell's Angels since birth. Hard, bitter . . . angry. "She was rehearsing. Gad, she was a smart-mouth, rebellious to the core, chain-smoking and swearing like a sailor." He shook his head and Ramsey looked astonished; he knew he shouldn't have said that much. "It was a summer play of Romeo and Juliet. She was Juliet, you know, and damned awful, but she had the passion, and I knew she'd be good with some training. What I didn't know was how good. I became—" he shrugged— "her acting coach, agent, and guardian, I guess."

" 'Twas generous on your part, Antony. But had she no parents to guide her?"

Anthony didn't answer, looking away as he remembered promises made long ago. "No," he said, bringing his gaze back to his newest friend and fought the urge to blurt out the truth. "If you want to know more," Anthony mumbled, studying his shoe—"you'll have to ask Penelope." He slanted him a cautious look. "Carefully."

Ramsey nodded thoughtfully and without his help the screen unthawed, images speaking, moving. Ram sank back into the soft tuffed couch, utterly entranced.

"In this she portrays an orphan, a novice sequestered in a convent since she was a child, raised under the thumb of nuns until her true father comes to take her back."

"Bloody bastard! Why in God's name did he leave his child in such a strict cold place?"

Anthony laughed. "He didn't know she existed, and remember, Ram, it's only a movie, just like a play. You *have* seen a play, haven't you?"

"Aye."

There it was again, that innocence, as if he were just born into this world. He'd seen a play but not movies, claimed to be a sea captain, yet arrived like a new baby, no modern clothes, no money, at least not what he had considered valuable currency. He was considerate and protective and proud and Anthony wondered when living under Penelope's roof was going to get to that huge pride. Or had it already and that's why he wanted his own flat? And you're going to risk everything for him, a voice nudged and Anthony rubbed his bearded chin, then smoothed his moustache.

Ramsey recognized his indecision. " 'Tis a matter you wish to speak on, Antony, be free with your words. We are friends."

Anthony smiled, feeling strangely honored, then took the control, pausing the film. "You might see something in print about your living here."

Ramsey suddenly looked like a pot about to boil over.

"Relax, it's common. Celebrities are subject to close scrutiny and Penelope understands this. Police reports are public record and once the reporters get a nibble, they chomp hard. That's one reason why I asked you to stay here, no matter what you read or what she says.''

"She will truly be in a fit?"

"A mild assumption. Deal?"

Ramsey's lips tugged in a faint smile. "You already have my word, Welshman, or would you prefer it in blood?''

"With that, I'll leave you. I've just enough time to catch my flight.'' Anthony handed back the control, stood, then tipped an imaginary hat and left.

Ramsey returned his attention to the screen, drawn into the small chapel, right beside the young girl clad in white and kneeling afore the altar. She looked all of nine and ten years, though he knew Penelope to be at least eight or nine years senior. The film progressed and he forgot 'twas Penelope, the events portrayed stirring a deep sympathy for the sheltered miss and her contempt for the solemn captors who hid behind a holy order and black robes. 'Twas not Penelope he saw, but Karinn, the woman-child forced to submit to harsh Catholic rule because of her lack of parentage. Yet Ram witnessed something else, a hollow ache in the girl's eyes he'd seen once in Penelope herself, the day they'd met aboard the *Diana*. His heart tore as Karinn begged God to give her hope of a life beyond the stone walls and he knew a kindred spirit as she was suddenly thrust into a world she never experienced afore. As the film concluded, Ram pushed his fingers through his hair, realizing how easily Penelope's portrayal had taken him away from the woman he knew, and into the life of young Karinn. She was talented, and he admired her for it.

But he'd yet to see his Penelope express such vivid emotion and wondered why she hid so much from those who cared for her. Were the moments with him a role she portrayed? The thought struck him painfully hard, then he cast it aside as he recalled the cool drape she affected when Bailey and the police were about. 'Twas a role she slipped into, he thought again, to keep the curious at bay. And she was a master at it. But still, the niggling wouldn't be suppressed. Who was Penelope Hamilton?

* * *

The film was just beyond the halfway point when Penelope paused outside the room, not at all upset that he'd made himself at home. She should be, but he looked too damn good, there on the couch, his legs stretched out before him, bare feet resting on the coffee table. Ramsey sipped from a tall glass of beer, his side parted hair, loose and shiny, shielding a view of his expression as he watched the screen.

She left a chunk of herself in that film. No one would ever know how much she would have given to have had a life like young Karinn. Penny never cared what critics said about her work; she knew when she lacked and missed the mark. *Habits of Nature* hit dead center. She wanted his opinion, but his tightly-clenched fist and soft wordless sounds of compassion was all she needed. Her heart soared. And in the next breath she told herself it shouldn't matter whether he enjoyed her work or not.

But it does. It really, really does.

She took a step, considering joining him, then stilled, looking down at the antique key clutched tightly in her hand. Her heart did a quick, painful drop to her knees and she jammed the key in her robe pocket, silently turning away. Her happiness was short-lived lately and a little voice inside her screamed at her to grab some before it was gone.

Chapter 23

She was dreaming. And dancing. No . . . swimming, but it was a dream, so what did she know? The faint haunting blends of the classical piano filtered to her sleepy brain. So soothing. In the pool? No. The ocean. She emerged from the frothy water, naked, walking slowly up the beach. Sand squished between her toes, her hips swaying deeply as her feet sunk into the sand. Ramsey. He was on the beach, watching her, his amber-dark gaze moving over her body so hotly it felt like his hands. Slow, infinitely sensual. Everything about the man oozed sex. Lithely he came to his feet and started toward her, his gait loose-limbed and graceful. He wore those skin-tight knee breeches and looked as he did when she'd first seen him, vulnerable, mysterious—swashbuckling. He reached for her, enveloping her in his embrace. Then he kissed her, slow, old fashioned, rolling and nipping. It was nice to know a man could still pack so much hunger in one kiss. Then his tongue came into play. He made love to her mouth, exquisitely, and Penny melted into the sand, taking him down with her as his kiss went hot and savage and all devouring.

A frown knitted her brow as the vision faded and the music became more prominent. She tried to draw him back into her dreams, but failed. Squirming on the couch, she thought of the soft bed upstairs and the man sleeping down the hall. Fabulous dream. Wrapping her robe more tightly, she let the wonderful comforting strands gently brush away the webs of slumber. Radio or CD, she wondered. Opening her eyes, she rolled onto her back and for a moment wasn't certain where she was. The solarium, she realized after her eyes adjusted to the pale light and she recognized the dome shaped ceiling.

She levered herself onto her elbows, frowning. The music was incredibly crisp, clear. She blinked when she heard a flat note, then a replaying. Grasping the back of the couch, she peered cautiously over the cushioned edge.

Her breath caught.

Ramsey.

Where he was seated at the black piano, she could see only to his shoulders, the dim light from the crystal chandelier radiating warm gold prisms that sparkled off his unbound hair. A broad snifter of brandy lay within his reach, the liquid vibrating with each note. He looked like a crazed composer, eyes closed, his head thrown back, the piece brilliant, yet tormented and mysterious. His talent was magnificent and never in her wildest imagination would she have thought he'd like music, let alone know how to play like a concert pianist. Her heart split a little and she let his clear notes seep between the tiny crack as she slowly moved off the couch.

Her movements hadn't drawn his attention and she savored the moment of seeing him so involved. Slowly he tilted his head forward, his long satiny dark hair tumbling across his face, his eyes still closed as the piece became powerful, nearly violent, then abruptly softened. He was lost to the melody, letting it sing through his blood. His pleasure was tangible and she shared it, her body humming as if drugged with mulled wine. There was something to be said about watching a man when he didn't know you were there.

Then his eyes opened and he saw her.

"Don't stop," she said before he could. "Please."

Ramsey smiled slightly, his entire body jumping to life at just the sight of her. His little sneak looked lovely, all sleep-tussled and bloody alluring. His gaze skimmed her flushed face, then moved lower, lingering at her breasts, the delicious bit of cleavage the dark-green satin robe exposed, then dropping to her bare toes afore returning to meet those cat round eyes.

"I was not aware I had an audience."

Penny swallowed. It was wickedly obscene, the way he looked at her. "I fell asleep on the couch." She gestured behind her. "I didn't know you could play."

" 'Tis a great deal of me you do not know, Penelope." His voice was rumbling and diabolic, suggesting there would be pleasure, immense pleasure within the discoveries.

"Who taught—I mean, where did you learn to play?" She moved closer, resting her palm on the gleaming black surface of the baby grand as she rounded the jutting edge to stand close. He looked heavenly, she thought.

"My mother. 'Twas her passion." His tender smile was laced with bitter grief. "She was a lady, proper reared and schooled, yet the pianoforte was her freedom, she claimed. She would have liked to play on this. The tone," he said, looking down at the keys, "is so gloriously rich."

"Pianoforte? This is a piano, Ramsey, a Steinway."

He nodded slowly, but she didn't think it meant anything to him.

"Do you play?" he asked.

"God, no. I'm lucky to bang out scales without sounding like a dying mule."

"Then why own such an instrument?"

One shoulder rose and fell. "Hank plays a little. So I keep it tuned, though it was in the house when I bought it." She watched his long tanned fingers glide over the keys, imagined them on her skin, then quickly blurted, "What's this piece?"

The gray silk robe shifted against his powerful shoulders. "Father called it her Night Song."

"Your mother composed?" Penny was incredulous.

"Aye." Defensive, but soft.

"Why Night Song?" she asked, brows drawn slightly.

His touch on the keys softened, the sound barely audible, but the tone, seductive and beckoning—was there, wafting around them. "She played for him, my father. Banishing the little ones to bed, he'd enjoy his pipe and watch her, waiting til it swept her."

She propped her elbow on the surface, cupping her chin. "I'm not sure I understand."

A devilish light flickered in his eyes, utterly mischievous. "I snuck below stairs once," he confided softly, as if someone might hear. "I was ten and two, not a man, but thinkin' I was. She was playing, and Father rose slowly, tapping out his pipe. She smiled at him. 'Twas a smile I'd caught atween them only thrice afore and didn't know what it meant til I'd had my first woman." Penny gave him a speculative look and he wiggled his brows. "Mother ignored him as he stood behind her. Father brushed her hair off her shoulder and kissed the spot and she went into his arms. He made love to her on the parlor floor."

Penny straightened, eyes wide, brows high. "You actually watched them?"

His lips trembled with a smile. She looked so adorably indignant. "Aye."

"Ramsey!"

"I was too scared over getting caught and receivin' the thrashin' I deserved." He shrugged. " 'Twas wild and swift and over before I realized it." His fingers stilled, the last notes vibrating to silence as he met her gaze. "About like you and I, Penelope."

Her skin fused with soft heat. "That was a mistake." Her mind screamed to retract the words.

He cast her sly look, plunking one key at a time. "Mayhaps a kiss or two could be considered an exercise in poor judgment, Penelope, but the sweet passion you found in my arms, beneath my touch?" He shook his head. "Never."

She drew herself up a little straighter. "Good God, you're arrogant, O'Keefe. Anybody ever tell you that?"

Ramsey thought of Tess and how she'd easily destroyed his finest seductive tactics whilst they dined aboard the *Sea Witch*.

"Aye, quite bluntly, I'm ashamed to repeat. But I shall take to account the lass was mad with love for another—" he flashed her a rascally grin—"therefore immune to my charms."

"And you're saying I'm not?"

Ramsey's gaze lowered to her breasts, lingering over the teardrop roundness, and the tiny locket resting atween. Her nipples plumped the satin, and he met her gaze swiftly and smiled, slight and mocking. "Your body knows me well, Penelope, even if your heart speaks nay."

He continued to play.

"Keep going, Ramsey." She folded her arms petulantly across her middle. "You're digging yourself deeper by the second."

His lashes lowered on a challenging gleam. "Shall I prove you wrong?" Ramsey tried to maintain his composure. But with the evidence of her desire blaring at him like friggin' trumpets, all he could think of was how those rosy crests beckoned for his attention. He could smell the exotic scent of her flesh and grew restless. God's teeth man, yer like a beast seeking to rut and 'tis bleedin' fortunate yer sitting down.

"Presumptuousness is not charm, Ramsey, and you have about as much charm as a Brahma bull."

He chuckled lightly. "And you, love, are transparent as oiled paper—to me," he stressed, giving her a lusty look.

Penny spun about, took a step, then rounded on him. "I thought your kind were all but dead."

"And that is?"

"A dyed-in-the-wool chauvinist!"

Ramsey frowned, not understanding, then recalled Tess's explanation of the word: *A man who thinks first with the contents of his breeches.*

He grinned. "A failing only where you're concerned."

"Lucky me," she said flatly and the silence stretched between them, tightening the air.

"Have you opened the trunk, Penelope?"

She drew a sharp breath, startled by the shift of conversation and the aura around him. "No."

His shoulders drooped and he ceased playing. "I thought as much."

"What's that supposed to mean?" But his disappointment was clear.

Ramsey picked up the snifter, swirled the liquor, then took a sip.

"Well?" she prompted, just noticing his gold signet ring.

Smoothly he drained the brandy, ignoring her presence, infuriating her, and she took a threatening step. He cast her a side glance, arching a brow.

God, she was beginning to loathe that measured look.

"What does it matter whether I open the trunk?"

"It does to the Blackwell who left it to you," he said, carefully placing the snifter on the piano's surface, watching his own movements.

"What about your package? What do you have to do with all this?" She'd heard him say he was a Continental Marine with the confidence of a judge and the impossibility made her feel as if she were being conned.

"I've opened mine." He was still staring at the snifter.

"What does it have to do with my trunk?"

"Naught and 'twas not to me the chest was gifted, Penelope." Edgy, soft.

"And I'm telling you I have *no* connection to anything as old as that trunk."

His gaze flew to hers, his dark eyes glacial and piercing. "Say naught was familiar to you, woman, and I will believe you are simply insensitive to a dead soul's last wish."

Penny reared back. She'd never heard him speak like that, so wintry, not to her. "Why are you hounding me like this?"

"Tell me!" he demanded, smashing a balled fist onto the delicate keys, making her flinch.

"Yes! Yes! The handwriting. It was Tess's. *My* Tess." She thumped her chest. "But it isn't possible, don't you see? She was only twenty-five and that thing's been sealed since 1839!"

"Then by Triton's will, woman, discard your fears and for the sake of the smattering of familiarity, go open the bloody trunk!" His anxiousness made his tone harsh and biting, yet she held his gaze, mutiny written in her expression and a sound of disgust snagged in his throat. "I see a coward stands afore me," he hissed, ignoring the burst of hurt in her eyes. "Did this Tess mean naught to you?" He rose slowly to tower over her. "Or mayhaps she went to her death because of a friendship she *thought* she had with you?" His viperous arrows pierced her heart with the accuracy of a cross bow.

"You bastard!" Her hand shot out, cracking against his face with a power that sent his head to one side. Slowly he turned back. She trembled, swallowing repeatedly. "Do you think I don't have a heart to break?" A tortured whisper, her eyes misting. "She was my only friend, Ramsey." The tears came, slow and burdened with guilt and he felt the muscles round his heart clamp like a vice. "For God's sake, we grew up together, we survived together! And I—" A hard shudder raced through her body, her ragged breath choking her words. "Oh God." Furiously she scrubbed her hands over her face. "It should have been me," she moaned, slowly lowering her hands, and Ramsey saw the wall about her crumble. "*I* asked her to steal, *I* changed places with her when those men were chasing her. Jesus—" she tilted her head back, staring at the ceiling—"I might as well have put a gun to her head." Slowly she met his gaze, tears falling. "If I'd been brave like Tess and just taken my shots like I *deserved,* she'd be alive." Her voice broke. "But she's not. And it should have been me who died!"

"Ah, nay love, nay." His features mirroring her sorrow, he reached for her. "She made her choice freely, just as you did."

"Don't patronize me," she warned in a bitter rasp, batting away his hand. "I can't take that! God, not from *you!*" The last an agonized plea before she whirled about to run. Ram grabbed her arm, dragging her back, his eyes fierce-bright as he crushed her to him. She has old shadows, he realized, and 'twere leading her down a path to her own private hell. By God, he wouldn't let it take her.

"Let go, Ramsey, please." She shoved at his chest, turning her face away. Her pulse quickened at the base of her throat. "You don't want to be near me . . . I'm poison."

He clamped a hand to the back of her head, forcing her to meet his gaze. "Then I shall drink a draught of your venom," he said and crushed her mouth beneath his, his kiss relentless and desperate, yanking passion from her cool figure, her tainted heart. It tore at him to see her like this. 'Twas not her hand in

Tess's disappearance that haunted her so deeply, gave her such a low opinion of her worth, and he was determined to find the source and destroy it. Yet if loving her body be the only way to reach her heart, then so be it.

But she fought him still and he refused to yield, his free hand sliding down her spine, roughly molding her trim hips, grinding her to his throbbing warmth, then skimming up and around to shape her satin covered breast. Her body softened against him. With deepening circles his fingertips worked her nipple to a tight throbbing pebble, and he absorbed her quick hot shudder.

She clung to him, gripping his silk lapels. It was happening again, she thought as he pushed her robe aside, his callused palm closing over her bare breast. *He wields his power. And I can't fight it.* She wanted to lash out at him, scream at the awful way he spoke to her, but she couldn't think of anything except the heady feel of his hands, his taut body against hers and how desperately she wanted to lose herself in him. With Ramsey, she could do it, leave pain and sorrow behind and be primal, wicked. Then she was, yanking open his robe to slide her hands over his chest, shape his coin-flat nipples, then smooth the ridged plains of his stomach to his arousal. The air left her lungs. He was brick hard.

"Ramsey?" She flexed against him.

He didn't speak, yet twisted around, pushing her down onto the piano. The disjointed keys sent a broken chime into the air. He kissed her savagely, wedging atween her thighs, and her legs immediately wrapped around his hips. His fingers found her, wet and hot and incredibly snug. He thrust deep inside and she gasped against his mouth, caught the satisfied look in his amber eyes. He'll pay for that arrogance, she thought, plowing her fingers into his hair, holding him while she blistered his mouth with flowing erotic strokes. The ivory keys bit into the soft flesh of her buttocks, yet she was blind to it, clawing his powerful shoulders. A delicious burn radiated through her body. Sinful. Luxurious. He made a hungry sound, nuzzled her throat and his fingers pushed, retreated. Again and again. He touched the tender core of her and Penelope threw her head back, satiny red hair splaying across the gleaming black surface like spilled wine. She was on the edge, ready.

And she took his breath away.

Ramsey wanted this as much as she, wanted the sweet explosion that came when their bodies melded and the incredible peace he knew he'd feel after. Yet he would trade it all to climb into her heart and push her secret pain out, taste them, know them like his own.

"See how you come alive in my arms, love," he murmured against her throat, lightly stroking her. "Why only here?"

"Shh, Ramsey, please." She drew him to her mouth. "I don't know. I don't care." She pulled frantically at the silken ties of his slacks.

"Do you want me truly?"

"Do *you* want *me?*" she countered, her breathing labored.

He held her gaze, his voice somber, reverent. "Aye, lady heart, always."

For a heartbeat everything inside her and around her froze, her gaze searching his features. "Then love me." She freed him into her palm, gasping at the incredible heat of him. His erection bucked in her hand, her legs pulled him closer and she guided him to the source of her need.

Eyes locked. And he plunged hard, driving her briefly off the keys.

"Oh—God!"

Her body grabbed him, wet velvet sliding, and Ramsey didn't think he'd last long enough. Too hard. Too hot. Her fingers stole over his ribs, grasping his sides, urging him, and he gave, clamping onto her hips and sinking deeply. He moved in desire's erotic symphony, the crescendo swiftly climbing. She demanded more, thighs clenching, her head thrown back. Ramsey laved her throat, her smooth shoulder, curving his long body and closing his lips over her nipple, drawing it into his mouth. He sucked hotly and she drove her fingers into his hair, curling her hips in sensuous little tucks. He felt her stormy eruption like cannon fire. Her hoarse cry spilled first and he received it into his mouth, his kiss keeping her pleasure within him, secret and hidden, then the exquisite tightening of woman-flesh pushed him over the edge. His hands moved in a swift provocative motion down the backs of her thighs, strong fingers curling beneath her knees and lifting them higher as he thrust deep and long, exploding inside her. Sweet heaven. Nothing was ever so glorious.

Nothing stole more of his heart.

She clung to him, whispering his name. His broad arms swallowed her in a fierce embrace, absorbing every shattering spasm.

Her breath dusted his chest, and after several moments she lifted her head, her lips curving in a soft wonderous smile.

"My God, Ramsey. Hearing the piano will never be the same again."

"Neither will playing it."

He bent to kiss her and noticed she still cried.

Chapter 24

He didn't mention her tears, yet kissed them away, slowly, the barest touch of his lips, and Penny closed her eyes tight, trembling from his tenderness.

And fear—of him and how much he affected her guarded emotions. She could reason it away that he'd barreled into her life when she needed someone, beyond Tony or Margaret or Hank, yet that was a lie. Ramsey knew her thoughts without speaking, saw into her soul, forcing a confession she never dared say aloud, then soothed her wounds with his incredible loving. Proving his power over her, again. She swore she'd never allow any one to get that close, yet a barren decaying part of her selfishly wanted to stay lost in his seduction a little while longer. For the moment would be shattered soon enough.

"Such a complicated creature," he whispered into her ear, as if just realizing the thought. Her lids lifted slowly and she gazed into searching cognac-brown eyes. She urged him closer, pressing her lips up the column of his throat, to the curve of his mouth.

"And you are undeniably the most erotic man I've ever met," she murmured, then kissed him deeply and he left her body, gently, with a finesse that didn't surprise her, fastening his clothes, then sweeping her into his arms and lifting her high on his chest. He was right out of an ancient fairy tale, she thought, wrapping her arms around his neck, his mouth on hers, blistering and hungry for more and only the silence of the house saw them ascend the stairs and enter his rooms.

Ramsey went directly to the bathing chamber, backing her up against the rain chamber door, shrugging out of his night clothes and stripping the satin from her body with an urgency that excited her. He would never have enough of her, he realized as he reached past her to turn on the water, his lips grinding a delicious path over her bare shoulder, her throat. Neither spoke. Passion claimed mind and body, enfolding them in the touch, taste, and sweet Jesus, the feel of her. His hands ran the length of her arms and grasped her fingertips as he drew her beneath the steaming water.

"I confess I've ached to share a bath with you since I first saw this contraption."

Not want or considered, but ached he said, like pain and Penny thought she'd melt under the heat of the spray. "It's sinful."

"Then share your crime with me," he said, grasping a cake of soap and dragging it down between her breasts, then around the slick globes in slow maddening circles.

She arched into his palms. "Has any woman *ever* said no to you?"

She gasped as he suddenly pushed her against the cool tile.

"None afore matters, Penelope," he murmured darkly as his soap traveled over her buttocks, then slipped around to dive between her legs. She inhaled. Suds slithered.

"Sure, right." Sarcastic, breathless.

"So distrusting you are, lass," he tisked, torturing her with his wet hands and warm bubbles.

"Well, you *have* just popped into my life, twisted it around your finger and now look where we are."

It hurt that she could not accept him freely.

"Can you not see that what we share, 'tis beyond the flesh?" he said. She made a sound, of disbelief and uncertainty and he tossed aside the soap, cupping her face in his palms. He gazed deeply into her eyes, his thumbs brushing across her cheekbones. "You consume me, woman."

"That's just wild sex talking."

"Nay, nay," he groaned, his expression sad. "Why can you not believe I am not here to take from you?" His heart tripped at the flicker of hope in her green eyes. "By God, Penelope, were I to walk away this night—" He inhaled, his fingers tightening. "*I* would need a part of you to survive," he uttered savagely and the strength of his words ripped through her, stripping away another layer of loneliness.

"Oh Ramsey, don't. Don't say any more," she sobbed against his mouth, kissing him with a possessiveness he never dreamed she'd bestow. He felt every morsel of her lithe figure, her plush wet breasts pushing against his chest, small hands flowing slickly over his torso, the satiny inside of her thigh sliding against his skin as she hooked her leg around him, her calf slippery over his firm buttocks.

Thick steam clouded the room, dripping with sensuality. Then boldly she clasped his erection, pushing down til the tip of him entered her.

"Again, Ramsey."

A plea of the heart, of the body, and Ramsey surged into her, his big hands holding her steady, eyes locked. Water cascaded between, settling and flooding past sealed skin as he moved, gave, and Penny accepted, tilting her body to his, sensitive and wanting. And the eruption suddenly snapped through them, a deep bone-racking shudder, a roaring flex of muscle and flesh. He held her, suspended like a wild animal caught in amber, his huge body quaking. His eyes, dark and hooded, never left hers, even as the last liquid spasm curled through her body.

His voice was thick with adoration when he said, "Ah love, you rob me of my pride when you give to me like this."

And I have none left when I do, she thought, as he slowly left her body. The soap in his hand again, he worked a thick foam over her flushed skin, his touch teasingly slow and retribution lit her eyes as she tried to take the cake. He held it beyond her reach, his smile blinding and Penny showed him she didn't need a handful of bubbles to torture him as they stood beneath the spray, falling into a heavy soul wrenching kiss til the water cooled. Shutting off the flow, he drew her out, wrapping her first in a thick towel, then himself. He didn't let her leave him and carried her to his bed and with another towel, dried her hair, her shoulders, rubbing her warm and cozy. He sat beside her, her legs draped across his lap, the towel working beneath his strong hands. He even dried her toes. Penny fell back onto the mattress. His unselfishness continually amazed her.

"'Tis an old wound?"

She glanced up, deliciously lethargic. "No. Well, I don't know. I've had it as long as I can remember." He was referring to the small purplish mark ringing below her left ankle. "I almost had it removed a while back."

Ramsey frowned softly. "Removed?"

"Yes. You know, plastic surgery."

He didn't, yet caught himself afore he looked the fool and realized 'twas likely possible in this age of medical advances. And what the ruddy hell was plastic? "Vanity does not suit you, Penelope." It was a statement.

She levered herself onto her elbows, smiling at the compliment. "I was doing a mystery-thriller film and the director thought it might be mistaken for a clue to the plot when the camera panned a body shot during a love scene."

Ramsey went still as granite, his voice tight, his grip on her calf tightening. "You actually made love—" he gestured to the air, mentally indicating the tapes he'd viewed—"with a perfect stranger for the bleedin' world to see!"

His fury was palatable and Penny wisely kept her voice calm. "Not a stranger, Ramsey, an *actor,* and there were twenty other people in the studio." His jealousy, the power of it, made her feel cherished.

"But you were—intimate?" His hesitation betrayed his heart and she almost cried, for if he knew what she'd done—suddenly she dropped back onto the bed.

"Kisses, touches, yes. Actual intercourse—" her gaze collided with his—"No, Ramsey. Never." Public nudity and *film* sex scared the hell out of her; how much was necessary for the work were usually contract breakers for her.

He hadn't moved, as if deciding whether or not it was truth, then finally his shoulders relaxed and he shook his head ruefully. "I fear I will never comprehend the ways of your world," he murmured as he crawled onto the bed.

The ways of your world, she caught, like he didn't belong. He didn't, she thought as he snuggled her beneath the covers, pulling the towels from their bodies, then tossing them aside as he joined her.

And she let him, sinking into the cocoon of warmth.

"I really should go to my room," she murmured sleepily.

"Do you wish to leave me?" He hovered over her, running his hand the slender length of her body, the blood freezing to his heart.

"You *do* make it hard to resist." She wiggled into the curve of his body, aware that the longer she shared this intimacy with him, the harder it would be to protect herself from him.

" 'Tis my intention." He pressed a whisper-soft kiss to her temple, his massive arms swallowing her in his embrace.

"Hah. I'm shameless, Ramsey, and you are leading me down the road to ruin."

His lips curved. "Lay the blame at my feet, love, for 'tis mine by right," he murmured into her damp hair. His voice lowered to a whisper. "Stay with me, Penelope, and I vow naught will ever wound you."

She didn't hear and Ramsey's gaze traced her delicate features as sleep took her. Such a lonely flower, he thought, tormenting herself with guilt. Yet her silent pain went beyond that, for 'twas the simple happiness of friends and family she denied herself, a punishment. Yet in his arms she was free and teasing and vulnerable. Patience man, he told himself. Those barriers have been in place long afore you and 'twill take time to crush them.

And he would.

One block at a time, if he must.

She smelled cherries and smoke and felt safe.

Humming, deep and comforting, and with it came the sensation of strong arms about her, protecting her and she knew she was happy and loved. A sparkle and a delicate touch scented with flowers. She strained to grasp more, see more, but the sensations faded, blackened into terror and pain and utter loneliness.

They didn't want you.

Ramsey jolted awake, blinking into the darkness, his gaze rapidly circling the room, then dropping to the woman lying next to him. She wrestled against him, her fists clenched over her ears, her body drawn tight and cowering. She trembled violently and he gathered her close, gently rubbing her shoulders, her spine.

"I'm here, love," he murmured close to her ear. "I'll not let anyone harm you. I promise you're safe." He spoke softly, over and over, his heart catching on her pitifully whimpered words.

"Don't leave me!" She gripped his arm like a vise. "I'll be good."

Ram's brows shot up. Her cries were that of a child, no more than a babe.

"Where are you, little one?" he coaxed. "Where?"

"Dark. Dark." Whispered fear and loneliness. "Hurts . . . Da!"

"Shhh," he hushed and she clung to him desperately. "You are safe, sweetling, safe. None will hurt you now. 'Tis over."

Yet 'twas not.

And he feared she would never let him close enough to help her.

Sultry air clung to his skin, sticking the white shirt to his back, and he shifted his shoulders, an annoying trickle of sweat dripping down his spine. The nonstop flight was brutal and Anthony knew he was in trouble when he didn't see enough military personnel in this part of the city to make him feel comfortable. Angela City, Philippines. A dozen years since he'd been here last, for Penelope.

Bone tired, he moved down a narrow alley, his oldest pair of boots marking the path of his friend Argarlo, strolling a few feet before him, a bit too casually for Anthony's comfort. But this was his home. The slim dark-skinned man knew everyone, everywhere. He could find anything—for a price, illegal or otherwise. Human or not. And Anthony couldn't believe he was risking arrest, his career, and maybe even Penelope's.

They passed huts, palm thatched, wood and tar papered, some tin roofed and rusting, most of the dilapidated shanties without a door and all closely fitted like a chess board. The foul stench of raw sewage in the rain-soaked streets was nearly unbearable, though one grew accustomed to the odor after awhile. They strode around a pretty girl of about thirteen squatting in the alley, washing herself, the soaped cloth passing beneath her bra and panties, which was all she wore. Anthony glanced away and nearly collided with Argarlo.

"You want a woman, too?" Argarlo asked, nodding to the girl as he slid a crushed cigarette between his lips and flicked a match. The yellow match light sparkled off the inky slickness of his shoulder length hair, the four unevenly spaced loops running up the side of the man's ear; his pale blue sarong was so transparent Anthony could see the stitching of his dirty tee shirt beneath.

"No. But thank you for the offer." He wouldn't insult Argarlo by showing his distaste.

Shrugging, Argarlo sucked on the smoke, leaning against the wall as he gestured to the cloth covered door. Anthony brushed back the faded drape and stepped inside. The scent of sweat, whiskey, and stale *San Migel* assaulted his nostrils. No one moved, yet several occupants tossed him a curious glance, then went back to their drinks.

"The bartender," Argarlo murmured in heavily accented Tagalog.

Anthony crossed the dirt floor and leaned against the bar, ordering two beers. There were no stools, nothing on the walls but a faded Coca-Cola ad. Women, girls really, were propped near the end of the wood slab bar, looking more frightened than pleased with their companions.

Argarlo saddled up beside him. Anthony spoke, his Tagalog stilted and bringing a faint smile from his comrade.

"Papers." He didn't need to elaborate. Word traveled swiftly and Anthony didn't doubt the man knew everything about him down to shoe size by now.

The squat bartender studied Anthony with a thin-lidded glare, then shook his head and moved away. Anthony casually slid several bills across the counter, as if paying for the drinks. The fat man stopped, his coal-black eyes widening at the American currency, his gaze shifting between the cash and the buyer. Anthony sweetened the pile and Argarlo stayed his hand before he added more, spitting words—soft and deadly, at the bartender. Anthony didn't see the knife Argarlo brandished beyond his line of vision.

The bartender stared at Anthony for a second, his breathing heavy, then he slapped a hand over the cash, dragging it across the counter and into his pocket. He gestured with his head to a door beyond him, the only one Anthony had seen actually made of wood and Anthony followed.

He had to and never considered what lay beyond.

Chapter 25

Penelope stretched, like a cat content with a belly full of cream and Ram smiled, watching her in the mirror's reflection, her willowy arms twisting above her head afore she opened her eyes.

"Good morn, love," he said, fastening his cuff, his back to her.

It certainly was, she thought, sinking into the bed, her gaze slowly traveling over his body clad in dark pleated trousers and the crisp white shirt. The brightness of it showed off his tan, the leanness of his waist, and she already recognized the style was his preference, collarless except for a narrow band, button front.

When she didn't comment he looked down at himself. " 'Tis not appropriate?"

"That depends on what you have in mind." Her expression spoke volumes and his lips curved as she slowly slid from the bed, dragging a sheet about her and exposing more than she shielded. He faced her, slipping his arms around her waist and pulling her up against him, kissing her heavily. His hands rode up her supple spine; her bare body, plush and warm from sleep tempted him to join her abed again. But the house was a'stir and he'd not let them be caught so deeply compromised afore the help. Reluctantly, he drew back, the question nagging him all morning tumbling out.

"What torments your dreams, lass?"

She stiffened in his arms and tried to pull away, but he held tight, gentling his intrusion with soft kisses.

"I don't remember," she finally said.

Her met her gaze.

"I never do." She shrugged. "I can't recall anything except feelings. I've been hypnotized, analyzed, and regressed and nothing helps." She avoided his probing stare. "I sort of live with it."

Such a horror to be taunted like that, he thought. "You were a child, a babe really," he said softly and her gaze narrowed. " 'Twas your voice, yet light of pitch, innocent."

"So I've been told."

He could tell by her tone she wanted the subject dropped and he let it.

"Going out?" She flicked imaginary lint from his shoulder.

"I thought to purchase a few books, mayhaps some sheet music," he whispered near her ear, then moistened a path up the curve of her throat. " 'Tis a fellow Rachmaninoff, I understand is quite the composer."

Penny thought he was making a joke and laughed softly. "I heard that, too."

The sweet joyous sound filled him like slow moving honey and he struggled to control his need of her, pressing his forehead to hers. "Would you care to accompany me on my outing?"

She moaned disappointedly. "I have accounts to go over before the courier arrives." She glanced at the clock on his dresser and inhaled sharply. "Which is in two hours!" She pushed out of his arms, nearly losing the sheet as she tossed aside fallen pillows and comforter, searching for her robe. The drooping sheet offered him a delectable view of her shapely hips and tight little bottom and Ramsey couldn't stand the alluring temptation. He swept her into his arms.

"Put me down!" she hissed. "I'm perfectly capable—" He

kissed her into silence, til she went liquid and purring against him.

"I am well aware of your assets, love." He headed toward her chamber. "But if I were to see you bare again, the courier would definitely be left waiting."

"Is that so?" Lord. He looked in mortal agony.

"God's teeth, aye," he groaned, releasing her legs, her body sliding deliciously against his hard length afore her feet touched the carpet.

"You're saying you *might* think of me today?" Flush against him, she ran her hand up the length of his thigh, sliding inward.

"Oh aye," came with feeling, his breath catching.

"Good." She straightened. He blinked. And she stripped off the sheet, giving him an unobstructed view of her naked body afore she pushed him back out the door and shut it in his face.

"Imp," he said, grinning at the sealed wood. He'd taken but two steps away when the door abruptly opened and she peeked around the jam.

"There's a connection to the trunk and that little chest Bailey gave you, isn't there?"

He recognized the challenge in her voice and 'twas a monumental effort to keep his features impassive. " 'Twas coincidence that we received the endowments together, Penelope. Even had we not met, Bailey would have arrived on your doorstep just the same."

She knew that, but ... "Will you ever give me a straight answer?"

He looked at the floor, then her. "This evening," he promised and knew he'd best be prepared for it.

The phone chimed as the receiver hit the cradle and Detective Pete Mathers tossed the pencil on his desk, then raked his fingers through his hair.

"Still won't give up any information, huh?"

Mathers glanced at his partner. "What the hell do you think?" he snapped. "O'Keefe doesn't exist according to my investigation, never did, and Lloyds of London won't break confidence as to how they know him."

Dave Downing whistled softly. "Sounds like an important client paying that bill. What about Scotland Yard?"

"Won't touch it either. They don't consider a man without a past their top priority."

"What's with you and this O'Keefe? He seems like a nice enough guy. And you have nothing on him. He hasn't committed any crime." Dave poured himself a cup of coffee and settled into the desk chair directly opposite.

"I can't figure him out. He doesn't have a job record, tax returns, nothing. He's like—well, it's like he doesn't belong here. I don't know if it's the way he carries himself or the way he talks—"

"You talk funny and we haven't thrown you in jail." Mathers glared at his partner and Dave grinned, then chomped into a jelly doughnut, silently admitting O'Keefe did speak like King Arthur.

"I should have locked him up."

"For what? Defending his woman? You can't blame the guy. You were a nasty son of a bitch to Miss Hamilton."

"They're keeping something," Mathers said, ignoring the censure and studying his reports. "Something big. Renfrew's connected to O'Keefe. I feel it."

"She's also dead."

"Lost at sea," Mathers corrected with a glance up.

"That's as dead as it gets, considering she was lunch for some shark." Dave cringed, not liking the image one bit. Helluva way to die.

"Consider that our source isn't known for his reliability," he reminded. "Just a bit squeamish." His tone implied that he didn't believe the story.

"Two sources. The *Nassau Queen*'s ensign saw the shark drag her away, too, and when he notified the captain, she'd already vanished under water. Tess Renfrew hasn't turned up in the Bahamas or anywhere else, for that matter. And neither the U.S. Coast Guard off the Keys nor the Bahama Air Sea Rescue Association have found any remains." Dave paused for a bite, chewed and swallowed before continuing. "The judge will declare her dead, Pete, legally, as soon as the cruise line's investigators finish questioning the passengers. We don't have any reason to put all our effort into this case. No surviving relatives, no massive fortune to dole out. No motive," he stressed. "No connection. A suicide."

"Bullshit. A woman doesn't relax on a luxury liner, then decide to kill herself." Mathers steepled his fingers, staring blankly out the window. Dust motes marked the stream of sunlight splashing across his desk. "What pushed her to travel under Hamilton's name, use her credit cards, and leave that expensive Jaguar on the pier with keys in it?"

"Which was delivered back to her garage the next day," Dave reminded, then sighed. "Okay, say it wasn't suicide. You don't have a body, lack suspects, no mysterious drug fortune to make it interesting, and no jurisdiction. Renfrew disappeared off Caribbean shores. That's Bahama territory, and you know their pace. Slow and slower." Mathers's determined look made him press harder. "Hamilton's a recluse. Everyone knows it. Maybe she was trying to get away from the press and her friend helped. It's no big deal. They sure as hell don't look enough alike to fool anyone. Renfrew never claimed to *be* Penelope Hamilton and the credit slips say she only purchased essentials, not spend the woman into debt. And she had Hamilton's permission."

"I read the report too, you know."

"You're digging in an empty grave, Pete." There was a long pause before Dave said, "People do a lot of strange things to get close to that particular actress."

Mathers arched his brow. "Threaten to carve her up like a melon? Shoot her lover in plain sight of everyone?"

Dave shrugged, giving him that much.

"Renfrew didn't jump either. At least not willingly."

Dave's hand paused, the cup halfway to his lips. "You think someone pushed her?"

Mathers smiled, nodding. He was coming around. "It would explain why one of Phalon Rothmere's boys was on that cruise liner, close enough to *see* her jump, yet didn't alert anyone until she was carried away. It doesn't wash."

Dave whistled softly, his chair creaking as he leaned back. "That's a helluva accusation." His voice was barely a murmur, his gaze darting beyond the glass walls for eavesdroppers. Suddenly he leaned forward, arms braced on the desk. "You better have evidence carved like the commandments before you breathe a word of this to anyone."

Mathers knew if he opened his mouth, it could cost him his job. "If you've got a better theory, pal, I'm open."

"His boy hasn't made bail yet." Dave grinned. "Want to borrow my rubber hose to test this theory?"

Mathers chuckled as the door opened and a young blond officer entered the office, shutting the door behind him.

"Give it to me quick and shit-can the fluff."

Dave frowned between the two men as the rookie flipped his pad and read aloud.

"Since Tanner dropped him off, he's been all over the city. Buying merchandise, paying with cash and having it delivered to the Hamilton estate. He was in the hall of records, archives, two museums, a library and checked out two modest apartments. Oh, and the newspaper morgue and a sport gun shop."

Mathers lifted his gaze to his partner, as if to say; *nothing to this, huh?*

"Did he talk to anyone?"

"No, sir, except the clerks and guides at each establishment."

Mathers toyed with his pencil. "Did he try to buy a gun?"

"No, sir, just looked them over. Like he was curious, nothing more. Didn't even ask to use the range in the sports mall." The cop examined his list. "He purchased a dictionary, several books on military sea power, strategy, and war history, clothes, wallet, watch, calculator, pens, binoculars, sheet music, had a diamond appraised—"

"A diamond?" Mathers interrupted.

The rookie looked up, straight blond hair falling over his brow. "Yes, sir. A single pear-shaped, deep pink. About five carats and very rare. Appraised three separate times."

"How much was it worth?"

"You wouldn't believe it, detective."

"Put it in the report," Pete muttered, waving in dismissal and the rookie left.

The instant the door closed Dave rounded on his partner. "I can't believe you put a tail on him! He's done nothing and you're wasting good manpower. God damn it, Pete, this is getting personal."

Mathers relaxed back into his chair. "A B & E and assault yesterday, and now O'Keefe, who was dragged out of the ocean days ago with nothing but his clothes, now has a diamond worth at least a half a mill. What do you figure I got, Dave?"

Dave told him. "Nothing. My gut says O'Keefe isn't that kind of guy. And Lloyds of London delivered a package to him yesterday. The diamond could have been in it." Mather's stared back benignly and it incensed him. "Did you know he rescued a little girl the other day? Climbed nearly fifty feet up a tree. Didn't stop to think just—" Dan thumbed the air— "less than a day after he was fished out of the water, clinically *dead* at the time. B.A.S.R.A. captain said he didn't even know who Miss Hamilton was. I figure either O'Keefe can't remember who he really is, or . . ." Dave finished off the dregs of his coffee, forcing Mathers to wait. "He was stranded on one of those uninhabited islands for a very long time. Maybe made a boat and it sunk." Dave shrugged. "All I know is you're looking in the wrong backyard and unless you want that high powered, highly *visible* attorney shoving court restraining orders up your ass, I'd back off."

"All right, all right. I get the picture. Christ, you make O'Keefe sound like a fucking saint." Mathers admitted he hadn't considered those possibilities. He'd attended the same high school as Tess Renfrew, though no one in his department knew, and he vividly remembered the energetic gymnast. For the sake of a teenage crush he was going to find out why she took a dive off a moving luxury liner.

"You're just jealous," Dave said. " 'Cause O'Keefe's got the woman every man wants—at least once, and you'd give your left nut to trade places."

"The right," he said, then reconsidered. "Nah." He shook his head. "Can't see waiting for the ice to thaw in that woman."

"You just don't have what it takes to—"

"Shut up, Dave," Mathers cut in harshly, his masculinity bruised enough. "Before I add ventilation to your forehead." He stood, arranging his reports and closing the file. "I'll leave O'Keefe alone, for now. But we still have to give the judge what he wants. Come on, grab your rubber hose." He slipped into his jacket, stuffing his gun in the shoulder holster. "Let's find out what Rothmere had to do with Tess Renfrew's death."

"*If* he had anything to do with it," Dave countered.

"*What.*"

"If." His partner opened his mouth to speak and Dave put up a hand. "I give up."

"That's the idea."

"She singing?" Hank asked from behind Margaret, his ear tuned to the soft melody drifting from the back porch.

"Yeah, all day. He's under her skin," she said quietly as he reached around her to steal a bite of fruit.

"Like me to you, ain't it, honey?"

"Go on with you, old man." She playfully nudged him aside, then sighed as he pressed his lips to the back of her neck. She turned into his embrace and kissed him with the passion of a young girl, his weathered hands smoothing over her round hips and up her back.

"Got an hour til I'm to pick up Ramsey." Hank wiggled his busy brows and smiled.

She shoved a piece of pineapple into his mouth before he could kiss her again. "Randy old goat."

"Uh-huh," he said around the food, giving her a hungry look that spoke volumes. He loved her and wondered when she'd ever let him tell Penelope about it.

Margaret recognized his expression. "No, we can't. Maybe soon though," she consoled when he scowled and stepped back. "Ramsey's in her life now and I don't want to desert her."

"You wouldn't have to," he replied. "Told you I'd agree

to stayin' on, but I've loved you for years, Meg, and I want to marry you.''

Her heart dipped. He said it often and always with every ounce of emotion he possessed. ''You know what I mean. Mister Wainright, me, you, we're all she's got now.''

''Enough for some folk,'' he muttered sourly. ''Look at Ramsey.''

''Where is he, anyway?''

He made a face at the change of subject. ''Hell, if I know. Dropped him off in the middle of town. Didn't want any company. Said he'd call.'' The singing stopped and the glass door slid open.

''Paper come yet?'' Penny poked her head inside.

''No. Sorry dear.'' Margaret raised a brow at the girl's attire, the gold Tarzan style bikini revealing more than it hid. That wasn't like her. She usually wore a simple tank suit with more coverage and slipped on a wrap the minute she was out of the water. ''I didn't hear you in the pool?'' Margaret went to a closet off the kitchen and brought back a stack of brightly printed towels.

Penny accepted the pile, yet didn't dry off. ''Let me know when—'' she hesitated—''when the paper arrives.'' She turned away, humming as she tossed the towels aside and dove into the pool.

Margaret smiled. ''She hasn't swam in there since—''

''Since Tess was here last,'' Hank cut in. ''She was the outdoorsy one.'' He frowned at Margaret. ''Why didn't you tell her the paper came?''

Margaret glanced out the glass doors, then covertly pulled it out of the trash, handing it to him.

''Believe me, the longer we keep this from her, the happier we'll all be.''

Hank turned his back to the glass door and unfolded the paper, shaking the damp coffee grounds into the sink. ''Damn sakes, she's gonna have a fit!''

Chapter 26

Coward.

Was Tess the only soul privileged enough to garner a space in your heart?

Did she go to her death because of a friendship she thought she had with you?

Harsh words to swallow. And they'd brought her before the trunk already twice today, and she'd gone so far as to remove three of the wax seals. Her bikini dripped water on the plush carpet of her bedroom as she fumbled with the beach towel, absently wrapping it around her waist, her stare on the mysterious box. The ribbon dangled from her fingertips, the key spinning, demanding she open the sea chest locked for over a hundred years. Rubbing her nose with the back of her wrist, she knelt and in quick motions, inserted the key, twisted and flipped the latch.

She held onto the sloping edge, hesitating. Then as if someone gave her a nudge, she quickly ran her thumbnail beneath the last wax seal, prying it off. With a deep breath she forced the lid upward a crack; the dankness of age immediately hit her nostrils, musty, dry.

Quit stalling and do it.

She shoved back the top, its leather hinge-straps creaking ominously before it thumped open. She gripped the lip of the trunk, her lungs pumping.

Oh God.

On the top of the disjointed pile was Tess's gaudy neon yellow gym bag, water stained, yet still as bright as when she last saw it. Just over a week ago. She reached, her hand trembling as she grasped the satchel and brought it to her chest. Penny closed her eyes, fighting the hot rush of tears, the renewed slap of guilt. *Oh God, bud, what did I do to you? How could Tess's property be in this trunk?* It was physically impossible. It should have washed up on shore somewhere. Loosening her grip and willing herself to relax or they'd find her frozen like this tomorrow, Penny sniffled, setting the bag almost reverently aside. She stared down into the trunk.

It was not filled as she'd imagined, then considered she never envisioned anything quite so—normal; thin balsa boxes in various sizes tied with ribbon, a tapestry covered book. Nearly everything else was bound in discolored tissue or muslin. Cautiously, she lifted out the largest box, freeing the still bright ribbon and removing the lid. She inhaled sharply, gently shaking out the lavish gown.

Dark blue watered silk rustled across her lap, surprisingly crisp and vivid, the fitted boned bodice studded with seed pearls and tiny crystals. It was breathtaking, the style old, just prior to the turn of the eighteenth century, if she hazard a guess; puffed sleeves narrowing to deep funnels at the elbow, a deep pointed waist tucking yards of billowy silk, the underskirting drawn with blue silk ribbon. The bottom of the box was filled with matching blue petticoats, delicate slippers, and a dainty little tulip shaped bag. *Feminine decadence,* Penny thought, shaking her head. *And what purpose did it serve to store this for so many years?*

Cautiously she folded it back into the box. That's when she saw the note hidden beneath the petticoats. Parchment? She tilted the thick yellowed paper toward the sunlight and her heart slammed against the wall of her chest.

Penn,
I've never had enough money to give anything really
special and when I saw this fabric I immediately thought
of you. Designed it myself, and I hope you'll give yourself
the chance to wear it someday. Maybe to that premier
gala next month?

Love,
Tess.

Penelope's gaze darted between the trunk, the dress, the note, and around again.

"Tess," she whispered and her sanity slipped another notch, the paper crunching in her grip. She grabbed the tapestry bound book and flipped it open. Tess's writing! The author instructed her to make certain she was reading the first book. After rummaging the trunk she discovered several more books, each numbered sequentially—each addressing her.

I can only imagine what you're experiencing now, the
confusion, grief and wonder. Don't grieve for me, Penn,
please. I'm fine and I'll try to explain as clearly as possi-
ble, so sit back, bud, 'cause it's a long story and tough
to swallow. I'll start from when we last spoke. I left on
the cruise liner and sailed to the Bahamas. I didn't stay,
knowing you'd be waiting to hear from me and was
on my way back when Rothmere's goons found me. I'd
honestly thought I'd slipped past their Radar. Arrogant
of me, huh? They were on the Nassau Queen, *dressed*
like waiters and pointing a gun with a silencer—at me.
Before they could pull the trigger, I jumped, or rather a
damn good ten point back flip, if you're keeping score.
The ship's propellers pulled me toward the blades and I
swear, Penn, I thought I'd bit the big one. I was drowning.
God, what a helpless feeling. Then I saw a dark fin. I
went ballistic, making my lungs fill faster, then suddenly
I was yanked to the surface and carried away by a dol-
phin. The strap of my Kmart special was caught in his

mouth and all I can say is, the big Kahoona was watching out for me, girl friend.

I hadn't scraped up what was left of my sanity when I realized the dolphin, [I named him Richmond] was pulling me AWAY from the ship. It hardly mattered, since Rothmere's gorillas stood on the deck, waving cheerfully, the bastards, and unfortunately over the deck festivities, no one noticed I'd jumped.

I was alone in the Caribbean waters, very aware that it might be days before I was rescued. Bummer, eh?

Now here comes the tough part.

I saw this black wall of mist. Jesus, this thing was alive, pulsing and swirling. Black as sin. Lightning flashed across the wall, and I could hear a storm on the other side. I know it's hard to understand, let alone believe, but I've never lied to you, Penn. This curtain reached up into infinity and it sure as hell wasn't there before I jumped. The dolphin dragged me toward it and no matter how much I pleaded or wiggled or fought, he and the current took me closer. I felt raunchy then, light-headed, my legs heavy, and I thought I'd lose my lunch any second. Then I was out cold, I guess. Hell, I don't know. I recall only bits and pieces of the next hours, but being tossed around in a storm and baking in the Caribbean sun did not make Tess a happy camper. Until I was rescued.

Penny reread the paragraphs, uncertain and totally confused. Then she closed her eyes and thanked God. She'd been saved. Alive! Staring at the trunk, she frowned. But then—how could her things be inside a two hundred-year-old trunk? And if she was rescued why the *hell* hadn't she contacted her? Frantically, Penelope read on.

I was saved from ending up as shark fodder by the captain of, get this, a twenty-four gun frigate. Honest. Just like in the old movies and the pictures in my Dad's office! I assumed the captain was just an eccentric playing out a pirate fantasy in his imaginary 1789. You know the type, money to burn and time to waste. So I played along. Nothing else I could do. Didn't hurt that they were damn good at it either. And no amount of reference to modern inventions would sway these guys from the game. You know those reenactor types, sticklers for detail? Well, this ship was incredible, authentic all the way down to the one hundred eighty man crew. Did I mention these guys did not take kindly to their captain bringing a woman aboard? But I'm getting ahead of myself. It wasn't until they were preparing for a mock battle that I got a feeling there was more to the hand-stitched clothes and the pattern of speech than just a game.

Because when it happened, the war was real. Christ Penn, a man chopped off another's hand right in front of me, then shoved a sword blade all the way through his chest! I puked my guts out. [I'll admit that only to you, bud] But the fire, the screams, the death, everything was terrifyingly real.

I pushed it out of my mind until the battle was over [survival was my biggest concern] and while I was helping the wounded, the crew talked of a black curtain of mist. Their description matched what I saw, except they saw a white ghost ship beyond the mist, sighted first in one direction, then seconds later in another.

The white ship was the Nassau Queen. *And the black wall was a rip in the fabric of time.*

Penny blinked and reread the lines again and again, then looked up, staring at nothing. Can't be true. A hole in the fabric of the universe that took you physically to another dimension, another century? That was only theory, nothing tangible ever proven, and a nervous laugh staggered in her throat.

But it's Tess's writing, Tess's words, Tess's affectionate "bud."

I know what you're thinking. Good ole Tess has water on the brain or something. I'm no rocket scientist, but I

*believe I was in that ocean, at that precise moment,
because I hesitated in Rothmere's office and got caught.
If I'd gotten away clean, I wouldn't have run and ended
up in the water in the first place. Hell, I can't explain
the unexplainable. But trust me, Penn, it did happen. I'm
living in 1789. And I love it.*

Penny settled back against the trunk and read swiftly, flipping
page after page, learning the events that unfolded after Tess
made her discovery, her determination to prove to the captain
that she'd traveled through time *without* using the contents of
her duffle, which would have made it easy. Tess wanted him
to believe *in* her before he believed her story. How like Tess
to go the hard way, Penny thought, then learned Tess had fallen
in love. And she married!

Penny sat upright.

Married Captain Dane Alexander Blackwell! Tess Renfrew
Blackwell! Anxiously, Penny thumbed through the other books,
briefly scanning the pages. Diaries of Tess's life. Her mind
fogged with all the thoughts and images Tess created for her.
The writings spanned nearly fifty years and she couldn't bring
herself to read the last entries. Her heart thumped up to her
throat. Swift air bellowed her lungs. Not possible, a logical
side shouted. Not real. Yet as her gaze swept the debris, within
the layers of papers she saw a water-stained photo. Cautiously
she slipped it free, a tender smile curving her lips. The Sergeant
Major and Lil. Tess's adoptive parents. Her fingers tightened,
paper crackling. This is the same photo Tess took just before
she left, Penny remembered, when Rothmere's men were just
outside her apartment.

Shaky fingers soothed her temples.

*Tess has done this for me. So I wouldn't wonder, grieve . . .
hope.*

And it meant she was really gone.

A convulsive scream boiled in the back of her throat and
she swallowed it down. God, Penny thought. Time travel. Two
hundred years. She didn't want to believe it, though the evidence
said otherwise. *The evidence is damned overwhelming,* a voice

in her brain shouted and her gaze dropped to the diaries. One lay open to a page she hadn't read yet, and without touching the book, she read of the birth of Tess's first child. Her heart immediately swelled with joy. A baby.

Childbirth is the pits, the pain indescribable, not to mention the inadequacies of this century. But I'd do it all over again after holding our precious son in my arms. He's beautiful and healthy, Penn. And Dane and I have named him for a dear friend. I suppose now that I'm confined to a bed [Dane's insistence] with nothing to do, I should tell you about our son's namesake, Ramsey.

The blood froze in her veins and she snatched up the book. She swallowed; moistened her lips. Can't be him. It can't be. She straightened, reading quickly.

The wall of time returned and wanted a soul, Tess wrote. *The sick feeling came again, like a calling card. No one else experienced the sensations but me. And Ramsey. An he let it take him.*

Because of Ramsey's sacrifice, I am here with the man I adore, enjoying a life I've dreamed of—the kind we fantasized about when we were lonely kids, Penn. Ramsey gave up everything he knew and loved for me and to this day the memory of him being sucked through the wall, breaks my heart. I'll never know if he's alive, where he went, for he passed through to the unknown, so I could stay with Dane. Ramsey lives for the next adventure, a real playboy, but I don't think he was ready for whatever was on the other side of that wall. If there's a chance in hell you come across Ramsey Malachai Gamaliel O'Keefe, be nice, and don't tease him about those ridiculous middle names.

She lifted her gaze from the book, staring at nothing. The journal tumbled from her lax grip. He passed through a wall over the ocean. It would certainly explain why they hadn't found Tess's body.

And found Ramsey instead.

Her thoughts pressed in on her with a crushing force, the day they rescued him replaying with amazing clarity; the sudden instantaneous loss of sunlight she thought she *imagined*, the way he was dressed, the weapons, his ignorance of anything remotely modern; how adored and comfortable he made her feel.

And that he'd lied to her.

His deep voice cut into her thoughts, sounding distant as he called her name, and she left the room running, tripping over the length of towel and nearly falling down the stairs.

He passed through into the unknown.

Heading toward the sound of voices, she felt dizzy and chilled, and bumped against the doorjamb leading to the kitchen, knocking over the trash can.

Absently she bent to right it, stuffing the garbage back in. Her hand paused halfway to the can, her gaze glued to the wet newspaper, the headline of the entertainment section, stained brown and crumbled. She straightened slowly.

Ice Queen of Hollywood melts for Captain Hook.

Beneath it was a grainy photo of herself dragging Ramsey toward the rented car, a second photo of them inside the Jaguar, beside the first.

Her blood thummed in her ears, her body going hot with outrage. Damn you, Max. The cut line read: *"Actress Penelope Hamilton whisks her mysterious beau from the paparazzi."* The article began with: "While in search of her missing friend, gymnast Tess Renfrew, Oscar winning actress Penelope Hamilton aided a man's escape from a Bahama hospital last Tuesday. Authorities refused to release the man's identity, yet sources report that Miss Hamilton first encountered the man earlier that afternoon near Crooked Island. Is her self-enforced seclusion over? Is this the man to do it? Or is *he* connected to the disappearance of gymnast Tess Renfrew?"

The article, a glorified gossip column, went on to speculate further, then mentioned her recent interview and the upcoming premiere of her latest film.

"Great Neptune's balls!"

Penny's head snapped up, the color draining from her face. Ramsey didn't notice. He was too busy devouring the ripe curves scarcely concealed beneath tattered gold fabric.

"For the love of God, woman!" he choked, glancing toward the patio, then back to her as he stepped inside, pulling the glass door closed. "Put some bleedin' clothes on!" Crossing the room, he stripped off his shirt as he went, then draped it over her shoulders. Good God, she was trembling! He rubbed her arms, thinking so scant her attire, that she must be chilled. She wasn't.

Penny stared, scarcely breathing. He'd lied to her. And kept lying. Even after making love, he'd kept on hiding the truth. Oh God, she thought, her body quaking. Was last night just another adventure for him?

Suddenly she shrugged off his touch, tossing the garment at him.

Frowning, he caught it. "What ails you, love?" Her cool look made Ramsey refrain from touching her again.

She glanced at the newspaper, envisioning the unwanted notariety that article would do to her life. Because of him. Because she let him in and allowed herself to be vulnerable to his chivalrous charm.

"This is your fault." She offered the paper.

Ramsey scarcely gave the article a glance. "I beg your pardon?" A chill crackled up his spine. Where was the warm woman he'd left this morn?"

"If you hadn't come into my life, your face wouldn't be plastered all over the papers and connected with mine." If he hadn't, you wouldn't know what it was like to be a woman again, a voice countered, and Penny slapped another brick on the wall sealing in her twisted emotions.

"What is—is, Penelope," he said with forced clam, not mentioning the invitation was hers. Anthony said she would be in a fit, but this was ridiculous. " 'Tis a matter that cannot be retracted now."

"True, but I can stop any more of this crap from being printed." She saw nothing beyond the danger he represented, and she wanted her privacy back, the warm blanket shielding her from feeling *so much*. Guilt and hurt raged through her, all she discovered pounding painfully in her brain; the trunk, Tess, Ramsey and his lies, the awful feeling of betrayal . . . she couldn't deal with the onslaught, not all at once and needed time to sort it out. Alone.

"I want you out of this house, Ramsey. Today."

Ram folded his arms over his chest, bare muscle flexing as he met her freezing stare and gave her a long slow study.

He felt a wealth of emotions, not the least of which was embarrassment and shame. He'd never been so rude a guest as to be asked to leave.

"Nay. I will not."

"Then I'll call the police and have you bodily removed."

"I don't believe I'm hearing this!" Neither pulled their gaze to the couple standing in the doorway. "Penelope! How can you do this?"

Penny slanted Hank a hard look. "See that *Mister* O'Keefe is off this property by this evening."

"Nay, thinks I," Ram said softly, though there was no question in his tone. " 'Twould force me to break my word."

"To who?"

"The Welshman. I have sworn to remain until he returns."

"From where?"

Ram shrugged insolently and her eyes narrowed to slits.

"What did you promise Tony?"

"My protection."

"For me?" She scoffed meanly. "I don't need it."

"You are certain?" He reached out, touching a finger to the cut left by her assailants. She jerked back, glaring at him with those devastating green eyes. Ramsey had never broken a bond promise afore and would not allow her or the ravings of some journalist to provoke him to such a dishonorable act. "By all manners then, call the constabulary. For I will remain—" his voice hardened—"at any cost."

She took a step closer and hissed in a low tone, "I swear if you do not leave I will tell the press, the cops, and the justice department, where you really came from.''

Bloody hell! She's opened the trunk, Ram realized, and Tess has mentioned me by name. ''And where might that be, Penelope?'' The corner of his mouth quirked cynically.

''You know perfectly well where.'' Her composure trembled and he leaned down, nearly nose to nose.

''Ahh, but do *you?*'' He arched a deep russet brow, the menacing look daring her to speak her thoughts aloud.

She was cornered. Not a soul on this planet would believe her. And what will you tell them? Tess traveled back in time and this man in front of you is her exchange student? They'd throw her in the nearest padded cell.

''There's the old carriage house, Capt'n?'' Hank suggested hastily, feeling the tension between the pair. Behind his back he clutched Margaret's hand.

''It's not fancy,'' Margaret offered. ''Needs a lot of cleaning, but—''

''Fine. Good,'' Penny cut in, grasping straws. ''Stay there, as long as it's away fr—''

''Enough!'' he exploded, posture stiff. ''I cannot offer protection from a league away!'' His gaze, dark amber edged with tempered fury, stung like a slap. ''Make no attempt to force my hand, Penelope,'' he warned in a threatening hush, his presence filling the room and her senses. ''For I will gladly bind you to that frilly bed if need be.''

She choked on her indignation. ''You just try and—what are you doing?''

Reaching into his back pocket, he pulled out a wallet, the scent of new leather wafting to her as he pried it open and without taking his eyes from her, withdrew several crisp one hundred dollar bills. ''Me lodgings are paid, *Mistress Hamilton,*'' came in a bitter rasp. He tossed the currency on the counter, his tone gone snide. ''Satisfaction should your *public* inquire.''

The silence lengthened, the air conditioned breeze spreading the money across the tiled surface. A heaviness hung atween them, a hard unchangeable energy circling, drawing the focus down to a single stare. Ramsey didn't know whether to shake her or hold her til it passed.

Ask me, his eyes begged of her. Ask and I will gladly ease your confusion. Yet when she said naught, Ramsey felt the bridge atween them crumble, and he bowed, formal and mocking, then quit the room.

Penny's gaze followed him. *Ramsey gave up everything he knew and loved for me,* Tess wrote. *Because of his sacrifice I'm enjoying the life I've dreamed about.*

Suddenly she rushed from the kitchen, sliding across the mosaic foyer and rounding the staircase to see him pushing his arms into his shirt sleeves, his ascension determined and angry-loud.

"Ramsey." She took the stairs two at a time. "Ramsey!"

Ram halted beyond the landing, yet didn't turn to look at her. From her rooms to his left, the uncapped sea chest blared at him like Triton's trumpet and Penny approached slowly, the flex of his shoulders cautioning her.

"No one out there—" she flicked her hand behind her— "has reason to hurt me." Implying he did.

He spun about so fast she nearly fell back down the steps. "Sweet Jesus, woman," he said in a raw voice, catching her shoulders. *"I* am not thy enemy!"

"But you lied to me!" she cried and his features yanked taut.

"Nay! *Never* have I spoken an untruth to you! You chose not to see!"

God, he was right, but . . . "what are you?"

It was the wrong thing to say and his pained look struck her square in the chest. He straightened slowly, lowering his hands to his sides.

"Oh God. I—I didn't mean it like that. I—"

"What I am," he cut in savagely, "is a man. And after last eve, I do not believe 'tis under question." He gave her that arrogant half-lidded stare she loathed. " 'Tis the whence I've come you cannot abide."

Her gaze searched his. "I don't want to believe this," came in a broken whisper.

His expression darkened as he grasped her wrist and yanked her into her room, forcing her to look at the open trunk.

"Tell me now you cannot believe!"

Penny stared at the bright-yellow satchel, the photo of Tess's parents, Tess's small neat handwriting marking the journals.

She moistened her lips. "You knew her, didn't you?" The fractured words tore from her throat.

"Knew her?" He scoffed bitterly. "I fancied myself in love with her."

Penny sucked in a sharp breath, snapping a look at him, but he was gone.

Chapter 27

Ramsey paced the study, a bottle of twenty-year-old whiskey fisted in his grip, his heavy footfalls muffled by the plush carpet. He paused and tipped the bottle to his lips, his Adam's apple bobbing as he drank, the dark gold liquor sliding smoothly down his throat. The spirits were more refined than he was accustomed to and he consumed nearly a third of the bottle afore he realized it. 'Twas no matter, he thought, swiping his lips with the back of his hand. He'd no one to visit upon him this night. Raking his fingers through his unbound hair, he strode to the desk and snatched up Dane's letter, skimming it, longing to speak with his friend, then tossing it aside.

Ram cursed Dane for finding Tess first, then cursed the sharp tongued female, for what e'ere Tess wrote, ruined what he'd just begun to understand.

Then Ram cursed the stubborn redhead with a heart of stone and a passion of ten women.

He felt damned alone, as if he'd lost his best friend. And he'd been in the study for hours, brooding like a temperamental child, feeling twisted and confused . . . and humiliated. Blast and hell, he thought, taking a long pull from the bottle, then resuming his pacing. After all her stalling why did she not wait for him to open the trunk? And what had Tess written about him in those books? *Likely yer worthless past,* he considered, then groaned, imagining what Penelope thought of him now. Not much a'tall, man, if she told you to leave her house, her life. And why, for the love of God, was she so bloody concerned over the speculations of a journalist? She was infamous. Was that not to be expected? Did Mathers not say people were interested in every aspect of her life?

He dropped into a chair, caught atween believing the woman was fickle as a tavern wench or that once she discovered who and *what* he was—[dear God, but that drove a spike through his chest just to remember her distaste] she wanted no such oddity near her precious career. Why else embarrass him with demanding he leave? That stung, Ram admitted, rubbing his chest as if to soothe the ache.

Ramsey'd never experienced aught like this afore. 'Twas far different than losing his family or a shipmate. And a horrible riddling sensation tore through his bloodstream every time he thought of how quickly everything had changed, how much he stood to lose. The receptive woman in his arms the night afore was gone, hidden beneath a layer of indifference. 'Twas understandable, for discovering her lover was a time-traveler had to be no less than a shock. But to simply not ask him? He took another pull of liquor. He wanted to go to her, to demand she cease this charade, but pride bade him keep his distance.

And his parting words to her were bitter jabs he'd have to soothe.

For all his years of experience with women, he didn't know where the bloody hell to begin.

For his heart was no longer his.

Her lover was a time traveler from the eighteenth century, Penny thought, hugging a pillow and staring at the open trunk.

My lover. Yet Ramsey had loved Tess. So much that he'd traveled through time so *she* could stay with the man she adored. How chivalrous. Was he so devastated by losing Tess to Dane that he couldn't be near her and leapt into the ocean? Had her rejection wounded him that deeply?

Despair swept her and she dropped back onto the bed, staring at the ceiling. God, what a disappointment that must have been, to find me instead of a life with Tess. Penny tried not to feel used, not to feel second best to her closest friend, but Tess's journals had told her more than she cared to know.

Ramsey was a playboy of the worst kind. A rakehell, his century named him. Spoiling for adventure, a good fight, a little pleasure, to ease the boredom.

Hedonistic charm and chauvinistic honor.

A privateer captain. A pirate for the cause.

God, he must have had a good laugh. But it was the markings of his century that attracted her to him, his inbred gallantry, the indescribable sense of cherishing her without ever knowing her. She could care less about his playboy past, for she didn't have any room to criticize, but it was the fact that he'd had several opportunities to tell her where he'd come from *and why* and didn't.

Right? Like you would have believed him?

She blinked.

If I'd fallen from the heavens into your world, would it matter? he said the night in the kitchen. And hadn't he promised to tell her this evening? Penny felt altogether foolish and contrite and didn't trust herself to go to him. Yet when she heard his deep voice belting out a lurid sea chanty she flew to the door, yanking it open as he thumped up the stairs.

He saw her, the song dying, and when she opened her mouth, he put up his hand. "Nay, do not speak to me, woman, for I've no taste for your wounding words this night."

"Well, you've certainly had a taste for something. You're drunk."

He blinked at her, swaying like a great oak. "A state I rushed to achieve, aye." His gaze traveled the length of her, the thin collarless shirt scarcely hiding her body from him. He tisked, shaking his head. " 'Tis a sad state of undress, lass. Careful." Wide eyed, his gaze searched the hall. "There could be a bit of your *public* about."

Penny fumed, any thoughts of offering the olive branch disintegrating.

"Good eve to you," he said with a slight stagger in his bow afore heading to his room. He grasped the knob like a lifeline, pressing his forehead to the wood.

"Twentieth century liquor too much for you?"

He caught her needling tone and cast her a half-lidded glare. "Do not concern yourself with a mere tenant, mistress, 'tis naught that a good retching won't cure." Ram pushed his way inside and as he shut the door, Penny realized because of her quick temper and insecurity, she'd lost him.

Flint-lock in hand, pan primed, Ramsey was off the bed and at the chamber door afore he realized he was naked and quickly snatched up the bedsheet, wrapping it around his waist. Abruptly he threw open the door, aiming at the metal contraption roaring in the center of the hall, the noise competing with the one atween his ears. He blinked, his bleary gaze focusing on the molded block with a pole protruding from its spine, its lungs puffed up like an angry child holding its breath in threat. Sweet Jesus, 'twas bloody loud, the teeth grinding roar grating on his last nerve and he jabbed the beast with the barrel, praying 'twould cease and he could sleep off this hangover in blessed silence. But his jolting merely tottered it to its side, the growl increasing in volume and snapping Ramsey's patience.

He leveled the gun and fired.

It exploded in a puff of gray smoke, whining to a slow death and as the mist filled air dissipated, Ramsey noticed Meggie standing on the landing, her hair and face dusted with a fine muddy powder. She looked from him to the gun, then to the whimpering contraption, then sent him a disgusted look, her hands on her hips.

"Well," the housekeeper snipped. "Aren't *we* crabby this morning." Then she marched over to the wall and yanked the vacuum cord from the circuit. The whine ceased and Ramsey shrugged, looking sheepish and guilty as he turned back into his room, hitching the drooping sheet over his bare buttocks.

'Twas the soft laughter that stopped him and slowly he turned, finding Penelope just inside her doorway, a sadistic almost triumphant smirk on her lovely lips. His gaze rolled slowly over her, his expression as bland as he could summon afore he turned back into his chamber and closed the door. He leaned back against the frame, his head throbbing mercilessly. *You be deservin' of it.* Wallowing in self-pity in the bottom of a bottle did naught to change the situation. His gaze dropped to the open leather chest, the diamond glistening from the dark velvet, and he pushed away from the wall. He'd a promise to keep and prayed that time in the rain chamber would ease the pain in his head, for he needed his wits about him. If anything, to keep from going to Penelope and foolishly confessing his heart.

His professional attitude always impressed Ramsey.

"She's sold jewelry, a few numbered prints and two of her four cars. There hasn't been a deposit in her account in over two weeks, which usually was steady twenty-five grand a month. Daddy's money," the dark haired man said, reading from a list. He paused to sip from the beer Ramsey placed before him.

"Your assumptions?" Ramsey asked, propping his feet on the low table and relaxing back into the stuffed chair. Ahh, the luxuries of this century, he thought, the cushions bracing his body perfectly.

"She's been cut off from the Rothmere money. And to keep up her lifestyle, she has to sell a few baubles." At Ramsey's arched brow, Noal Walker added, "She's gotten herself into one hell of a jam and Phalon Rothmere isn't helping her this time. I don't know why." He shrugged. "He always has before. And no, I don't know what she's done."

"What say you of the crimes she has committed 'afore?"

Noal was getting used to O'Keefe's manner of speech. "Not crimes exactly. Well, she sent his yacht into a pier during a drunken party, her lover was arrested for insider trading—" Ram nodded even though he didn't know what the bleedin' hell that was. "His money kept it out of the papers." Noal braced his forearms on his knees. "Regardless, Captain O'Keefe, it hasn't affected her lifestyle, at least she hasn't let it, yet. She's at Derringer's nearly every night with a crowd."

"Have you met the lass?"

Noal sank back into the cushion and laughed shortly. "No-ho, she's too rich for my blood."

Ramsey smiled, despite the odd tinge of bitterness he caught in Noal's tone. 'Twas decadent wealth then, for Noal Walker had a bleedin' corps of detectives working for him. He'd resources Ramsey couldn't begin to understand, and though Ram attempted for two days to find the information himself, his ignorance of this century's advances and lack of time to learn, drew as much attention as did his manner and speech. Neither were aught he could rectify and at all costs, his journey through time must be kept secret. And potential for repercussions on Penelope was a risk he refused to take. He needed assistance and with Hank's help, found Noal by using the yellow phone book, calling each agency and slyly mentioning that their competitor offered more for his money. On each occasion, this man's agency was mentioned. His agency was the best this state had to offer, his sterling reputation stemming from efficiency, absolute discretion, and a low profile. And he garnered results.

"Have you naught else for my money, Mister Walker?"

Noal grinned. The man paid well, offered a bonus for quick work and came through each time. In cash.

"Rothmere's man, Owen, is still in jail, being held on a minor parole violation, but I think it's for his own protection. He's singing to the cops, if he's stupid as I think."

Ramsey stiffened in the chair. "Are you insinuating giving over the truth is not wise?"

"Who's to say it's the truth?" Noal spread his arms and shrugged. "He's in jail, Rothmere's out. Let me warn you, Captain. Rothmere's is a respected family in this town, and Phalon Rothmere's even bigger. Sloane causes him trouble all right, but it's more than any bad press reaching his doorstep. His name is clean."

"But?"

The man was too insightful for his own good, Noal thought with honest admiration. "I don't have proof, but I know he's got the ties and could have that man's throat slit with one phone call."

Ramsey swallowed that bit of news with bitter resignation.

This venture was becoming dangerous. Sloane was the one he needed to speak with, yet doubted she'd confess her crime of blackmail. But 'twas against Penelope and she'd involved Tess. Why be so vindictive? He wasn't about to discuss this with Walker, even though he trusted the man. Penelope's secretiveness was her choice. He would respect it, for as long as he could.

Was he wasting his time? Was the battle atween Rothmere and Blackwell dead after two hundred years? Ramsey thought not.

Noal stood and dropped a thick packet on the table. "My intel man says this is everything that's ever been printed about a Blackwell since the city started keeping records. Newspapers, certificates of birth and death, their shipping business, there's even a police report." Ramsey's brows shot up. "Read it and you might understand the circumstances, 'cause I sure as hell can't. A B & E with nothing stolen? In that house? Christ the doorknobs are worth a small fortune." He shook his head. "It's vague, too vague, if you get my drift."

Ramsey glanced at the broad packet. Was it about Tess? He didn't think a Rothmere would involve the constabulary if he had the power to go around it and the detective already told him unsolved cases were not public information.

Noal moved away, blue eyes staring out the living room window. "That other matter we discussed?"

"Aye?" Ramsey rose, his body suddenly tense.

"Nothing documented before twelve years ago."

Ram cursed under his breath, then stared intently at Noal's profile. "By God, how did you discover such so quickly?" Ramsey had asked only this morn.

"I've done this one before," Noal said lowly, bringing his gaze back to Ramsey, tempted to ask why he wanted this information, but ethics forbade it.

"For who?"

Noal's expression was unapproachable and without explanation he headed for the front door, yet when he paused to shake Ramsey's hand, he knew the man would not let the matter die.

"Are you aware there's a reporter hanging in a tree across the street with a long-range lens camera?"

"At least he has obeyed my wishes to stay off the property."

"He can't see anything from there," came from behind and both men turned as Penelope walked into the foyer. "Too many trees," she added, her gaze sharpening on the slender blond man beside Ramsey. "Noal?"

"Hello, Penelope." His appreciative gaze swept her as she moved closer. God, she looked good, all sleek and leggy in that snug little tank dress.

"It's been a while."

"Yeah, too long," he murmured, and her gaze shifted immediately to Ramsey, instantly suspicious. He met her stare unflinchingly, his expression bland despite the jealously slithering through him like a hot coil. 'Twas more than business they shared, if the way Noal was looking at her was any indication. Ramsey wanted to fire the man, but wisely kept his emotions under control.

Noal glanced at Ramsey, nodded, then returned his gaze to Penelope. "Take care, pixie," he said, then left.

Penelope sighed softly, almost dreamily, and Ram's control slipped. He shoved the door, the slam making her flinch.

He stared at her across the small foyer, the five foot separation feeling like miles.

She hadn't seen him in three days. No, she corrected, she hadn't been this close to him, but she'd seen him; learning to drive with Hank, swimming in the ocean off the end of the pier, planting scrubs with the gardener, but never speaking to her. And from the look on his face he wasn't pleased to see her now, as if he'd marked a line in the dirt, daring her to cross it. He lived here, but didn't live with her. Made love to her, but never loved her. And she was miserable, wishing he'd say something, yell, rant, do anything to break this horrible silence. But words wouldn't come.

For Ram was dying inside, his imagination running wild and his eyes thirsting for the sight of her. Dark fathomless brown eyes absorbed her lush curves enhanced by the black dress like a man starving. God, he would never grow accustomed to seeing women display so much unencumbered flesh in public, he thought, his arms throbbing to hold her, make peace with her. But his bruised pride and the encounter atween the detective clouded his mind and he grew hot with rage thinking they might have been lovers. Or had Noal worked for Penelope? He opened his mouth to speak, then snapped it shut, spinning on his heels and snatching the envelope off the low table, heading above stairs without a backward glance.

Penny watched him go, the urge to call him back hovering on her lips. But she didn't. His hurt was too fresh and she considered he might not want her, ever.

In his chamber, Ram slapped the parcel down onto the table and faced the window, focusing on the rushing sea and not on his anger. By God, he wanted to smash something and clenched his fist in an effort to restrain the urge. He drew in a full breath, then released it slowly. This jealousy would serve him naught. And he realized whate're was atween Noal and Penelope, she looked upon it with the fondness of a sweet memory, and had naught to do with the woman she was now. At least he hoped.

For that a simple look from her could bring him to his knees boded a sorry future if he were to lose her. Yet if she wanted him in her life, truly a part of it, enough to risk her heart to his tender care, she had to come to him.

'Tis a reeking fix you've made for yourself, he thought, then glanced at the fat white envelope. And spending the afternoon discovering how Dane's family had died off would not better his mood either. Resigned to a thoroughly ruined day, Ram dropped into a stuffed green chair and tore open the envelope, dumping the contents on the table. He read.

At least Noal was correct, Ram thought hours later after pouring through the stack of papers. The Rothmeres were the epitome of society, respected, sought for funding for museums and hospital wings. And Ram had to admire that Phalon was not at all like his ancestor. He was generous with his wealth as Dane and Grayson had been. His lips quirked. He wondered what Dane would think to know his personal effects were under glass in a museum. Even the ships logs Tess had deciphered were there. Outraged likely, for Dane was a private man. Ramsey pushed his fingers through his hair, dislodging the ribbon holding it back and he snapped it free, frustrated.

What Sloane used to blackmail Penelope was unimportant. Yet if Sloane's vendetta stretched for over ten years, had it reached the father, or had she gained this intense hatred from her sire? For other than purchasing the Blackwell house when the shipping business was about to declare bankruptcy, he could find no connection, incriminating or otherwise, atween the families afore twenty-five years. Afore Sloane Rothmere's birth.

Chapter 28

Anthony stood at the far end of the sundeck, gazing up at the roof. Bare chested and barefoot, Ramsey knelt on the gabeled ledge, replacing the scale style gray shingles, his hammer slamming with a power that rattled the windows. He worked with a vengeance, driving the nail home with one blow, and Anthony detected suppressed anger in his moves.

He waited til Ram paused to wipe the sweat from his forehead and drain a plastic bottle of water before he called to him. Ram glanced down and smiled, then immediately tossed the hammer aside and descended from the roof with surprising balance and agility for a man his size. He dropped to the deck with a thud, snatching up a towel and swiping at the sweat raining over his chest as he crossed to Antony.

Ram's gaze sketched his face, then he carefully grasped Antony's wrist, raising it, examining the bandaged fingers with a critical eye.

"You tucked your thumb inside," he judged, his lips tugging. "I pray your opponent suffered worse."

"He was facedown in the mud last I saw."

"You are too old to engage in fisticuffs, Antony." Ram noted with concern his swollen lip and blackened eye.

Anthony threw his shoulders back. "Hah, look who's talking. I'm only fifty."

Ram's eyebrows rose. In his time the man would be naught but decaying bones in a grave, but the Welshman looked no more than a half score older than himself.

"Where's Penelope?"

Ram inclined his head toward the sea behind him and Anthony looked past in time to see Penelope vanish along the shoreline near a strand of sea oats.

Penny slipped through a break in the shrubs and sea oats, wanting to escape, for no matter where she went, she felt Ramsey glaring holes in her back. And she simply couldn't stay inside anymore, the house suddenly too crowded with him in it and Margaret and Hank's disappointment showing in every pointedly delivered glance didn't help either. She regretted treating Ramsey so rudely, but she'd panicked. The newspaper, Tess's books, learning that he loved Tess and had actually traveled through time for her, was too much, yet now, with nothing else to think about, she wanted some answers. But Ramsey, well, he . . . he was being the perfect gentleman, was what he was doing.

It was as if he knew where she was at any given moment, for she would see his fading shadow or glimpse the edge of his shoe as he slipped off around a corner. Perhaps it was best they weren't near each other, for that man could push her buttons and make her feel every bit like a petulant child.

She bent to pick up a shell and felt the warmth of the hand a split second before it closed over her mouth. There wasn't time enough to scream as the man slapped his arm around her waist and slammed her back against his chest. His grip was smothering, her lungs working to draw back the startled air.

"You listening?"

Penny nodded best she could, terrified, her arms pinned to her sides. Dampness seeped into her clothes.

"I want the diamonds." She made a sound of protest and he jerked her tighter. "Don't even try it. I'll let you know when and where, but if you don't—'' he paused for effect, and it worked, her imagination running wild—''someone you love will pay.'' There were two of them, she realized as a gloved fist shot out in her line of vision, a delicate flower resting breathlessly in his palm before his fingers curled, crushing it nearly to liquid. Yeah, she got the message. Now if only she knew why they thought she'd have their *diamonds*.

Suddenly her captor released her, her freedom so abrupt she stumbled forward. Penny twisted around, but there was nothing there expect a strand of sea oats, their long slender reeds whispering toward the ocean. Her gaze shot around her, to the watery footprints in the sand and she headed in the opposite direction, toward the open shore line, then bolted toward the house.

Someone you love will pay.

Dear God. Margaret, Hank.

Ramsey.

She tore open the back porch door, running through the long butler's pantry. ''Margaret! Hank!''

Margaret stepped into the kitchen from the front of the house, dropping the laundry to catch her. ''For the love of Mike—''

''Are you all right? Are you!'' she demanded, breathless, shaking her when she didn't answer.

Margaret frowned. ''Sure, honey, sure.''

''Hank!'' Penny called.

''Here girl,'' he said, coming around the corner.

''Oh thank God!'' Penny stretched out one hand for him and he took it, recognizing her fear and wrapping his arms around both women. ''I thought you were hurt,'' she said, hugging the housekeeper, fighting sudden tears.

''We're fine, honey.'' Margaret patted her back like a lost child. ''We are.'' Margaret frowned at Hank and he shrugged. ''Now what happ—''

Ramsey burst into the house, Anthony at his heels and the group separated, Ram's gaze immediately lighting on the red hand print across Penelope's cheek and mouth.

His eyes darkened to near black, his body coiled tight. ''Are you harmed?'' he said in a chilling whisper.

She shook her head and even across the kitchen table she could sense him, his escalating fury, his quick breathing, the flex of muscle as he drew a plain black tee shirt over his head and chest while she told him what happened. And though Margaret, Hank, and Anthony were firing questions at her, Ramsey didn't so much as blink.

"Stay here." He pointed at her, then left the house.

"But they're gone," she tried to tell him, following. He ran across the beach, his head twisting and turning. A man approached, wearing cut-off jeans and a tank top and Ramsey towered over him, his biting tone recognizable even at the distance. Immediately they separated, searching for several tense moments before Ramsey called out.

Penny and Anthony came upon him bent over a prone body, gently helping a surfer sit up.

"I was so close and didn't see him," she said, numbly bending to pick up the flower her assailant crushed.

"I'll call the police," Anthony said.

"Nay!" Ram pressed a handkerchief to the man's bloody temple. "He works for me."

"I didn't hear him, Captain, sorry," the surfer said, reaching out to pluck a blood-stained rock from the sand. "Must have used a sling-shot to get me that far way."

"Ramsey." A frightened demand, and he twisted a look up at her, his gaze dropping briefly to the bruised yellow flower she offered.

"They are here to protect you, Penelope, for I cannot be everywhere."

Except with me, she thought as Cut-offs approached, speaking into a hand radio, looking around, then motioning to people she couldn't see. Then did. Four men and two women, dressed in an assortment of swim trunks, bikinis, and work clothes came from different points on the grounds. And they had guns.

"How long have they been here?"

"Nigh on a week. Noal selected them." He rose to his feet, ignoring Penelope as the bodyguards helped their own.

Anthony rubbed his sore jaw, his gaze shooting between Penelope, Ramsey, and the retreating guards. Ramsey knows something the rest of us don't, he thought as Penny caught Ramsey's arm, forcing him to look at her.

"You couldn't spare a minute to tell me," she said, her voice edged.

"You did not seem interested in the happenings of others, nor this household."

Her eyes narrowed to mere slits, the dig too close. "If I'd seen one of theses people lurking around the house and called the police, they could have been hurt and then we'd all look like fools."

"God forbid your public think you aught but a human being," he growled down at her and she lost her grip, her face flaming.

"Damn you, Ramsey," she hissed softly. "This is my property and—"

"Your house. I am well aware of that, but as you can see, 'twas necessary." A pause and then, "You promised not to leave the grounds."

"I needed to get away."

From you, she was saying. God did she despise him that much?

Her eyes widened suddenly and she closed the space between them. "You've known all along what they wanted."

His gaze drifted above her, still searching for intruders. "Since the attack last week, aye."

"How?"

"Tess." He brought his gaze back to hers. " 'Twas her theft that started this in the first place."

"No. I did."

He didn't comment, a muscle working in his jaw as he waited for her to confess, but she offered naught. "Speak naught of this to anyone," he ordered, then spun about and stalked to the house. Penny watched him go, too stunned to move.

Diamonds. That's what was in the packet. No wonder they chased Tess for so long. It's my fault. Oh God, does he know about the evidence, she wondered frantically, then traced his footsteps up the back porch and into the house.

Anthony limped along, and she slowed her pace, frowning as she held the back door for him.

"You look like you kissed the bumper of a semi."

"Took you long enough to notice."

Her expression turned affectionately contrite, enough to satisfy him, yet as she shoved her hair off her forehead, Anthony noticed the dark circles beneath her eyes. Whatever was going on, or rather *not* going on between her and Ramsey, was having a definite effect on her. The moment he arrived, Anthony felt the tension, as if he'd walked into a crystal room, everyone treading on tiptoe to keep the walls from shattering. That an attack on her didn't break it, told him Penny and Ramsey had a long way to go to get back to each other.

"What diamonds were they talking about, Penelope?"

"Evidently in the package Tess stole for me—"

"I warned you that was going to explode—"

"—had a little something extra," she said through gritted teeth, painfully aware of her mistakes coming back to haunt.

"Phalon did this," he indicated the attempt on her life. "Sloane isn't smart enough for the slickness of that assault."

She stopped and looked at him. "Don't put anything past her, Tony. She's had it in for Tess and me since college. Because of one lousy dinner date years ago, she thinks I ruined her chances with the love of her life."

His expression was doubtful. "A bit far for the woman scorned, don't you think?"

"Who knows how her mind works? He dumped her to date me."

He fanned his fingers beneath his bearded chin. "But it didn't last."

Nothing does with me, she thought, then said, "We both had our reasons, but I can't be held accountable for her insecurities. God, I wish she'd just grow up."

"Do you realize what this could do to your career," his voice was hushed, "if anyone discovers what Tess did for you and why?"

They'd know she was weak and worthless, without control, not to mention the spotless reputation she'd struggled for years to keep would be ruined. "I'm very aware of the consequences, Tony." She looked him in the eye. "And I don't care anymore." His features tightened. "It already cost me my best friend. I can't—no, I *refuse* to allow my problems to hurt Margaret or Hank . . . or Ramsey."

Anthony rubbed his beard, chin whiskers rasping and he was glad she finally had her priorities straight. At least he hoped.

"So, why did you slink off and not tell me where you were going?"

Subject dropped, Anthony thought, watching her move down the back hall toward the study.

"I was in the Philippines."

Penny paled and spun about. "Jesus, Tony! What the hell for?"

Ramsey poked his head out of the study, a dark scowl shaping his face and Anthony glanced cautiously between the couple.

He'd heard it all, Anthony thought, then nodded to the study. "Perhaps we should discuss this in private."

Ram stepped back, waiting til they passed afore shutting the door. Folding his arms over his chest, he leaned back against the wood, staring at Penelope with an uneasy mix of fury and longing.

"Why did you go there again?" Penny demanded the instant the door closed.

"For Ramsey."

Slowly Ram lowered his arms and straightened. "You were beaten to a pulp for me?"

"Hardly." Anthony smirked. "But you needed this." He dipped his hand inside his coat and withdrew a wide slip of paper.

Penny stared at it, and she was suddenly fifteeen again, needing a name, a birth date, a new life. "It's a birth certificate," Penny said without opening it. She turned her gaze to Ramsey. "It makes you legal, proof of who you are. And it's forged."

"What!"

"Of course it's forged. There isn't any record of you, Ram."

"So you took it upon yourself to invent one?" His face went molten with suppressed rage. "My God, man, you're a barrister.

'Tis breakin' the law! And by Jesus, I'll not have to prove who I am to anyone!''

"Yes, you will," Penny said, stepping between the men, facing Ramsey. "If you want a driver's license, a checking account, a house or do damn near anything."

"And Immigration is looking for you," Anthony put in. "The Bahama Air Sea and Rescue Association had to register your rescue *and* your lack of papers. There were two calls on my machine from an Agent Torres of the Justice Department. He's given us one week to supply him with proper documents or Immigration steps in. A copy if this—" he flicked the paper—"was sent to him by overnight express today."

"Damn you to hell, Welshman," came in a grating hush.

"Ramsey." Penny moved closer but he ignored her presence, his gaze on Anthony. "Tony risked his life for that. The Philippines, the area he had to go, is not the safest in the world." No effect, not even a flicker. "Look at him, for heaven's sake! And he called in a lot of favors to get that certificate slipped into a file somewhere."

Ramsey's features remained sharp and glacial, his gaze knifing the Welshman.

"Ramsey, look at me."

He did and her heart twisted; he looked as if he could eat glass. He was an honorable man, more than any she'd met before, and it hurt somewhere deep inside her to see him this torn. "There wasn't any other choice and you know it."

Ram lowered his gaze to hers, reason and logic racing through his brain. 'Twas true, but it soured in his mouth to live a lie. Finally his shoulders sagged and he accepted the certificate, smoothing his thumb over the raised seal of the state of Massachusetts. "At least you've aged me proper," he muttered and Penny and Anthony exchanged uneasy glances.

"There is another alternative," Anthony said and waited until Penny and Ram looked at him. "You two could get married."

"Forget it," Penny blurted and her doubtless answer felt like a blade pushed deep into Ram's soul.

"Aye, for I will fight to remain in me country." He looked

down at her, his hurt manifested in his harsh tone. "But I'll not spend me life with a chilling wench for wife."

"Especially when I'm not the one you want," she returned hotly.

A denial trembled on the edge of his tongue, but her rejection bit it back. " 'Tis no matter then. For Antony has returned and my promise is fulfilled. I shall be gone afore night fall." Ram bowed and turned to leave and Anthony saw panic strike across her face.

"As much as I *don't* want to get into this," Anthony said with enough volume to make Ram stop—"I do have a life and a string of clients who need pampering. I can't stay." Anthony looked at Penelope, his tone that of her lawyer. "Short of laying land mines on the beach, this house is vulnerable and if you do not let Ramsey see to your safety, then I'll call the studio and this place will be swarming with security within the hour."

"You wouldn't."

His look warned her not to press him. "They don't pay those outrageous insurance premiums for nothing, Penny. You're under contract, an asset, and until you finish your next picture, you belong to them."

Her lips thinned with distaste. "Stop treating me like I can't take care of myself. I have, for years, and you know better than anyone I've survived much worse without his—" she flicked a hand toward Ramsey—"protection."

Ramsey advanced on her, scowling like black thunder, stalking her until she backed up against the mantel. He reached passed her head, his hand coming back with a flower identical to the one her assailant had crushed. 'Twas sadistic satisfaction as her face drained of color and he arched a brow, waiting for her to comment on how easy one could gain access to her. No matter how many guns and men surrounded her. She brushed him aside, leaving her jailers alone, venting her embarrassment and anger by slamming the door.

Anthony whistled softly and smiled.

"That is the most stubborn hard-headed woman!" Ram hissed, his gaze on the door.

"Just finding that out?"

Ram scoffed, rubbing a hand over his face.

"By the way. I know who you are."

Ramsey stiffened, lowering his hand to look at Anthony. Apprehension slithered through him. "I should hope so, after all you've done on my behalf."

Anthony rested his hip on the edge of the desk. "You're from another time."

Rams's eyes flared, his body still as glass.

"I don't know how you got here, exactly, but I suspect it has to do with Tess and her *disappearance.*" When Ramsey looked as if he'd deny it, Anthony pressed. "You can't hide it, Ramsey, not from me, at least. You're marked by your time. And it's all too pat, you turning up in the Bahamas, the coins, the endowments from Lloyds, your initials on the chest. And that astrolabe. There hasn't been one discovered in such perfect condition in a hundred seventy-five years."

The two men stared across the opulent room.

A door closed somewhere.

"How long have you known?" Ram finally said.

Anthony let out a long breath, his face wreathed in a smile. "I suspected the night I showed you the television."

Ram couldn't look more astonished.

"I didn't want to say anything til I was certain she knew." A moment and then, "Took the news with her usual finesse, huh?" Anthony chuckled softly, but Ramsey didn't find the situation humorous and dropped sullenly into a chair.

"The woman wants my head on a pole, I'm thinking." Ramsey glanced at Anthony, his expression self-depreciating. "She accused me of lying, called me a *what*—as if I be a thing that ought be on display! And fool that I am, I mentioned I'd a *tendre* for Tess."

Anthony contained his excitement over learning that Tess had lived, long enough to say, "I bet it isn't your skull she wants on a pole then."

Ramsey made a pained sound and Anthony settled into the matching chair, bracing his ankle across his knee. He met Ramsey's gaze. "So. Where would you like to start?"

* * *

Maxwell studied the mayonnaise dripping from the base of his burger and on to the plate as if it were the NATO reports. "Is this a trade in information, Lieutenant Mathers?" He said the name loud enough to draw a few odd looks.

If he was trying to keep a low profile, the kid just blew it. "Answer the question."

Maxwell looked up, his sharp eyes assessing the detective. "He committed a crime?"

"He pulled a gun on you."

"I didn't press charges and that was in Bahama territory. You don't have jurisdiction."

"Listen, Maxwell," Pete Mathers leaned across the table. "You've had your skinny butt planted outside those gates since he got here. I want to know what's going on and any photos you have."

Maxwell slanted him a condescending smirk. He needed a court order to get his photos, yet Max knew it was wise to stay on the good side of the local police, and his apprehension stemmed from O'Keefe himself. He liked the guy. No matter how hard he tried to hide in the trees or disguise himself, O'Keefe saw through it, saluting the tree or climbing up to join him, instead of blowing up and tossing him on his ass. Once he stood beneath the tree and very quietly asked the bark if spying on his daily habits made a man thirsty, then offered him a beer.

"You sit and watch and you'll see the same as me." High octane tension, he thought, returning his attention to the meal.

Mathers started to reach across the table, then remembered who this man worked for.

Max saw the move and saved his ass.

"The estate is armed like a prison."

"What?"

"Jesus, you deaf and stupid? God help the city." He lifted his head and stared, feeling like he was betraying an old friend. "Somebody got onto the estate, and no, I didn't see anything.

Just a lot of commotion,'' Max said when Mathers looked excited. "But he's hired more security and locked her inside.''

"How do you know *he* has hired them?''

" 'Cause they don't do anything without his okay. Not even the mailman gets in.''

"That shouldn't matter to her, she likes privacy.''

But it did, Max thought, for he'd seen O'Keefe stop her from leaving the grounds alone just yesterday and she was furious, like a caged animal slowly going mad. But he wasn't about to tell Mathers that.

"What else is he up to?''

"Maybe he's trying to take over the goddamn country,'' Max snapped sarcastically. "How the hell should I know? Ask him yourself, Lieutenant. I'm not doing your job for you.'' With that Max tossed his burger on the plate with a wet splat and stood, then left the diner.

A half hour later, Mathers was parked outside the Hamilton estate. The kid was right, he gave him that. Mathers noted the license of each car that managed to get past the gates, which wasn't many. Who'd threatened her life again, Mathers wondered, and why didn't he call the department and report it. *Like you would have offered that kind of help?*

A knock on the window sent Pete's stomach to his knees and his head snapped to the side. Ramsey O'Keefe stared down at him between his arms braced on the car's roof. Mathers rolled down the window, glaring his best even though he knew his face was flaming red.

"Should you not be out searching for the bastards who attacked my lady last week?''

"Clues are slim and sometimes they return to the scene of the crime. Have they?''

Ramsey didn't answer, maintaining a dark, even stare, yet he seemed about to say something.

"When you gonna trust us to do our job, O'Keefe?''

Ramsey dropped a paper sack filled with sandwiches onto Mather's lap as he said, "Mayhaps when you cease having *me* followed,'' then turned away, signaling the guards afore he scaled the wall.

Chapter 29

"There's the car." The guard pointed to the red '65 Mustang as he jammed on the brakes. Ramsey released the harness and opened the door.

"Take yourself to the road that she does not elude you again," Ram said to the guard, his low voice ringing with authority and threatening the lot of his comrades with dismissal. He left the Jeep in a rage.

She'd outsmarted him, the little witch, slipping off the estate whilst he was closeted in his rooms, pouring over the material about the Rothmeres. He'd yet to wade through the newspaper clippings on the Blackwells when he discovered she'd stowed in the back or the rear bonnet of her car as 'twas removed from the estate for repairs. He knew little of what was necessary to maintain the contraptions and she used his ignorance to her advantage. 'Twas admittedly clever, but by God, he'd fulfill his threat to tie her to her bed this time. She tempted his patience daily, and for the love of the Almighty he couldn't understand what purpose served in coming here, to the docks.

Familiar scents and sounds soothed his foul temper as he studied the throngs of people lined outside the yawning entrance of a warehouse. Though its appearance was well kept, its patrons were not. 'Tis the poorest of my country, he thought, the hopelessness in their expressions like those of friend and foe during the revolution.

Slipping around the side of the building to a pair of open doors, he cautiously ducked inside. The heat was smothering, sweat immediately bursting 'cross his brow as his gaze rapidly scanned the interior. Rows upon rows of cots covered nearly half of the immense bare stone floor, personal effects neatly tucked beneath. Children and adults sat quietly, their low murmurs humming on the damp warm air. 'Twas desperation in their eyes, he thought, his gaze drifting from face to face. And hunger. He'd recognized the like afore, in himself.

His gaze moved rapidly, searching, his brain trying to comprehend why she would be here, amongst the salt of the earth. But he couldn't find her and his anger catapulted into fear. Had the guard been wrong in his assumption? Had she misled them intentionally and lay hurt elsewhere? God, he couldn't take that, not with the wedge atween them festering by the day. He swore if he—Ram spun about, his gaze frantically searching beyond the line of people carrying small trays, atween the steaming kettles and swift moving workers.

He swore he heard her voice.

He shifted his way atween the people, the scent of unwashed bodies reminding him far too much of his days aboard ship as he neared the galley area. He stopped abruptly, his heart rolling loosely in his chest. He would have never recognized her. Clad in brown abbreviated trousers and a black sleeveless shirt, she wore no paints or powders on her face, no jewelry, only a smudge of dirt on her chin. Her deep-red hair was pulled back, covered with a small cap, the wide bill facing backwards. Perspiration glossed her skin, now warmly tanned from spending hours in the sun, avoiding him.

She hovered over steaming basins, spooning food onto the trays, smiling, making conversation, pausing only to draw a pan of buns from a massive oven, then tending to her serving.

Ramsey stepped back out of her line of vision and watched her, watched as she filled a plate and left the food line to bring the meal to an old man sitting hunched and decrepit. She forced the utensil into his hand, her lips shaping encouragement as she coaxed him to eat. He did and she smiled, a smile he'd rarely witnessed from her. She worked tirelessly, sending her coworkers off to rest as she took charge. They did not seem to know who she was beyond the offer of food and shelter, he realized, for 'twas not the same as when she was accosted in the streets by her *fans*.

A woman in a white coat approached, addressing Penelope, yet she continued to ladle and pour, nodding, then turned her utensils over to another and followed her. Ram slipped behind support post and around cots, tracing their steps. Keeping hidden, he found Penelope nestled on a cot, a small black haired child in her arms.

"I won't lie, the needle is going to hurt." The child cringed and Penny soothed her. "But it will make the big pain go away."

"Don't want no more hurt, Rusty," the child sobbed helplessly and Penny closed her eyes, her heart wrenching as the boney little girl trembled in her arms.

"I know, honey," she murmured against her hair, nodding to the doctor to prepare the syringe. "How about I take a shot just to show it isn't so bad, okay?"

"I can't allow this."

Penny's gaze jerked to the young physician. "I could use a little vitamin B," she said, her tone brooking no argument, and, as the two women fought a silent battle, the pale cherub face tilted up, round dark eyes blinking.

"Honest, Rusty?" She shuddered heavily. "You will?"

Penny recognized the look. Suspicion. No one had sacrificed so much as a smile for this child. "Have I ever lied to you, Peaches?"

Numbly Peaches shook her head and Penny stretched her arm, nodding to the doctor. The child shrank when the needle pierced her skin, but Penny didn't blink, smiling. Peaches looked between the doctor and her savior, then gingerly offered her arm.

And Ramsey realized 'twas broken, the bone threatening to protrude through the skin. The child sank into a painless sleep afore the physician withdrew the needle and Penelope shifted, settling the girl as she stood. The doctor went immediately to work setting the break.

"Damn, Rusty, I wish you'd quit putting me on the spot like that. It's dangerous."

"She's alone and terrified. What would you have me do, Renee? Lie? Strap her down while she screams herself into shock?" She didn't respond. "And don't swear in front of the children, Renee."

Ramsey slipped back out of sight as Penny strode across the compound to the food line, taking up her position, her smile bright and full of hope.

"We missed you yesterday, Rusty."

"A girl's gotta make a living," she said with a soft smile.

"I here yah," the man said, shuffling past.

"How's your son, Lana?" she said to a woman after a few people had passed.

"Still coughing. Barks like a seal sometimes, I'm afraid he'll wake everyone at night."

"Have Doc Renee take another look." She swiped damp tendrils from her cheek with the back of her wrist. "Tell her I sent you over," she added when Lana looked to protest. Ram watched her for a moment longer, his pride of her swelling, then slipped outside, out of her sight, yet kept watch, his senses atune to her presence. 'Twas the worst place to see her protected, he thought, just as someone tapped his shoulder. Ram whirled about, fists primed and a young man flinched, lurching back.

"Christ, wound up a little too tight today?"

Ram's expression remained unchanged.

"Sorry. I'm Jake, and I could use some help, if you don't mind."

The young blond scarcely in his twenties gestured behind himself to the open truck filled with boxes. Ram glanced inside the warehouse, then back to the lad. He nodded once, then leapt onto the tailgate, hefting the stores and stacking them inside a small brick building. Each time he passed the side door he glanced beyond, assuring himself she was still there, still safe.

And Jake noticed.

"Looks different, don't she?" came in a whisper and Ram snapped a look to the side, shifting his grip on the box.

"How is it that they do not recognize her?"

Jake shrugged, walking beside Ramsey to the storage shed. "Some do, I guess. But most of these people don't have enough money to eat, let alone spend seven bucks to see a movie." They deposited the crates, then went back for more. "Everyone knows she doesn't come here to be the star and keep her identity quiet. Sort of like a family secret."

"She's here often?"

"Yup. 'Bout three, four days a week," Jake said, grabbing another box, his eyes widening when Ramsey hefted three without so much as a grunt. "And she don't let the press know the locations, says people here need to keep their dignity. So don't give her away or she'll be pissed."

Mad, he deduced. 'Twas an effort on her part, to keep her affiliation with this establishment secret. "Do you live here, lad?"

"Not anymore," he said proudly. "Her foundation gave me a grant and I'm in college now, but come back to help out."

"She finances this?" Ram waved to encompass the warehouse and its occupants.

"Yeah," came cautiously and Jake recognized his shock. "Jeez, what planet you been on?"

The unloading complete, Jake rapped on the trunk and as it rolled away, he dropped some coins into a soda machine and bought them both a cold one. "Want to meet her?"

Ramsey drained the soda without stopping, thoroughly enjoying the tingling in his mouth. "Nay," he said, crushing the can and pitching it into a bin marked for metal trash. "We are acquainted."

"Not as well as you thought, huh?" Jake murmured on laughing.

Ram's lips curved, his expression chagrined. "Apparently not."

As the lad bid him good day and thanks afore heading inside, Ram took up position near the entrance and spent the remainder of the morning keeping vigil on the woman he adored, yet was discovering all over again.

Penny let out a yelp when she sank into the car seat and found Ramsey sitting beside her. Her first instinct was to club him into Silly Putty until her fear subsided, but instead gripped the steering wheel.

"How did you find me?"

"All that matters is that I have." His gaze sharpened. "And you are safe."

"I was never in danger here. God, can't you take a hint?" This was a part of herself she wasn't prepared to share with him, not this much at once. "If I'd wanted you here, I would have told you about it." *But you'll have to, a voice challenged, if you want him.*

Stung, he leaned forward in her face, his low voice cutting into her temper. "Meggie and Hank were half mad with worry for you." Her brave front wilted and he was glad she felt at least a measure of regret. "Therefore you'd best suffer the consequences like royalty, lass, for your inconsiderate actions have brought you a personal protector." He sat back. "Rouse the beast," he said, gesturing to the dashboard and she turned the ignition. "Where e'er you go, I go."

"Great," she muttered, supposing she deserved that, so hot to get here without his notice she forgot completely about telling Margaret. Damn, she hated it when he was right, she mulled, throwing the car into reverse and making him scramble for his seat belt.

Ram shot her a narrow look and she smiled sweetly, speeding out of the parking lot. The woman should not be allowed full rein in a temper, he decided. Avoiding the scenery racing past with nauseating speed, Ram kept his gaze on her, aware it made her squirm with indignation. She'd bathed and changed into a simple blouse and skirt and his gaze drifted to her bare legs, muscled and tanned as she depressed the pedals, then shifted the stick, wandered back up to her face.

"Why put *you* on this act?"

She frowned, confused. "I act before a camera, Ramsey."

"Then is *Rusty* a character you portray for them?"

She glanced to the side in surprise.

" 'Twas a warm and caring lass I saw today, not the cold—"

"—bitch?" she cut in and he looked appalled.

"I would not even think such a thing," he hissed, angered by such a self-depreciating remark. She was far more faceted than any female he'd known; a tyrant with her independence, a temptress in his bed, and a samaritan of the downtrodden. He adored every part of her and besides, he decided, the only person privy to her icy contempt was him and he'd no desire to fight with her.

"Yeah, right. Well," she huffed into the tense silence, ignoring the bait. "You've seen for yourself the chaos recognition causes," she said without a trace of arrogance. She slowed to a stop at a light, glancing in the rearview mirror, then staring out over the hood. "I have my reasons for secrecy."

And he had his suspicions as to why, but wanted her to come to him, tell him, and said, "But you will not reveal them—" he leaned closer, hovering, the interior shrinking around her and Penny dared a look in his direction, gazes colliding— "Even to me, love?"

Love. If only he did.

But he was a man of his century, believing women were on earth for men to protect and adore, gently reared and pure women, like his mother. And Penny didn't even come close to qualifying. And she didn't want him to know about that part of her life, for she couldn't bear to see disgust in his eyes. But she hungered for him, missed him, and suddenly wanted to jerk the car off the road and kiss him, and be kissed back, one of his smoldering pulse-stealing kisses, the kind he put his whole body into giving. She ached for the on-the-edge breathlessness that came with touching him, the freedom, the delicious feminine rush through her body that she'd never known before Ramsey. This dance they did to avoid each other long enough to fling a veiled dig or two was wearing on her. She wanted him back. But she didn't know how to ask.

Tell him, trust him, completely, a voice said, and she almost blurted out her feelings before she recalled he wasn't being honest with her either. And then there was Tess and his love for her.

"Maybe I will . . . when you tell me what Noal Walker is doing for you?"

Ram blinked, sitting back, disappointed in the fire so quickly extinguished. "I hired him to investigate."

"Ramsey," she warned, accelerating the car through the intersection, trying to shake a tailgater.

" 'Tis the past association of the Rothmeres and Blackwells he seeks on my behalf."

Penny tried not to panic. Was it her he was investigating? "Tess's family I can understand, but the Rothmeres?" She gave the rearview a glance. Still there. A midnight-blue Mercedes, dark tinted glass, and familiar.

"I believe Tess has gifted me with one of the diamonds she stole, Penelope."

"Gee, news to me, Ramsey." He gave her that insolent *you weren't interested before* stare. "And?"

"I believe Rothmere knows I have it, or rather *we* have it." Ram cursed himself for having the bloody thing appraised, alerting anyone of its existence.

"Oh God." Her gaze darted to all the mirrors, unease hiking her panic. When had the tailgater suddenly vanished?

"He wants them back, all of them, and God knows what else he'll do to see the fortune his again."

She was in danger. Real danger. And so was he. They didn't have the diamonds. Tess did.

"Ramsey." She swallowed, her fingers whitening on the steering wheel. "They tried to kill Tess to get them back."

His brows furrowed. He recalled Tess saying as much, yet thought 'twas feminine dramatics. "You are certain?"

"Look at your seat," she said, elbowing the back when he stared at the bottom cushion.

Ram twisted, his features stretching taut as he pushed his finger into the hole in the leather cushion.

"This is—was Tess's car." His gaze glazed over the interior.

"I've had the rear glass replaced. It had a clean bullet hole through it. That seat and the body still have to be repaired." She darted a glance at him. "There are at least three bullet holes."

"The constabulary? They know of this?"

She shook her head, making a left turn. "It happened *before* Tess left in my car." Before we burned the evidence.

"Tell me what happened that night, Penelope."

Penny slowed, waiting for some children to cross the street into the park.

"She broke into the Rothmere Estate, stole a packet and was caught. It was a set-up," she said with absolute conviction. "Or those diamonds wouldn't have been inside." Damn you Sloane, she thought, her eyes widening at the sight of the Mercedes pulling out from a side street behind them. "They chased her to her apartment, and I knew she was in trouble, tried to help, but only managed to convince her to switch clothes and cars with me." She came to an intersection and stopped, her fingers flexing on the wheel. "She wouldn't tell me what was inside the packet." Behind them, the Mercedes engine revved. "She hopped the cruise liner I was going to take and sailed to the Bahamas. She was headed home, believing she'd eluded them til she saw them on the ship. They were going to shoot her, right there in front of hundreds of people. So she jumped."

The light changed and she gunned the engine, forcing Ramsey to grip the door handle. "You know the rest." She made a right, a left, then cut across a mini mall parking lot. "I can't understand why she just didn't give them the diamonds?" She thumped the heel of her palm against the steering wheel. "Why did she hold onto them?"

Ramsey glanced to at the side mirror, memorizing the carriage number.

" 'Twas likely her only bargaining power, should she be taken captive by those men."

"You see them, don't you?"

Only his gaze shifted out the window. "Aye."

"They've been following us for—"

"I know. Go as you must." He gestured ahead.

"I've already made two extra turns."

The Mercedes rode their bumper. "Oh jeez! What do we do?"

"We must either outrun them or confront."

"Confront? Be serious, Ramsey. This isn't 1789. Confrontations on the streets of Coral Keys is not a daily occurrence."

"We could head to a populated area," he suggested, scanning the area for a way out. "Your fame could aid us."

"No." She shook her head for emphasis. "No way. People could get hurt. We don't know what these guys want or why they're following or what they are capable of. No."

"I've ascertained your point, Penelope." His dry tone lacked impatience.

"They're coming up along side." Panicked, urgent.

"Allow them to come about and be prepared to evade."

"Evade?" she squeaked. "Listen *captain,* you have no crew and they're probably armed and—oh jeez, what are you doing?"

He jerked up his pant leg, slipping a knife free from a scabbard strapped to his calf. He grinned. "Never a harm in being prepared."

"I should have known," she muttered, glancing at the side view mirror as the car rode the shoulder to get closer.

"We're bumper to bumper," she said, swerving.

"Keep it steady." He maneuvered his big body sideways.

"Ramsey, they could shoot you," she called when he pushed his torso out the window. The Mercedes pulled up close, scraping the Mustang.

"Turn, woman, turn!"

She made a hard right, heard a pop and in the side mirror saw the Mercedes swerve out of control and screech to a halt. Ramsey slid into the seat so hard the car bounced.

"You hit the tire!" She blinked at all the mirrors.

"Drive." He gestured ahead, then looked behind them.

"You actually hit the tire!"

"Drive, Penelope," he said in a calm voice, grasping the wheel and pulling the car back to the right of the road. She was breathing rapidly, excitedly, and Ramsey couldn't keep from smiling. But they weren't out of harm's way yet. The dark car was pulling back onto the road, limping but still coming.

"In there." He pointed to a deserted warehouse, its tin walls and a third of its roof pushed in by storms or vandals.

Penny jerked the wheel and the car listed, tires squealing.

" 'Tis my desire *not* to bring attention to ourselves and this blatantly obvious carriage."

"Sorry." She shrugged, sheepish. "It's my first car chase." She shoved her hair out of her face as he directed her to pass the first two doors of the gaping warehouse.

As they did, Ramsey found what he sought, another entrance on the side. "Turn right, then sharply right again, Penelope."

She did and the maneuver put them inside, up against a corner wall. She cut off the engine, looking around.

There was a wide open door at the end of the car's bumpers and she couldn't understand why he wanted the car in such a vulnerable spot, for she could see the empty street between the gaps in the dented wall.

"Make haste," he said, climbing out, and she snatched up her purse, leaving the car and following his heated gesture to get into the darkness of the warehouse as he tugged on a corrigated steel door. Rusted, it wouldn't budge without waking the dead and he scanned the area for something to cover the car.

"This will work," she said, quickly gathering up moldy wet cardboard boxes and laying them against the back of the car. Ram instantly joined her, hiding the vehicle from sight.

"Enough, enough, hurry," he urged, catching sight of the dark car atween the wall gaps as he grabbed her hand, pulling her along the perimeter.

Penny felt a rush of excitement like she'd never experienced.

"This way." He gestured up a metal staircase that looked more like a fire escape. She went first, climbing the dozen rungs.

"Why don't we just wait in the car?"

"And if they decide to destroy the car, assuming we are in it?" he countered.

"Oh—right." She reached the top, stepping onto a narrow catwalk. "Oh Jesus," she hissed as it swayed noisily. "This doesn't seem much safer." Fear wavered her voice.

"Head to that opening," he pointed to a blackened square in the wall. "And put one foot afore the other and 'twill sway less."

She glanced back over her shoulder. "You're sure?"

He could tell she was scared. "Trust me. 'Tis like rigging."

She did, holding the rusted rails and she made it to the opening a lot sooner than she imagined, ducking into the darkness, feeling her way for something to grip. Ramsey was there, his feet on solid ground, his body tucked close.

"Do not step further," he whispered close to her ear. "I fear this place is as unstable as it looks."

Light flickered between the broken seams of the warehouse, yet not enough to see his face clearly.

"It smells like oranges."

"Aye, rotten ones," he agreed. "Nay, do not move. Lean back against me." She did and he held her as he settled to the floor, then shifted her atween the wedge of his thighs.

"How long do we wait?"

"Til the bastards cease circling."

"They are?" She strained to look, and he pushed her head back.

"Aye, 'tis their second time."

A noise and then, "What was that?"

"Shhh."

With his back against the wall and his shoulder to the door frame, Ramsey had a clear view below and to the right of a goodly portion of the warehouse floor, the hood of her car and the door they passed through. Yet beyond that, he would have to make himself known to see. If he were better armed than with a knife and alone, he would have risked the confrontation, but not with Penelope here.

Ramsey hedged the opening, then jerked back.

"They are examining the damaged wheel."

"Great. Let's hope they don't decide to change it here because they'll notice the car."

She shifted against him, digging in her purse.

"What are you doing?" he hissed, her fidgeting grinding her softness to his groin.

"Looking for my cellular phone."

"Do not bring the constables into this, Penelope."

"I'm not, but Claire will kill me if I miss another appointment."

"Claire?"

"My dressmaker."

In the dark Ramsey rolled his eyes. Penny muted the sound and dialed, whispering into the phone. She cut the line, tilting her head back to look at his silhouette. "You sure you don't want me to call the cops? We can at least scare them off."

Silence.

"Ramsey?"

"I'm considering."

"Well, consider that those meat chunks want something from us and I'll give you two guesses as to what it is? And the first one doesn't count."

Ramsey grinned. Cheeky lass. "Why would they believe we would have them with us? Bloody hell. 'Twas a king's ransom in gems. Only a fool would take such a risk."

"Phalon isn't a fool. Sloane is—debatable. I don't think they know for sure if the diamonds are still around. Even if the police knew, they would have to assume they went down with Tess."

"Yet I saw them."

"In 1789, and who knows what happened to them since, except for the one Tess left you." She shifted, her voice a conspirator's whisper. "The way I see it, the diamonds are either undeclared wealth or they don't belong to Phalon in the first place."

"Mayhaps Sloane's? She, after all, put them there."

She smothered a snicker. "If she knew what they were worth, she would never have let them out of her sight. Even I know the value of colored diamonds."

"The gems have a past we must discover." He sighed, his breath brushing her hair. "By Triton, we are in a fix, lass."

"You know, I could buy more diamonds and set a trap."

He stiffened. "I think not," he hissed near her ear. Her idea sounded much like Tess's need to bait Phillip, with herself.

"Why?"

"The culprit has no face yet, and one must know his enemy afore he can strike." He edged for a look at the pursuers and saw the car moving beyond the crumbling walls back toward the street.

"You sound like it's an everyday thing, to be fighting someone."

"You forget that the land you ride upon everyday was Spanish territory, not yet in statehood, in my time. Your Louisiana was French ruled, territory beyond undiscovered. Land changed hands many times, lass. When Dane's father bought their home in 1762, I believe, 'twas no more than six rooms, once owned by a fat poppenjay," he said with undisguised disgust, "some official of the Spanish government. Spanish law prevailed then, til . . ." he paused, thinking back, "1783, then 'twas ruled by the British."

"Wow," she said, thoroughly fascinated. "I hadn't realized."

" 'Twere Seminole Indians about, too, magnificent warriors, but unwilling to allow passage, nor recognize anyone's ownership. 'Twas dangerous to travel the roads without full escort. We'd English spies and saboteurs to tend with, and always the thief or felon. The sovereign thought America his private dumping pile for criminals," he added sourly. "The village streets brimmed with the likes of those." He inclined his head to the warehouse.

She took a minute to absorb that. "What was it like?" came softly. "Finding yourself two hundred years in the future?"

He was wondering if she'd ever ask. "Terrifying. Mesmerizing. A pull like I've never experienced afore." He looked down at her, shifting her to stare at her profile outlined in the dim threads of light. "Know that I wanted to see what lay on the other side of the wall, Penelope. I accepted the risk freely." His lips quirked. "Though I'd no notion my arrival would nearly kill me." He sounded amused, she thought. "But 'tis all too fascinating to ever go back."

"As if you could."

He gave her a considering look. "I arrived, did I not?"

"You don't really think that's possible . . . again?" Apprehension bolted through her. Could he be taken away as easily?

"The question is, would I go."

A stretch of silence, then an urgently whispered, "Well?"

"I like your century fine, lass," he said on a chuckle, loving that she sighed with what he hoped was relief, then dared another look for their hunters. "I believe we have successfully eluded them."

"Castration's sufficient punishment for this, don't you think?"

He choked, then shook his head, rueful. " 'Tis cruel side to you, woman."

"That's self-preservation," she said. "If I don't look out for me and mine, who will?"

"Me," he said, tilting her face to the sultry gray shadows. "When will you trust me?"

"If I didn't, I wouldn't be sitting in a smelly warehouse with bugs trying to climb up my skirt."

His voice was low and silky. "Shall I seek and destroy the little beasties for you?"

She laughed softly as he stood, helping her to her feet. "I'll get back to you on that."

"Be assured I shall ask again," he said close to her ear.

God I hope so, she thought, as he poked his head out the opening, then guided her onto the catwalk.

"I know, one foot *afore* the other," she mimicked and moved cautiously toward the escape stairs. Ramsey waited until she was off the ladder, then took the easy route swinging over the side, hanging, then dropping to the ground.

"Show off," she said and he herded her to the car. He checked the empty street and yard afore climbing into the car. Penny cringed as she started the engine, the rumble echoing in the barren warehouse and she muttered a half dozen Hail

Marys as she pulled the car out onto the road and didn't breathe until they saw other cars and people.

"Well," she huffed a sigh. "That was exciting."

"Having our lives threatened is not a game, Penelope." His gaze still searched around them.

She maneuvered the car into the driveway before a modest house, using Claire's van to shield the red Mustang, then yanked up the break. She stared out over the polished hood for a moment, then shoved her hair off her forehead.

"Maybe the diamonds do have a past and it's in Tess's diaries?"

"You have not read them?"

"Not all." She glanced at him briefly. "I guess I know when I reach the end, I'll read how she died."

" 'Tis a fact we cannot escape, love," he said, his eyes soft with sympathy. "Read them all and put her to rest."

Penny stared at her lap. Once again he was right, but she couldn't help feeling that if she did read it, a part of herself would die, too. "Are you going to tell me what else she left *you?*" She glanced at him through a curtain of dark red hair.

" 'Tis naught but personal possessions," he said matter of factly, wiggling the signet ring on his finger. "Dane and Tess thought 'twould bring me comfort were I alone in the future."

But you aren't alone, she wanted to say. I'm here. But it was Tess he'd loved, and the thought that he still might clawed through her chest like a raging animal. She hated feeling this way and tried pushing the stabbing pain under tight control.

"Come on. Let's get this over with."

She retrieved a box from the back seat and Ramsey frowned at the sudden sadness in her green eyes. "Penelope?"

"Claire hates it when I'm late," she said, ignoring his concern and leaving the Mustang. "And even a car chase won't be a good enough excuse."

Ram followed, damned confused and determined to pry loose some answers.

Chapter 30

A tiny bell chimed above his head and Ram paused to examine the street afore closing the door. 'Twas the dressmaker, he realized, the open room filled with bolts of fabric filed by shade in a Queen Anne armoire, spools of trim neatly arranged in glass cabinets and surrounded by artfully placed reticules and matching slippers. He recognized the Hipplewhite chairs and tables and though Ram did not frequent such establishments afore, the shop reminded him of his century.

A short, slim woman greeted Penelope with a bright saucy smile, her gaze drifting briefly to Ramsey afore she escorted Penelope beyond a set of doors. Ramsey followed on her heels til the seamstress gave him a quelling, very territorial look, fairly shoving Penelope's box into his hands, her meaningful gaze directing him into another room.

A dull red crept up his neck. Though he'd rather not have Penelope from his sight, he did as she bade, yet not afore he caught Penelope's scarcely masked smile.

Ducking to the room, his discomfort heightened, for surrounding him was a man's imagination in feminine frippery. Puffed and ribboned curtains graced the tall windows, lacy sheers moving with the conditioned breeze. Delicate glass shelves bearing porcelain creatures of the forest variety flanked the doorway, and his every step shook the cabinetry and he nearly tripped on the thick pile rug in his effort to tred lightly. Catching himself afore he went crashing like a boar into furnishings, Ram hastily took a seat on a small settee, the daintily carved wood creaking with his weight, his knees banging the low polished table. He set the balsa aside and rested his hands on his thighs.

Across the room from him, the joint of two walls were covered with mirrors, magnifying his conspicuousness, and as carefully as he could manage, he braced his ankle across his knee and sat back. He shifted uncomfortably, feeling like a clumsy giant and was about to do his waiting outside when a petite girl of about nine and ten entered the sanctuary to offer him coffee or a soda. The latter he accepted, his ears tuned to the murmur of voices. She was back there, he realized, down the dimly lit hall that held some mystical place where women dominated and men never dared.

"Go on out and see what you think of this one," he heard afore Penelope appeared in the archway, her hair swept off her neck.

The air left his lungs and he straightened in the seat. Only in his dreams has he envisioned her like this. Why would she dress in such a manner? Certainly not to please him.

Penny stepped onto the pedestal, fluffing the dress out around her, concentrating on the gold creation in the mirror and not the man behind her. Rooms always felt smaller with him around, and she busily tucked and shifted the heavy gown, wondering why he was looking at her so oddly. Then she understood. And her gaze jerked back to the mirror, the dress.

It was a style from his time. His century.

The neckline plunged deeply, accenting her tightly laced ribs and waist, the sleeves snug, fountaining in long funnels at her elbow. It was lovely, a mist of gold chiffon laying over the heavy gold brocade and the entire mess was heavier than her sofa. It was a costume from her last film, one of several shipped by the studio for her selection and as much as she did not want to attend the premier and the party, it was an obligation in her contract. A costume ball, with tons of celebrities, reporters, and hype, and hourly she cursed Tony for not deleting the clause from her contract. He'd done it deliberately, she suspected.

Before she could catch Ramsey's gaze in the mirror, the dressmaker entered the room, tape measure slung around her neck.

"How's it feel?" Claire said.

"Like I'm wearing a pontoon boat, but fine."

"Well something's wrong." The dressmaker's professional eye judged her reflection.

" 'Tis the wrong shade," Ram's deep voice cut in and Penny's gaze jerked to his in the silver glass.

"But I wore this before, in the movie."

"Regardless," Ram said, slumping lazily in the chair, his legs stretched beneath the table. " 'Tis nearly the same shade as your skin."

"That's it," Claire gasped. "Your tan makes you look . . . washed-out." Her words slowed as she sent Ramsey a quizzical glance, her brows drawn.

"Good, let's try another, *lighter* one."

"You know the way." Claire indicated the dressing room and Penelope immediately marched off only to return moments later in a deep pink creation. She was fairly bursting out of the bodice, the neckline cutting just above her nipples.

Ramsey admired the spilling bosom long enough to be noticed by both women, then in a light voice said, "Too garish. You look more the courtesan, than the lady."

"And you'd know the difference," she challenged tartly and he favored her with a rascally grin.

"I've an education on the subject," he said with a hint of pure masculine arrogance and she rolled her eyes. "And 'tis unnecessary, those ribbons and flowers," he added distastefully, waving at the profusion spilling over the panniers.

"Without being on the movie set, it does look a little overdone," Penny agreed after a glance in the mirror and Claire joined her on the pedestal.

"I could remove them," she said, then checked the stitching, lowering her voice. "All right, who is he?"

''My friend and,'' her gaze met his in the glass—''body-guard.''

''You ought to be guarding him,'' Claire murmured. ''He's incredibly fascinating.''

''He does have a way about him,'' Penny said, not at all pleased Claire, *the viper,* was interested.

''Mind if I—''

''Yes I do,'' Penny cut in quickly and Claire laughed, soft and knowing.

''I was just kidding,'' Claire said as they stepped into the privacy of the dressing room. ''No one could get past the way he looks at you.'' Penny stared at her seamstress. ''Good God, Penny, you can't be that blind. He looks like he wants to eat you alive.'' Penny cast a furtive glance down the hall, then turned her back to Claire so she could help her out of the monstrosity.

She returned wearing another gown, this one of deep claret.

'' 'Tis the same shade as your hair,'' he commented and she sighed, dispirited.

''My hair was powdered in the movie and no—'' she shot Claire a defiant look—''I will not attend looking like a frosted strawberry.'' Gathering up the folds of fabric nearly to her knees, Penny huffed into the dressing room and Ramsey noticed she was perspiring, her upswept hair sagging to one side.

With the next gown, she didn't bother to step onto the pedestal and simply stood beneath the archway, awaiting his comment, then at the shake of his head, she blew a wisp of hair off her forehead and trotted off with all the elegance of a dockside barmaid.

She returned in yet another, in deep forest-green.

''This is the last one,'' she reminded and without taking his gaze from hers he tipped the lid to the box she'd given him and drew out the dress.

''Where did that come from?'' Claire rushed to see.

''It—ah . . . was a gift from an old friend. Be careful, Claire. It's not a copy.''

Claire gasped, carefully shaking out the dress. ''It's magnificient! Oh and look at this.'' She lifted out the corset and petticoats of deep blue, inspecting the lacings, ribbon work, and hand stitching. "It's in excellent condition. What gives?" When no comment was forthcoming she looked up and found her customer and her bodyguard staring at each other in a way that made her feel like an intruder.

Ram didn't turn his gaze away as he said, "Preserved like any antique," his lips curved—"with a bit of tender care."

Penny laughed, more to herself, and Claire didn't even bother to figure that one out.

"Well, the seams will have to be reinforced, but the fabric will hold up." Like they were listening, she thought as her shop bell chimed. "Susan will get it." A timid voice called out and Claire frowned, then just as quickly her features smoothed taut. "Shoot, she's on break," she apologized.

"Go, Claire, I can manage."

Claire's gaze moved between the couple as she laid the gown aside and left, smiling and wondering if she'd find them rolling on the floor when she came back. God, the steam those two created was enough to melt wax!

Once Claire was gone Ramsey left the settee to stand before Penny. His gaze roamed her face, his hand coming up to brush the damp tendrils at her forehead.

Her breathing quickened.

"Thanks for your help. I suppose you are the expert." She plucked at the skirts. "Would I be accepted, like this . . . in your time, I mean."

Ramsey felt her emotions laying on the edge of her words. The woman had no consciousness of her beauty. "I do not doubt you'd bring your suitors to their knees, begging favor."

She laughed uncomfortably . "I don't think I'd go *quite* that far."

"I would." He took a step closer, smothering the air around her.

She swallowed, overwhelmed. "I suppose I should see if that fits." She gestured sluggishly to the gown.

"Allow me." He motioned for her to turn around and pinched the zipper slide. " 'Twould have made my life simpler then," he said, chuckling, pulling it slowly down. Penny's flesh jumped to life, his seductive tone smoothing over her skin like warm oil. "By God 'tis an erotic sound."

"Ramsey," she glanced covertly at the door. "We—you shouldn't be, you know, helping me."

She was in full view of the wall of mirrors, her gaze caught in his. "I have seen you lain bare and brazen as you will ever be, love." She closed her eyes, briefly, remembering the way he made love to her last, in the shower; the water and heat and his slick warm skin sliding against hers.

Dizzily she opened her eyes and found him staring at her, a sensuous promise darkening his eyes. Slowly he peeled the dress off her shoulders, his breath fanning the skin there and Penny experienced a tense rush from his nearness and for an instant sagged back against him. He held her, her back to his front, and in the mirror she watched his hands briefly frame her waist, his fingers tugging at tapes and a confusion of ribbons as his head descended. He dropped moist grinding kisses up the length of her neck, then nuzzled the skin behind her ear.

"I have missed the scent of you," he whispered and a tiny moan worked in her throat. His hands rode lower, shaping her hips, pushing the gown down, then he lifted her out of the pile of gown, panniers, and petticoats, setting her to her feet.

His hands remained on her waist, thumbs smoothing the silk fabric. Cognac-brown eyes prowled slowly over her from head to slippers; her garments authentic down to the tiny bows on her garters. As his gaze climbed, Ramsey wished they were truly alone, for he wanted to take his time removing them and adoring the treasures beneath.

"Don't even think it." His gaze flew to hers, the heat of it singing through her veins.

"You can read minds?"

"More like signs." Her gaze lowered to his trousers, the bulge hinting beneath the fabric.

He flashed her an easy grin. "My state of unease is your blame," he said, then afore she could protest, deftly unfastened the modern hooks of her corset, stripping her of the stays, then quickly lacing her into the other.

"My my. You are rather skilled at this," she tossed back

over her shoulder as he threaded the lacings and gave them a tug. He met her stare in the mirror.

"Would you have me lie?"

Her expression withered. "No, the truth is bad enough."

He stilled, frowning. "What has gone afore matters not, Penelope."

"You're expecting me to trust that answer?"

He forced her to face him. "As you have trusted me?" he hissed, the festering wounds atween them swelling, and she remained silent, mutinous. " 'Twas it not you who asked me to leave your life?" The shame of it still stung, the evidence of wounds inflicted lingering in his eyes. "Was it not you who saw a freak of nature in the same man you let love your body a night afore?"

Regret and misery swept her. "I'm so . . . sorry." Her voice threatened to break and he smoothed his hands down her bare arms. "I was terribly confused—"

"I know—"

"And scared."

"I know—"

"There isn't any excuse for treating you the way I did."

His shoulders sagged and he pressed his lip to her forehead and murmured, "How can you trust me with your life, Penelope, and not your heart?"

She looked up sharply and he saw the haunting question in her green eyes.

"Ask me aught and I will tell you gladly." Urgently, pleading.

After a few false starts, Penny moistened her lips, her eyes glossing with sudden tears. "Did you really love her, Ramsey?" came in a fragile whisper. "Do you still?"

"Nay."

Her trapped breath breezed past her lips and the simple gesture nearly gutted him. How could she not know how he felt about her? He tipped her chin, gazing into her eyes and hoping she trusted what she was in his. "I thought 'twas love, for 'twas as I wished, yet Tess knew me upon first greeting, aware I sought a bit of excitement and not a lifetime."

Although her stiff posture softened, her gaze held a full measure of doubt. "Did Dane know how you felt?"

"Aye. Threatened to run me through if I did not leave off." His look was sheepish. "He was on a dire quest for vengeance that would see him dead if she'd not come into his life then. And her odd ways, her candid manner, 'twas what he needed to bring him back to his mates and kin." His smile was reminiscent. "I dare say Tess humbled him, and so us all, with her plain speech and absolute defiance of the rules."

"Sounds like my bud." Penny smiled. "I bet Dane had a fit."

" 'Twas a fit he reveled in. He was ready to love and be loved, Penelope. 'Twas his time." A pause and then, "And I knew 'twas naught but her saucy ways that attracted me."

"She had a few things to say about you, too."

He made a pained sound, half laugh, half moan. "Splendid. My reputation is in tatters for a bit of flirting."

"Flirting, my ass."

He quirked a brow, a grin tugging. "Tess does not have a flicker of the cheeky impertinence you possess."

"We are very different women." Green eyes dared him to compare.

He wouldn't dream of it, but couldn't resist saying, "Well . . . I'd kissed her once—" His head, his lush mouth, drew closer—"and 'twas nary a scrap of what we share."

She jerked back, a tapered red brow lifting. "And that is?"

His arm snaked around her waist and he pulled her tightly against him. "Passion enough to swipe that icy look from your face," he murmured into her mouth afore his lips covered hers, his muscled arms crushing her to his long frame and lifting her off the floor. Her response was unchained, hot and bold with her need and he drank, thirsted, kissing her with the love fighting its way out of his chest. His broad hands swept down her spine, memorizing her hips and buttocks and she clung to him, her tongue sinking into his mouth and her fingers sinking into his hair, holding him for her possession. Ramsey feared he'd see his own heart broken if he did not make this woman his, forever.

He loved her and it tore at his heart that she might never return it.

"Oh! Excuse me," a voice said and Penny jerked back, her skin reddening. But Ramsey was not the least bit ashamed and slowly let her feet touch the floor. He felt her struggle against his hold and released her, stepping back. His gaze never left her, even as she murmured something about trying on the antique for size and swept up the overflowing box, nearly running beneath the archway.

"Guarding that body real well, aren't you?" Claire murmured with a quick glance at the man, then followed Penelope.

Penny was feeling dizzy by the time she strapped on the harnesses and petticoats. She experienced an odd sensation as Claire fitted the gown about her, a chill running the length of her spine and legs. Ramsey residual, she thought with a private smile.

"Step into the slippers. He has to get the whole effect." Claire carefully laced up the dress.

"I'm not doing this for him."

"Right. After that kiss? Girl, I'm surprised my fabrics didn't ignite."

Penny laughed at that, her body threading with fresh desire. Volcanic eruption was more like it, and she avoided his gaze, composing herself as she stepped beneath the archway and up onto the pedestal. Yet as Claire fluffed the dress out and adjusted the tight bodice, Penny couldn't resist seeing his reaction. She lifted her gaze, meeting those dark brown eyes in the silver reflection, feeling them like the warm stroke of his fingers as they lingered over her bare shoulders, her waist, trailing down the curve of her spine to the length of deep-blue fabric fountaining behind her.

"Face me, love." Whispered words carried across the room and Claire's gaze shot between the two as Penny turned.

"Tess has great taste, huh?"

" 'Tis the woman within who has given the fabrics their appeal." His voice bore a schoolboy's raspiness, for to see her so elegantly clad, in the garments of his time, robbed him of air.

Every inch of the deep-blue gown enhanced her beauty, bringing her natural vibrance to the surface. The bodice fit as if fashioned for her; off the shoulder and deeply heart shaped, the neckline plunging atween her breasts, yet revealing only the fullness of her figure against the beaded edge. Tiny crystals were scattered 'cross the creation as if dusted by morning dew, yet more of her smooth shoulders and arms were exposed than 'twas proper, he thought possessively, the funnel sleeve at her elbow a whisper of watered silk. The pannier was slimmed down, the fabric about the pointed waist smoothly draped instead of puffed and nipped. She looked regal, yet bewitchingly exotic and he left his seat, striding toward her, offering his hand. She accepted it, stepping down to meet him.

The look of awe on his face left her breathless, dreamy.

"Ramsey?"

"God almighty, Penn." His fathomless gaze swept her hotly. "Who must I duel to keep from showing another man what my eyes behold?"

Something bright and warm sang through her blood just then. "Well," she said carefully, briefly biting her lip. "You could join me."

Both his brows shot up in question.

She threw her shoulders back, drawing a fortifying breath. "I'm asking you for a date, Ramsey. Come to the premier with me."

Ramsey gazed into her green eyes at length, searching, desperate to see what he hoped, and aware that he must tred cautiously. Yet he knew that inviting him to join her, afore her public, afore the reporters and such, was a step he'd only dreamed she'd take for him.

Slowly he bowed over her hand, dropping a kiss to the back, then lifting his gaze. " 'Twould be an honor, lady heart." He straightened, drawing her closer, his stirring gaze caressing the lush bounty of skin she displayed. "Remind me though, to attend armed to the friggin' teeth."

"That might not be so bad," she said carefully, wonder and fear in her voice. "The celebration is at the Rothmere mansion."

Chapter 31

Margaret O'Hallaran adjusted the grocery bag, then shoved the Jeep Cherokee's hatch closed, moving around the side to unlock her door. Tossing her purse in before sliding into the driver's seat, she inserted the key in the ignition, then raised her arm to adjust the rearview mirror. But it was gone, broken off.

"That the hec—"

An arm around her throat cut off her air and her assailant jerked her, arching her back against the seat.

"Don't," he hissed in her ear when she tried to sound the horn. "I said—" Margaret felt the gun barrel at her temple and inhaled sharply, putting up her hands.

"I don't have any money." She was surprised at her own calm, even though no one could see she was in trouble. The windows were tinted too dark to see inside the Jeep.

He snickered nastily. "Shut up. You didn't tell her, did you?"

A moment's hesitation, then, "No."

"One more chance and we're coming for *her*." He tightened his grip and Margaret's vision sparkled with white dots.

"She doesn't have them," she gasped.

"We have proof. Convince her with this," he said, and the pistol stock cracked against the side of her head. Pain exploded there and Margaret slumped to the side, grabbing her skull. Warm blood wet her fingers.

Distantly she heard the car door open, the rustle of clothing, then the screech of tires and she righted herself enough to see a dark car speed away.

She closed her eyes against the pain, digging in her purse for a tissue. The blood was running free, staining her shirt. They're going to know, she thought, blotting the wound, then starting the car. She blinked, backing up and carefully weaving her way into traffic.

Penelope would never forgive her.

"I'll get this one," Penny called out, crossing the foyer as the chiming bell drifted into silence. She threw open the door and found Noal, his hands braced behind his back.

"Hey, Pixie."

"Please don't call me that," she said not unkindly, backing away to let him in.

"Sure." He looked her over, frowning. "He's expecting me."

Like a brass band didn't announce his arrival already, she thought, for no one could get within yards of the gate without being questioned like a potential serial killer.

"Well, I haven't the foggiest notion where he is." She waved, indicating the house, a book clutched in her hand, her finger marking her place. "Somewhere in here."

"A little testy today?" Noal flashed her a disarming grin and she returned it with an teeth-gritted smile.

"Ha! Get in line. You're the third person to have an appointment with my house guest." And that was just today, she thought, closing the door.

Clarissa Two Leaf left a half hour ago, smiling, a new one for her; Anthony was here with a broker, arguing with Ramsey over God-knew-what, except that Tony thought it was worthless. And now Noal, whose presence always hiked her suspicions. Although he was a private detective, with the emphasis on private, his association with Ramsey made her nervous.

Of course, she couldn't test the theory because she hadn't seen the man much since the dress fitting two days ago, except in passing; passing in the hall, passing as he left to do whatever or passing someone who had an appointment with him. For a man who'd just arrived in this century he'd certainly acclimated himself well and was awfully popular.

And secretive.

That, she tried to push aside. It was really none of her affair, but she discovered this latent nosy streak of hers kept rearing when anything concerned him. Reminding herself that he'd take off in a dead run if he knew she was nothing but a fake didn't help either. She was walking a tight rope, and knew she should have never stepped onto it. She knew! Her balancing act was wobbling, and the unsettling feeling that she was about to fall terrified her. She couldn't bear to see his disgust when he found out and it weighed against the urge to just disappear before he could. She was a coward.

But Ramsey meant too much to her. The realization coming in the warehouse when he'd looked at her as if he'd challenge the world to keep her safe with him. She didn't want to lose him, but she didn't really have him either. And Penny knew a time would come when she'd be forced to either cut all ties or give up her heart to him, without question or reservation and accept the consequences.

Her palms perspired, the skin of her neck dampening as she thought of losing him completely. To catapult her emotions, Ramsey appeared, striding across the living room from the solarium, Anthony and his broker at his heels, still in a heated discussion. Ramsey's step slowed the instant his gaze lit on her, those smoldering amber dark eyes caressing her from head to toe and back and her heart leapt, pumping so much blood she felt her skin go warm and bright. Why did it feel like weeks since she'd seen him last?

He maneuvered around a statue, coffee tables, between a pair of sofas, and her attention dropped to his lean hips and long legs.

She'd never seen a man fill out a pair of jeans quite like he did.

He strode directly up to her, gazing deeply into her eyes and her senses throbbed with energy, contouring to the width of his chest, his cradle of his hips, the corded thighs she knew were ropey with sculptured muscles. She wanted to run her hands over them and her body gravitated to his warmth, the heady look in his soulful eyes. His message was clear.

And Ram's hands flexed against the urge to touch her.

"I'll admit this is enterprising," Anthony was saying, "and I understand your reasons, but honestly, Ramsey, you simply can not take a risk like this."

Ram didn't spare him a glance. "If you do not care to handle the transaction, be assured I will."

"Gad, and have them take you for everything you've got, hell no." Anthony looked at the broker, nodded toward the door, then left, with Ramsey still staring down at Penelope.

"Your appointment, sir." Though her manner was formal, her words came on a breathless hush.

His brows drew close. "Forgive the chaos I've done to your household."

She moistened her lips. "Stirring excitement seems to be your forté."

His grin was slow, carnal, his gaze dropping briefly to her scandalously-sheer blouse. He breathed deeply. "I am not alone in that task."

"Would you two like to be alone?"

They both looked at Noal, who was failing miserably to hide his smile. Penny blinked, then hastily stepped back.

"Sorry," she murmured, red faced, then turned away. She could feel Ramsey's gaze on her back and her steps slowed as she headed toward the kitchen, pausing at the wide entrance and opening a small shallow cabinet. She studied the rows of keys, finding one out of place, corrected it, then selected a set.

"Ramsey," she called and he faced her. She jingled the keys, then tossed them across the foyer. He caught it, frowning at his palm, then to her.

"They're to the study. You need it and I never go in there."
She tilted her head. "It sort of suits you."

Suddenly he was there, inches from her, his eyes searching
hers. "Why?"

Her shoulders lifted and fell in a gesture of uncertainty. "I
thought you'd be more comfortable there," her lovely lips
curved, "an antique surrounded by antiques."

His smile lit his features and he gathered her against him,
crushing her mouth beneath his. His kiss was quick, a wild
slide of wet tongues and warm lips, utterly possessive and
devastatingly erotic. She felt her feet leave the floor and didn't
care that Noal looked on, didn't care if anyone saw them, only
that Ramsey was holding her. His hand roughly rode her spine,
slipping familiarly low before he set her down with a thump.
His gaze dropped to the book she still held, and he lifted her
wrist, reading the title: *Life in the Eighteenth Century.*

His heart fairly leapt out of his chest. "You needn't read that,
love, for you've a reliable source within your tender reach."

'Twas a plea, an open door and he'd wait an eternity for her
to step inside, he thought, then turned toward Noal, nodding
down the hall to the study.

Clutching the book, Penny sagged against the wall, breathing
heavily, thinking she was a fool to get in this deep, yet wanting
to dive another thousand feet with him.

Noal was a gentleman and made no comment about what
just happened, but the sexual tension between those two was
hot enough to make him squirm in the leather seat. Penelope,
it seemed, had met her match. He'd known her for years, done
some investigating, some dating, but her high recognition didn't
mix with his need for a low profile status. Yet he'd never seen
her that . . . electric. Not toward anyone.

Ramsey dropped an envelope on the desk, and Noal looked
up.

"Your services are no longer needed."

Noal reached for the envelope, opening it and fanning his

thumb across the crisp currency, whistling softly. "This is too much."

Ram merely shrugged.

"You have any problems with my men?"

"Nay. 'Twas Penelope who broke her promise to remain on the grounds. I cannot fault them for her cleverness. 'Twas not expected. I shall remain at her side." It infuriated him, his inability to protect her.

"Til these guys are caught or something gives, I don't think it's wise to let up."

"I am not, but—"

He heard Penelope scream his name, the sound of rapid footsteps, and he left the study in a dead run. The front door was thrown open, a guard carrying Meggie over the threshold, Penny matching his steps. She turned frightened worried eyes to Ramsey and he cleared the sofa of pillows, letting the guard lay her out.

Penny knelt beside Margaret, stroking her head. Her hand came back covered in fresh blood. Penny shot to her feet and ran to the kitchen, filling a pitcher, dragging out towels, ice, a bowl and aspirin, clutching them to her chest as she tore back into the living room. She pushed her way between Ramsey and Noal, setting the items on the coffee table as Ramsey propped up Margaret's feet, then shifted around to hover over the back of the sofa.

Penny checked Margaret's eyes. "She's unconscious."

"What!" a voice said and Penny glanced up to see Hank striding across the room, panic struck across his weathered face. Hank sank down beside her.

"Talk to her, Hank," she said, enfolding the ice in a towel, then tucking it beneath Margaret's head. "She has to wake up. Now."

Hank grasped Margaret's hand, patting it as Penelope gently washed the blood from her head and neck.

"In the butler's pantry, under the sink is a first aid kit," she said to no one in particular and within moments it appeared before her vision. She suspected it was Ramsey.

Penny assessed the damage; not deep enough for stitches,

yet she had to clip away some of Margaret's hair to afix a butterfly.

I saw Tess do that, Ram thought, watching her work with swift efficiency. Her concentration was fixed, her movements practice although her hands trembled, and he remembered Tess caring for Dane in much the same manner, the morning he was caught in the broken mast and received a concussion that nearly killed him.

"Try harder, Hank," Penny urged, applying ice to her wrists. Margaret stirred, moaning and reaching for her head.

"Open your eyes, Margaret," Penny commanded, restraining her hands.

"Aw, Meggie, darlin'," Hank said softly when her eyes fluttered open, and Penny glanced to the side, her frown deepening. There were tears in his eyes. Penny's gaze slid to Ramsey, then Hank and Margaret.

"What have you gone and done now, woman?" He bent a kiss to her forehead.

"Oh hush up, you old goat," she slurred, "and give me some air."

Margaret looked around at the small crowd, her eyes tearing when they fell on Penny.

"Can you tell us what happened?"

Margaret's lips quivered and she glanced at Ramsey. He rested his hip against the back of the sofa and grasped her hand.

She told them, and at the mention of the dark car Penny's gaze swept up to lock briefly with Ramsey's.

"Why didn't you tell us they'd made contact?"

"It was a note, an ordinary letter, addressed to me, not you," she said to Penelope. "I didn't think much of it, thought it was junk mail, no postmark, no return address. I didn't even go through it til yesterday. I never dreamed—oh, I'm sorry. You've got to believe me, I would have said something but I was afraid for you."

"It's all right," Penny soothed. "As long as you're safe." Penny leaned close and kissed her cheek, blinking rapidly. "I would die without you," she whispered and Margaret offered a tremulous smile.

"Where is the letter, Meggie?" Ram asked.

"In my rooms, on my dresser." Margaret tried to get up, but Penny held her down.

"Downstairs," Penny said to Ramsey.

"No, I'll get it." Hank kissed Margaret once, short but passionate and Penny's gaze followed him til he disappeared beyond the kitchen. It struck her then that they were in love. She wasn't so blind that she didn't realize there was some affection between them over the years but they were madly, deeply in love, like teenagers.

Cutting herself off from the public, maintaining that precious privacy, she realized, made her an ostrich with its head stuck in the sand. For she'd lost so much in the process. Yet that the two people she adored most hadn't told her, had hidden their love from her and . . . well, it hurt, and made her feel like a selfish demanding *bitch*.

Oh, Margaret, she despaired, after all they'd been through.

"So, is he going to make an honest woman out of you or are you just going to keep living in sin?"

"Look who's talking about sin," Margaret managed, her gaze flicking meaningfully to Ramsey.

Ramsey tried to look affronted. "Meggie, you're a shameless tart."

"Yeah, yeah, but a damn good cook, too," she said. Ram chuckled, squeezing her hand, then nodded to Noal, who stood discreetly back, near a window. The two men met in the foyer.

"I fear I've been hasty in releasing your services."

"No problem. But we have to get a hold of that letter. If there is anyway we can trace where it came from, we'll have *some* proof."

Ram shook his head, a gesture delivered more to himself for the wonders of this century continued to amaze him. Follow the path of a slip of paper?

And where was Hank?

As Noal went off to speak with his men, *hired guns,* as Penny had come to call them, Ramsey passed through the galley to the set of stairs leading to the cellar. Even as he descended he'd wondered why Margaret chose to live below, until he saw the rooms. 'Twas teaming with light and lovelier than he'd imagined, white walls, pale-green carpet and several tall plants filled the parlor. A door to the left led off to the housekeeper's bedroom and tucked beneath the sleekly sculptured stair case was a small serviceable galley. Ramsey was impressed, yet his pleased smile fell when he saw Hank standing afore a shelf, his arms loosely at his side. Ram could feel the despondency in the man and he frowned.

"Mate?"

Hank turned around, sniffling as Ramsey strode close.

"The letter?"

Hank handed it over and Ramsey examined it. 'Twas thin paper, a quality common in this century, he'd come to know, and was not marked except for the address and Meggie's name. He opened it and read.

Coral Keys Park
Near the bird sanctuary.
1 P.M.

His suspicions were confirmed. Whoever was in that dark carriage had been waiting for them to deliver the diamonds and Ramsey was surprised they'd gotten away with their lives.

"That could have been stuck in the mailbox by anyone," Hank said, defensive. "Won't find any fingerprints worth anything either, too much handling."

Hank turned his gaze to the shelf and the framed photographs lining the wood.

"'Tis Penelope?" Ram said, stepping closer, consistently intrigued by this process of capturing images on paper.

"She's four or five in that."

Ram was struck by the dark weathered look on the child's face, as if she were an adult in an adolescent's body. It gave him pause to wonder what had happened to make her appear so unapproachable, even then. Her thin arms were folded over her chest, a mutinous dare on her face. No smile, not even the devilish pleasure of the innocent.

"She wasn't a happy kid," Hank said as if to himself. "Didn't know her name, but then she didn't talk either. She was a pitiful thing, skinny and with all that red hair. Only thing she had was that dang locket and wouldn't let it go, chewed on it even." He shook his head, almost chuckling. "Margaret found her behind a store, sleeping in a grocery cart, having one hell of a nightmare." Ramsey looked horrified. "Yeah, that's how they knew she could talk, 'cause she screamed. Sometimes she'd lash out violently, try to hurt herself." Hank shrugged, not understanding. "I think she still has nightmares, but 'course she wouldn't let on."

Yet she refuses to face what e'er is the cause, Ram thought, for to ask for help would be a sign of weakness to her.

"Thinking she was doing right, Margaret took her back to child welfare. See, she'd run away from a foster home we found out later, her third. She checked on her, tried to get some doctors to take a look at her, did once, but she took off. When Margaret found out," he blew out a breath—"she took to the streets, searching. The first words that child said was 'don't let them hurt me.' " His voice fractured and Ramsey's heart wrenched for the frightened little girl. "Margaret wouldn't give her back to them when she knew they didn't care."

"Was she with Meggie long?"

"A few years, even when Tess came along." Hank chuckled sadly. "Tess, sort of, moved in without an invitation. God," he said shaking his head, his face wreathed with pleasant memories. "She was all smiles and jokes and too quick with locks for her own good." His expression withered. "Got her into trouble, that cleverness."

Ram's gaze studied the photos, wanting to know more of the woman he loved. "And this one?"

Hank squinted. "Sorority sisters." He pointed to the Delta PI symbol, then picked out Penelope, Tess.

Ram recalled that Anthony said Sloane Rothmere was a sorority sister and asked.

"That's Sloane. Pretty, huh?"

"If one cares for blondes."

Hank slanted him a sharp look. "You love our Penelope, don't you?"

Ramsey's brows rose into his forehead.

"Hell, I know you do. Aren't many men who'd put up with

that frosty bite of hers to find out what she's really like." Hank chuckled, more to himself, then gestured to a large photo. "That's their college graduation."

College, Ram realized, stunned. 'Twas a man's privilege in his time and he'd thought mayhaps Penelope and Tess attended a school for women, not a university.

"But I understood Penelope was older."

"She is, but she missed a lot of school." His tone hardened. "Sloane never let her forget that either." Hank turned away, rubbing his hand over his face. "Case you hadn't noticed, I don't like the Rothmeres. Sloane especially. She's a spoiled brat with a mean streak as wide as her bank account."

Ramsey frowned. "You've seen this?"

"The damage it did? Yeah." Hank nodded, folding his arms. "When Miss H. was in college she was cruel to her and when Tess attended, the pranks and viciousness got worse. Always directed at Tess." His tone bit with anger. "Neither of those girls did anything to hurt Sloane," came with absolute conviction. "She just didn't like them 'cause in her eyes, they were nothing but white trash and didn't belong in her *world.*" He flicked his nose for emphasis. "The more Sloane and her friends tried to beat them down, the tougher they got though. Miss H. is harder on herself than anyone was to her."

"I noticed," Ram said unnecessarily and Hank smirked.

"Tess was a national champion." He gestured to the famed magazine cover of *Gymnastic World.* "And Pen—Miss H., she was valedictorian as well as having an acting career that beats Meryl Streep's all to hell."

A father's pride speaking, Ram thought, smiling tenderly, his gaze sweeping the apartments. Margaret's shelves and walls were covered with photos of Penelope, clipped from newspapers and magazines.

Yet 'twas the open book on the low table that drew his attention and Hank slammed it shut, sending Ramsey a warning look. But Ram caught a glimpse of its contents.

"Margaret would do anything for Penelope," Hank said defiantly.

"Even lie?"

Hank stood rock still, his fists clenched, his pale aged eyes daring Ramsey to make another remark.

"Go to your woman, Hank," Ram murmured, his compassionate gaze speaking for him. He would not press the matter now. And the old man's shoulders sagged. He turned to leave, stopping short, tension leaping into his spine.

"I'm sorry, Miss H." His expression slackened. "Aw honey, I didn't mean to—"

"It's all right, Hank." Penny smiled gently, forgivingly, before she inclined her head toward the stairs. "Margaret's asking for you." He sprinted past like a man half his age and Ramsey watched Penelope ascend the stairs with her usual grace.

"Are you through prying?"

"I but listened." She made a soft sound of doubt and he crossed to her. A quirk of his lips and then, "And you were eavesdropping."

"It's kind of hard not to when I heard my past spilled out for examination."

"What e're occurred 'twas nay your fault."

Her gaze slid from photo to photo, remembering Margaret's tender care and her thirst for it. "I was a scared little girl with nowhere to go."

"You should be proud, Penelope," he said to her profile. "You have come far."

Her gaze jerked back to his. "I don't want your pity," came in a guarded voice, her shoulders stiff. "So I had it tough? Big deal. I don't remember most of it before Margaret, so don't ask anymore."

He wanted to shake her and drew on his patience. "I do not care from whence you've come, only that it still has the power to wound you."

Silence, chilled air swirling around them and Ramsey took a step closer, his voice beseeching. "When will you see that I've not come two hundred years into the future to resurrect your past for the world to view?"

Her stiff posture withered and she met his gaze. "I know." She covered his hand resting on the bannister.

"Our past shapes us into who we are, love, the young given to faults in order to learn."

"What faults can be so bad that a parent would abandon their child?"

She blames herself, he realized. "Are you certain you were abandoned?"

"Yes, that's all I know, all I feel." She rubbed her arms. "Sometimes there's a sense of safety, it comes with a strange smell, like fruit, but then it's gone, before I can figure it out."

"What else do you recall?"

"Darkness, and a voice telling me they didn't want me back." She shrugged, appearing much the forgotten child. "Do you know what that does to a kid?" She briefly looked to the ceiling, breathing deeply and Ramsey realized she was terrified of being loved and hurt like that again. "God. Sometimes I wish I could remember so I could blame something tangible for making me feel so discarded." She turned toward the stairs, mounting the first few.

"I wonder if my own son would have thought of me in that manner?"

Penny froze, then turned. "Your son?"

Ram nodded, bracing his hip against the bannister. "His mother and I were but a passing fancy, and I'd thought not to see her again. Til word came again that I'd made a child with her." His throat worked. "I returned from a voyage in time to put her in the earth."

"And the child?" She moved quickly down the steps. "Did you leave him back there?" Her tone accused and worried at the same time.

"He took his last breath in my arms." He lifted his gaze, his expression utterly miserable. "My only true regret is he died without my name."

Her green eyes held his, slowly glossing with tears. "Oh, Ramsey." She descended the last step, sliding her arms around his waist and holding him. "I'm so sorry."

He pressed his lips to her hair, squeezing his eyes shut. "Til then, I thought the stripping of my back by a slaver's whip was the worst pain I could endure."

She tilted her head to look at him. "A slaver?"

His voice was devoid of emotion when he said, "I angered the wrong people, it seemed, and was kidnapped off my ship, clapped in irons and sold as a slave in the Turkish market."

"Dear God, that's horrible!" She'd thought those scars had something to do with the British.

"I was there until Dane and his troops rescued me."

"Troops?"

"Aye—"

"Wait. You really are—were a Continental Marine?"

"Aye." His shoulders stiffened as if he were waiting for her to make jest.

But she didn't, infinitely proud of him and the courage it must have taken to endure life back then. "You're not the least bit ashamed of those scars, are you?"

"Nay." He hooked his thumb in his belt loop. "For without the reminder, I'd become naught but a cocky bastard."

She grinned. "Like you aren't already?"

Chapter 32

Halting on Margaret's staircase, Penelope sent Ram a frown back over her shoulder, then inclined her head toward the open door. Ramsey followed her gaze up the remaining cellar steps to where Noal was waiting, arms folded, his expression oblique.

As Penelope emerged to cross the threshold, Ramsey didn't mistake the suspicious glare she dealt the detective afore she swept past to check on Margaret. Noal seemed oblivious to her censure. Did she suspect him of eavesdropping, and how much had he heard that would be damaging?

Ram stared at the paper briefly. Were he in his time he would have confronted Phalon or Sloane at the point of sword, without regard to the consequences. Yet 'twas not so, and it forced him to step carefully. 'Twas a thin rope they trod, he thought, afore handing the letter over to Noal.

"Computer paper, and a common font," Noal said, holding it up to the light. "I doubt we'll get a print." He met Ramsey's gaze. "I've wired the phone but I don't think these guys are going to risk it. Too slick. Extra camera surveillance and ten guards ought to be enough." Noal sighed, glancing briefly away. "But I get the feeling it's wasted manpower."

Ramsey rolled his shoulders, his impatience to solve this

puzzle and be done with it making his tone sharp. "Speak, man, I'll not risk another getting hurt."

"I realize you hired my team for protection and some paperwork, but I can't help, if I don't know who I'm fighting."

He'd no proof this mess was the makings of a Rothmere, nor could he say aught about the missing gems, for to do so would force him to tell how he'd come to know of their existence in the first place.

"I fear it would put you in a difficult position were you privy to all the facts." He would not discredit Tess's reputation, nor Penelope's. 'Twas her choice to keep whate'er the deuce she was hiding from scrutiny and he'd respect it, for it mattered not to this situation. Nor to him.

"All right, all right," Noal said, almost angrily. "That I can understand that. But at some point, you've got to trust me completely."

Noal turned away and Ramsey caught a glimpse of Penelope crossing the foyer. And he headed toward the study, stopping short on the threshold, frowning, his gaze on the journals stacking the desk. Quickly crossing the room and reaching for the first, he hesitated when he saw the slip of paper tucked in the bind. He slid it free and read, his smile slow and incredibly pleased.

> Ramsey,
> I can tell you're restless. Don't ask me how, but I can. Maybe a little light reading will help.
>
>   Penelope

He opened the book, his gaze skimming. Tess's journals. The impact of Penelope's offer struck through his heart with a sweet poignancy, for trusting him with her most precious friendship scripted in these journals told him more than he'd hoped. Running his fingers over the neatly printed words, he tried to imagine what Tess was thinking when she set about to prepare the trunk for Penelope. With it came the vivid picture of Penelope, confused and helpless over the discovery, lashing out at her only target.

Such an obstinate lass, he thought with a smile, the moment shared below stairs giving him a deeper view of her soul. He would not gainsay her sense of abandonment within the darkness of her dreams, for he'd witnessed her torment, yet what e're haunted her sleep owned the blame for such a low opinion of her worth. Poison, she once called herself, not good enough to be loved and he wanted to shred the soul who made her feel so unworthy. And without friends to speak of, not even casual visitors, nor taking a moment for herself in a simple pleasure, Ramsey recognized how much Tess's friendship must have sustained her.

'Twas difficult to believe the two women were so close, for Tess was fearless, bold and defiant, and absorbed life with a zest everyone felt, whereas Penelope was stubborn and reserved, shielding herself like a punished princess. Holding the world at bay.

She was generous with her wealth and home, but her heart was another matter. She guarded it so carefully Ramsey felt she were doling out portions of herself to him.

And greedy son of Triton that he was, he wanted it all.

Penny hung up the phone, numb. "Where's Ramsey?"

"Outside." Margaret shrugged, her gaze on her needlework. "Replacing shingles or building me some flower boxes or probably digging a new pool. Heck, I've never met a man who liked backbreaking work more than him."

"He's going to put me out of a job," Hank said, walking into the solarium, a lunch tray in his hands.

"Not a chance," Penny said almost absently, then came to her feet, giving her spot beside Margaret to Hank.

"What's the matter, honey?" Margaret asked from the sofa, frowning. "You look like you've seen a ghost."

"That was for him," she said, gesturing to the phone, her gaze searching the scenery beyond the wall of windows.

Margaret and Hank exchanged uneasy glances. "Who was it, dear?"

"Tony." She swallowed. "It seems that Ramsey has an

appointment,'' a pause and a deep breath, ''with Alexander Blackwell.''

Margaret paled and Hank grasped her hand.

''He's sailing from Corpus Christi. He lives on a boat.'' She brought her gaze to the couple. ''Do you believe that? I thought they were all gone and now—'' Something jittered in her stomach. A Blackwell. She wanted to meet him.

''Well, you'd better go tell him,'' Margaret said softly.

Hank snapped a look at Margaret and she nodded sadly.

Penny didn't notice and walked toward the door. ''Hank, if she gets up off that couch again—'' She paused on the threshold, turning to look at the couple—''kiss her til she gives up.''

Forcing a smile, Hank looked back at Margaret, nudging her. ''Go on, try it,'' he dared, but nothing could break her gaze from Penelope's retreating figure.

''She's going to hate me, Hank.''

''You're acting like the rest of the world, underestimating how big that heart of hers really is.''

Tears welled in Margaret's eyes. ''I know. But I'm scared.'' And Margaret wanted to call her back, confess, but she wasn't strong enough and watched the child she'd raised reach for the door.

Penelope opened the front door and found the guard clutching her mail. Her gaze narrowed on his face, the quick shift of his features. If she hazard a guess, he'd been caught examining her correspondence. Was he expecting a letter bomb, she thought cynically.

''I'll take that,'' she said, hand out. He gave it up, then moved further down the steps. She was about to toss it all on the hall table when a large envelope caught her attention. It was too plain, no return address and she opened it, sliding the contents free. Her breath caught.

Damn. Oh damn.

Not again. Please, not again. She searched the envelope again, inside and out, for a postmark, for anything that would lead to who was doing this.

Nothing.

But she knew. And Penny tore the photo in half, then again

and again, exacting vengeance in ripping tiny pieces, then flinging them in the trash.

Breathing raggedly, she pushed her fingers through her hair,
her gaze on the waste basket and she saw her life, what she
had with Ramsey, unraveling because she was once young and
stupid and desperate.

No more!

She needed to tell him, end this ghost chasing away her
chance for happiness. She needed his strong arms around her,
to hear his eloquent voice. She needed to feel like she always
did with him, like nothing else mattered.

Like she was home.

Ramsey rubbed the cloth across the mare's back, marveling
at the even silver opulence of its coat. Majestic beast, he
thought, giving the animal's neck a pat, then forcing its weight
to the side and turning back a hoof. He picked clean the dung
and hay, humming a sea chanty. Sweat trickled down the center
of his bare chest and back, yet he enjoyed heated confines of
the stables, the scents and labor familiar. After reading Tess's
descriptions of his time, all that was common to him yet exciting
to her, Ramsey needed to feel a part of his century, to touch
and work it beneath his hands. And he found it in the stables,
the inside plain, dirt floors, wood walls. 'Twas the only area
on this estate that he'd not an annoying set of modern contraptions to understand afore he could perform a simple task. He
felt at ease here.

Dane had always allowed him the freedom of *Coral Keys*
and more often than with a willing wench, Ramsey could be
found within the stables. But 'twas the home he envied, he
knew, the sense of belonging, a rightful place for all who
came afore and would come after. 'Twas not the heirlooms or
furniture inside which made a stone and wood structure a home,
but the lives it sheltered, the bodies it kept warm in the coolness
of fall, the privacy and protection it gave lovers and innocent
babes. Ramsey ached for that, a place to plant his feet firmly
and call his home again, yet Penelope's home was just that,

unmistakably hers. Though his pride was already in a shambles over the woman, for he'd do aught to be with her, he wanted to provide for her.

The sea captain needed work.

And he wanted a wife.

A stubborn, cat-eyed redhead with a reluctant heart and a passion unequaled.

And babies, he decided. Lots of them. That she might already be carrying his child made him grin hugely as he moved into a empty stall and forked the bale of hay, spreading it sparingly on the dirt.

The mare nudged his shoulder. "Patience, lassie, I've chores to finish afore we can play."

Smiling, Penny stepped quietly into the barn, her panic easing with just the sight of him. Bare to the waist, his breeches and seawater stained knee boots made him look every inch a man of his century and seeing him in this rough setting gave her a vague look to the life he'd once led. No luxury, no idle hours. He did everything with a vibrance for life and living, yet with an ease of familiarity. And Ramsey never let up. An eighteenth century workaholic, she thought, watching him spear and spread hay.

"Did you have the irresistible urge to sweat and stink today, or what?"

He turned sharply, his features immediately softening and he propped his arm on the top of the fork handle. "Does a body well to do a bit of hard work."

"Obviously," she said, her warm gaze lingering over his bare muscled chest. She needed his nearness, the solid testimony of strength and assurity, and it drew her like a magnet.

"Off with you now." He shooed her back. " 'Tis no place for a lady."

He received the reaction he'd expected, God love her, and Ramsey admired the confident authority in her every long-legged step.

"I never said I was a lady."

"Nor could you disclaim it." She looks upset, he thought and tried not to frown his concern.

"Anthony phoned." She plucked a sprig of hay from his hair. "Why didn't you tell me about Alexander Blackwell coming to see you?"

"Excellent," Ramsey said, incredibly pleased Dane's family had not completely perished. "I did not know any Blackwells still existed. I merely wished to purchase the shipping company."

"Why? It can't be more than just a name on paper after twenty years, if that much."

"Mayhaps." He shrugged. "His arrival is but the beginning. I owe a great deal to Dane, and to see his legacy survive is but a small effort for all he's given me."

The affection in his voice touched her. They were like brothers, she realized, and he misses him. "I wish I'd known Dane. He seems like a remarkable man."

"He'd have liked you, Penn, if aught for that you've let me envision 'tis more than life on the sea."

"What an honor," she said, her heart hammering. "Though I don't believe you had any real help from me." It hurts just to look at him and know it might end soon, she thought, fighting her despair and trying to muscle the nerve to tell him everything.

Ram searched her eyes, his concern magnifying. "Penelope." She looked about to cry and he reached to brush her hair from her cheek, then saw the dirt coating his hand and drew back.

She slapped on a bright smile. "Where's the trainer?" she blurted and his brow furrowed, unease skipping down his spine.

She wasn't fooling him. A'tall. "Mister Crane has left to be with his child."

She nodded, sinking into his dark eyes and finding peace. "Oh yeah," she said as if just remembering. "She had a competition today." Ram frowned his ignorance. "She's a gymnast. In fact, she was one of Tess's students."

Ram smiled, pleased she hadn't distanced herself from her employees as he imagined. "I offered to complete his tasks in his stead."

"That horse is worth a fortune and needs constant care, Ramsey."

He braced a hand on his hip. "Are you implying I am not qualified?"

"No." Penny wrinkled her nose. "You certainly smell like you are."

Mercilessly, he moved within a hair's breath. "When was the last occasion you rode the beast?" came in a husky tone and her insides jingled with excitement.

"Them?" she said. "They're racehorses. Professional jockeys ride them."

"Evidently not well enough. I see no ribbons." He inclined his head toward the empty trophy wall even as his gaze rolled down her body with a hot possessiveness.

"They're tax write-offs." Her claim sounded like that of a child cornered by the town bully.

"A possession owned but never enjoyed." He hurumphed, turning his back as he switched his fork for a shovel, systematically scooping and dumping horse dung into a bucket.

"Considering I don't ride, it hardly matters."

He cast her a sly look she couldn't quite decipher, then dumped another pungent pile afore he hefted the bucket and strode toward the rear of the barn.

Every inch of him was defined and prominent and the muscles in his back rippled and flexed as he pitched horse crap into the bed of a truck parked out back. Her fingers clenched. The pale scars at the base of his spine glistened, arresting her for a brief instant. Whip scars. A slave. It was hard to imagine a proud man like him submitting to anyone, and deep inside she hurt for him and all he must have suffered.

"Why are you doing this, Ramsey? It could have waited."

He bent over the sink to wash his hands and arms, lather foaming. "I needed to touch my time," he said, soaping his face and neck, then surprised her by dunking his head beneath the faucet's spray. He rinsed, splashing water across his chest, then straightened, flinging his head back and shaking like a puppy before pushing the hair out of his eyes and meeting her gaze.

"You miss it, don't you?" Her eyes followed the path of

water streaming down his chest, breaking over his flat coin nipples and soaking his trousers.

Slowly he shook his head, the pattern of her gaze leaving its telling effect on his body. "I find this century has much to offer this lowly seaman." He returned her stare, heady and captivating.

There was *nothing* lowly about him, she thought, yet knew he hadn't known luxury, spending the better part of his life fighting in the revolution, enslaved, or aboard a ship in small cramped quarters with rotten food, doing backbreaking work.

But who he was made her love him more.

Penny blinked, glancing away from his possessive stare. I do, she thought, a smile tugging, and she met his gaze. I always have. Archaic down to his knee boots and hippie hair, she loved him.

And she would lose him if she didn't give up diamonds that no longer existed in this century. She knew she'd do anything to keep that from happening. She wanted him forever.

Ramsey halted midstride, the look on her face catching him in the gut. Sunlight peeled into the barn, a bright wedge in the cool dark, and his sudden need to hold her close and tight and sheltering nearly overpowered him. He wanted to take her away from whatever was upsetting her and drew her horse from the stall, then slipped on a bridle.

"Wh-what are you doing?"

"Exercising the mount," he said patiently.

"You aren't supposed to ride them. Crane takes them to the track for that."

He arched a brow in her direction. "When you have a perfectly good stretch of beach?"

"Ramsey," she delivered his patient tone right back at him. "That horse costs too much to be a pleasure mount and isn't it dangerous, leaving the grounds?"

He ducked beneath the horse's neck and stepped into a stall, coming back with his pistol and a powder horn and small sack dangling from a leather strap. He dropped the strap over his head and shoved the flint-lock in his waistband.

Her gaze lowered to the barrel and its obvious direction.

"Living dangerously, I see." She took a breath and lifted her gaze. "All that unstable fire power."

"Me or the weapon," he said, grinning lecherously, then with an agility that shouldn't have surprised her, swung up onto the horse's back. Just to see him up there, powerful and commanding, drove an unspeakable heat through her blood.

"No saddle?"

He shook his head, his eyes never leaving hers as he controlled the eager horse with one hand and offered her the other. "Come ride with me."

"No." She stepped back as the horse pranced regally.

"Mayhaps yer afraid to be alone with me again?"

The challenge made her smile. "Of course not, you arrogant antique. I'm not dressed to ride." She flicked a hand at her short leather skirt and Ramsey admired the length of leg exposed, the coltish limbs enhanced by her heeled shoes. The skirt, or what there was of it, was black and hugging, contrasting to the billowy sleeved white blouse. She looked delicious enough to ravish.

Still, he held out his hand. "Come with me, Penelope." The horse sidestepped impatiently. "Place your foot atop me boot and join me." She started at the mentioned boot, biting her lip. His voice was smooth and coaxing. "Be free with me."

Penny lifted her gaze, excitement singing through her. It had been years since she'd done anything reckless. Except maybe, making love with him on the piano, in the shower, or hiding in a rickety warehouse waiting to be attacked.

Ramsey sucked air in through clenched teeth when she shimmied the shirt up her thighs and placed the ball of her foot on his instep. He lifted her onto his lap, sideways, sliding his hands luxuriously down her bare legs and prying off her shoes.

"I despise spurs," he said in an intimate tone, tossing them to the floor, then shifting her leg over the horse's neck. With her skirt hiked to the top of her thighs, her position invited his touch and his hands itched to roam her warm flesh. Blood rushed to his loins, hot and quick, and he wisely repositioned his flint-lock in the back of his breeches and concentrated on handling the animal and not the bulge crowding his breeches.

"Ready?" came in a strained whisper.

She glanced back over her shoulder and nodded as Ramsey slipped his arms around her waist and adjusted the reins. "Hold tight, love." A smokiness hung in his voice as he said, " 'Tis a remarkable pleasure having such a powerful beast surgin' atween ones legs."

She colored, her lips curving in sweet innocence, her hand coming up to lightly pat his jaw. "I believe I've already experienced that."

His deep laughter joined the dust behind them as the horse jolted out of the barn. Hooved feet clattered on the stone drive afore Ramsey angled them toward the lawn and knead the beast faster, leaving clumps of Tennessee bluegrass sod chopped and scattered in their wake. They skidded down the tree dotted slope toward the beach, heading for the azure shoreline. The animal was swift and sure-footed, fountaining sand and water glistening the silver coat, a salty mist sprinkling the riders as they raced the hemmed coastline.

"Oh God, this is great!" she shouted, laughing, her hair fanning across Ramsey's chest and shoulder as she leaned back into him.

The charger's hooves dug into the sand, laboring to capture the pleasure never allowed. Waves splashed, foam churned, their own breathing excited and swift, and Ram felt suspended in air, felt her pleasure of freedom, and then she shrieked a laugh, clear and bright and clean.

"Faster, faster!" she begged and he pulled her tightly against him, bending low as the thoroughbred took the head. Their ride was nearly soundless, the splash of waves coating their speed. They raced until the horse tired, then walked for a pace to cool the mare. Ramsey stopped and slid from the animal's back, then helped her down, holding on until her legs adjusted to her weight.

"That was incredible," she said, falling against him, breathless, cherry cheeked and lush. "Thank you."

He didn't know whether or not 'twas seawater or tears he saw. " 'Tis me pleasure, lass." The reins caught in his fingers, he brushed whispery strands from her face, her delight like an aphrodisiac.

"You were right, about the surging beast. Sort of like foreplay."

"Foreplay?"

"All those wonderful things you do to me before you—you know—"

He chuckled, catching her full against him. "Afore you beg me to take you?" he murmured silkily, nuzzling her ear.

"Something like that." She dragged her tongue across the line of his jaw, down the column of his throat.

"Afore I push inside you," he went on mercilessly, taking her mouth beneath his and she moaned against his lips, backing up the beach. The horse nudged his shoulder, urging them along.

"I think she's jealous." Penny's hands couldn't be still, sweeping his chest, down his tight ribs.

"She smells it," he murmured into her mouth, passion building.

"What?" She gripped his waistband, pulling him up the beach to the seclusion of brambly trees.

"The hunger," came in a deep rumble as he tossed the reins over a bush.

"Smart girl." She jerked him against her, the tight contact of hip to hip fueling awareness, and she flexed against his hardness, her gaze liquid and her breath rushing along the width of his chest as her tongue circled his flat nipple, sliding up the carved muscle to his throat. She was restless, impatient, her hands stroking the firm curve of his buttocks, her mouth and tongue wreaking havoc over his skin.

Suddenly he gripped her tightly and backed her up against a gnarled tree.

"I love when you're wild for me," he murmured, his head descending. She stretched to fill the space and his lips covered hers with a crushing force. His tongue thirstily outlined her lips, and she opened for him, the intensity of his sharp thrusting tongue making her purr with pleasure.

She was a tempest in his arms, grinding against him and

Ramsey felt her urgency, a desperation, and the canopy of shade did naught to shield the heat raging atween them. She was untamed, her desire racing without control, frantic and consuming and she clutched him, molding his damp muscled back, his waist and lean hips. She drew the pistol from his breeches and let it slide to the ground, then stripped the powder horn from his chest, tossing it aside afore she brought her hand to his breeches, shaping and molding his arousal with a boldness unmatched, prying at the buttons.

"Ramsey," she gasped against his mouth. "Come to me." Her body's cadence drove him wild, her touch pushing him to the summit and he swiftly unbuttoned her blouse, shoving the fabric off her shoulders, then peeling the delicate lace cups from her breasts. She arched, offering, the locket atween the lush swells of flesh as he bent, taking her nipple into the heat of his mouth, drawing deeply. She gasped and pleaded, holding him there, driving her fingers into his hair.

"Ramsey, I need you now, I do," she whimpered, hips thrusting. "Please."

Her body wouldn't wait; he could feel it edging the explosion, in her ragged breath, her restless shifting. He sank to his knees, shoving the leather skirt up to her hips and hooking his thumbs in her delicate panties, drawing them down. She flexed and rocked, his every touch pushing her closer to the edge of rapture and Ramsey tossed the scrap aside and tilted her hips, spreading her afore he took her softness beneath his mouth. She cried out and he pinned her hips to the tree with fistfuls of leather and devoured her, savoring her climax, spreading her wider and tasting her sweet erotic pleasure. She quaked, a bone racking shudder. A low guttural groan sanded in her throat and she urged him to his feet, tearing at his breeches, driving her hand inside and freeing him into her palm.

"More, more," she breathed. He cupped her buttocks, lifting her and she wrapped her supple legs around his waist, sinking onto his fullness.

Ramsey surged, imprisoning her against the tree and she laughed and choked and panted, her slickness gripping and drawing and he fought for some control in the wildness of wet sex and untamed lust. He thrust, her sleek body answering his rhythm. She clawed at him, bucked her hips to smash his and Ramsey had never tasted anything so wicked and free and passionate as Penelope when she wanted. He drove into her and she gripped handfuls of his hair, gazing into his eyes as each dark plunge brought them there again. Exploding. Rushing. Savage. He held her suspended, watching her climax unfold in her eyes, feeling it wrap him and squeeze and tear the last of his heart from his chest. They stared, for what felt like hours, the moment unchanged, breathing slowing. Then she smiled, pleased and sated.

A tear rolled down her cheek as she brushed his hair from his forehead, watching her movements. "You know," she sighed, "you are just plain dangerous to be around."

He chuckled deeply, glancing meaningfully at the scratches on his shoulders. "Dangerous for who?" Her legs gripped once and quick and he grinned at the threat, smoothing his hands over her bare buttocks. Slowly he left and she inhaled, sharp with pleasure. He kissed her deeply, letting her legs lower to the sandy ground. He worked magic over her mouth and Penny sank into the heady kiss, moaning when he pressed a cloth between her thighs. Did she ever know anyone so caring and giving, she wondered as he adjusted clothing, still kissing her, still holding her.

He lifted his head, his expression serious and dark as he gazed into her eyes.

"I want you."

She moved against him. "Again?"

"Nay, Penelope. I want you—forever."

She lowered her gaze to the damp center of his chest. "You don't know what you're asking."

"Aye, I do. I am too old to play games, lass, and too old not to know my heart speaks for you alone."

She pulled her shirt closed, tilting her head back against the bark. "Don't, Ramsey, you'll ruin it." She closed her eyes. Not yet, please.

"Me?" He cupped her jaw in his hands, forcing her to

confront him. "By God, woman, I am not the one desperately ignoring what is so obvious to everyone else."

"I'm not ignoring anything." She covered his hand with her own. "Don't you know that I can feel you, taste you, without touching or seeing you?"

"Then why are you so afraid of loving me?" His tortured look pushed the words past her lips.

"Everything I've done is coming back to destroy me. And it'll hurt you."

His hands dropped to her shoulders. "More than you are bleeding me now? Damn it, Penelope, I am not the parent who left you to rot in the street so do not make me pay for the crime. I am not going anywhere."

Her gaze searched his, rapid, unsure, and she saw all her hopes hanging on a thread about to snap. "You say that now."

"Great Neptune!" He stepped back suddenly. "Naught will change how I feel for you, but I will not have my heart held hostage by your past," he declared harshly. "Speak of what keeps you from me, from everyone, and be done with it!"

He looked so threatening, so angry, and a sob caught in her throat. "I'm scared."

His stern expression faltered and Ramsey waited, waited for her to come to him, feeling his future with her about to crumble into dust. He gazed deeply into her green eyes, praying she saw the love he wore like a part of his skin.

Penelope swallowed thickly, her breath filling her lungs. "I was a drug addict," came in a rush and his brows lifted a fraction. "Cocaine." She edged away from the tree, turning her gaze to the horizon, offering him her profile. "I'd run away from Margaret. We'd had a huge fight and I was too stubborn to admit I was wrong."

"That does not surprise me."

Her lips curved for a brief instant. "I lived on the streets, always avoiding the cops, because if they picked me up they might arrest Margaret. Her custody of me, well, wasn't legal." Memories rushed and she sank to her knees in the sand. "I stayed away so long, I couldn't go back. Too proud, too determined to do *every damn thing* alone."

She picked up a twig, digging in the sand. "God, you wouldn't believe the places and things I've seen; people so drunk they slept in their own vomit, addicts shooting heroine straight into their veins, kids younger than I was turning tricks in alleyways," she cast him a side glance as he lowered to the ground, "boys and girls. I learned to pick pockets, shoplift, just about anything to get what I needed, food, money, drugs. Christ, I even rolled my friends to get money for my habit."

She shook her head, damp hair shifting over her shoulders and she felt choked with shame, her words coming from a dark hollow place in her chest. "I posed naked for a photographer, Ramsey." He made no comment and she swallowed, afraid to look at him, but forcing herself to meet his dark gaze. His expression was unreadable. "I did it for money." She had to make him understand. "For *more* goddamn drugs!"

She gasped for air, misery weighing her voice and knew she might be destroying the only happiness she'd ever had. "After the first click of that shutter, I knew I'd sunk as low as it got. Later, I stole the film and split," she said on a tired sigh.

Ramsey treaded carefully, aware of how fragile she was, unwrapping her faults and failures for him. She took the drugs to escape her loneliness, he thought, admiring her for walking away from the temptation, for he'd experimented with opium, knew the blissful oblivion it brought.

"Christ, Ramsey." She jabbed at the sand, not looking at him. "Will you say something!"

Her hidden tears clawed his heart as he pried the twig from her tight fingers, gently caressing one hand. She risked her heart for him, for them, and he would not fail her. " 'Twas when you met Antony, aye?"

She nodded sullenly, sniffling behind a curtain of hair. "A few months later. He was more of a savior than he realizes. I tried so hard to clean up." She thumped her thigh with her fist, clinging to him with the other. "I had a second chance and didn't want anyone to know what a waste of human life I'd been, a no guts lowlife who'd hurt the people around her for another ten minute high."

Sweet mercy, Ram thought, she could not have been more

then five and ten at the time. " 'Tis not as damaging as you might believe. Remind me to tell you of my occasions as a slave and all I did to survive.''

She shifted toward him, her face a mask of regret and shame as she lifted her gaze. "I know that must have been hard, but don't you see? I lost control, of my life, my values, of my body—everything! *I* lost it.'' She poked her chest. "No one took it from me. Good God, Ramsey, it wasn't bad enough that I did it, but there's proof!''

"Children are given to faults in order to learn,'' he repeated his words from the day afore.

She scoffed. "I stopped being a child the first time I snorted a line of coke.'' She held his gaze, needing him to know everything. "Those negatives and photos were the bait in the packet Tess stole.'' His look said he'd already come to that conclusion. "It gets worse.''

His gaze sharpened.

She licked her dry lips. "I received a copy in the mail today.'' He scowled, annoyed she hadn't told him. "Whoever sent it said they'd give it to the newspapers if I didn't give up the stones.''

Ramsey silently fumed, not wanting his woman exposed for the world to see, but 'twas a matter they'd deal with then.

"You do not impress me as a woman who'd hide for the sake of what others will think.''

"Well, I did. For a long time my career was all I had. I didn't want to be famous, but acting came easy. I never imagined I'd get so much attention and it terrified me. They hounded me, made up stories, but I found that money made it easy to control my surroundings.'' Her lip quivered. "It's all so pointless, not when it can hurt you.'' She searched his eyes, soft amber-brown and gentle and prayed she wasn't imagining the emotion she saw there. "Oh Ramsey, I've made such a mess of things and I don't know how to fix it.''

"Aw, love.'' He reached, tenderly cupping her jaw, sliding his fingers into her hair. " 'Tis all but one thing you can do.'' His thumb swiped the tear moving down her cheek. "Tell your tale afore she can.''

She looked horrified at the idea and on his knees afore her, he held her shoulders, staring deeply into her eyes.

"Nay, do not speak and listen to me. Let them hear it from your lips, in your words. None have died from embarrassment, love." He gathered her in his arms. "Take the power away from her and you've lost naught."

A moment stretched. She swallowed. "It could get ugly." She gripped his biceps. "Will I lose you?"

Her heart lay afore him, bare and bleeding, waiting to be gathered into his tender care. And he shook his head. "Never. I have defied logic and reason and the laws of science to be with you." He smoothed the hair from her face. "Can you not feel we share the beat of one heart? Your pain is mine. Your breath, I breathe." His voice lowered. "Your passion is my blood."

"Ramsey," she whispered, searching his handsome face, tears welling in her eyes.

"Open your heart and take, Penelope, for naught can come atween us. We are destined." She whimpered, biting her lip, and he closed his arms tightly about her, driving his hand up her spine to cradle her head. "I have traveled two hundred years through time for you. To *find you.*" The conviction in his voice made her insides shift, hope blossom, spread. And he took a breath. "I love you," he said fiercely. "I love you so much I will perish without you."

A sob worked in her throat and she wet her lips. "Well, we can't have that."

He trembled. This big imposing man suddenly trembled like a frightened child.

"Do not speak the words," he warned softly, licking his lips. "If they are not in your heart."

"But they always were." She laid a hand to his chest, feeling the wild pump of his heart. "I've nothing to hide behind. You've stripped me bare." A breath and in a feathery voice, she said, "I love you, Ramsey O'Keefe." A ragged breath shuddered through his lungs and she realized he was as scared and unsure as she. "I love you."

He smiled, heart stopping and joyous, the corners of his eyes crinkling. "Again." He sprinkled kisses over her face.

"I love you."

He kissed her deeply, thoroughly, sinking to the ground and taking her with him.

"You love me," he marveled, pressing her into the sand.

"Yes, I *really* do."

Ramsey laughed, a delicious rumble of thunder as he smothered her with his love and Penny hungered for more, for the incredible freedom it gave her.

And the horse nickered, turning his big head and casting the lovers a mild glance as they rolled over each other on the pink sand.

Chapter 33

"Where have you two been?" Hank demanded like an angry father when Penelope stepped through the door, Ramsey behind her.

"Why? Is Margaret all right?"

"I'm fine," Margaret said, coming up behind him. "He's just being overprotective."

Hank looked them over, noticing the relaxed set of her shoulders, the way she held Ramsey's hand. And the hay in their hair.

"Lose your shoes?"

Penny looked down at her feet as if just noticing, then glanced at Ramsey. He simply smiled like a satisfied lion at his newly-won lioness.

He'll be hell to live with now, Penelope thought happily.

"And how'd you get all sandy?"

"Geez, Hank, leave 'em be," Margaret said, nudging him aside and moving to stand before Penelope. Margaret plucked a blade of straw from the girl's tangled hair and Penny blushed. "Get." She inclined her head toward the staircase.

Penny dropped a kiss to her plump cheek. "You should be resting," she said softly.

"If I laze around anymore I'll go nuts."

Penny slipped past, and Ramsey tried to follow but Margaret blocked his path.

"You aren't taken another step in this house with those boots, Ramsey O'Keefe. Shuck 'em," Margaret said and he did. She handed them over to Hank with a sour face and before she could say anything, Ramsey sprinted up the stairs.

"Mayhaps I'll keep these," Ram said from her doorway and she looked up from her position on the edge of the bed, smiling widely. Til her gaze dropped to the article dangling from his fingertip. It was her panties, black and stringy.

Her skin fused cherry red. "A trophy of the day?"

He stuffed the delicate scrap in his pocket, advancing, kicking the door shut, then pushing her down on the bed and covering her slim body with his own.

"Tell me again. Tell me."

"I love you."

"Why?"

"Because you're just so damn ugly."

He grinned. "Tell me again."

"Because you have to have the biggest feet I've ever seen on a man."

He chuckled, then kissed her thickly, hotly. "Again."

"I love you because you have an appetite—for food," she amended quickly, "that rivals the entire NHL hockey league and 'cause you don't know what that means."

He buried his face in the flesh of her throat. "But I'm sure you'll enlighten me."

"Of course," came breathlessly. "I love you . . . because . . ." She looked to the ceiling, thinking, and he dug his fingers into her ribs. She squealed and arched, then settled warmly against him. "Because you're strong and gentle and patient and forgiving and gallant." Her voice softened with each word, her fingertips brushing adoringly over his cheek, his lips. "I love you, Ramsey O'Keefe, because you see beyond everything and you never give up."

"Never, my love." His hand slid up her bare thigh, beneath

the skirt and she pushed into his touch. "You've sand all over you."

"Not *everywhere*."

He blinked. She arched a tapered brow, daring.

A moment later, he discovered she was right.

Tess's journals spread across the kitchen table afore him, Ramsey peered over the one he was reading, watching Penelope forage in the cupboards.

"Oh good," she said, removing one tall slim box after another and setting them on the counter. She studied her selections and Ramsey set aside the journal, tilting his head to read the brightly-printed words as he stood and came to her.

"It's cereal, normally for breakfast."

"That shouldn't matter to you," he commented dryly. Loving always seemed to give *her* the ferocious appetite to rival the teams of ice skaters.

"Here's one you'd like." She smirked a smile, setting a box before him. "Captain Crunch."

He chuckled, working open the package.

"With crunch berries," she added with zeal as he popped a handful into his mouth.

"Dewishous," he mumbled around the food and she shook some into a bowl and poured on the milk, shoving a spoon into the cereal before handing it to him. "Go, sit, eat."

"Aye-aye, Capt'n." He saluted her with the spoon and he took his seat, enjoying the crunchy cereal as she prepared herself a bowl of *Lucky Charms*

"I've a likin' for the wee marshmallows," she said with an Irish accent that was intolerable, then joined him at the table.

They crunched and munched, each taking up a journal, reading and relaying a passage aloud. "Listen to this," she said and read. "I can't seem to have anything but boys, little black haired ruffians with a penchant for trouble." She looked up, frowning. "Now does that sound like Tess?"

"Nay," he said, finishing off the cereal and pushing the bowl aside. "But she has been in my century long though."

He checked the date; eight years. "Mayhaps she's merely adapting."

She had to agree. "I hope you don't lose it, the way you talk, I mean." She tilted her head. "I can't imagine you walking around saying *totally awesome dude,* with any ease."

"I shant think so." He looked appalled at the idea and Penny grinned, returning her attention to the books.

She shifted uncomfortably, then stretched out her legs and he hoisted them onto his lap, rubbing her soles as he read a disturbing passage.

I know this will seem bizarre to you, Penn, but I am happy for you, for today I discovered you lost your heart to the biggest chauvinist on the face of the earth.

He closed the book, confused, casting it off as a secret atween the two women, then picked up another journal.

"I don't think Tess would have used the diamonds," she said into the silence and he looked up. "You know, for money. I know her. If they weren't hers, she wouldn't have turned them into cash. And they can't be legit if Phalon hasn't had me arrested, yet."

"He has no proof."

"How 'bout the stone you had appraised?" she countered, and he realized his mistake again. "Diamonds can be traced, Ramsey, like fingerprints." He leaned forward, interested. "They have flaws and dark spots that mark their quality and even if they are cut again, they can be identified. They're graded in their value, by the carat. Colored diamonds, blue, yellow, even pinks are rare. Pinks are especially valuable and the deeper the color, the rarer it is."

"The stone she left me is as red as your blushes."

Only he would make a comparison like that, she thought, her heart catching. "Except that if we don't know where they came from in the first place, I think it will be like fishing in a pond to find out. We have nothing to start from."

"If that is the case. Mayhaps Noal can discover—"

"No," she cut in sharply and he frowned. "I don't trust him that much."

"I'd assumed you knew the man." There was hitch in his voice he hated.

"I did, a few years ago, but—" She chewed her lip.

"What troubles you?"

She laid the journal on her lap. "If he's so good at his job how did those guys get close enough to whack Margaret and get to me?"

"You left the estate without permission," he reminded with a scowl, "and Meggie was not guarded. 'Twas my fault in not realizing *anyone* could have been a target."

She conceded the point, contrite over her part.

"Why do you not trust him?"

"He knows too much. He investigated my past for me. Tried to find out where I came from." A dull red crept up his neck and she sat back. "You had him do it, too," she accused.

"I saw that the dreams caused you such pain, love, and only tried to seek the source."

She stared at him, wondering why she wasn't as upset as she ought to be, then realized that Ramsey would never do anything to deliberately hurt her, or hurt anyone.

"Well, even a hypnotist couldn't help me. It doesn't really matter anymore." Her shoulders lifted and fell negligently. "I'm satisfied with my only link." She held up the locket and he examined it closely. "I didn't know my name, so I took it from this." He squinted, trying to see past the teeth marks. "P. H." she told him.

"Nay, love." His gaze shifted to hers. "The second letter, 'tis either an r or a b."

She blinked, her features gone slack and she gaped at the locket. "You really think so?"

"Aye." He rubbed the ink from a pen across his thumb, then squeezed the locket afore stamping his thumb on a pad of paper laying on the table atween them. Penny hovered over the paper, noting the slight curve in the engraving, then looked up, her face a portrait of disappointment.

"Gee. I'm not even a *real* fabrication," she whispered unhappily, comparing the dented locket to print. "Margaret will be surprised."

Ramsey tipped her chin, gazing into her eyes and wishing he could give her the heritage she so desperately wanted.

"I love *Penelope Hamilton,* and I'll fight to the death any soul who says otherwise."

The corners of her eyes crinkled, tears brimming. "I just bet you would."

She squeezed his hand, sniffled, then as if dismissing the incident, picked up the journal and continued to read. But Ramsey wasn't fooled. She was as he'd been when he first arrived, without connection, except she'd lived with it all her life. Her loneliness was not so much her own making, for 'twas in the wounding dreams she rediscovered her abandoning pain. And it pushed her into privacy, protecting herself from being hurt. The shadows of the night are the paths to our own hell, he thought and his heart wrenched for the child she was, for the woman he'd first met and the one he knew now. She was changing. He could see it, every moment he spent with her and he was arrogant enough to feel 'twas his love that gave her this glorious radiance. But he knew, 'twas just her time.

"Ramsey, look." He did and she showed him where the journal was coming apart at the back. "Oh, this is awful." He leaned close, prying up the edge, studying the binding. He picked up another, examining it closely, then handled hers again.

" 'Tis thicker, this side," he said and pressed the leaf page. It felt spongy, a crackle deepening his frown. He pried the edge further. " 'Tis false." He tugged and the leaf gave easily, only the corners tacked and Penny gasped as he slipped a piece of heavy paper from the back of the journal.

"Why would she do a thing like that? I would have never noticed it. It was one of the last ones, Ramsey." She might never have gathered the nerve to open the book if he weren't with her. Ramsey unfolded the parchment slowly and she leaned closer. "God, I can't even read that."

" 'Tis the words of my time. See the way the spelling is different and some letters are reversed. 'Twas a difficult feat for me, learning to read in this century."

"Really? I didn't realize." He sent her an amused smirk. "Amongst other things, huh?"

"Like how much I love you," he said and she leaned over, kissing him heavily on the mouth.

"Yup, now read."

His gaze slipped over her face afore he returned his attention to the paper. " 'Tis a document, legal words and such. Mayhaps a will."

"And?"

"I am unsure, but I believe it states that the Blackwell house, the grounds, and," he cleared his throat, "a certain painting, are to never leave the hands of a Blackwell descendant."

"The house? You mean Phalon has to," she jerked a thumb to the door, brows up.

"According to this, aye. Unless he can prove he is the rightful heir."

"When hell freezes," she said defiantly, then scanned the paper. "That's Tess's signature, and Dane's and—" she inhaled, her gaze flying to his—"does that say what I think it does?"

He frowned. She was suddenly tense, eager. " 'Tis but the signature of their barrister, love."

"Did you know him?"

"Aye. I've tipped a few pints," he grinned, "and did a bit of wenching with the man. Takes a muck of ale to loosen him up though." Ram chuckled, remembering. "And it never remained in his gullet overlong."

"You got drunk with Thomas Jefferson!" she fairly shrieked, coming out of her seat.

"Penn, my sweet, calm down." He tossed the document aside and pulled her onto his lap. "He was not quite the paragon of virtue."

"And what part, dare I ask, did *you* have in destroying that image?"

He sent her a mild glance. "I saved my prowess for deflowering virgins, robbing nunneries, and pillaging the coast," he said dryly and she blanched.

"Sorry."

"Beg for my forgiveness," he told her, regally looking else-where and she slid her hand beneath the folds of his robe.

"You'll tell me when I have it, huh?" She kissed his throat, his broad chest.

"Mayhaps."

"Is this foreplay?"

"Everything you do is," he growled, then covered her mouth with his. Her hand sank beneath his silk trousers and he flinched when she enfolded his arousal, warmly stroking him. "Penel-ope," he gasped.

"It's midnight and I've never made love in the kitchen."

"We could be discovered."

"Isn't that half the excitement?"

"Penelope," he pleaded.

"Then take me somewhere where there's a door. And hurry."

He lifted her in his arms and carried her to the nearest room, the one with the television, and set her to her feet long enough to tear away their robes and the lacey chemise she wore.

She laughed softly, pulling on the drawstring of his silk trousers, baring him for her eyes, then shoving him onto the couch. She slid to her knees and before he could wonder she took him into her mouth.

"Sweet Jesus!" he groaned, gripping pillows and her tongue slid mercilessly over the moist tip of him. "Penelope, nay, nay!" His long body shuddered like quaking earth and Penny laughed, soft and deliciously pleased, teasing him again, and he suddenly grasped her arms, dragging her up the length of him, then jerking her legs round his hips.

"By God, you unman me," he said, his wide chest heaving, his hand busy finding the moist source of her need and returning the torture.

"That'll never happen," she replied, her hips taking motion, his fingers playing. "Oh God, Ramsey, oh, oh—!" He bucked, shoving himself deeply inside her and she cried out, throwing her arms around his neck and clinging. She rocked, stealing the life from him and Ramsey drew his head back a fraction to watch. A wicked smile of pure sexual pleasure coasted across her lips, her slim body like liquid rhythm, undulating to the quick tempo of her passion. Her green eyes held him, her love of him teaming in the emerald depths and Ramsey knew rapture, knew why men dueled and died for the love of one woman. Suddenly she jerked, her muscles convulsing around him, thighs squeezing, fingers digging and only then did Ramsey fulfill his own need, wrapping his arms around her and jamming her downward. She moaned and squirmed, draining him of his fire, trembling. Her ragged breath whispered in his ear, a soft rushing feminine sound he adored.

She went slack and warm against him and he rubbed her spine for a few moments afore she leaned back slightly, fingering his hair off his forehead.

"I love you, Penelope." He caught her hand and kissed the palm.

"Why?" she said, yet no teasing smile graced her lips.

"Because thou art *you.*"

Her gaze flew to his.

"I need no reason, no words to define the workings of my heart. I simply do, my sweet."

Her lips curved, her look one of peace and serenity as she leaned in for a kiss.

"And of course, because you've the most beautiful breasts I've ever seen on a woman." She chuckled throatily as his big hands swept up her body to enfold the lush swells.

"An asset, I'm sure."

"Because you ravish the cupboards after you've had your pleasures."

God, she loved the way he talked. "Speaking of food . . ."

"Again?" he said and she wiggled off his lap, the separation nothing short of painful. She grabbed up her robe, slipping it on and disappearing out the door, leaving Ramsey disheveled, dismissed and feeling much the man who'd lost control. A few moments later she returned to his side with a tray laden with iced cans of soda, a tall glass of chilled beer, cookies, potato chips and a bowl of popcorn. She offered him the corn and he made a face.

"Pilgrim fodder," he muttered distastefully and she folded over with laughter.

"Oh Ramsey," she said happily. "You are definitely one of a kind."

"Permission to come aboard," Ramsey called from the dock.

"Granted," came from somewhere inside the vessel.

Ramsey strode up the gang plank, glad his legs could still adjust to the rock of the sea. 'Twas a modest ship, not even sixty feet or so, but two masted and low slung like a sloop. A cabin cruiser, the harbor master had told him, named the *Annora.* Unlike most of the other vessels in the harbor, which were mostly white and of fiberglass, a definition which eluded Ramsey, this craft was a fine piece of workmanship, constructed of dark wood, her deck polished to a high shine, her rails smooth and slick from a fresh coat of varnish and wax. The winches and pulleys gleamed of new brass, her sails a soft brown and rolled tight with leather strips instead of twine. Ramsey felt instantly at home and as he ducked beneath rigging, he decided he wanted one. 'Twould be a fitting place to take his bride, he thought, once she agreed to wed him. He stood midship, waiting, trying not to show his impatience when a slender man climbed the passageway, pausing half in, half out.

They stared for a moment, and Ramsey recognized the carved features of a Blackwell.

"You're the one who's buying my company, aren't you?" the man said, half accusing, the wind whipping at his silver hair.

"Aye. I am—"

"I don't care who you are." He turned and ascended. "Come below."

His chilling response arrested Ramsey, yet he followed, backing down the narrow passageway, the coolness of the air flushing his skin as he ascended into a modest stateroom. 'Twas not elaborate, the room, but comfortable, bespeaking of constant use. The walls were dotted with framed photos and mounted weapons and Ramsey thought he recognized the silver cutlass slung over a sagging sofa. Yet beneath his feet was a well worn piece of Aubusson carpet, and against the far left wall, an armoire from his century. The touches here and there told him of a family of wealth and power. Naught was left but this man and his vessel, Ram realized despairingly . . . and the animosity he felt in Alexander Blackwell from across the room as the man selected a pipe from a rack on the desk.

"I understood you wished to sell, sir. If 'tis not the case, then I shall not trouble you again and bid you good day."

"No," Alexander said with a sharp glance, looking him over thoroughly. "No. I just can't understand why you want it." Alexander gestured for Ramsey to sit, then dipped his pipe into a humidor and filled it. "There isn't anything left, not of marketable value. Some stock, a couple of warehouses, and the dockyard."

"I am aware of the risks."

"Wainright said you intend to keep the name, why?" He brought the pipe to his lips as he depressed a silver cylinder and Ram's brows rose at the instant fire.

" 'Tis a legacy I wish to revive."

Alexander glanced up, critically judging him and the ponytail didn't escape his attention, even at his advanced age. "It's dead." He puffed. "I wish you'd let it be buried."

"My honor bids I cannot," Ramsey said and the conviction in his soft tone made Alexander straighten. He'd an odd foreboding the moment he saw this man standing on his deck, and it just got stronger.

"Your family business was no small effort, and I ask afore we go further, if that is the case, to tell me how this happened?" He wanted to know of the police report. "I could find naught to guide me, Mister Blackwell."

Alexander settled slowly into a chair perched aside the desk. "Call me Alexander and no, I can't tell you."

Ramsey sighed, trying not to show his disappointment and Alexander conceded, though not at all sure why.

"I wouldn't cart oil."

Ram looked up, frowning.

"I wouldn't fill my ships with OPEC oil. It's too risky to the ocean, the chance of spilling that stuff into the sea. The sea was life for my family for a hundred years. I felt obligated to see it stayed clean. Did you know my ancestors started out building ships?"

Ram nodded, wondering what this man would think if he knew he'd sailed one of those magnificent vessels.

"I had contracts signed, but when I saw what it was doing to the sea, to the environment, I couldn't take it on. I lost a helluva lot of money and employees when I wouldn't give in."

"It appears you stood on personal conviction."

Alexander scoffed, the pipe clenched in his teeth, the swirl of smoke haloing his gray head. "Shipping by boat isn't as lucrative as it was fifty years ago. The recession, cargo planes, took care of that. I went to building pleasure boats." He gestured to his floating home. "It wasn't what we needed to get moving again." He shrugged. "It was a bad business move."

"Surely it didn't destroy the company?"

"No. Just made us weak enough that when we needed money—" Alexander stopped abruptly, breaking his gaze to stare somewhere beyond Ramsey.

Ramsey twisted to see where he looked and his features tightened.

"That was my wife, Annora."

"She is lovely," Ramsey said and 'twas not a lie. The woman was dark haired and statuesque, her hair twisted high and sleek, ringlets softening her aristocratic features. In her arms was a child of about one or two snuggled in frilly blankets and lace.

"She's dead, they both are."

"You have my sympathy, sir." 'Twas the photo Meggie had clipped from the papers. He brought his gaze back to Alexander and saw sheer agony and loneliness in the man's pale-green eyes. Ramsey couldn't bring himself to press him further.

Suddenly Alexander shook himself. "Well, if you want to buy nothing, I guess you'd better look it over."

Ramsey frowned, coming to his feet as Alexander did.

"Come on," he said, crossing the cabin and mounting the ladder. "I get the feeling there's sailor blood in you." Ram followed on his heels. "Prepare to cast off."

Ramsey grinned. "Aye, aye, sir." On deck he shucked his

jacket and rolled up his sleeves, then leapt to the dock to release the moorings.

Alexander manned the rudder, nothing short of astonished as his companion raced around the deck, releasing the halyard line, adjusting winch and boom. The man knew ships and it made him feel a bit more comfortable about selling off what was left of his family's business.

"I suppose I should know your name, mate," he finally asked.

"Ramsey O'Keefe, sir."

Alexander blinked, a skin-drawing chill running up his arms. No. Had to be an ancestor, he decided rationally, then said, "Let's take her out by sail, Ramsey."

Ramsey nodded, realizing this craft could be powered by machine if need be, and manned the stern sails, feeling the wind on his face as he sailed from Coral Keys harbor once again, with a Blackwell.

The two men strolled companionably within the shipyards, the long shoremen gone, the cranes and pallets empty. 'Twas in sad disarray, the proud name of Blackwell fading on the front of a massive warehouse. Inside were racks for drydocking smaller boats, the pleasure ship section that failed twenty years ago.

"What do you really want with this place?"

"To build ships, again."

"It isn't equipped for steel carriers, if that's what you—"

"Nay. I've discovered there is a great deal of wealthy people in this country and they are all willing to spend phenomenal amounts of money on their pleasures. I plan to build ships meant to be sailed by the skill of the hand and wind and not mechanics." Ramsey could only do what he knew, and he knew sailing.

"Good luck. Most people are lazy."

At his cynical tone, Ram cast him a glance, stone crunching beneath his boots. "I would not allow the unskilled to venture a fathom without a seasoned captain. Me," he said with a grin.

Alexander suddenly understood. "Like the dude ranches or joining a cattle drive?"

Ram nodded. "And afore you ask, I know 'tis not lucrative, but I've enough money to see myself and my woman comfortable."

Alexander snorted at his possessive tone. "Woman, huh?"

"Aye, Penelope Hamilton. I plan to make her my wife."

"The actress?" he said, stopping in his tracks.

Ram frowned back at him, pausing. "Aye."

"I can't imagine—it's just that she's a notorious recluse."

"Merely private," Ramsey defended.

The corner of his mouth quirked. "I never stay on shore long enough to see movies, but I hear she's incredible."

Ramsey could only agree, yet noticed a darkening in Alexander's features, a sadness, and he wondered what he was thinking to bring his mood so low. "She'd like to meet you."

Alex looked up sharply. "Me? What the heck for?"

"I've a confession to make, Alexander." Ram stopped and faced him. "Penelope Hamilton recently received an ... endowment from an ancestor of yours."

"Tess Blackwell," he said without missing a beat and Ramsey's brows shot into his forehead. "God, she was legendary for doing stuff like that. And a loon, if you ask me." Ramsey's look disapproved and Alexander laughed for the first time since they'd met that morning. "I remember my grandmother telling me some stories. One of her sons was in trouble, kidnapped or imprisoned—" he shook his head, trying to recall—"and her husband wouldn't allow her to come along to the rescue, so she stowed away on a ship and as the story goes, she was the one who orchestrated the rescue. If you can believe that?"

Ramsey did. 'Twas just like Tess not to be left out of the battle.

"She had to have been at least fifty at the time." Alexander sighed as they walked back down the pier. "She left a couple of *endowments,*" came with a rueful twist of his lips, "to a few strangers. And I'll spare you the rest of my ancestors skeletons, but let's just say she made us interesting back then."

The matriarch, sharp tongued and rebelling against society.

And a bonafide flake, he thought, for although she was well loved, by her family and the old township, her claim of time traveling was a family secret. But his mother had believed it and so had his grandparents, insisting there was proof, and when he was a kid, so had he. But not anymore. He didn't believe in anything except the good die young and happiness is fleeting.

"Why did Tess leave anything to an actress? She lived two hundred years ago."

"I fear I am not at liberty to reveal that. Mayhaps Penelope will offer—"

"No thanks." He shook his head, putting up a hand. "Being a Blackwell hasn't been an asset in my lifetime." He was cutting all ties by selling the business, so what did it matter? He'd no one to pass it on to and there were enough Blackwell relics around to insure the name wouldn't be forgotten, at least by a museum curator or two.

"You know," he said thoughtfully, leaping onto his boat. "My wife always believed her ghost haunted our house."

"Ghost?"

"I know, it's crazy, but after Annora died, something comforted me in that house." He flicked a glance in his direction before he checked mooring and manned the rudder. "Or someone. I would have gone completely mad if I didn't believe I wasn't totally alone."

His voice fractured and he cleared his throat, turning over the engine.

"I'd read a police report, Alexander, for a theft?" Ramsey ventured and the old man suddenly looked as if he'd crumble into dust, aging a hundred years afore his eyes. "I apologize, I didn't realize."

"No, no." He waved him off and busily steered the boat away from the pier. "You see, too much information on other unsolved cases was getting out to the public, and thinking they had a leak, the police made two reports, filing one, the captain keeping the other, hoping to catch whoever was making them look like fools. Frankly, I was grateful. I needed it that way." He flipped open a small compartment to his right, removing two beers and tossing one to Ramsey. They broke the seals and Alexander finished off half afore he spoke again. "I knew Annora couldn't take reporters and cameras invading her misery."

Ramsey held onto the mast, trying not to drain the beer in one swipe in his eagerness, for he sensed, for Alexander, 'twas excruciating to even speak of the incident.

"Our child was kidnapped from her playroom. Just vanished. One minute we could hear her laughing and tossing toys and the next . . ." He shuddered heavily before he continued. "At first we thought she'd simply found one of the passageways in the walls. I mean, the house was old as time, and though most of them were sealed up, even I didn't know of all the secret panels leading out. But somebody did. That was the only way they could have gotten in." He seemed to be trying to justify his part in his child's disappearance and Ramsey said naught, aware of the narrow passageways of the Blackwell mansion, and how he'd used them to leave the house unnoticed for a private horse ride or a tumble with a maid, without embarrassing Dane with his behavior.

"A ransom demand came. Three million dollars."

"Sweet Jesus!" The can crunched in Ramsey's broad fist.

"I know, it might as well have been twenty." Despair weighted his words. "I didn't have that kind of money, not that wasn't tied up in investments or my company. Then they demanded it in diamonds or they'd kill my little girl."

Ramsey's features yanked taut and his spine tightened, his gaze narrowing on Alexander.

"Colored diamonds, the greedy sons of bitches." He mashed a hand over his face. "I took everything I had, mortgaged the house, the lands, sold every damn antique, the horses, cars, and I did what they asked. I kept the police out. They had my baby, for God's sakes!" His throat worked violently and it was a long moment afore he could speak again. "All I got back was a tiny bloody sneaker. It was hers, and the blood type matched. So I knew—oh Jesus." He cut the engine low and he dug the heels of his palms in his eyes, his words muffled. "I never saw her again. And Annora, God, she just gave up. She couldn't

take knowing our baby spent her last hours screaming for us
to help her, her last breath being *tortured.*'' He ran his fingers
through his gray hair, his expression so wretched, Ramsey
experienced and remembered his own agonizing pain, of a
father standing by, helpless as his child perished. ''Why did
they have to hurt her? I paid. I paid! Why couldn't they have
given her back?''

Ramsey crossed to the old man, his heart twisting in his
chest.

''God almighty, Alexander, I am sorry for making you relive
this,'' Ramsey said, dropping his hand to his shoulder with a
gentle weight and when he tilted his head back to the sun,
Ramsey saw the sheer of tears.

''God, I wish I'd died, too.''

''Nay, nay,'' Ramsey soothed, giving him a soft shake.
''Have a bit of faith, man.'' Ramsey could not offer an explanation for he did not understand the feelings assailing him, yet
beyond the diamonds, his story stirred a faint memory he
couldn't grasp.

''I knew this would happen if I came back.''

''I did not mean to pry so deeply, Alexander.''

Alex scoffed. ''You didn't. I haven't spoken about that to
anyone since Annora died. I couldn't, to be honest. It's why I
left. I lost everything that night and here,'' he waved to the
shoreline. ''There's just too many memories.'' He breathed
deeply, struggling for composure, then cast Ramsey a suspicious look. ''You can have the company, Ramsey. No charge,
take it if that's what you want, but it's cursed, I tell you. It'll
destroy you.''

Chapter 34

Now that was a ship, she thought as the vessel breezed into the slip, and she studied Ramsey as he lowered the sail, securing in neatly, methodically, then hopped to the dock and tied the lines. He looked comfortable in the surroundings, incredibly energized and she knew why he wanted to be aboard a ship again, doing the excursions. He was a seaman. He needed it and it was good for their relationship that she didn't get seasick. Because he wasn't going anywhere alone.

Her gaze shifted to the older man working beside him. He wore faded jeans and a short sleeved sweatshirt and a Greek fisherman's cap covered gray hair she could see grazing his collar. Then they strode toward her and her gaze went to the man beside her lover.

Alexander Blackwell.

Her palms perspired as the pair drew closer. He had to be at least sixty, his features tanned and weathered, his eyes the palest green she'd ever seen. Almost too pretty to belong to a man, she decided.

Ramsey met her first, and she tore her gaze from Alexander and looked up into his handsome face.

"I missed you," he murmured softly, bending to kiss her heavily on the mouth.

She gripped his biceps, standing on tiptoe. "God, you look good out there," she said, her voice throaty with sudden desire. He grinned knowingly and kissed her again, hotly, possessively, a slick push and taste of lips and tongue.

"Had I known 'twould offer such a reaction I would have kidnapped you and kept you aboard a ship til you succumbed to me."

"What an interesting idea," she said and he threw his head back and laughed. Penny hugged him and over her shoulder she met Alexander's gaze.

Ramsey felt an immediate change in her, a tightening of her posture and slowly he released her, turning to face Alexander.

They stared, a questioning look knitting her forehead and Ramsey watched the odd by-play atween the pair. Penelope never took her gaze from his face, his eyes. But Alexander's gaze slid over her rapidly, curiously to the point of rudeness.

"Penelope, this—"

"I know." Her voice was soft and inviting. "It's a pleasure, Mister Blackwell," she said, offering her hand.

Alexander stared at her slim fingers, his gaze traveling upward to her face. "Alex," he corrected, then grasped her hand.

Her breath caught and she frowned at the warmth of his grip.

Alexander blinked, trying not to look like an idiot before the famed actress.

Ramsey didn't miss the exchange.

A phone buzzed and Penny flinched, then smiled at Alexander, excusing herself as she turned toward the Rolls. Hank lowered the window, scowling at Alexander as he handed her the cellular phone.

Alexander studied Penelope, then looked at Ramsey. "I've seen photos of her when she was a teenager." A pause, a glance in her direction. "She's turned into a real beauty."

Ram shifted restlessly, his thoughts aching to have voice. "The beauty is but a shell," Ram said as Alexander continued to stare. She cast him a quick glance, smiling as she spoke into the phone.

"She doesn't fit the image the tabloids paint." Alexander looked as if he wanted to question her and Ramsey tensed.

"Alexander?"

Both men faced her as she cut the line, handing the phone to Hank before she spoke. "Would you like to join us for dinner tomorrow night?"

"Thanks, I'd like that," he said without hesitation, glancing at Ramsey, then back to her. "Maybe you'll show me this endowment from my crazy ancestor?"

Her gaze flew to Ramsey and he shrugged, a bit sheepish.

"Then maybe you'll tell me why you think they were nuts?" she countered with a smile. "I'll send a car for you about six," she added, her voice trembling slightly. She cleared her throat and looked at Ramsey. "That was Tony. He's at the house, impatient to see the document."

Ram nodded, his gaze shifting to Alexander. "Til the morrow, Alexander." He held out his hand and Alexander grasped it firmly.

"Have Wainright draw up any papers he likes."

Ram nodded and they remained on the dock as Alexander turned and strode back toward his ship.

"He seems like a nice man."

"Aye. Made me mind weary to know he's Tess's great great great great great grandson."

She blinked. "I hadn't thought of it quite like that."

Penny ducked into the car, enfolding Ramsey's hand as soon as he dropped down beside her. He brought their clasped fists to his lips, but she seemed to ignore his attentions, glancing out the rear window, watching Alexander, a frown wrinkling her brow before she turned back and sighed.

"Love?"

She met his questioning gaze. "I don't know. I get a strange feeling about him. He seems so . . . lost."

"He's had a tragic life."

Ramsey was fain to speak his thoughts, but as she crossed her slender legs and his gaze caught on the dark scar circling

her ankle, he knew they could not wait til she saw Alexander
again.

Alexander rummaged in boxes, peeling through his files,
seeking the ownership papers of his company and deeds to
property. He found them exactly where he expected and was
about to leave the small storage compartment when his gaze
fell on a small wood and leather chest, tacked with brass studs.
A memory flashed and he recalled seeing it in his great grandmother's rooms. No one was allowed to look inside, no men, at
least. It was to be passed on through the hands of the Blackwell
women. He found a seat on some boxes and drew it to his lap,
flipping the latch and opening the lid.

Annora had put this in here, he thought, knowing that all
these years he could never bring himself to look inside. Just the
image of her brought him to his knees. He riffled, recognizing a
piece or two of jewelry, her girlhood diary, a silhouette of a
Blackwell female, certificates of birth and death and marriage.
It was all he had left of his ancestors and Alexander felt his
own mortality.

He wished he hadn't disappointed his forebearers by losing
all they'd held dear. Lifting out a rolled piece of brittle parchment, he loosened the faded ribbon binding the cylinder, unroll-
ing it carefully. It was a marriage certificate, of Dane Blackwell
to Tess Renfrew—

Renfrew? Why did that name sound familiar, he considered,
staring off for a bit, then returning his gaze to the paper. They
were married in the islands. Good God, in a pirate's lair, he
thought with a chuckle. His features slackened when his gaze
fell on the date, not of the marriage, but of Tess's birth. August
twelfth, nineteen sixty-four. Nineteen! It was the proof his
grandmother mentioned.

Good God.

She wasn't crazy.

And if this legend was true, then what of the story of Ramsey
Malachai Gamaliel O'Keefe, the portrait, and his legendary
sacrifice for his family?

Alexander was suddenly glad he'd been invited to dinner. He had a lot to ask O'Keefe. A hell of a lot, he thought, rummaging further in the box, plucking out piece by piece. Something drove him; a deep seeded notion he couldn't put into words, a nudge in the recesses of his brain, guiding him. Impatiently, he dumped the contents on the floor, sorting, dropping item by item back into the chest. He suddenly stilled, his gaze on the bottom of the box. He frowned at the worn ill-fitting edge, running his finger along the velvet seam. It wobbled and he withdrew a penknife from his back pocket, flipped it open and pried up the corner. Beneath the false bottom, he found a slip of vellum, yellow and brittle, its wax seal obviously replaced several times. It wasn't the Blackwell seal, he realized as he lifted it toward the light, but Rothmere.

Anthony gaped at the document, bringing it under the light and adjusting his glasses. "My God," he whispered. "My God!"

"Antony." Ramsey smiled at being so thoroughly ignored as Anthony felt the paper, turned it over, searching the back for God knew what, then examined the lettering again.

"Considering that I am older than Thomas, and therefore a more valuable antique," he quipped, winking at Penelope when she laughed—"mayhaps you could give me your attention?"

"Oh yes, sorry," he said, shrugging sheepishly. "It's a codicil to a will, and I'd have to look up a few laws to know for certain if it's legal, which it should be. But you were right. He states, by the original owner of the house and lands, that it will never leave the hands of a Blackwell and should circumstances cause it to do so, this—" he waved the paper, then cringed when it cracked, threatening to crumble, "revokes any agreement and if the opposing party fights it, it turns the house and lands over to the state as a historical landmark."

"Talk about covering all the bases."

"Excellent."

Penny's gaze sharpened on Ramsey. "What are you planning?" She left her seat to stand before him.

He smiled at her mutinous stance, arms akimbo, chin tilted.

"To lure Phalon."

"Where?"

"Anywhere he desires," he said cryptically.

"Ramsey," she warned. "He's not someone you provoke unnecessarily."

"I agree," Anthony put in. "He's only sent out a light warning so far. I wouldn't want to tangle with him when he gets a little heavy-handed."

"It wasn't heavy shooting at Tess, or damn near killing Margaret?" Penny snapped and Ramsey slid his arm about her waist, hushing her, his lips pressed to her temple. "Damn," she said, briefly closing her eyes and letting her temper simmer. "I get the feeling this is all going to blow up in our faces." And it's all my fault, she thought, opening her eyes and looking up at Ramsey. "I think we should go to the police."

He faced her fully. "I do not."

"Ramsey."

"Penelope," he began patiently. "He must tip his hand afore we can do aught. We have no proof that is of value. None we can show anyone beyond this room."

She gripped his arms, squeezing. "But it's dangerous. And we have to walk into his house, his *lair,*" she said disgustedly— "in four days."

He'd almost forgotten about the premier. "Mayhaps Sloane is a weaker link."

"Like a gorilla maybe—"

"While you two fight this out—"

Penny jerked a look at Tony. "We aren't fighting."

Ramsey chuckled and Anthony smirked, dropping the papers transferring ownership of Blackwell shipping on the desk.

"I'll take this to the museum, see if I can find anything out." He slid the will into his briefcase, then snapped it shut. "Maybe Clarissa can help?"

"Clarissa, is it?" Penny said, on a turn to face him.

Anthony grinned. "Too young?"

"No comment." She inclined her head toward Ramsey. "The man I love is as old as they get."

Suddenly Ramsey wrapped his arm about her waist, jerking her back against him.

" 'Tis proof then.'' He nuzzled the flesh of her throat. "Age has naught to do with the heart,'' he murmured and she twisted in his arms, melting beneath his fevered kiss, neither noticing Anthony leave. Yet when she was languid and compliant he murmured, "Please do not fight me on this, Penelope.'' He scattered heart-weakening kisses over her face and throat. "I cannot take this darkness clouding over us another moment.''

Us, she thought and it hit her that she wasn't alone in this world anymore. "I'm going with you.''

He stiffened, his gaze narrow. "I think not.'' She opened her mouth to protest, but his warning glare made her clamp her lips shut. "This *incident* began two hundred years afore you were born.'' His eyes were hard, nearly black with suppressed fury. "And I plan to put it to an end.''

He was looking forward to doing battle with Phalon, she realized and decided it was wise to stay out of the line of fire.

A secretary led him into the library and as soon as she closed the door behind him, Ramsey strolled the room, recognizing the changes in the interior over the years and trying to recall exactly how the house appeared in his time. Afore his travel through time, it had been three years hence he'd set foot in Dane's home and though the polished wood walls and shelving were the same, as was the fireplace and the treatment of windows, the furnishings were different, new with the look of old.

The door opened and Ramsey turned as a well dressed man strode in, ignoring him until he was behind the desk. He shuffled papers, then finally lifted his gaze, and Ramsey saw the eyes of his enemy in the twentieth century man afore him.

"I am Ramsey O'Keefe, present owner of Blackwell shipping.''

"I know,'' Phalon said, looking him over as if he were meat on the block for chopping.

It set Ramsey's teeth on edge.

"What do you want?''

"Only what is rightful." Ramsey dropped a sheaf of papers on the desk and Phalon pulled them across the desk, scanning with a critical eye. "This house and the lands surrounding." Phalon nearly choked. "And every stick of furniture that lay inside this home afore 'twas taken from Alexander Blackwell."

Phalon shoved the documents back across to Ramsey. "You demand an awful lot for a man without a past, or a job."

Ramsey merely arched a brow.

"I know who you are. A nobody, a nothing. Only her lover," he said with distaste and Ramsey stiffened, taking a threatening step. "Get out, Mister O'Keefe. I have nothing to say to you. And the Blackwells are all dead."

Ramsey couldn't mention Alexander's arrival, fearing 'twould put the old man's life in jeopardy. "I am offering to buy back the home, Mister Rothmere, not steal it." His tone implied 'twas Phalon's method.

Ramsey made a generous offer.

"No."

He sweetened the pot.

"I said no. This is my house, my lands!"

He sounded too much like Phillip for his comfort and Ramsey stepped back, his gaze glacial, predatory. "This land was never yours, Rothmere. Never," Ramsey hissed. "You preyed on the misfortune of a desperate family."

Ramsey dropped a copy of the codicil on the desk. "And the Blackwells have come back from the grave to regain their home."

Phalon immediately snatched it up, frowning as he read, a dullness creeping into his skin. "This means nothing." He flipped it back within his reach. "And I'll drag you through the courts until you're as dead as all the Blackwells."

"Your arrogance makes you a fool," Ram said matter of factly, stuffing the copy inside his jacket. "And you would not be in this home if the ransom was recovered."

None but Alexander and Phalon knew of the diamonds, and Ramsey wanted Phalon to put himself in the center of the crime.

Phalon picked up a pen, tapping it on the desk. He was almost certain this man had the *Red Lady*. Almost. But to confirm it with the jeweler who'd appraised the stone would bring attention Phalon didn't want. And how was he going to get them back without incriminating himself?

"It never surfaced."

"And hence, neither did the child."

Phalon stared, a muscle clenching in his jaw, and Ramsey could have swore he saw a flash of regret in his eyes.

"That was twenty-five years ago. What do you know about that?"

Ramsey scoffed and let his gaze drift to the painting hanging behind the desk, then slowly bringing it back to meet Phalon's piercing blue eyes. "I know your heritage, Rothmere," came in a growl as deep as the ocean floor and Phalon paled, his body gone deathly still. "It seems for two hundred years the Rothmeres are still vipers on the flesh of the Blackwells."

"Give it to me," came in a sinister hiss and Ramsey instantly realized he *wasn't* referring to the diamonds. He tried not to show his confusion and without a word, spun on his heels and left, brushing past a slim blond woman. Ramsey froze, twisting, his gaze sweeping her once afore he bowed at the waist, then continued down the familiar hall.

"Who was that?" Sloane said, advancing into the room and closing the door.

"Trouble," he said, pacing. He paused, flicking a hand toward the phone. "Make the call."

Penelope stood on the threshold of the study, gazing at Ramsey. He looked as if he were carrying the weight of the world, she thought, bracing her shoulder on the frame and folding her arms. He sat behind the desk, elbows resting there, his head clutched in his hands, his fingers sunk into his hair.

"You've been awfully quiet since we left the docks yesterday."

His head jerked up, his dark scowl evaporating. Smiling, he fell back into the chair, extending his arm in invitation and she flew to him, sinking onto his lap and curling one arm around his neck. He covered her mouth with his and she opened for

him, the embers of desire flaming hot and bright. His tongue
slid between her lips, sweeping wildly, his hands mapping her
slender curves with a hunger that bordered on desperate. When
he finally drew back, their breathing was labored, bodies eager
for more.

"What? What is it?" She brushed at his hair. "I can feel
it, something is wrong."

His gaze traveled her face. "God almighty, I love you," he
rasped fiercely, tightening his embrace, burying his face in the
curve of her shoulder.

"I know, Ramsey, I know," she soothed, rubbing the knotted
muscles in the back of his neck, his shoulders.

It was several moments before he lifted his head to look at
her.

"You're scaring me," she said, gazing into his dark brown
eyes.

He released a long breath, smoothing his hands up and down
her arms and wishing he could postpone this. "Afore Alexander
arrives I've a confession."

"You say that like you're going to the guillotine."

Her tender heart bade him move with caution, fearing this
first step would hurt her beyond repair. "I've discovered where
the diamonds originated."

"And it's not Phalon or Sloane," she answered for him,
searching his eyes and he nodded. "I knew it, I knew it! Where?
Why?"

His hands slid up to cup her lovely face. "Those gems were
the price of Alexander's only child, Penelope."

Her eyes widened and she inhaled sharply. "A ransom!"

Afore he could respond, Margaret poked her head into the
study and Ramsey lowered his hands, disappointed.

"Hank's pulling into the drive with Mister Blackwell," she
said and Penny frowned at the sadness in Margaret's expression.

"She's upset." Penny hastily climbed from his lap and
headed to the door.

"I need to speak with you on this, Penelope."

She glanced back, reaching out to straighten a vase. "Tell

me after—'' She inclined her head towards the door indicating their visitor. ''In bed tonight.''

He smiled crookedly, his gaze sweeping over her body clad in the slim fitting dress. '' 'Tis an invitation?''

''No, Captain, an order,'' she said, then disappeared around the jamb.

Ram's smile faded and he forced himself out of the chair. I could lose her, he thought, simply for finding Alexander first.

Chapter 35

It was a moment he'd dreaded and anticipated since he'd laid eyes on her. She'd asked how he'd become the last surviving member of his clan and he'd told her.

And the tears in her eyes nearly broke his heart.

"Oh Alexander," she whispered, covering his hand with her own. "I'm sorry I asked."

He stared down at her slim manicured hand, and when she started to jerk back, he wrapped his fingers around hers. "It's all right." He gave her fingers a quick squeeze, releasing a long slow breath. Talking about it twice in two days was going to make him a very old man, he thought. "I sailed away and never looked back."

"You didn't have reason to," she said, letting go of his hand.

"Well . . . now that I'm in a seat, coveted by *millions of adoring fans,*" he said with a reporter's vibrato and she made a sour face—"tell me how you got so famous."

Tension leapt into her body, her gaze wary.

Ramsey leaned close and she lifted her gaze to his sympathetic eyes.

"You've naught but time, love," he said for her ears alone, recognizing her old resistance.

Penny turned her attention back to Alexander, who was fighting between a frown and a smile, and she knew she had to start somewhere, start releasing that part of her life. And though the ease of conversation, of the instant comfort they felt in the other's presence didn't escape her, or him, she wasn't ready to tell him. He was a virtual stranger. Tomorrow was soon enough, she thought, smiling, tilting her head.

"On a whim, I auditioned for summer stock . . ." she began and after a few minutes, Ramsey stood and left them alone.

Penny sank into the wicker sofa with a huff. "That was fabulous, Margaret," she said and the men surrounding her agreed. Margaret smiled, a smile not quite reaching her eyes, Penny thought as she poured coffee. She wouldn't talk with her before, claiming she was running behind in preparing dinner and Penelope knew from experience that Margaret was the most efficient woman on this continent.

"Let me know when you're ready for dessert."

Ramsey looked at Penelope and smiled. "Cheesecake," they said with feeling and Margaret's laughter joined Alexander's as she headed back into the house.

Penny sipped her coffee, letting the warm breeze smooth over her skin, then suddenly kicked off her shoes and stood, walking to the pool and dropping down on the edge. She sank her feet into the glittering water, the pool lights painting the liquid a translucent blue-green.

Behind her Ramsey met Alexander's gaze, then rose, crossing to Penelope. "I've the need to check the grounds," he said, bending to drop a kiss to the top of her head.

She caught his hand, searching his dark eyes. "You'd tell me if there was trouble, wouldn't you?"

"Aye, love." He squatted aside her, kissing her quick and heavy and Alexander smiled as she watched Ramsey return to the house. But he wasn't a stupid man and though he didn't mention the armed guards at the door or the surveillance equipment, it was obvious something was stringing the people of this house as tight as a full blown sail.

And something was about to snap.

"You look happy," Alexander said suddenly, softly, the realization pleasing him.

"I didn't know I could love someone that much," she replied before returning her gaze to the pool. "I'd just about given up when Ramsey came into my life."

"You're too young to crawl into a hole and hide."

"I thought I had good reason." She glanced back over her shoulder, her smile teasing. "And look who's talking."

He flashed her an easy grin. "Sort of makes you believe in fate."

"I believe in a lot more than just fate," came on a short laugh. "Nothing means the same anymore." Not her outlook towards herself, towards her career, and she didn't care if she ever landed another prime role again. She had other plans. "But something's been bothering me." Penny twisted to look at Alexander and his expression encouraged. "How did a Rothmere end up owning your house?"

Alexander's features sharpened and he looked at his lap, then took a sip of coffee, replacing the cup on the saucer before returning his gaze to Penelope.

"When my world was falling apart he came in and rescued it."

"How can that be, if *he's* got your ancestral home?"

Alexander leaned forward, bracing his elbows on his knees and clasping his hands. "The city was going to take it all, and he bought the note, promising to leave the house and lands as they'd been for two hundred hundred years." He shrugged. "The company he couldn't do anything about. Phalon didn't know enough about shipping, then."

She swung her legs out of the pool and stood, her footprints marking her path back to him.

"Why him?" She sank into the wicker sofa.

He shrugged negligently. "He was family."

"What?" She straightened, eyes wide.

"My wife, Annora," he eyed her for a second or two, "was Phalon's sister."

Penny fell back, the wicker creaking. "How interesting."

"What's going on here, Penelope?"

She looked up.

"This place is tighter than Camp David."

"There have been some threats." She couldn't meet his gaze, the half-truth sticking in her throat.

"Who's trying to hurt you?"

"I've done some stupid things in the past," she hedged.

His pale-green eyes flared. "You're being blackmailed."

Her skin reddened. "Products of a misspent youth," she said with a shrug as he withdrew a leather envelope and pipe from inside his jacket, holding it up in question. Penny nodded her permission, watching as he filled the pipe and brought it to his lips to light it. "It won't work for long. I have a—" She went still as glass, her body tightening as the smoke haloed his head. She inhaled, her gaze narrowing, a strong sense of déjà vu' sweeping her, holding her. For an instant she could see nothing but his face engulfed in smoke and she flinched violently when someone touched her.

"Ramsey," she whispered, relaxing, her gaze dropping to the books in his hand. He handed them to her and she stared at Tess's journals, smoothing her fingers over the corners, then took the first, checked the sequence, and handed it to Alexander.

Alexander didn't open it, staring at the space between his feet, puffing on his pipe.

"Tess Renfrew was my best friend, Alexander." His gaze jerked up. "And in Seventeen Eighty-nine she married Dane Blackwell."

"I know."

Penelope's gaze bounced between Ramsey and Alexander. "Do you know how she—"

"Time shifted?" came with an arching brow. "No. And for over fifty years, I never believed the stories," he lifted his gaze to Ramsey's—"not until I saw your name on the sale agreement. It matches the signature on the marriage certificate."

He was waiting for an admittance and when no comment was forthcoming, Penelope nudged him.

Ramsey swallowed, lowering himself beside Penelope and

curling his arm around her shoulders. "I fear I am laying my future in your hands, sir."

Alexander leaned back in the cushion and rubbed a hand over his face before looking at the couple. "It's safe . . . Ramsey *Malachai Gamaliel* O'Keefe."

Ramsey's lips quirked and as Alexander opened the first book, he stood, drawing Penny with him and ushering her toward the house.

She tilted her head close to his. "What on earth possessed your parents to give you all those names?" she whispered, and Ram chuckled lowly.

"I was a tiny thing when I was born, love."

She gave his big body a speculative glance.

"Mayhaps they imagined I'd grow into them."

"Well . . . parts of you did," she said in a throaty purr and he laughed, stepping into the coolness of the house and leaving Alexander to learn of his heritage.

They found him pacing the wood deck and when the glass door slid back he ceased, his gaze narrowing on the couple.

"Phalon didn't have anything to do with the disappearance of my child," he said with absolute conviction. "He . . . adored his sister. And would *never* do anything to hurt us like that." He shook a paper at them.

"I'm not accusing," she said, crossing to him. "But how do you explain them having the diamonds in the first place?"

His gaze knifed her. "Hell, if I know. The police didn't even know I turned the money into diamonds. But they're gone. Everything's gone! So what does it matter!"

"Alexander," Penelope said calmingly, pushing him gently into a seat. She laid a hand on his forearm. "We didn't tell you this to upset you. I felt you had a right to know about your family." She got the distinct feeling he was hiding something.

His wrinkled fists clenched and unclenched, his lips pulled tight and it was a tense moment before he spoke. "Is this codicil of any value?"

"Aye, Wainright verified the signature. And as the Welshman said, the constitution has held up for two hundred years, why not this?''

The older man chuckled, short and deep and Penny smiled at Ramsey, her relief relaxing her.

Yet when Alexander's gaze fell on the codicil still in his hand, his expression turned grave. ''You should let this die, Ramsey. It's not worth it.''

''I cannot.'' Alex's gaze flew to his. '' 'Tis a matter of honor.'' He took the codicil. ''She entrusted me,'' he glanced briefly at Penelope, ''*us* to right this wrong.''

''It doesn't mean the same, without Annora,'' he said softly, his gaze flicking to Penelope.

''I do not mean to be unfeeling, but an injustice has been done, to more than you.''

Alexander knew what he meant and stood, face to face with Ramsey. ''Without the diamonds, you don't have a leg to stand on,'' he reminded.

''Sloane's penchant for blackmail has naught to destroy us after the morrow.'' He glanced assuringly at Penelope. '' 'Tis the entire cache they believe Tess gave to Penelope.'' Ramsey dug in his trouser pocket, then held up his fist, opening his fingers. The thumb sized deep rose hued diamond dropped like a hanged man from a gold chain. ''And she did not.''

Penny stared at the spinning stone, momentarily trapped by its fiery brilliance til Alexander caught the diamond in his palm and tilted it toward the porch light.

''The Red Lady.''

Ramsey scowled as the older man rubbed his thumb over the cut stone.

''This one belonged to Annora.'' His gaze jerked to Ramsey's. ''It wasn't one of the group I bought to exchange. It belonged to my great great grandmother.''

Ramsey released the chain into Alexander's hand. ''You're certain?''

''Annora never took it off.'' He looked at Penelope for a long moment, then slowly brought his gaze back to Ramsey's. ''And I can prove it.''

* * *

His body slid smoothly into hers, again and again, her hips tucking to take more. His broad hands swept leisurely down her sides, pushing her legs around his waist as he lifted her back off the bed, and they melted, mouth to mouth, breast to chest. Yielding femininity to masculine strength.

She rocked and he cupped her buttocks, feeling her motion, savoring the quick shots of rapture racking her body. Her breath choked and she clung to him, gripping his shoulders, grinding down. She was always so wild for him, throwing her head back and begging for speed and power, and Ramsey bucked, finding his release in hers. He held her, her slick body arching tightly against his as spasms wrenched her, snapping through her like a brush fire.

After a long moment, she softened against him, kissing him slowly, liquidly, and Ramsey thought he'd perish into dust from her tender loving.

"Marry me, Ramsey," she said against his lips. "I love you. Marry me."

His brows rose and he pulled back, his gaze searching hers. " 'Tis usually the man who asks."

Her look was petulant. "Not in my century."

" 'Tis hardly the proper spot to be doing the asking."

She was suddenly still, her expression falling. "Is that a no?"

"Nay, nay." He sighed miserably, running the tip of his finger across her bare shoulder and watching his movements. "I'd never thought to love enough to speak the words to anyone," he met her gaze, "and wanted to do the asking."

She arched a tapered brow, her lips tugging. He was pouting. "Want me to withdraw the offer?"

"Nay!" Appalled and a little afraid. "I'll be your mate."

Mate, how apt. "You make it sound like a chore."

"I will make a fine husband," he said supremely, adjusting his arms about her. "You'll see."

She gave him a cool look, yet her eyes sparkled with happiness. "Think so?"

He pushed her onto her back, thrusting deeply into her lush body. "Ahh, you've that doubtin' look about you, temptress."

"Assure me," came on a gasp.

"If it takes a century, my love."

Her smile was bright, her eyes tearing. "I can hardly wait."

She smelled cherries and felt safe, cocooned in softness, in the place of a child's dreams, a warmth and gentleness she only vaguely remembered, surrounding her. She saw hands, manicured, slim and feminine, reaching out to touch her. She loves me, she thought, and struggled to see more. A dark green dress, a length of ribbon and lace. And a flicker of light, quicksilver and pink as a spring rose. A deep voice whispered lovingly, humming a lullaby.

Then she glimpsed a face, brief, hazy, like a puff of mist, and she hungered to recapture the vision.

But it slipped away like a breeze, dissipating.

Then it came again, familiar, dark. Suffocating.

Terror rode through her blood. She was not alone. Her arms were bound and she couldn't cry out, couldn't move her lips. Sweat moved beneath her clothes, tears streaked her cheeks. Heavy footsteps marked a rhythm with the air punching from her lungs. An odor, brittle and musty, filled her nostrils and wind howled, slow and whistling, as if through a crack in a window. Hands gripped her, tight and punishing. And she feared the threat. Then the words came, hateful and knifing.

They didn't want you back.

I'll be good.

They didn't want you back.

A sob caught in her throat. Pain lanced her ankle and she was running, limping, running, breathless and terrified. The rush of heavy footsteps sounded behind her, closer, closer.

She was alone in the dark, every sound ringing hollow, the odor fetid and rotten.

Why didn't they want me back?

She smelled cherries again and cried, confused, heart sick,

her senses jumping between spine-jarring fear and uncondi-
tional love denied.

She felt hands on her back, sliding warmly, a deep voice, a
new voice, calling her name and her eyes flashed open, her
body taut as a bow. Her lungs worked frantically.

"Penelope. 'Tis me, my love." His expression was infinitely
sad as he brushed at her wet cheeks.

"Ramsey," she managed, clinging to him, gasping for new
air.

"Ahh, love." He sheltered her in his strong arms. " 'Tis
killing me to see you suffer."

"No, no." She shook her head, pushing back. "It was different this time." He waited as she caught her breath and wet her
lips. "I kept smelling cherries," came in a rush, "and I saw
a face." She held his gaze. "It was familiar." Excitement made
her voice eager as she braced her hands on his shoulders. "I've
never seen a face."

Ramsey knew the value of the vision, for her *never,* was
over twenty-five years of her life.

Suddenly she flopped back, stuffing a pillow beneath her
head, wiping her cheeks, sniffling. A tissue appeared before
her vision and she smiled, accepting it and wiping her eyes.

"Tell me all that was different."

The heat of his body comforted her, calmed her. "It's always
so vague, just feelings." She spoke to the ceiling. "Pain, loss
fear." She shrugged. "If I felt safe it was only a sensation,
never a clear image." She turned her head on the pillow to
look at him. "Like ghosts. Sort of, you know, it's there but
you can't understand why." He propped his torso on one bent
elbow and she reached out to brush his hair off his face, tucking
one side behind his ear. "Dreaming always hurt so much,
because I knew I was happy in the beginning. And felt like I'd
done something to ruin it."

"And now?"

"Oh, it's the same." She returned her gaze to the swirled
ceiling. "But I saw hands, a woman's hands, the collar of a

dress and something glittering.'' Her shoulders moved, unsure. ''And a man's voice, humming. Then the dreams turn mostly like before.

''Mostly? You said afore you recalled naught but sensations.''

Her brows furrowed as she concentrated, remembering details that had always escaped her. ''I smell dirt and old wood. It's windy, like howl through a half open window.'' The words tumbled from her lips. ''I'm restrained and can't talk because there's something in my mouth. And it makes me sick and dizzy.''

''Tied and gagged?'' he suggested and she nodded as the pieces fit.

''It feels as if someone is hitting me in the stomach, and the hits are in syncopation with footsteps. The footsteps sound like when you're the only person walking into a church. You know, echoing.''

''Mayhaps you were tossed over a shoulder and carted into somewhere that was open, barren?''

''A warehouse?'' She jerked a look at him. ''But that means—''

She clamped her lips shut and his gentle voice coaxed. ''Relax, love, 'twill come to you, do not fight it.''

Her eyes bloomed with fresh tears. ''Oh God, Ramsey,'' she whispered, her voice fracturing. She licked her lips. ''I was stolen.'' Suddenly she sat up and kicked off the covers, staring at her ankle, rubbing her fingers over the dark scar, remembering. ''I climbed out a cellar window and caught my foot on metal. It hurt, I cried out. It alerted *them*,'' she said with utter hatred. ''And I kicked off the shoe to get free. But this one,'' she touched the other ankle, ''still had a shoe. A white polka dotted sneaker,'' she said into the darkened room. ''I ran and ran and fell, then hid in a trash can. I knew I had to be quiet. So quiet,'' came in a sinister hiss as if someone were listening. ''If they didn't want me back, then I wasn't going. I wasn't going to tell them anything. I wasn't going to remember how much it hurt to be left behind.'' Her lip quivered and she sniffled, rubbing her arms and rocking back and forth. ''Oh

God, oh God,'' she sobbed quietly. ''I wasn't abandoned. I was kidnapped. They took it all away. Damn them, they took my life away!''

''Penelope.''

She put up a hand, effectively holding him off, not looking at him. ''I know, Ramsey. I know.''

Ramsey waited, the air trapped in his lungs, the misery in her voice tearing his heart from his chest.

''He got back a bloody shoe. The sparkle was the Red Lady. He said she never took it off.'' Her tone dared him to contradict, her restrained cries grinding through her throat, flexing her shoulders. ''Oh, dear God.'' She covered her face with her hands and sobbed helplessly, years of bitter rage and loneliness racing for release. ''I'm a Blackwell. I'm Alexander's daughter.''

Chapter 36

Penny stared across the breakfast table at Ramsey.

When she'd wanted to call Alexander last night, he'd told her three in the morning was a breech of good manners and made love to her, hurriedly, wildly. When she agonized over the life she'd been denied, he promised her a new one filled with excitement and endless loving and then he'd made love to her again. And again. Until she could do nothing but sigh into a dreamless sleep. Her first in too many years.

"You knew."

Ramsey looked up from his cereal bowl. "Only after I'd heard the story from him, aye." His eyes crinkled as he smiled. "You bare a striking resemblance to your mother."

A dish crashed to the floor and they looked up to see Margaret, her face pale as snow. "I—I—"

Penny left her chair, ushering the woman away from the broken crockery. "What is it?" Urgent, frowning as she pushed her into a seat.

"I'm sorry."

Tears welled in her eyes and Penny sank to her knees, grasping her hands. My God, Penny thought, she's shivering. "It's only a dish, Margaret."

''No, no.'' She glanced hesitantly at Ramsey, then back. She stammered twice before she blurted, ''I'd suspected for years you were his girl.''

Penny jerked back. ''What!''

''I was never sure,'' she rushed to say, blinking rapidly. ''The thought never occurred to me til she died. Her ... Annora's picture was in the paper—'' she struggled to control her tears and face the devastated look in Penny's eyes. ''And the disappearance of her girl was a one line mention. That's when I thought you might be ...'' her voice trailed off for a moment, her expression crushed. ''You wouldn't talk, honey, and not even the child services could find out who you were. Only had that,'' she nodded to the locket, ''and the welfare insisted you dug it out of the trash.''

''Why on earth didn't you say something?''

''What if I was wrong?'' she wailed. ''I saw what being abandoned did to you, those awful nightmares. You knew you belonged *somewhere* and I couldn't get your hopes up like that when I'd nothing to prove it with. Not even the police would take me seriously.''

''The police?''

Margaret nodded miserably. ''No one would listen to a drunken vagrant, 'cause that's what I was then. It was just a hunch and I only had a newspaper picture to go by.'' Her shoulders sagged heavily, reaching out to stroke her hair. ''God, you were just a tiny thing—'' She jerked back, suddenly, but Penny caught her hand, bringing it to her cheek.

She'd carried this burden all these years, Penny realized.

''I lived every day thinking they'd come take you away from me any minute and the older you got, the harder it was to even think about it. Once I ran a picture of you in the paper and some ads, but that was all I could do back then. You've got to believe me!''

''Of course I do,'' Penny said without question. I made it so hard for her, she thought, her vision blurring.

''I *had* to be sure, honey. You were my world and I wasn't going to give you up to just anyone.''

Penny blinked, tears rolling down her cheeks and Margaret lifted the corner of her apron, gently blotting them away.

"Some things will never change, huh, Margaret?" Penny caught her hand.

"No, honey. I'll always love you like my own."

"But I am yours and you're mine. Don't you see?" Her gaze frantically searched Margaret's. "You're my mother." Margaret's eyes flared, her features slackened. "You loved me and cared for me without reason. You were the only one I could ever really count on." She gripped her arms. "*You* were my family."

Margaret stared at her, her lips quivering, then she broke, heavy sobs shaking her shoulders and Penny held her, softly insisting all was forgiven, as Margaret had done for her, her entire life. Beyond her, she saw Ramsey, blinking rapidly, a deep shuddering breath expanding his big chest. And Penny thanked God he'd fallen from the heavens into her life.

In less than an hour the house was overflowing with a news crew, entertainment division. The production staff were unwinding electrical lines through the halls and out the front door, wheeling in metal camera cases.

"Ramsey," Penny hissed motioning to him. Bless his heart, he was fascinated but he was getting in the way.

"Amazing," he said, drawing his gaze from the chaos, to her and noticing the warm flush of her skin. Since he'd called Alexander for her this morn, she'd been unusually quiet, edgy. "Are you well?"

"Sure." She tried to look unaffected, fiddling with her locket. "Just the biggest moment in my life."

He grabbed her hand, dragging her down the hall and into the study. He pushed the door shut and backed her up against it. "I thought last night was the grandest moment of your life."

She smiled widely, looping her arms around his neck. "Well, I do recall a dream or two, and then yes," she looked thoughtful, "you did make love with me a couple of times.

He pressed her harder against the wood. "*Several* times."

"Several. Of course. But," she shrugged, "other than that—"

"Do not think to tease me now, woman," he said in a low growl and kissed her, savagely, deeply, and when he drew back she was gasping for air. "I adore you, Penelope," he said, enfolding her jaw in his callused palms. "And I promise you'll never be alone, never want for the love of family, for we will make our own."

"Babies," she said on a breath of air, covering his hands with her own and gazing into his dark eyes. The thought of having his child made her deliriously happy.

"Aye, but first you should speak vows with me."

God, she loved the way he talked. "Today soon enough?"

He chuckled, pulling her tightly to his long frame, smoothing one hand up her spine and around to cup her breast. "Aye, afore you grow big with my child and cause another scandal."

She leaned into his touch. "Mmmm. Heaven forbid."

A knock rattled the door and Ramsey groaned, lowering his hands. Penny smothered a giggle and stepped away from the door."

"Penelope," came from beyond the wall and her gaze flew to Ramsey's.

"It's Alexander." A whisper sharp, timid.

Ramsey saw the tension leap into her body like a new coat of skin and when he went to open the door, she put up a hand, halting him. He frowned and watched as she smoothed her clothing and primped her hair, then nodded. Ramsey opened the door.

They stared, for a long moment nothing passed between them beyond the recognition and realization in their eyes.

Alexander swallowed. God, his arms ached. For over twenty years his empty arms throbbed to hold his little girl. He'd missed a lifetime, of lullabyes and scraped knees and birthdays and watching her grow into a woman. And he ached. His eyes burned, a lump swelling in his throat. His fingers flexed. She was so beautiful. Her features hinting of Annora, but it was her eyes, cat-green, that marked her a Blackwell. He wet his lips.

"I've missed you, poppet."

A whimper caught in her throat and Penny crumbled, her legs going weak and Ramsey reached out to catch her. She sagged against his strength, still staring at Alexander. Lost memories flooded. And the vision of her dreams cleared; Alexander as a young man, holding her in his arms and dancing with her around a grand room, humming a tune in her ear.

She took a step away from Ramsey.

"Hello . . . Da."

Alexander choked, his lips quivering as he titled his head and raised his arms. "Are you too big to hold?"

Penny flew into his open arms and buried her face in the curve of his shoulder, sobbing helplessly.

Alexander squeezed his eyes shut, crushing her. "Oh God, I wish your mother was here," he murmured brokenly.

"You are and that's enough. Oh God," she sobbed, "it's enough."

Ramsey felt the ache of her loneliness, the years she must have spent feeling unloved and unwanted, washing away in her soft cries. And Alexander murmured to her, assuring words of a father, of a man who been unjustly denied the love of his child, a man who needed her as much as she needed him.

They stood there in the center of the study, renewing the love that came with touch and hope and Ramsey smiled, the corners of his eyes crinkling and sending a lone tear down his face. Ahh Tess, he thought, can you see what you've done for her? Are you up there with Dane watching the rebirth of your family?

"It was your pipe smoke I remembered. It smells like cherries," he heard her sob childishly, and Alexander's soft happy laughter followed Ramsey as he slipped from the room.

Sound checks and lighting went on around him as Justin Baylor adjusted the mike clipped to his lapel, watching her, easily pinpointing the differences from the last time they'd met.

If anything that she couldn't stop staring beyond him to the long haired man leaning against the back wall.

"You sure they're no restrictions, no dangerous territory?" He still couldn't believe it and didn't want to ask the wrong question and find himself chopped off at the knees by her or his producer.

"Baptize me with your worst," she said, bringing her gaze to his and his frown deepened despite her smile.

"Why did you ask me to do this? The premier's tomorrow and last time I wasn't exactly," he shrugged, "you know . . ."

"Polite? Tactful? I saw that interview and was pleased that what was important didn't end up on the cutting room floor. And this has nothing to do with the premier." Though the studio thought it would be great press and supported her. She tilted her head, smiling. "I hear you got a promotion."

"Getting the interview of the century had a little to do with it." He appeared suddenly shy, staring at his papers.

"Well, make this good, Justin. It's my last."

His gaze snapped up from his notes.

"After my next film, I'm retiring, for lack of a better word." He signaled the cameraman to get this on tape. "Why?"

Her gaze drifted past him to Ramsey and his dark eyes held the warmth and energy she needed to do this, to expose herself. His gaze lingered over her and she felt her skin heat as the memory of last night replayed sweetly in her mind. She loved him, so much it almost hurt to look at him. But looking had its pleasure, she thought, for nothing turned her on more than that man, in a plain white tee shirt, tight across his chest and arms, and jeans, button fly, no belt. God, he was sexy.

"Miss Hamilton?"

Penny dragged her gaze back. "Huh?"

He smiled, inclining his head to Ramsey. "He the reason?"

She straightened in the chair. "I'm going to marry that man."

The heavy camera suddenly swung around to get him on tape, a hand held flashing in his face. He didn't so much as flinch, his gaze tight on Penelope and when the news crew failed to gain a response, attention shifted back to her.

Where it should be, Ram thought.

"You going to fight me for time with her?"

Ramsey chuckled shortly afore he looked at Alexander. "I only wish to see her happy."

"We barely got started when they," he made a sour face at the production crew, "butted in."

Ramsey knew he'd have most of his questions answered afore the interview was complete, yet said, "If you are impatient, mayhaps you should speak with Margaret O'Hallaran." Ram nodded to the woman standing just off to the side, watching. Alexander frowned quizzically, aware she was the housekeeper. "She saved her life."

Alexander immediately crossed the foyer, and Ramsey watched as Meggie back-stepped a pace, her manner wary. Alexander spoke softly to her and Meggie smiled, sudden and relieved, and with their heads together, they spoke, pausing long enough for Meggie to hunt down Hank and bring him into the discussion.

The call for quiet spent through the house and Ramsey's gaze returned to Penelope. Bright lights filled the living room, and a woman adjusted a smattering of hair over Penelope's shoulder afore slipping out of the vision of the camera. From his vantage point Ramsey could see her, her image in the wide square lens of the monstrosity of a machine. She shifted her head, gazes locking across the room and Ramsey knew this was hard, knew she was releasing her ghosts afore her public. And he loved her more for her bravery. She was crossing swords with far greater a foe that he's ever drawn upon.

Penny caught his wink and smiled, taking a deep breath and focusing on Justin. She wasn't normally nervous, the camera a secret place she lived inside, but this time, she'd brought it into her home, her life, in the hopes of breaking open a new one. Freedom. From Sloane and her threats, from hiding her past.

"This will air tomorrow morning on *Talk Florida,* by the way," Justin said and she sputtered, "What!" just as the camera's red light flicked on.

As Justin spoke his introduction into the camera, Penny looked at Ramsey and recognized his disappointment. She shrugged helplessly. He understood the consequences before she even called the studio. She couldn't pick a time slot, and if Phalon or Sloane had a habit of watching the local midmorning news/talk show, they'd be alerted, even though she had no intention revealing the blackmail source.

Justin turned to her.

"You arrived into the film industry, at the tender age of seventeen, a child with the talent of a seasoned adult." Penny nodded her thanks for the compliment. "But there isn't a scrap of information on you prior to your summer stock audition. Why?"

"It's a complicated story," she said, and then she told him.

And Alexander listened as she revealed the ugly details of her youth, the drugs and vagrancy, and the things she'd done to survive. With each word he felt his heart ripping from his chest, agonized over the pain and loneliness she'd suffered. He relived the rage and the emotional torture of losing her, feeling it move thickly through his blood, yet without a place to vent the blame. He felt as helpless as he did twenty-five years ago and could say nothing, do nothing, for she'd grown beyond it.

"Cut," a voice said into the stillness and Justin sagged back into the chair, aware that if he turned around to see the staff, there wouldn't be a dry eye in the house. How had she been able to hide her colorful past was beyond him, but he saw her through his viewer's eyes. They'd admire her, not so much for revealing a blackmail attempt, but for her compassion for the homeless, and for being an ordinary person, suffering loneliness, destitution, addiction, then overcoming it and giving something back because she knew what it was like to be desperate. The nude photos would keep her name in the papers, add to the hype, but her fans would forgive her as they remembered she was young and alone.

Christ, did she know how lucky she was not to have died, not to have slipped beneath the crush and end up a bag lady or a hooker or a dealer? She had an unshakeable strength, and the insight to recognize when she'd fallen too far and Justin admired her for the courage, to open herself up for scrutiny before the entire world.

"I think this is enough," he said softly. "Off the record—" She arched a tapered brow, the austere woman he last interviewed leaping to the foreground, "do you know who's doing this?"

Her gaze darted to O'Keefe. "I'd rather not say."

But he had an idea. The police reports were public record; the judge's ruling on Tess Renfrew's disappearance as a death by drowning because there were witnesses, an ensign and muscle working for Rothmere. That *muscle* was the connection. Rothmere wasn't stupid, but add Sloane and the sorority rivalry since, and he had one hell of a link brewing between her, Sloane Rothmere and Tess Renfrew. That Hamilton had admitted her part in the catalysts leading to Renfrew's disappearance would exonerate her, at least in the viewer's eyes, but Sloane Rothmere was another matter. Her history for costly screw ups and border-line criminal activity was going to reek mayhem on her families reputation. And Justin was going to do a little digging.

"Is there a chance of interviewing Mister O'Keefe?"

She glanced at Ramsey and laughed to herself. "There are some things I still need to keep private, Justin," she said, before returning her gaze to Baylor.

Justin smiled, genuine, expecting that answer. "Then I'll see you tomorrow night."

"Good. I'll introduce you to my father."

Justin blinked, stunned. And Penny inclined her head to the man standing a few feet from Ramsey. Justin twisted for a better look around the cameras, his feature pulling tight. He snapped a look at her. "He looks familiar."

Penny stood, winking at Justin. "I'll give you time to do some research," she said, then quickly stepped over cords and equipment and into Ramsey's arms.

Alexander placed the worn jewelry chest in her hands. "Do what you think is best with what's inside. There's mostly pictures and letters. We sold off all her jewelry." Sadness marked his features.

Penny smoothed her fingers over the top, glancing at Ramsey, then Alexander.

"Thank you." She leaned out, wrapping her arm around his neck and hugging him, yet as she stepped back, her locket chain snagged on the box. Alexander immediately freed it, his gaze shooting between her and the dented oval.

"Annora put this on you a few weeks before you were taken." He smoothed his thumb over the gold. "I didn't want you to wear it because you were too little and kept putting it in your mouth. I thought you'd choke."

"She still puts it in her mouth," Ramsey said, flinging an arm around her shoulder and Alexander smiled.

Penny kissed him once more, clutching the locket and leaning against Ramsey as he turned and strode down the steps. She couldn't convince him to stay the night and she wouldn't press it. It was a lot to take in one day.

Ramsey closed the door, urging her up the stairs.

"Dare I ask that you let that rest til the morrow?" He nodded to the box.

"I can't." Her eyes pleaded for patience and he sighed, his lips curving slightly as he urged her into his room.

"You have me bewitched, you know that." He took the box, setting it on the dresser afore pulling her into his arms. His gaze slipped over her upturned face. "By God, how can I see you and still miss you?"

Her hands molded the ropy muscles of his broad back as she nuzzled the warm curve of his broad back as she nazzled the warm curve of his throat. "I've neglected you today, haven't I?" she said against his skin.

"Aye," came on a groan as her hand swept around to the fastenings of his breeches.

"I didn't say I had to open the chest right now?" She jerked on the waist band of his jeans, flipping open a button.

"Nay, you did not," he rasped.

She pried a second button and wet her lips, her gaze locked with his. "Think of anything we can do?" Her fingers dove beneath the waist band, seeking, her teasing making him suck air in through his teeth. Suddenly she yanked his tee shirt from his jeans, shoving it upward, baring his chest to the touch of her lovely mouth and Ramsey trembled, clutching her as she drew slow maddening circles around his nipple. He peeled the shirt off over his head and let it drop, then made quick work of the buttons of her blouse.

She arched against him, moving impatiently and she unzipped her skirt, shoving it down, kicking off her sandals with it. Her blouse joined the pile, and Ramsey struggled with the hooks of her lace bra.

"Sweet Jesus," he hissed against her lips.

"Rip it," she told him and he did, tearing it from her body and burying his face atween her breasts. She dropped her head back, laughing and he clutched her tightly, backing her up to the bed and pressing her to the mattress. Her hair fanned across the coverlet as he kissed her and kissed her, his mouth wide as if to devour her. Penny whimpered, loving his anxiousness, feeling it in her blood and she opened his jeans, shoving and pushing, urgent to feel the heat of him, but his lips were on her breast, laving her nipple, drawing it deeply into his mouth and she gasped for air.

"I want you, Penn." His hands moved frantically over her naked skin, her thighs, scooping beneath her buttocks and grinding her to him.

"I know." She drew her knee up, rocking.

"Nay, now." He caught the strings of her panties and tore them from her body. "Now!"

She freed him from his jeans and he spread her, sinking long and solid into her softness. She was like wet fire.

"God almighty!" He withdrew and plunged again, hooking her leg with his arm, pushing it higher, wider, his bonejarring thrusts driving her across the bed. She gripped fistfuls of sheets, his mouth and body smothering her and she abandoned herself to his hunger, their climax quick and shattering, over too soon.

Ramsey collapsed against her, panting. "Forgive me, love," he murmured, raining frantic kisses over her face and throat. "I did not mean to be so—"

"Savage?" she finished, breathless, and he leaned back, a

dull red creeping into his face. That was part of his attraction, his utterly masculine allure, the reckless wild side of him he kept tamped down for her century. "I like seeing you lose control."

"Are you saying 'tis only me?" he challenged and afore she could answer, added, "I do recall a wild lass pushing me onto a pile of hay and taking her pleasures with me in the barn, where anyone could have come upon us."

Her smile admitted her guilt. "Must have been all that—" she pushed him onto his back, straddling his hips—"Rocking and riding," she said, then did it again.

Ramsey was restless. 'Twas nearly two in the morn and his brief sleep in Penelope's arms would not restrain the energy building in him. He was impatient, for this bloody premier to be done with, for the interview to air, for the threats to either fade away or explode. He needed to either beat the bloody hide off a Rothmere or ride, and chose the latter, striding across the drive to the stables, eager to take the silver mare for a run down the darkened beach.

Horses whinnied, stomping, hooves hitting the wood stalls and Ram hesitated at the entrance, frowning at the flicker of light. One of the guards, he thought, yet slipped his knife free from his boot just the same. "Who goes?"

The flicker disappeared, rendering the barn in darkness but for the crooked streams of moonlight. Cautiously Ramsey stepped inside, edging the wall, his gaze moving to all corners as his eyes adjusted to the dark. He heard the rustle of hay and gripped the blade, inching toward the center of the barn, to the string left suspended to turn on the light. His foot connected with solid matter and just as he bent to examine it, pain detonated in the back of his skull. He dropped abruptly to his knees, struggling against his sinking consciousness and lost, sagging forward against the solid mass.

Beyond the screaming pain he realized he lay across a horse, the metallic scent of blood filling his nostrils, smearing his clothes. Rage burst through him and he tried to push himself up, but his body refused the order. He fell against the butchered animal, catching a glimpse of a narrow beam of light on a pair of feet afore all was gone.

Chapter 37

Hank flattened himself against the edge of the outer wall, the gun close to his body. He glanced left and right, then slipped around the wide open doors, tucking himself into a dark corner. He blinked, impatient for his eyes to adjust to the blackened interior when movement near the backdoor caught his attention.

He took aim and pulled back the hammer. The door flung open, sending a gray fracture of moonlight into the barn. Air locked in his lungs, his trained eye searching corners and rafters. No shadows moved, no one advanced, but the ribbon of light spilled over the figure laying across a fallen horse.

He immediately recognized the ponytail and inched close enough to kick at Ramsey's boot, softly hissing his name. Ram stirred, rising like an uncoiling serpent, slowly staggering to his feet. He swayed, his hand flying immediately to the back of his head.

"Get over here." Hank darted out into the light enough to grab a fistful of shirt and pull him into the darkness.

Ramsey sagged against solid wood, trying to get his bearings. "What the bloody hell are you doing out here?"

"I got up for a drink and noticed the alarm sensors around the grounds weren't on."

"I did not shut it off." Cannon fire rung in his head and he winced, snatching a rag off a hook and pressing it to his head. "I fear I forgot."

"Well, that—" he nodded to the horse—"should have woken everyone for two blocks."

They were against a stall wall, shoulder to shoulder, Ramsey out.

"We've been betrayed," Ram rasped, angry.

"Yeah, I figured as much and we ought to know who any second. I turned everything back on except this place. Here." A rustle of clothing and Hank pressed an object into Ramsey's hand. 'Twas a knife and as Ramsey figured the shape of it, realized 'twas an extremely big one.

"Sweet Christ, man."

"I know, but it'll do the trick." A pause, a sniff, then, "Jeez, smells worse than ever in here."

"Bowels and blood. By Triton, 'twas damned useless that." He sighed over the waste of magnificent horse flesh, then glanced at Hank, noticing the unmistakable outline of a gun. "Do you always skulk about the grounds with a loaded weapon?"

"In my nature. I used to be a Marine. Served with Tess's father."

"Well, Marine," Ram said, grinning in the dark. "Let us seek and destroy."

"That's kick ass and take names, Capt'n."

Ramsey led the way and Hank slipped behind him, the men crisscrossing out the barn and around the grounds. Tension rode him, making his head throb and Ramsey was glad Hank had turned on the sensors for 'twas too much ground for the two men to cover. They moved beneath trees and around shrubbery. Hank nodded to his right, indicating he'd search toward the north wall gate, and Ram moved left toward the sea, darting from patch of darkness, to refracting light from the solarium windows, avoiding the pattern of beams close to the house. His head pounded mercilessly, forcing him to concentrate harder and pause to seek a source of noise.

He heard the scatter of pebbles, the muffled rhythm of feet

on sand afore he saw a shadow edge along the white brick of the surrounding wall. They were fleeing by water, like the first intruders, Ram thought, pausing to toe off his boots. He quickened his pace, yet atween each step he searched the area for a partner. For none could have gotten onto the estate without help.

Unless they were already there and knew the way of it.

Ram opened his stride, his need to exact punishment riding up his spine and he caught up with the intruder, tucked in the cover of the sea oats, hovering over a small stack of equipment, light bending across silver and glossy black.

With no boat in sight, Ram had no notion of what he was about, yet even above the crash of waves, he heard a short hiss of air, a grunt, then saw him attempt to heft a large cannister onto his back.

Ram lunged, grabbing a fistful of cushiony leather, jerking him upright and pressing the blade into his side.

The intruder froze.

"I shall kill you, make no doubt," he murmured darkly.

A dejected sigh and then, "I'm not armed."

"Remove that," Ram commanded and the intruder slid the pack from his back. It jerked his arm and just as Ram realized it must be extremely heavy, he swung it at him, hard metal impacting with Ram's side.

Ram staggered, losing his grip and the man ran to the sea, dragging the cylinder onto his back. Ram gave chase, splashing water and latching onto his shoulder afore he could dive beneath the surface. He held tight to the spongy fabric, jerking the man around and sending his fist into his face.

Blood exploded from the first blow, his knuckles feeling the separation of cartilage. Even as the alarms sounded like a herald's trumpet, Ram did not cease, the knife gripped so tightly it cut into his palm. The pain in his head, and his failure to expose this bastard, bred power as he drove his fist into the intruder's ribs, forcing the air from his lungs. He gasped, folding over, then came upright, clenching a black knife and stabbing at Ramsey. Ram jerked to the side, the blade slicing through his shirt and he blocked a second strike, then twisted his wrist, bringing the back of the massive knife down on the his assailant's arm, the honed silver grazing his chest and cutting open the black skin of his suit.

He howled, dropping his weapon. The alarms went silent.

"No more," the intruder gasped, staggering under the weight of the equipment and Ramsey cut the straps, the cylinder dropping heavily to the sand as he jerked him close and tucked the blade beneath his chin.

He stared into the eyes of Noal Walker and tasted the bitter gall of betrayal.

"My God, man why?"

Regardless of the knife, he turned his head and spit blood. "I owed him."

Ramsey wanted to smash his face in. "No debt is worth murder!"

"He's powerful, influential."

"And you are a coward!"

Noal struggled and a shot rent the air.

Out of the corner of his eye Ram saw a figure freeze, hands up.

Hank approached from the darkness, driving the barrel into the partner's back, the man's face misshapen and bleeding. "Sorry. He got away from me." Hank shrugged, dug the gun and the intruder lurched forward.

Suddenly lights flashed on from the house, flooding the shore and grounds.

Penelope appeared at the rear door, tentative. "Ramsey!" Fear and anger tainted her voice.

"Come," Ram called, not taking his eyes off his prey.

Hank advanced, murmuring to his captive how much he'd like to *do* him, then moved in close to Ramsey, grabbing the knife off the ground and fitting it with another already in his waistband before he reached out to flip open the buckles to their weight belts. He scooped up the straps and flung them into the sea.

Ramsey's gaze flitted from Noal, the second man, to the unfamiliar equipment strewn on the beach and his ignorance made him angrier. "Find aught to shackle them, Hank, and a suitable prison," Ram said and the older man grinned.

"Got just the place." Hank backed up as Penelope approached. "Here, honey." He forced the gun into her hands, adjusting her aim. "Keep that right between the eyes."

"I can't believe this happened again." Penny blinked, her feet sinking into the sand. "How did you know they—?" Her green eyes widened when she managed a look at Ramsey. "Oh my God. Ramsey—" She swallowed, shaking—"Tell me that's not your blood."

Ram glanced down at his chest; his shirt front and sleeves were soaked red. His gaze pierced Noal's and he released him with a shove, moving to Penelope's side. "He slaughtered your horse."

Horrified, her gaze narrowed on the man in the dive hood, his face smeared with blood. She squinted. "Noal!" She took a step, holding her aim. "How could you do this?"

Ramsey made to take the gun and she nudged him. "No, I like this—power," she said, her temper rising. "And if anyone shoots him, by law it has to be me."

Ram scowled, bloody tired of deferring his masculinity to the ways of this century.

"Why?" In cutoff jeans and a baggy tee shirt, Penny gestured with the barrel. "Why!"

"Rothmere hired me to find out what you know."

"Not good enough. Sloane is behind this," Penny said and Noal shook his head, peeling off the hood.

"The first time maybe, but not after that." He clutched his bleeding side. "Christ, I wish I never met either of them." His eyes shifted between the pair. "Don't you see? He owns half my agency like he does half this town! And you've pissed him off."

Her expression remained unchanged.

"Give him what he wants, Penny."

She arched a brow. "And if I don't?"

"He'll hurt you."

She scoffed.

"I tried to warn you."

Her eyes flared. And loose pieces fit; the keys out of place in the rack, her beach attacker in a wet dive suit, the crushed flower *in* the house, how they lead Ramsey to the shelter. "You helped them."

His partner snickered. "I could have killed you in your sleep," he said and Ramsey's arm shot out, his fist connecting with a soft jaw so hard they heard it crack afore the man dropped to the sand like a dead fish. Ram stared down at the unconscious fool, hands clenched white, his breathing labored. "By God, it ends now!"

"Ramsey?" His gaze flew to hers and she recognized the suppressed fury in his dark eyes. "What are you planning?"

"I have done as you wished, followed the rules and ways of your century." He straightened to his full imposing height. "'Tis time to play this war by mine."

Hank returned, Margaret beside him and together they bound the intruders.

"He's bleeding," Margaret said, looking at Ramsey.

"A friggin' shame." Unsympathetic, cold. Hank jerked them to their feet, taking the gun from Penelope and prodding the attackers toward the old boat house. "Hope you don't get seasick."

Ramsey eyed Hank briefly, a faint smile curving his mouth afore he gestured to Penelope to come along to the house. She took a few steps, then stopped.

"Wait," Penelope called to Hank as she crossed the sand to stand before Noal. Ramsey advanced, cautious of her vulnerability and saw a strange look pass in her eyes, of regret and outrage and a dead friendship. Then suddenly she drew back her fist and hit Noal square in the nose. "That's for hurting Margaret." Noal cursed, nose bleeding harder, eyes watering as he shook his head against the pain.

Ramsey choked on his amusement as he waited for her to join him.

"Your law gave you permission to shoot him."

"I know, darling, but I detest violence." She shook her hand, blowing on her knuckles and Ramsey smiled, his anger receding.

"Come." He bent and kissed her gently. "Dress in black and find one of those cylinders that holds the light."

She smiled, glad he wasn't leaving her behind. "A flashlight, Ramsey. We really should work on your technical education."

"Excellent. Mayhaps you'll tell me how those men proposed to swim at night with all that ballast."

Phalon snapped awake, struggling for air, but a heavy pressure on his chest kept him from filling his lungs. His eyes flashed open and he tried to turn his face away from the unexpected blast of light, but a huge bowie knife prevented it.

"Who are you? What do you want?"

The knife pressed against the tender flesh of his cheek, dragging slowly to the base of his throat. He felt his heart beat pulse against the cold steel.

Unable to see beyond the light shining in his face, Phalon realized there were two, one was sitting on his chest, knees pinning his arms to the mattress. He could see the vague position of the assailant's arm, ready to drive that knife into his throat at a moment's notice.

Any number of his enemies could have hired these two.

Suddenly he felt a presence beside him, level with his head, his ear. But the silence reigned and Phalon struggled. The knife pierced his skin and the warmth of his own blood moved slowly down his neck.

And when the voice came, the low rasp sent a chill down his spine.

"I am your nightmares come to life, Rothmere. I am your past."

"Go to hell." How did they get in here with out setting off alarms or alerting the dogs?

A chuckle, dark and sinister and Phalon swallowed thickly.

"What a pitiful creature you are." A wonderous whisper. "Prey on the weak and see now how you tremble?"

"You're the one hiding behind the darkness. Show yourself."

"Arrogant fool," came calmly, with a hint of laughter.

"I've come to kill you. I want to gut you like a squealing pig, lay your entrails for you to see."

Phalon's eyes widened and he tried unsuccessfully to look to his right.

"Or burn you alive like your ancestor."

Phalon stilled. "What do you know about my family?"

A hand appeared before his line of vision and he squinted to focus. "Is this what you seek, Rothmere? To hide your lineage from the world?" Long fingers turned the brittle square of paper and Phalon felt his heart stop. "Are you afraid you will follow the path of Phillip has set?"

"Where did you get that?" A panicked hiss, of terror and joy.

"Your sister speaks from her grave."

"Impossible!"

"Is it?" The fingers flicked the proof and Phalon's gaze shifted from the darkness to the aged parchment and he watched as the hand withdrew, taking the precious letter. "Tell me why *you* fear a scrap of paper?"

Phalon's features sharpened. *"Never."*

"Tell me!"

The knife jabbed.

"If you have it, you know it!"

"The truth!" came in a voice as black as the night.

"I loved her. Dear God, I adored her . . . and she betrayed me."

"Like Phillip loved Elizabeth?"

A stretch of silence and, "She had that . . . letter. The Blackwell women . . . they passed it along like a ritual. A promise to keep it hidden. She threatened to destroy me, my family, *our* family. For them!" He struggled to rise, and the pressure on the knees increased, the light neared his face. "Give it to me!" he hissed through gritted teeth.

"Why did she threaten you? What did you do?"

He tilted his head back, sacrificially exposing his throat and looking at the ceiling. He swallowed over and over, licking his dry lips.

"Phalon?"

"I tried . . . to love her."

A soft gasp and his gaze flew to the light, and he attempted to see beyond the glare, yet could make out nothing but a smooth silhouette of black against black. They knew, before he said anything, he realized they knew. He was mortally ashamed of the advances he'd made toward his sister, an embarrassment he blamed on his heritage, bad blood. And he had to get the letter back, the proof that the sick nature ran in *his* veins, and destroy it. Then it would be clean . . . he would be.

"What do you want from me?" he begged and hated the weakness in his voice.

"Bide your time, Rothmere." The voice lowered, thick with dark promise. "The Blackwells have returned."

The light clicked off, the pressure on his chest suddenly gone and he took a long full breath before he realized he was alone. Phalon sat up, tried to throw back the covers but his arms were numb. He shook them impatiently, then climbed from the bed. Feeling hadn't fully returned and blindly he sought the drawer and the gun inside. Armed, he snapped on the light, glancing around the room. Not even a drapery stirred, the large bedroom cold and vacant. He lowered the weapon, then tossed it back in the drawer and rubbed the circulation back into his arms.

How they got their hands on the letter, he didn't know, but the memory of Annora reading it to him, holding it up for proof, a threat against his ever touching her again, materialized in his brain. She knew exactly how much his lineage meant to him, to keep the dirt off the Rothmere name. He'd hoped Alexander had destroyed it in his grief as he'd done to most of her things, hoped it would have stayed buried in the past.

For an instant last week, he entertained the idea that O'Keefe possessed it, then dismissed his fear as groundless, the casual remark that he knew his heritage as nothing more than common knowledge of the old feud between the families.

He dropped to the bed, his shoulders sagging with the burden of his past mistakes, costly mistakes. God, he could see it on the front page headlines. This will be worse than anything Sloane could have done.

Sloane. He left the bedroom, nearly running down the wide

long hall to her rooms, shoving open the door. His gaze went immediately to the bed and she twisted softly on the sheets, assuring him she was fine. Sighing deeply, he returned to his bedroom, slipping inside and closing the door.

How had they gotten inside without a sound, he still wondered. All but two passages were sealed. Pushing away from the door, Phalon decided he needed a drink and moved to the étagère. Suddenly he stopped short, his gaze focusing on the barren center of the dark carpet. He inched closer, his heartbeat accelerating with every step. Dear God. The letter. He snatched it off the floor, feeling it almost reverently. The Rothmere seal, the seal Annora had fixed, was still intact.

Then why question him, threaten, then leave it for him to find, Phalon wondered, feeling as if he were a death row prisoner granted a reprieve. Immediately he strode to the empty hearth and struck a match. He didn't read it; every word was engraved in his brain and took a deep breath before holding the two hundred year-old paper over the flame, watching it catch and flare.

Then he tossed it into the hearth and smiled.

Ramsey pulled her through the trap door in the barn, lifting her to her feet, then went about concealing the tunnel.

"Think he'll know?"

He hushed her, kicking hay, then grabbed her hand and made his way across the grounds to the spiked wall. He hoisted her up, letting her stand on his shoulders and when she was over, he followed. They stripped off the *borrowed* dive hoods and headed into the woods, avoiding the news vans claiming their territory for the ball tomorrow. Excitement and adrenalin rushed through her blood as she leapt over fallen trees and ducked branches, and she squashed the urge to laugh outloud.

When they were well out of sight and earshot, she said, "I told you he would be desperate enough to tell us the truth."

He flung his arm about her shoulder, pulling her close and kissing her temple. " 'Tis amazing, such a big brain in that pretty head."

She elbowed him for that, then unlocked the car. "What made you think Phalon wanted that and not the diamonds?"

Ram looked left and right afore dropping into the seat. "He likely craves both, yet my first conversation with him I mentioned his heritage and he became—"

"—unglued?"

He flashed her a smile, fastening his seat belt. "Aye. And when you found the letter, I recalled giving the like to Tess aboard the *Sea Witch*. 'Twas in the pouch of diamonds. How it made such a circle through time, I do not know." She started the car, waiting for his signal to pull away. The side street was empty at four in the morning. "Mayhaps Elizabeth intended to give it to Tess whilst she was Phillip's prisoner and slipped it to her during the chaos." It was the only explanation he could manage without making his brain ache. "Duncan said he found it with the diamonds, yet all was collected in a gilded box, with the rest of the Blackwell fortune Elizabeth returned.

"But *if* it was in the pouch, then who put it there?"

"Mayhaps Sloane was aware of her father's past."

"Sloane wasn't even born then. She could have heard rumors, but Phalon didn't want anyone to see that." She shook her head sadly. "Elizabeth was a strong woman to rise above the abuse she suffered." She shivered at the horrible images Elizabeth's letter offered. "Phillip was a deranged creature."

"Aye. Mad, utterly mad," Ram said softly, remembering the crime he'd done to Dane's sister, Desiree. "Phalon likely thought he'd the taint of his blood." Ramsey shrugged, checking the view in the mirrors. "Beyond some odd Blackwell tradition, I knew Annora had to have another reason for keeping that letter. 'Twas about her family, too."

She agreed, but, "The entries in her diary only mentioned being uncomfortable around Phalon, nothing specific."

"I suspect she did not tell Alexander what Phalon attempted."

"And we won't."

He smiled sympathetically. "He likely knows, love, and left it for you to find."

He was probably right, she thought, eyes on the road. She couldn't imagine Alexander having that jewelry chest for so long and not opening it. And he did tell her to do what she wanted with the contents. "What was Phalon expecting to get from Noal? I mean, he didn't trust him enough to even tell Noal what to look for. That's if Noal's telling the truth, of course."

Ramsey was thoughtful for a moment. "Phalon could have given a description, but as terrified as he was this eve, he would not have revealed the contents, implying retribution if the seal was broken."

"So you heated the wax back up."

"Let Phalon have his peace. Naught will come from allowing the secret to die."

She and her *uncle* had that in common, neither wanting their mistakes aired, but Penny only hurt herself by hiding it.

"I agree," she said with feeling, steering the car through her gates. The absence of guards and guns was comforting. And watching Ramsey disarm and dismiss them earlier was satisfying.

" 'Tis not over yet, love."

"Why not?" She braked, threw the gear into park and turned off the motor as she spoke. "Phalon has what he wants, give Noal and his pal over to the police. Crane will take care of the horse."

He shifted to face her. "Have you forgotten those diamonds belonged to your father, your family, and they were in the possession of a Rothmere the night Tess stole them."

"But they're gone, lost between here and . . ." She waved at the darkness beyond the windshield, indicating the universe— "wherever."

When he didn't respond, she met his gaze.

And slowly Ramsey shook his head.

Lt. Pete Mathers pointed the remote control at the television and stopped the videotape from recording further, then tipped back in his chair, tapping the control against his lips.

"That didn't seem like the same woman we met."

"Yup."

"How 'bout that story?"

"Sort of sinks my theory all to hell," Downing said, not the least bit upset.

"Think she's on the up and up?"

"I sure wouldn't tell the entire English speaking public shit like that if I weren't desperate."

"I told you Renfrew didn't jump. She was forced over the side with the threat of murder."

"Sounds like it to me," Downing said, flipping through a report and pretending to read. "And since you can't arrest a dead woman for B & E, go after the living."

Pete rewound the tape. "Hamilton's an accessory."

Downing's head jerked up. "Think you can make it stick after that?" He gestured to the T.V. "We're supposed to be the good guys, Pete. The evidence was burned and five will get you ten, if there's any truth to what Hamilton said, we'll find a few bullet holes in that Mustang of Renfrew's and link it to Owen." They both reached for their jackets as the office door flung open.

The precinct captain poked his head inside.

"See the interview?" They nodded. "Catch that guy in the background?"

Mathers frowned, pausing in shrugging on his jacket. "O'Keefe?"

"Nah, the older one, gray haired."

Mathers grabbed the control and flicked the T.V. back on, watching the tape in rewind, searching the fast moving figures.

"Some detective you are," the captain said sourly, not stepping inside as if he would lose his authority if he did . "There," he pointed and Mathers paused the tape, leaning out to examine the figure.

"Yeah, so?" Looks like one of the news crew, Pete thought.

"That's Alexander Blackwell."

Pete stared blankly at his partner, then at his captain.

"I was a rookie when he was a big deal in this town. Take

into consideration that interview, that he was thought to be dead, was heavily connected to Rothmere, and now he's standing in Penelope Hamilton's house like he lives there." The captain flung a heavy confidential file on Pete's desk. "Then read that."

Chapter 38

Five sets of theatre doors burst open, news crews rushing out, each eager to get their story on the air first.

A slim blond woman, poised before a camera, nodded to her director.

"We go live in five, four, three, two—" He pointed.

"Here at Universal Studios, the premier release celebration begins," the reporter said into the mike the instant the red light blinked on. "And what a party it will be! *The Gold Masque* has already been dubbed the must-see film of the year. Majestic locations, detailed costumes and an intriguing plot of love cultivated behind the illusion of a mask and denied in public. Commoner and nobility clash in tempestuous passion, and believe me, the sparks fly from the screen, but nothing today compares to the surprise attendance of *Gold Masque*'s star, Penelope Hamilton and her mysterious escort, Ramsey O'Keefe." Behind her spectators waved and shouted at the camera. "The energy here is incredible," she fairly shouted over the noise, holding her ear piece in, "and lends to Miss Hamilton's unusual appearance and, even after the revealing telecast this morning, her receptiveness to the media. She's chatted with fans, signed autographs and did several spot interviews, proving that something has definitely changed for the reclusive actress.''

She took a breath as the electrican signaled the roll of footage taped earlier, then adjusted her sequined dress, waiting for the countdown to live air. ''Though her escort, O'Keefe, hasn't spoken a word on camera, he has not once left her side. And she doesn't seem to mind.'' In the background the crowd roared to new life and the reporter scanned the area, then motioned to the camera man. ''There is no doubt that Ramsey O'Keefe has stolen the heart of Florida's most celebrated resident.''

Striding down the center walk between velvet ropes, Penny paused, taking the offered paper and signing her name as she talked with a fan. She handed it back and noticed the young girl hardly spared her a glance, gazing up at Ramsey in wrapped awe.

She leaned close and whispered, ''I think she's in love.''

Ramsey smiled down at a girl of no more than five and ten and moved closer, taking her hand and bringing it to his lips for a kiss. She sighed dreamily and when he straightened and winked, she screamed, bouncing wildly. He flinched, lurching back and Penny laughed, pulling him toward the limousine, waving and smiling over the top, then winking into Max's lens before ducking inside. She dropped into the seat, instantly kicking off her heels and wiggling her toes as Ram fell in beside her, shaking his head.

''That was very sweet, what you did.''

''That child is going to rupture something.''

Penny laughed softly, patting his thigh. ''At least tonight will be calmer, I hope.''

Hesitantly he waved out the window, then dismissed the crowd, turning his attention to her, enjoying the sight of her sleek stockinged legs as she worked a kink out of her ankle. His gaze traveled upward, to the dark green dress covered in beads and scandalously strapless. A cocktail dress, she'd told him, and too short and exposing far too much flesh, he decided, yet she was unbelievably nervous afore they'd departed and wisely kept his comments to himself.

He leaned over and pulled her into his arms. "I am, again, humbled by your talent, love."

His praise meant everything and she scooted closer, swinging her legs over his thighs. "Liked the film, huh?"

"Aye." His hand soothed over her calf. "I'm fond of an enchanting romance." He wiggled his brows. "Ours."

She leaned up to give him a quick kiss. "But admit it, you were embarrassed during the love scene. I saw you squirming."

His skin darkened. "I felt much the voyeur." He wanted to stop the playing of the show, but knew 'twas impossible and suffered in misery as a goodly portion of her body was bared for hundreds of eyes.

"It was necessary for the plot," she consoled, smoothing the lapels of his black dinner jacket. He looked magnificent in a tux, dashing, to-die-for classy. She wanted to undress him right now, and the only thing stopping her was the windows weren't tinted for privacy.

"This, I believe, is true," he said thoughtfully, then met her gaze. "But I do not care to see you in the arms of another man. A'tall," he clarified darkly. "Regardless if 'tis an actor."

His jealousy was endearing and she knew he was suppressing a healthy, likely raging, chunk of his discomfort for her benefit. Though the scenes were tame, more sensual than skin, exposure like that was hard enough for any man to handle, let alone one fresh out of the eighteenth century.

She cupped his face in her hands. "I won't do it anymore, if it makes you that unhappy."

He groaned, brushing his lips to hers and drawing her hands to his chest. "I cannot ask that of you, 'tis your work."

"I know, but I offered, and love scenes hardly seem appropriate just now." Her fingertip circled his shirt button, her gaze on her movements and he felt her sudden trembling.

He frowned softly, tipping her chin. "What say you, love?"

"Well," she breathed. "I mean—" she swallowed nervously—"I'd have this big belly to work around."

Ramsey's chiseled features yanked taut, his eyes searching hers. His grip on her hands tightened. "Say it," he breathed.

"I'm pregnant, Ramsey."

He simply stared and her heartbeat accelerated as she watched his dark eyes gloss with slow tears. "God almighty," he choked and leaned close to kiss her, a kiss unlike any other, reverent, unspeakably cherishing, and she felt him struggle with his emotions, his great shuddering breaths. "Oh sweet *sweet* Jesus," he murmured against her lips, deepening his kiss, cradling her on his lap.

"You never fail to surprise me," she said, her arms around his neck, loving him for his vulnerability.

He rubbed his cheek against the inside of her arm, and chuckled shortly, sniffling. "Nor you, my heart." He smoothed hair from her forehead, stroked her cheek, felt the pattern of her lips. "God, I love you, Penn," he rasped.

"And I thank God for it," she cried softly, sinking into his kiss.

The limousine sped down the highway, sheltering the lovers, and Ramsey rejoiced.

The coroner unzipped the black body bag and Pete Mathers cursed as he recognized his prime witness. "Your assumption?" he said sarcastically though the bullet hole in Owen's chest was obvious.

The coroner snickered. "Time of death is no more than fifteen hours, if I had to guess." The coroner checked nail beds and teeth like he was inspecting a horse for auction. And Pete thought he'd lose his lunch right there. It didn't matter how many bodies he saw, it was still horrible.

The coroner sealed the bag, then waved at his assistants to cart the remains into the truck.

"Anything we can use?"

"He was cleaned out, no money, no I.D., no labels in his clothes, even his shoes were plain, common."

"Give me something I can use, Braddock."

"I won't be sure until I've done an autopsy." Pete made a hurrying motion; he knew the routine and wanted something to lead him in the right direction.

"He was with a woman, either before or during."

Pete arched. "You mean he got nailed while he was nailing her?"

Braddock smirked. "Don't quote me."

Phalon Rothmere stood beside the window, watching the constant influx of caterers, florists, work men, musicians, and their tons of equipment delivered into his house. The last thing he needed now was an entourage of press, movie and T.V. stars and their staff, along with the Lt. Governor and a few congressmen in his house, but since the movie was shot in a sound stage duplicate two years ago, he'd agreed, bound by a contract signed two years ago. It wasn't that he had to spend a dime; her studio was paying the bill, but the press had camped out outside since yesterday, and the phone hadn't stopped ringing. His only consolation was his unexpected visitor last night and the sacrificial burning of his family's lurid past. He felt confident and mostly relieved.

Except that Noal hadn't returned, nor called to give him a report. He had to know if Hamilton had the diamonds, if Renfrew had somehow left them in Florida. He *had* to know. The Red Lady in the hands of any who knew its history could destroy him. Even if Hamilton had them, his only recourse was to ignore it, for laying claim publicly would incriminate himself, even if the statute of limitation on grand theft had run out. But the implication was still there.

He was almost glad they were ten fathoms under the Caribbean sea. Another mistake swiped away. No diamonds, no knowledge of them, and he could never be linked. Then again, he'd lost a few million in the process.

"Did you see it?" Sloane said, bursting into the room. When he simply scowled, his gaze dropping briefly to the videotape in her hand, she raced to the far corner and threw open the cabinets, shoving the tape in the VCR. She grabbed the remote and stepped back, clicking on the screen. The tape played.

Together they watched. "Well, then," Phalon said when Penelope told the entire world what happened the night Tess

Renfrew vanished, "you must look your best when the police come to arrest you."

"Me? What for? She didn't name me."

His gaze shifted from the T.V. "Not on screen."

"They have only her word."

"Penelope Hamilton hasn't received so much as a parking ticket in twelve years and before that, well, you're right, we have only her word since there's nothing to verify that she even existed before then."

"I didn't break in here, *I* didn't take shots at her, or chase her through the city, or step onto her property. *I* didn't lay a hand on the precious starlet."

"You set up the blackmail and Tess Renfrew is dead, a judge declared it with that ensign's testimony. There is such a thing as accessory with intent to commit bodily harm, accessory after the fact, attempted murder, contract murder. Take your pick."

Sloane fumed. "If I go down, so do you, *Daddy.*"

He smirked, looking her over. "Nice to know I've been invited to the hanging."

"She has them, or why would she go through all this," she flicked a manicured hand toward the T.V., "if not to throw off suspicion."

"Do you actually believe, if they turned up, that I will forgive you for this?"

"Why not?"

"Hamilton didn't break the law."

She put her hands on her hips, petulant. "And you haven't scraped the thin line across it before?"

"A woman is dead!" Phalon raged.

Her skin brightened, her fists clenched white. "You mean your obsession is dead!"

His gaze narrowed to mere slits and he advanced, but she smiled, smug, calling out for her maid. He stopped and she spun about, heading for the door.

Dead, she realized, was not buried.

And she'd find a way to seal that grave. Tonight.

* * *

At the base of the staircase, Penelope paced, her mind frantically going over the possible scenarios to this evening. The premier showing had gone well, almost too well, but Phalon wasn't there. She would have to face him, Sloane, and walk into the house meant to shelter her. And Alexander? How was he going to feel, being a guest in his house after all they'd discovered?

"Oh my God," Margaret said and Penny stopped, frowning over her stunned expression, then turning to follow the direction of her gaze.

She inhaled, watching Ramsey descend the stairs, tugging his cuff.

Her heart thundered wildly and she saw him as he was born to live, the man of the eighteenth century, dignified, gallant.

The costume he'd selected was him, elegant yet took nothing from his masculinity, the rich brown velvet coat smoothly hugging his broad shoulders and torso, long and flaring at the hem. An ascot of flawless cream silk fountained from his throat, the long tapered vest of gold and brown brocade snugly accenting his lean waist, making his chest look accceptionally big. But it wasn't even the flint-lock pistol shoved in his waistband that drew her sudden attention, but his knee breeches, tucked in tall black boots. They were leather, the shade of turned earth, laced instead of a fly, and formed to his body like a second skin.

And she couldn't decide whether or not to march him back upstairs and either make him change or see how fast she could get those laces open! As he drew close, she realized the breeches laced down the side of his thighs, the ties flicking against his own boots.

Penny thought her legs would liquefy right there. No wonder Tess warned her about him.

He stopped afore her, tipping her chin and smiling into her green eyes. "If you continue to look at me thus, my love, we will be late."

"Oh Ramsey," she whispered. "I wish I'd known you in your century."

There was a look of awe in her eyes and he moved closer, frowning softly and searching her gaze. "Why then?"

"This," her glance swept his clothes, "makes me realize what you gave up, the life, and how much you've had to adjust."

He pushed a curl from her forehead. " 'Twas only a meager life of one man."

"But what you saw, what you did, the people you knew, it *is history.*"

"Yet in another century hence, this," his gesture encompassed her time, "will be that of our children's." He gathered her in his arms, and she griped his biceps, feeling the velvet. "This is our time, Penn, *ours.*" He pressed his forehead to hers. "I regret not a moment of leaving my loneliness behind."

"I hardly think you were *ever* lonely," she said with a faintly jealous smile.

" 'Twas my heart that called me through time, my sweet. To you."

What did I do to deserve this man, she thought as his hands circled her trim waist, broad fingers smoothing the corset stays beneath the blue gown.

" 'Tis not too tight, this?"

She smiled, toying with the ribbon holding his hair back. "Is your concern already directed at our baby," she whispered.

"Nay, nay," he assured. "My God, Penn, I look at you, knowing you will be the mother of my child, *our* child, and I—" Air hissed in through his teeth, his warm gaze caressing her luxurious figure.

"Get excited?"

"Aye," came in a gush.

"Better calm down then, 'cause in those pants, every one will know it."

He chuckled, kissing her quickly, then moving to her side and offering his arm. "Your carriage awaits, m'lady."

"And he ain't kidding," Margaret said, gathering her skirts, Hank at her side, both dressed in period clothing.

Penny frowned and Ramsey flung the front door open. She gasped, racing out onto the porch.

Behind the stretch limousine in her driveway, beneath the

warm glow of the lights, was a gleaming black carriage, four dove-gray horses harnessed to pull. A masked driver tipped his tricorn to her, the cloaked footman hanging on the back nodded, and Ramsey pressed a hand at the small of her back, guiding her down the steps. " 'Twas an opportunity I could not let pass, love, to share a bit of my century with you this day,'' he whispered close to her ear. ''Mayhaps the last.''

''It's beautiful.'' She smoothed a gloved hand over the polished wood, then glanced at him. ''And I get a taste of your century every time you open your mouth.''

He chuckled, handing her into the carriage, then alighting after her. ''But Margaret and Hank,'' she said, catching the sill and the older woman came to the window, offering her a pair of masks.

''No, honey, we talked.'' She glanced at Ramsey and smiled. ''The car needs to clear the way. You can't imagine the strings he had to yank to get this thing on the road.''

Penny looked at Ramsey, arching a brow.

''Alexander,'' was all he said.

" 'Sides, it's been a while since I rode in a limo.''

''Yeah,'' Hank said, giving her waist a squeeze. ''We can neck.'' She swatted him with her fan and he made a big show of being wounded as they climbed into the limousine. Chuckling, Ramsey rapped on the roof and the carriage lurched, rolling out the gates.

Penny leaned back into the leather seat. ''This is wonderful, Ramsey, thank you.''

''My pleasure, love.'' The blue gown gave her skin a soft radiance, or was that his child growing in her, he wondered with a smile. Her hair was curled, swept off her neck and artfully arranged to frame her face. 'Twas his first occasion to see it so meticulously styled, he realized, then noticed she adjusted her gloves for the third time.

''Frightened?''

''Yes,'' came with feeling. She was afraid for him, but he didn't need to hear that now. ''I have the irresistible urge to act out this night.''

''But?''

"I just got off *that* stage and I don't intend to go back."

"Then be as you are." He took the mask, afixing it afore his face. "Ramsey O'Keefe, m'lady, captain of the American frigate *Triton's Will*. At your service," he said, bowing as he drew away the mask.

She laughed softly, stuck by the easy flair when he did that. "And I am?"

"Penelope Hamilton Blackwell, lost heiress, come to retake her birthright."

She tilted her head. "I'd rather be Penny O'Keefe, wife, mother, and part-time couch potato."

Ramsey blinked, then laughed, giving her a quick kiss as the coach headed afore the mansion. The way was clear and Ramsey knocked on the roof and the carriage sped up the long torch lit drive, coming to a jingling halt afore the crowd.

"Well, this is certainly a grand entrance."

She reached for the door handle.

"Wait." He dipped his hand into his pocket, withdrawing the gold chain, holding it up. The deep-pink diamond swirled before her vision. She met his gaze and he motioned her to turn.

"This is going to drive Phalon absolutely mad, if he recognizes this," she said.

"He's a Rothmere, he will." He fastened the clasp, then kissed her bare neck. "Alexander wanted you to have it."

She looked back over her shoulder. "Is he coming, Ramsey?"

There was almost a childish plea in her voice and he hated to break her heart. " 'Twould be a grave humiliation to be a guest in his own house."

She nodded, staring at her lap. Oh Da, how this must hurt you, she thought as Ramsey gave her a squeeze. The footman flung open the door, then placed a wood box before the entrance. Ramsey left the carriage first, and onlookers screamed so loud he cast them a curious glance afore turning to help her. The crowd gathered went wild, cameras flashing, bright lights turned high as she stepped out of the conveyance.

She smiled and waved, her attention shifting to the wide

arched door way, the thick oak wood, carved and thrown open
for tonight's guests. The house looked like a Spanish castle,
gothic, swirling black iron balconies, pointed arches over the
windows, crenelations shielding the roof and she half-expected
to see rifles or arrow tips poke over the edge. Strewn across
the doorway and draping the steps were boughs of ivy, clusters
of herbs and wildflowers of blue, purple and magenta nestled
in their shiny leaves, splashes of gold ribbon peeking from the
green. The air hung with the splendid fragrance and Penny
imagined what it must have really been like to live then, with
Ramsey.

"Oh Ramsey, I forgot how beautiful this house really is."

"Have you ever been invited inside?" His wink meant in
the light of day, considering their adventure the eve afore.

She looked appalled. "Are you kidding? Me, in her house?"

Ramsey leaned close, offering her mask. " 'Tis the home of
your family, Penelope. *Your* ancestors."

Penny stared at the mansion, imagining Tess arriving with
her new husband, raising her children here, growing old and
she felt a pull toward the magnificent structure, a need to
connect with it somehow, and a hope that a childhood memory
would surface.

"Are you well?"

Her gaze jerked to his and she smiled. "Better than well,"
she said, linking her arm with his. Behind them, Margaret and
Hank followed. Security kept fans back, a select few of the
press already inside in a special room, and as they donned their
masks and swept through the entrance, Penny stopped short,
her grip on Ramsey's arm tightening. He frowned softly, following the direction of her gaze and stared into the lifeless eyes
of Sloane Rothmere.

Chapter 39

"That was some performance this morning."

Sloane's biting blue gaze rode over her gown, her face, briefly shifting to Ramsey, her manner inspecting, and finding them lacking. Her sight ended on the pear shaped diamond. Her gaze flew to Penelope's.

"I wasn't acting. Have a problem with it?"

The photographers went wild, the flashes blinding, people calling out questions as Margaret and Hank flanked the couple.

Sloane didn't spare them a glance. "Well, I'm still here, aren't I?" Sloane shrugged elegantly clad shoulders. "So you see, you did it for nothing. Now they know you're just white trash."

Penny didn't so much as flinch. "What I am, is happy. And I did it for me, Sloane, not you. You got exactly what you wanted. The world knows where I came from." She tilted her head. "Aren't you thrilled?"

Penny knew she hit a nerve when Sloane's carefully outlined lips tightened. She wanted to do the exposing, be the orchestrator of her maliciousness. That the power was gone made her a dangerous woman.

Sloane's gaze shot to the cameras lurking, yet she knew they couldn't be heard. She leaned closer, her voice a viperous hiss. "I'll be happy when both of you are shark bait."

Penny felt her skin shift on her bones and had the irresistible urge to rub her arms. There was no conscience there, no heart, only bitterness.

"Careful, Sloane, your fangs are showing." Penny continued to smile. "And the only reason you're not rotting in jail is that I haven't pressed charges, *yet.*"

Sloane scoffed nervously. "Like they could stick."

Penny's smile was brittle. "Think so?"

There was change in her just then, a desperate, almost pleading in her expression. "Where is he?"

Penny reared back, arching a brow, cool, patient.

"What have you done to him?" she said, grabbing her arm, nails digging. Penny looked down at her touch, her gaze rising slowly to meet strikingly pale-blue eyes. God, she was pathetic.

Ramsey immediately intervened, peeling her hand from Penelope's body. *"Never* touch," came with suppressed savageness and Sloane's features slackened briefly, then tightened with sharp beauty. "Enjoy the evening, Mistress," he said with a mocking bow, gently maneuvering Penelope into the grand hall.

"Thank you. I wanted to belt her across the chops so bad I could taste it."

Ramsey's lips curved. "Ignore her, love, she is naught but a mouse in this game." Oftimes she dropped all reserve and polish and returned, he could only assume, to the child of the streets and he'd lay odds she could dress a few hides if need be.

A tugging on his arm and Ram realized she'd stopped, her gaze sweeping the grand room. "You remember," he whispered.

"I see it empty, only the sun lighting it, and a little tape player in the corner." She gestured to the far left, then looked up at him, her eyes glossing. "And Alexander is holding me, humming." She looked back at the room. "And my mother is watching us." Ramsey leaned close and pressed his lips to her temple and she closed her eyes. "This was my home," she whispered, as if just believing it, then sighed, eager to be inside and perhaps, discover more.

They moved into the ballroom, the guests masked until midnight and already on their way to a having a grand time. Soft lights splashed over the elegantly-costumed people ringing the dance floor, dining from the scatters of tables heaped with huge chunks of beef, whole pigs, several turkeys, and an abundance of fruit, cheese, and vegetable dishes. Lilting strands of Mozart wafted from the orchestra, and dancers swirled, the rustle of petticoats and rich fabrics melting with the music. Profusions of flowers filled dusky lit corners, draped windows and Penny inhaled the pungent fragrance, smiling and introducing Ramsey as they strolled. The guests were immersed, the costumes and aura of the century taking hold. One man waved a turkey leg as he spoke, pausing long enough to tear at the meat like a Viking, while another chased a female servant, trying to steal a kiss.

A liveried servant passed and Ramsey snatched two fluted glasses of champagne from his tray, offering her one. She shook her head, discreetly touching her stomach and Ramsey grinned, draining one goblet afore handing it to a passing waiter, then swept his arm about her waist, leaning close.

"Do you see him?" He saluted her with the crystal. Above her head, his gaze scanned the dancers, catching on a figure poised against the wall, then moving to another who kept looking behind himself.

"No, but I wouldn't even recognize anyone with all these masks."

Ram finished off the champagne. "Relax, love," he whispered, recognizing her impatience. " 'Tis all the more interesting a night."

He deposited the glass on a waiter's tray.

"You aren't going to tell me what you're planning, are you?"

" 'Twill be best for your safety." His look said 'twas his utmost concern. "Aside that you cannot leave the guests. Your presence will be missed."

A man approached and Ramsey immediately recognized her acting partner, her costar. An Englishman, Ram recalled.

"Don't you look lovely. Positively radiant," he said as Penny leaned out and he peaked a kiss to her cheek. He looked at Ramsey, offering his hand. Ram accepted it, smiling. "We're to mingle, orders from the high-ups. Terrific costume, Ramsey. Press meeting in one hour. Have you met our host?"

Ramsey wondered how this lad could maintain the rigidness of a play when he talked so bloody fast.

"Josh, calm down." It was his first big picture and she could feel the rush of adrenalin in him. They'd worked together before, as teenagers, and their innocent friendship had started the vicious rumors, sending her into privacy.

"I keep trying," he flashed her a boyish smile, "and you always did mother me." Ramsey watched as he drew closer, the energy settling for a moment as Josh Randell stared into her eyes. "Thanks for the chance, Penny. I know your request for me landed me this role."

"Oh, Josh, don't underestimate yourself. If you weren't good, nothing I could have said would have mattered." She gave him a warning look. "And you know it."

He sighed, encouraged. "Save me a dance?"

"Is it in my contract?" she replied and he laughed, turning away and melting into the crowd.

"Miss Hamilton?"

Penny turned to find Justin Baylor standing close, dressed as a pirate.

"Or should I say Blackwell?"

Penny checked for eavesdroppers, then stepped close. "Ah . . . Justin, can I ask a favor?" He simply looked at her and she sighed. "I promise to give you an exclusive about my . . . parentage, if you refrain from asking any questions until this evening is over."

His guarded expression said that was obviously *not* his plan.

"Dire circumstances force us to keep this information private for a bit longer," Ramsey said lowly and Justin realized he hadn't heard him talk before. "I bid you grant us this and we'll see you are the one to reveal the tale, if that is your wish."

Justin glanced between the two. Penelope Hamilton could have called anyone for that interview, had her pick of the network name draws but she'd called him, personally, and given him the scoop of the decade. But it was the look in O'Keefe's eyes that grabbed his attention and the beat reporter in him knew there was much more to her name than any one would know, unless they told it.

"Exclusive? Not a word about who you are to anyone?"

"You doubt my honor?"

Justin chuckled, eyeing O'Keefe. "I'm a reporter, I doubt everyone. But yes, I'll keep a lid on it. Though if I hear even a hint . . ."

Penny sighed, relieved, and Ramsey held out his hand. "Our thanks, Mister Baylor." He bowed lightly and Justin's lips crooked in a half smile. O'Keefe was a strange one, he thought, watching them walk away and deciding he liked him. Real personable guy. And he'd revealed just enough to perk Justin's snooping instincts.

They circled the room, greeting and chatting with politicians and businessmen, costumers, grips, cameramen, script writers, and directors. Beyond the masks there were no distinctions and Penny had to laugh at the Lt. Governor, dressed like a pansy in red satin and scratching at his white wig. But it was Ramsey who intrigued them, his speech, his masculine grace and dignity turning several heads. And Penny noticed their host was nowhere in sight.

"I'd recognize that regal carriage anywhere," a voice said and together they turned to find Anthony, with his date, Clarissa Two Leaf, clad predictably as an Indian princess.

Ramsey bowed to the coin dealer, then looked his friend over from head to toe, chuckling as Antony tipped his feather-edged tricorn. He wore the uniform of a British officer.

"Do we cross swords on the lawn, my friend?"

"Hell, I half-expected you to be dressed as a Continental Marine."

Ramsey smirked. "The uniforms itched."

Anthony blinked, again realizing who Ramsey truly was and

he edged closer, his gaze dropping briefly to Ramsey's flintlock. "One of these days you'll have to sit and suffer my questions."

Ram smiled. "Agreed, mate."

Penny cleared her throat and the men looked at her. "Come on, Clarissa," Penny linked her arm with the quiet woman's. "*I'll* be a proper date and introduce you around. To all the *single* men," she said pointedly to Tony and he flanked Clarissa protectively, his sword flapping against his leg. Over her shoulder she looked back at Ramsey, her expression frightened, warning him to be careful as she inclined her head ever so slightly to a darkly-dressed man near the doors, his features completely covered in a hood. He scanned, found the subject, then looked back at her. He mouthed, *I love you,* then meandered his way across the room.

Beneath the hood, his gaze followed the tall man in brown velvet as he moved through the crowd, pausing to greet and chat, then continue. Pushing away from the wall, he traced the same path, slowly, as to not bring attention to himself.

As Ramsey O'Keefe slipped beyond the tall open doors, he was a few yards behind him.

A gloved hand depressed the lower portion of a panel, the wood giving under the soft pressure. The hinge creaked as he pried it open, then edged the narrow opening and slipped into the darkened corridor. Cobwebs draped the interior like veils of spun silk and he brushed them aside, pushing the brittle lever and sealing the passageway. He moved quickly, his penlight flicking a narrow beam off the walls and floor as he turned corners and climbed ladders. When he reached his destination, he paused, closing his eyes, listening. A scuffling of shoes against wood, a creak, and he wondered who else knew of theses passages. He waited for the sound to fade, then suddenly jerked the lever. It made no sound, no clatter of age and he frowned, then pushed open the panel, stepping into the darkened room.

It was empty, the only light cast beneath a painting hung high on the wall.

Phalon Rothmere strolled casually amongst the guests, occasionally watching her progress around the room. O'Keefe was not difficult to mistake for he towered over several guests. Phalon spoke to business partners, a senator and a talkative producer looking for backers until Phalon excused himself, pausing to address the congressman he'd help put in office. He listened with half an ear, covertly pinpointing Hamilton in the crowd, his gaze on the thumb sized diamond resting above the swells of her breasts. Her gloved hand rose to touch it, caress it and Phalon knew a burning desire to rip it from her throat.

The Red Lady.

Annora's prize.

Phalon experienced a tantalizing mix of lust and greed and utter remorse. The rare gem was his, all he had left that Annora loved.

Dismissing the congressman in midsentence, he headed toward her, then froze, suddenly realizing O'Keefe was nowhere in sight.

Chapter 40

Discarding his mask, Ramsey stood in the center of the grand study and stared at the painting.

"What a muck you've left me, woman," he said to Tess's image and did not doubt the clever woman realized two hundred years afore, that this night would come. Rounding the edge of the desk Ramsey lifted the painting off the wall, running his fingers over the cloth back, the frame, searching. 'Twas the only thing Tess was certain would be evergreen and the over-powering feeling he'd experienced the day he saw this portrait again, made him believe her spirit possessed this room, urging him to seek beyond the plain and simple. He let loose a captured breath when his fingers grazed a roughened spot and he tipped the back toward the light, plucking at a break in the thick frame. 'Twas a misshapen square divide in the wood, and he jiggled the piece, then impatiently withdrew his knife from his boot and pried the edge. It gave, the small fitted section splintering a bit.

His gaze darted to the door, afore he worked the block loose. Suddenly it popped free, and he inhaled, relief pouring through him. Bless you, lass. A small velvet pouch lay inside and Ramsey's fingers shook as he removed it.

The door thrust open, hall light streaking in and Ram stilled, not the least bit intimidated by the man standing in the doorway. The time to end this was now.

Phalon scowled with fury, his gaze darting to the blank wall, then to the pouch of velvet in O'Keefe's hand. His gaze shot to the painting. Damn! It hadn't been removed, except for cleaning, to his recollection, in two centuries, so how did this man know there was anything in there?

"I could have you arrested."

Ramsey nudged the phone across the desk. "Please do." When Phalon simply stared, Ramsey calmly replaced the block, then returned the frame to its proper place. He faced Phalon, hefting the sack.

"Whatever is in this house is mine." Phalon crossed to him, flicking on the desk lamp, glaring at the man.

Then O'Keefe opened the sack, withdrawing a single oval of pale-blue.

Phalon wet his lips, watching the soft light cast through the diamond.

"Did you intercept the stones—" Ram's gaze sliced to Phalon's—"therefore preventing the kidnappers from returning the babe?"

Phalon's eyes narrowed, his features sharp. "What do you mean?"

"Tess left one gem behind."

The Red Lady. And Hamilton was wearing it. "You have no proof of anything, and *you* have the stones."

"But Alexander was not a stupid man, Rothmere, these stones were photographed, each flaw and silk marked. Only three people knew the ransom had been turned into diamonds. Alexander, Annora . . . and you. And since they've never been cut and were discovered here . . ." Ram arched a russet brow, dropping the stone into the bag.

"No one saw you come in."

"I did."

Sloane emerged from behind the half open door, a small gun in her hand, its barrel acceptionally long. She held out her hand for the diamonds and Ramsey tossed them to her.

"No!" Phalon lerched and she pointed the gun at his chest.

"I wouldn't, *Daddy,*" she sneered and Phalon ground his teeth, disgusted with his offspring. Perhaps if her mother had lived . . .

"You put this into motion, Sloane. Even Tess had enough compassion to ignore your petty revenge."

"Tess, Tess! Christ, I'm sick of hearing that name! This is your fault. You paid too much attention to her, her *career.* She was a nobody! I'm your daughter. I AM!" she shrieked.

"But she made something of herself, and you had every advantage—"

"I lived under her shadow! You couldn't see her for what she was, because of that!" She jabbed the barrel at the painting. "Tell him," she said smugly. "Tell him how you've been obsessed with a ghost because she looks like Tess." Her father advanced, the point of the barrel stopping him. "Do you know how much I've hated you?" she taunted. "That's why I did it. Expose Penny and get Tess thrown in jail, then you'd see her for the trash she was."

"Shut up, Sloane."

"Go to hell, Daddy! I've listened to your crap about bloodlines and family and honor when you never had it! Elizabeth, the sainted matriarch," she said dramatically. "The bitch didn't bear heirs, she bore weapons! Your affection were conditions, Daddy, to be levied. The damn Blackwells cared more for family than money, and all you wanted to do was destroy them!" Her stance relaxed, the gun barrel waving as she spoke. "But taking their house wasn't enough, huh?"

"For God sakes, Sloane! Be quiet!"

"You took their baby, too."

A stretch of silence. Phalon's shoulders drooped. Sloane smiled thinly.

"I didn't want to believe it," came from far off.

Phalon watched as a figure slowly emerged from the darkened corner of his study. His gaze dropped to the tricorn in his hand, then shot to the face. He frowned, confused, and the man slowly peeled off the simple dark mask.

"Alexander," Phalon whispered, joy and horror in his voice.

"How could you do it? She was our baby."

"I—I didn't take her, Alex, I swear. I tried to help find her."

"Liar!" Alexander roared, taking a threatening step. "They knew the passages! They stole her from her bedroom!"

Phalon swallowed, horrified. "No, no, don't you remember, after the drop-off, my men found where they were keeping her, but she wasn't there. She'd escaped, vanished. And there was blood everywhere."

Alexander shook his head. "I trusted you, Phalon. Annora and I trusted you with our daughter's life, but they never got the ransom. Did they?"

His Adam's apple bobbed, sweat beading his upper lip. "I killed the kidnappers."

"And you kept the diamonds! You took my house, my land, all that I had left, because you were greedy!" Alexander's fists shook with his fury. "Good God, Phalon, I would have given it all to you just to get my baby back! You had underground connections then. We could have found her." His voice lowered, dark with unfulfilled threat. "But you knew Annora would never give you the letter." Phalon's features went slack. "She would never forgive you for trying to rape her and she was terrified you'd touch our baby!"

Phalon was sickly-pale. "Oh God, Alex, I wouldn't, I—"

"No! No more! You wanted to hurt her because she rejected you, because she loved me!" Alex drew a deep breath, twenty-five years of rage unleashing. "And you let her die. You watched her give up and you just let it happen!"

"Don't you think I've lived with that? But it was too late. The child was dead."

Alexander's fist connected with Phalon's face, sending his head back and blood splattering across the walls. Phalon dropped to the floor.

"No, Phalon, she wasn't dead, just lost, and its taken twenty-five years for her to come home."

Phalon scooted back, swiping his nose as Alex loomed over him. "Wha—what do you mean?"

"Annora's baby is alive."

Phalon's eyes widened, and his gaze shot to Ramsey. "No," Phalon whispered. "Not her!"

"Who?" Eyes turned to Sloane, only Ramsey still aware she held a loaded weapon. "A Blackwell is alive?" Her gaze darted between the men, the painting, then slowly coming back to Ramsey. "Penelope," she hissed, her face contorting with fury. "Well, I can fix that." She made to turn.

A panel opened, a figure slipping out, gun first. "I don't think so," he said, yanking the hood from his head. "Drop it, Miss Rothmere."

The gun shook in her hand, her gaze frantic between the men. Behind her Downing entered the room, yet before Ramsey could withdraw his flintlock, she swerved and said, "It was fine til you came," then pulled the trigger.

The shot was soft, an almost soundless thump as it impacted with Ramsey's chest. He staggered, a second shot firing elsewhere as he smacked the wall. He slid to the floor, hearing Penny's scream as she raced into the room.

"Oh Jesus! Ramsey, Ramsey!" she called, her hands skimming over his chest, covering the hole in his vest. He opened his eyes, blinking, then struggled to sit up.

"No, don't move! Someone call the paramedics."

Alexander hovered over her, dialing the phone as Mathers picked up the fallen weapon. Downing slapped handcuffs on Phalon, unsympathetic to Sloane's bleeding arm.

"Penelope, love, I am fine."

"You got shot, you're not fine, you're—" she looked down at her hand—"not bleeding." Her gaze flew between the hole and his face. Ramsey sat up and she tore at his shirt and brocade vest.

"A bulletproof vest!"

Alexander apologized into the phone, Mathers chuckled, and Ramsey looked at the man over the top of her head. "The detective suggested I don the heavy thing." He met her gaze. "To be honest, love, I did not think it would work."

"You brought the police in on this without telling me! I've been a nervous wreck and you—!"

Penny stared at him, battling between tears and anger. Finally she punched his shoulder, then punched him again and again until he caught her hands and held her. She sobbed in his arms and Alexander sighed, settling his hip on the edge of the desk.

"Got a temper like her mother," Alexander said.

"Hush up, Da," she mumbled into the crook of Ramsey's neck.

Ramsey chuckled, gently pushing her back, climbing to his feet afore helping her from the floor. He kissed her, then stripped open his coat and shirt, working the vest off over his head. Examining it, he plucked the squashed bullet, handing it to Penelope. She clutched it as he adjusted his clothing and faced the police officers.

"My thanks, Pete," Ramsey said, offering the vest. Mathers tossed the velvet sack at Alexander before taking the vest, a smirk on his lips as he nodded to Ramsey's pistol.

"Well, you needed it, with that antique."

Ramsey withdrew the pistol and pointed it to the hearth. He fired, the ball shot lodging in the brick.

Mathers blanched. "Christ." Shaking his head, he nudged Phalon and Sloane out the door, Downing withdrawing a hand radio from his back pocket and clicking it on. As the faint squawk of the radio faded, Alexander turned to Penelope. She melted into his arms, recognizing him as the masked footman on the coach.

"Welcome home, poppet." He kissed her cheek and left them alone.

She faced Ramsey, her hands on her hips. But her gaze flicked to the painting, dismissed it, then returned sharply. She tore across the room, staring up at the portrait. He told of finding the gems there.

"It's beautiful. She looks so serene—" her hand traced the dried paint down to the signature and she jerked back, turning wide eyes on him. "You painted this?" she shrieked.

His lips twitched. "Tess had the same reaction."

"What other talents are you keeping from me, Ramsey O'Keefe?"

"Many, love. Come wiggle them out of me." He opened

his arms. She didn't move. "Forgive me?" He gave her that
little boy shrug and she flew to him, kissing him lovingly.

He held her snugly in his arms for a long moment and when
the sound of voices rose from below stairs, Penny opened her
eyes. She gasped, leaning back and nudging him to look.

Ram turned, frowning at the tall cheval mirror, a fine crack
in the left side. The glass was foggy, a haze of shape beneath
the silver and they both glanced about for something to reflect
the image. But there was nothing.

"Do you see it?"

"Aye," he said in awe.

The fog cleared and as if through rain-wet glass the figure
of a woman, about thirty-five, materialized, children playing
at her feet. She reached out to gather the smallest, a girl, into
her arms, then stilled as her gaze touched on the mirror, her
smile soft as she tapped the man sitting on the floor with five
dark haired boys. His green gaze flicked between his wife and
the mirror. She spoke to him, but neither Penny or Ramsey
could hear.

"Tess," Penny said, taking a step, hand out. In the glass
Tess smiled tearily, her gaze drifting to Ramsey. Suddenly Tess
laughed without sound and Dane nudged her, his lips twitching
no matter how much he tried to look scolding.

Dane nodded to Ramsey and he returned the gesture, then
moved directly behind Penelope, slipping his arms about her
waist as the image faded.

Now he understood the strange passage in her books, he
thought, sighing.

"Goodbye, Tess," Penny said under her breath, sniffled,
then glanced back at Ramsey.

"Dane is a very handsome man."

"And what am I?" he said with false indignation.

"After what you just pulled?" she said. "Pilgrim fodder."

EPILOGUE

Ramsey stood at the helm of the *Lady's Roque*, steering the sixty foot craft, his seasoned gaze assuring him of sail position afore dropping to where Penelope lay stretched out on one of the benches fashioned in the hull of the vessel. The wind lifted strands of her hair and he thought her asleep til she brushed them back, one hand smoothing over the tiny back of their daughter. He didn't think he could love her more and then she presented him with an auburn haired girl. Megan was the light of his life, and it oftimes brought tears to his eyes to see them together, safe and happy. Penelope was more beautiful and alluring than the day he'd clapped eyes on her.

"I like it when you look at me like that," she said, rising slowly, cradling the newborn against her chest.

"And that is?"

"Like you want to rip her clothes off," Alexander said as he passed, climbing toward the bow to set jib.

"Da!" Penny said, trying to look indignant.

He chuckled, hidden by sail and rigging, and Penny moved carefully to Ramsey's side. He draped his arm around her shoulder, and she sighed against him.

"I love it out here," she said, tugging the frilly bonnet about Megan's face.

" 'Tis your turn at the watch," Ram said and she rested her head back on his shoulder, staring into his eyes.

"You just want to wake her up and play."

Ram grinned. "Aye," he said without a hint of remorse. "Now, man your station, mate." He gently took hold of their child.

"You enjoy giving me orders far too much," she commented dryly as he tucked the baby against his shoulder. Megan scarcely filled his broad hand.

"Bloody hell," he muttered. " 'Tis the only time I can." Penny laughed softly as Ram settled to the bench, his broad back keeping the wind off his daughter. He watched his wife at the helm, her feet braced, her attention on the sea, the sails, thoroughly enjoying the sight. Her hand at sailing was remarkable and he adored her for learning just for him. She was tanned and muscled, her figure lusher since Megan's birth and he ached for a little privacy. It had been a while, and he was thrilled to discover that if she took but one pill, he could love her and not get her with child. Although she wanted more children, soon. Even after the pain he witnessed, which was a startling opportunity he'd never forget, he couldn't believe she'd suffer that again.

Women, he decided, were a grand bit stronger than men. Thank God.

Margaret poked her head out of the hatch. "Chow in twenty minutes. Eating up here?"

Ram nodded, smiling when Hank peered behind her. He was an attentive husband, Ram thought. Penny had gifted them with her Victorian house on the couple's wedding day, then after the courts tried and sentenced Sloane and Phalon, the Blackwell estate returned to the possession of Alexander. But he didn't want to live alone and Ramsey and Penelope agreed to move in. Ramsey did not care where they resided, as long as 'twas together.

Megan fussed against him and Ramsey hummed to her, pressing his lips to the top of her head. His heart swelled every time she made one of those sweet baby sounds.

"You're a pushover, Ramsey."

He met Penelope's gaze, smiling one of his heart-stopping smiles, and it pleased her like nothing else to see Megan's big imposing daddy holding her, reading to her, or telling her outrageous tales of his exploits.

"I do have a soft spot for redheaded lasses." He stood, coming to her, kissing her deeply, thoroughly, afore handing over the babe. "Nay," he pleaded afore she could move. "Sail with me, love." He grasped the wheel, hemming her in and she sighed comfortably into the shelter of his body.

The wind loosened her hair, fanning it across his chest. The sun began its slow descent, showering the sea with a rich red gold.

"I never imagined I'd ever be this happy," she said, thanking God for the chance. "Who would have thought we'd have found each other like we did?"

He tipped her face up, lightly pressing his lips to hers afore gazing into eyes that would look upon him for the rest of his life.

"I always knew, my love. Always."

Aye, Ram thought. He'd found his true heart mate and a love to last beyond centuries. All it took was Triton's will and a leap of faith, in love.

HISTORICAL ROMANCE FROM PINNACLE BOOKS

LOVE'S RAGING TIDE   (381, $4.50)
by Patricia Matthews

Melissa stood on the veranda and looked over the sweeping acres of Great Oaks that had been her family's home for two generations, and her eyes burned with anger and humiliation. Today her home would go beneath the auctioneer's hammer and be lost to her forever. Two men eagerly awaited the auction: Simon Crouse and Luke Devereaux. Both would try to have her, but they would have to contend with the anger and pride of girl turned woman . . .

CASTLE OF DREAMS   (334, $4.50)
by Flora M. Speer

Meredith would never forget the moment she first saw the baron of Afoncaer, with his armor glistening and blue eyes shining honest and true. Though she knew she should hate this Norman intruder, she could only admire the lean strength of his body, the golden hue of his face. And the innocent Welsh maiden realized that she had lost her heart to one she could only call enemy.

LOVE'S DARING DREAM   (372, $4.50)
by Patricia Matthews

Maggie's escape from the poverty of her family's bleak existence gives fire to her dream of happiness in the arms of a true, loving man. But the men she encounters on her tempestuous journey are men of wealth, greed, and lust. To survive in their world she must control her newly awakened desires, as her beautiful body threatens to betray her at every turn.

Available wherever paperbacks are sold, or order direct from the Publisher. Send cover price plus 50¢ per copy for mailing and handling to Penguin USA, P.O. Box 999, c/o Dept. 17109, Bergenfield, NJ 07621. Residents of New York and Tennessee must include sales tax. DO NOT SEND CASH.